A Pallid Moon

BRAD FARLEY

Cover Art Designed by Mike Fauls Studios – http://www.mikefauls.com

Contact Mike: artbymike@yahoo.com

ISBN: 1539178781
ISBN-13: 978-1539178781

DEDICATION

For Mike: thanks for believing in me,
and for all of the great artwork, buddy.
The Raven says HI!

CONTENTS

CHAPTER ONE

The ship floundered like a wounded beast in the surf as the waves slammed into it. Tiny figures could be seen running to and fro on the decks, trying to right the vessel but it was a lost cause. The rain fell like thick sheets of lead and the spray from the sea swept more than one man away like so much debris. It was a northern ship as anyone could plainly see. Called by some long-ships and by others dragon-ships, and others gave them more fanciful names such as frost-reavers or iron-bearers, although the latter appellations were as often applied to the men who sailed such vessels as they were the ships themselves. Such names were used with fear and loathing to describe the barbarians from the north who preyed upon other ships and coastal settlements.

None of this made a bit of difference now, however. Neither their fierce reputation as warriors nor their peerless skills as sailors were going to help them now. It was obvious to any onlooker that the ship was doomed and there were, indeed, onlookers. Several men on horses watched the scene from a nearby cliff, saying nothing amongst themselves. They sat in their saddles back among the stunted pines that grew there, gaining some little respite from the stinging rains and the biting wind. Spring had recently come to the region, though it felt much more like winter still and spring had brought with it the vicious storms so common with the region. It seemed madness to sail in such weather and very strange truly that the north-men who were acknowledged even among their enemies as skilled mariners risk sailing now at this time and so far from home.

The observers still said nothing but simply watched, swathed in thick wool cloaks, their breath misting forth. After a time, one of them turned to face the others but another, a tall man in a faded blue cloak held up a hand and silence still reigned. The other man nodded and looked back out at the drama that was coming to an end upon the sea.

The ship was being tossed like a child's toy and it was clear that the battle to right it had been lost. Shouts and screams could be heard as rocks reared before the craft like the teeth of some primordial beast. The sound of the jagged rocks tearing into the hull of the vessel was a terrible one. Now, men weren't just tossed from the ship but most were leaping into the frigid ocean waters. The ship was rapidly taking on water and before long was sinking. The tiny figures in the water struggled there but most were soon lost among the whitecaps.

The blue-cloaked man made a clucking sound to his horse and the mount dutifully moved forward, its head held low in the rain. The other men followed, murmuring amongst themselves and he reined his horse in.

Looking back at the others, his voice rasped, "We will go down." He said it simply and quietly but his was a voice used to command and they said no more.

Below, the ship finally sank from view with a groan, as the sea claimed it's due. Within moments, it seemed as though the vessel had never even been there and there was only the storm tossed ocean.

The beach was littered with debris from the destroyed ship. Here and there were bits of flotsam in the water still as well. Much of it was broken wood from the ship and its cargo. There were still figures here and there, as well. Human detritus that the sea hadn't swallowed or perhaps had spat back up, depending on one's beliefs. The storm had passed but the sun had still not come out and it was likely that it wouldn't show itself at all. The sky was a lighter gray now, though and in the distance it was a darker shade. There would be another storm later this day or perhaps the next.

"At least the rain's stopped." One of the cloaked men offered.

"For now." Another replied in a terse voice.

It was obvious that they were on edge and the man in the blue cloak spoke in calm tones then. "It may rain later in the afternoon but we've time before another storm hits."

The other men nodded and agreed and said little else. They were spread out around him like chicks around a hen. In another circumstance, their leader might have chuckled but their situation did not lend itself to humor. They were, none of them warriors, and they all knew it. True, they clutched weapons and looked ready to use them but they weren't fighters and everything from their stance to their expression revealed this. They didn't want to be down here among the dead and debris, and the man in the blue cloak knew that they didn't understand what they were even doing here. Perhaps he should have explained it to them but he rarely explained himself to his subordinates. It was a bad habit to form and a hard one to break.

"Spread out." The man in the blue cloak ordered. "See if any of them are alive."

The others obeyed him but they still stayed bunched in smaller groups of two or three. There were half a dozen of them and none of them seemed in a hurry to be separated from their fellows. As they moved along the beach, they checked on the bodies lying there.

The man in the blue cloak pulled his hood back and surveyed the scene. His face was angular, tanned and weather-beaten. He wasn't young but neither was he truly old. Dark, thoughtful eyes seemed to take in everything.

His close-cropped hair was salt and pepper and he was clean-shaven, though stubble showed that he'd been unable to shave

3

recently. He was a trim man, though not overly thin, and he'd kept from developing a paunch because he was active. This was due mostly to his profession more than any vanity; although it was pleasing to him that he looked better than many men his age.

"This one's still breathing!" One of the men cried suddenly. The others hastened over, their weapons forward. They looked ready to finish the work the sea had started.

"Stop!" It was a simple command that their leader shouted but the men lowered their weapons and backed a pace or two away. They looked afraid, as if they'd found the carcass of a monster washed up and not the prone form of a man.

"Venaro, he's still breathing." The man who'd found the survivor offered as their blue-cloaked leader strode up to the group.

The man called Venaro nodded as he looked at the cast-away. What he saw was a large man with blonde hair. He was clad in rough spun cloth and a leather harness. There was an empty sword sheath on his side but there was no sign of it or any other weapon on his person. It was obvious that the survivor was a fighting man even unconscious as he was. His powerful physique and scarred forearms betrayed his profession and heritage as one of the feared sea-reavers.

Some of the men were muttering among themselves. There was no love lost between them and the northerners, who they considered barbarians. Many of them had lost family and friends to the depredations of just such north men and it was obvious they'd just as soon run him through right now.

One of the men, a stout fellow with a full beard, stepped forward, a short handled axe clenched tightly in his fist. "We should kill him, Venaro!" He hissed fervently. "His kind killed my son two years ago when they pillaged Bernholt!" Rage and fear warred with each other in the man's voice.

Nodding, Venaro answered in a calm voice. "Yes and many north-men have died on our spears as well, have they not, Callum?" He knew that the other man had lost kin to the barbarians as had some of the others. It wouldn't do to ignore that fact. "Still, this man has done nothing that we know of, has he?"

Outraged, Callum gritted his teeth and in a strangled voice, said, "I have no doubt that he's a murdering bastard like all the rest!"

Now, Venaro shook his head. "We're not about to kill a man who survived the ocean because of his race." Venaro's voice was firm and yet somehow still reasonable.

He knew all too well that his voice was a large part of the reason for his success. He held up a hand to forestall any further argument. "We're going to see if there are any other survivors and we're going to take them back to camp."

Now, the others all wore unhappy looks and gripped their weapons more tightly. They grumbled and shook their heads and a couple of them cursed freely.

Callum stepped forward now, his shadow falling over the prone barbarian. "You can't be serious!" He grated.

Venaro rose and faced his subordinate. He was taller than the other man and used both that and his rich, booming voice to his advantage. "Have you forgotten who is in charge here?" Venaro's voice carried easily and could be heard even over the crashing waves. "Have you forgotten our situation?" He asked the second question in a more subdued voice and now he could see them thinking. Every one of them was thinking on his words. Venaro didn't let them think long but imperiously pulled his blue hood up over his head. "The storm will be rolling in soon enough." He intoned, looking out over the waves at the dark clouds that were a bit closer now. Their heads turned and they saw he spoke truth. "I don't intend to be on this beach when it gets here."

He saw that he had convinced them as they quickly fanned out to look for any more survivors. Venaro was a master of persuasion and it had made him quite a bit of coin in his life. Causing their attention to focus on the incoming storm and not the Northman had given him the edge. They were used to following orders and were followers by nature.

Callum, however, lingered. "You don't know...you don't

understand…" He was muttering beneath his breath.

Stepping close, Venaro looked the other man in the eye. "I understand you have lost…" He began consolingly.

"You don't understand anything!" Callum snorted, an ugly gleam in his eyes. He looked down at the Northman with hatred. "You're not from here, how could you know?"

Venaro only nodded for a moment and in a low voice said, "It's true I'm not a native of this region but that doesn't mean I don't know about loss, Callum." Something in his voice made the other man look up and lock eyes with him. "I was at the burning of Entraci." His voice was sad.

Callum's eyes grew troubled at the mention of the fallen southern city. "I…I didn't know…"

Venaro nodded again and continued speaking, his voice sad. "I lost friends and family and barely made it out alive myself." He stared into the other man's eyes until Callum looked away. "Your countrymen left few enough of us alive after the sack of the city."

Callum stammered for a moment and then feebly said, "I…I wasn't there…I'm no soldier."

Nodding briskly, Venaro clapped the other man on the shoulder. "Neither am I, my friend. I'm not fool enough to blame someone because of what their rulers or fellow citizens do." Despite himself, Venaro was remembering Entraci now. "Now, this man may be a hardened killer, a rapist and a pillager but we don't know that and I want to speak with him if he lives long enough to get back to camp." He looked down at the unconscious Northman. "He may not survive long enough for me to do that and I promise you I'm not going to endanger our lives but I won't allow him to be slain out of hand because he's from somewhere else."

The other man said nothing else and it was clear that he was troubled. Callum had been with Venaro for quite some time and knew that Venaro was from the south. That he'd been at Entraci and survived the atrocities committed there had never come up. It was well known what had happened there and even though their countries had been at war and national pride being what it was, strong men had blanched at what the victors had done to the citizens of the city.

As the other man walked away, Venaro let out a long breath. His mind was now reliving that bleak day and he forced himself to look out over the waves and calm himself. His father had once said that men do great evil to one another for many reasons. Some of them are reasons that are easily understood and others are not. Venaro had always reminded himself of this as he traveled the land and it had kept him alive and profiting when others were blinded by hatred or fear.

It turned out that there were no other survivors and the men loaded the massive Northman on one of the horses across the saddle yet he still never awoke. On closer inspection, two things were made clear. The first was that he had suffered a blow to the head at some point and the second was that he was younger than he first appeared.

As the storm approached land, the group was already wending their way up the cliffside path. Venaro felt certain that they'd be back at camp before the storm hit. He made sure that it was he that led the horse that carried the barbarian, just as he made sure the man was tied securely to the saddle.

He also kept a close eye on Callum as they rode. One can never be sure of what lies in another's heart, his father had always said. It was good advice and one of the last things his father had ever said to him. He had died at Entraci.

When the storm slammed into the coast, it was even worse than the one that had sunk the Northman's ship. However, this time, there was no one there to witness it.

The camp was well situated among a clearing. Anyone with familiarity with the outdoors could tell it was a very old campsite; the stones around the fire-pit had been there so long that there was moss at the lower edges and stumps from where the clearing had been enlarged. The same individual would have also noted that it wasn't the best time to be camped this high in the hills.

Venaro, of course, was all too aware of all these facts. Necessity had forced him into this location and situation and his men knew it as well. By the time they arrived back at the camp, the spring storm hit, just as he knew it would. It was a driving rain mixed with sleet that was miserable and they were all glad they'd made it back to camp.

It was a good enough spot; for all that it was cold up here. Here and there, snow still clung to the ground beneath the trees. There were cut trees serving as barricades and wagons were circled around the perimeter interspersed with them. Nearly a dozen tents made up the innermost ring within the clearing, some old and patched and a few newer. More of Venaro's men stood guard about the clearing, though as the storm hit, they ducked inside tent flaps or wagons. There was a low fence of cut green saplings to keep the horses inside and they were huddled together.

As the other riders dismounted and saw to the disposition of their mounts, Venaro continued riding through the camp with the pack horse and its burden trailing behind. He saw the looks of consternation on those who hadn't been with them at the cliffs, just as he heard the whispered explanations from those who had. He could see Callum talking with Bandur already. The two wore grim expressions as they watched Venaro ride into camp and Venaro knew that would be trouble. Bandur was a tall, stocky ex-soldier and the only real warrior that Venaro had hired for security. The two watched the horse carrying the Northman intently as it passed them.

For a moment, Venaro thought they wouldn't say anything but then Bandur stepped forward. He wasn't quite blocking the way but Venaro reined his horse in anyway. The two locked eyes for a moment and then the former soldier glanced back at the burden slung across the horse behind.

Arching an eyebrow rather eloquently, Bandur asked, "What's all this then, sir?" His clipped manner of speaking as well as adding sir when addressing Venaro betrayed his past as a soldier.

Pulling his blue hood back, Venaro grimaced as the sleet and rain pattered off his head. He was too tired and too cold to be his usual charming self. "There was a shipwreck off the coast." He glanced back at Callum briefly. "As I'm sure you've heard there was a survivor." He let the statement stand for itself. He'd be damned to the lowest abyss if he was going to explain himself.

Bandur hesitated then, looking around at those nearby. "Well sir, I understand but he's a bloody barbarian!" There was heat in his voice as he said it but it was obvious Bandur was being cautious. After all, they both knew who paid who.

"Yes, he isn't from around here, I am well aware." Venaro answered drily. "Then again, neither am I."

Bandur hesitated again, choosing his words with care. "Aye, sir but that's different…"

The former soldier didn't get to say more as Venaro cut him off. "I'm not going to debate this, Bandur." He looked around at the other men and raised his voice, not enough so that he was yelling at Bandur but so the others could easily hear him. "He's a cast-away and I wasn't about to leave him to freeze to death. That's the end of the matter."

"But sir!" Bandur protested. "Surely you know these north-men are savages not to be trusted! He'll cut your throat for your trouble!"

"I said that's an end to it!" Venaro snapped. He was angry now. "You will follow me to my tent. NOW!" He snapped the reins to his horse and Bandur was forced to step aside or be knocked aside by the girth of the horse.

Bandur dutifully followed but he glared around him as if daring anyone to say a word. The others, all more than a little intimidated by the ex-soldier said nothing, busying themselves about their chores.

A short time later, Venaro was seated in his tent with a mug of mulled wine. He hadn't drunk much of it but just breathed in the warm scent. He had changed into dry clothes after he had made Bandur and a few others carry the Northman into his tent. The man had been none too happy about the task but had said nothing. From time to time, Venaro caught him glaring at the prone figure of the barbarian but that was all. Now, with a fire going and the chill leaving his bones, he was a little more at ease.

Motioning Bandur over, Venaro nodded toward a nearby stool. "Have some." He said, offering some of the mulled wine to the man.

Showing that he, like any soldier anywhere in the world, was not above taking a free drink, Bandur took a mug and drank. "It's good." He offered simply.

Venaro nodded at the other man. "That it is." They sat and drank for a few minutes before he spoke again. "Do you think I'm a fool, Bandur?"

The other man hesitated and then shook his head. There was a troubled look in his eyes, which strayed back to the prone giant lying nearby.

Venaro laughed out loud, despite himself. "But you think I'm being foolish now, don't you?"

With a shrug, Bandur gruffly replied. "I think you're a wise man and a good merchant, Venaro." Then after a moment, he added, "But that doesn't mean you're never wrong."

Taking a sip of his wine, Venaro nodded. "Go on." When the other man hesitated, he snapped, "Oh come now! I want you to speak your mind!" A wry grin creased his face. "You were quick enough with your words out in front of the men."

"It's true, sir. I think you're making a big mistake here." Bandur looked into his mug as if for the proper words. "I know you've traveled all over but I don't think you know how dangerous the northern barbarians are."

"All men are dangerous, Bandur." Venaro said in a terse voice. "Where I come from there are men who will smile and call you their friend and slip a dagger into your ribs all in one smooth move."

Nonplussed, Bandur nodded. "Aye and there are such men here as well but these barbarians are different, sir." His glance made its way over to the prone Northman again. "They fear nothing and they live for slaughter. We can't trust him!" His voice was raised slightly but there was honest urgency there more than anger. "We should at least bind him securely!"

Shaking his head, Venaro set his wine down. "No, that wouldn't do at all." He too looked at prone figure. "I know more about the north-men that you realize, Bandur. If he wakes up bound, he'll never trust us."

"Then let's kill him now!" Bandur hissed.

"NO." Venaro said it simply but firmly, as if he were talking to a child. This wasn't lost on the other man but the merchant didn't care.

"I want his goodwill and we'll not get it by tying him up." Venaro spoke as patiently as he could. "If I wanted him dead I could have let them kill him at the beach or more easily let him die of exposure."

"Why?" Bandur asked, almost plaintively.

"How can you ask that, knowing our situation?" Venaro queried.

With a snort, Bandur replied haughtily. "And how can this man, a barbarian that we can't trust, help us?"

"We don't know that we can't trust him and perhaps we can't. Perhaps he's a mad dog killer and we'll have to put him down." Venaro raised a hand to forestall another outburst. "However, we don't know that and I think we'll find quite the opposite. Whether you realize it or not, the north-men are not men without honor, though I'll admit their sensibilities are quite different from ours. At the very least, I am going to talk with him."

Bandur leaned forward. His expression showed that he knew he wasn't going to win the argument but he stubbornly refused to quit. "It's a mistake, Venaro."

"Enough." The merchant was done with the whole conversation now. "I've heard you out but it's time for you to remember who is in charge here." Bandur leaned back then and Venaro continued. "I hired you and your comrades to protect my wagons and you've done an admirable job. I'm sorry that your friends didn't survive but as you remember, we lost a lot of men when the orcs attacked. Now it's just us and a handful of drovers' left with a tribe of the green-skins between us and civilization."

Bandur nodded slowly. He well knew their situation and seemed at a loss for words.

Venaro, however, was not. "You said yourself that we could never get through with just you and the others." He stood then. "Now maybe, this barbarian is a crazed murderer as you say but then again, maybe he's not. Maybe, he'll see that we pulled him from the sea and be grateful enough to help us!"

Bandur didn't try to interrupt, though it was clear he still wasn't convinced, judging by his expression.

Venaro didn't care because he'd realized something in the last few moments. "Maybe, now that he's woken up, we can talk with him."

"Derku's beard!" Bandur spluttered, naming the deity and clambering to his feet. Whirling around, the former soldier saw what Venaro had. The Northman was awake and had sat up while the two were finishing their conversation.

Bandur's hand crept toward his sword hilt but Venaro hissed, "Keep that blade sheathed, sergeant." Now Bandur hadn't been a sergeant in years, since his days in the army but something about hearing his former title used made him listen.

Venaro smiled then. Knowing people and how they worked was his specialty. He took a step toward the Northman cautiously, his hands before him, palms raised to show he bore no weapons. "Greetings." He said simply to the barbarian.

The other man stood to his feet then, towering over Venaro and even the taller Bandur. They looked briefly at each other then and Bandur's look had a mixture of panic and anger. Then, the barbarian spoke, his voice a deep baritone. "Food." He said it as both question and command.

Bandur fumed and would have spoken but Venaro intervened. "Of course we have food." He turned a stern gaze on Bandur then. "Go have the lads prepare some food for our guest."

It was a mark of his training as a soldier that Bandur went out without a word but his expression showed that he clearly thought he'd come back to find his employer dead. Venaro fervently hoped that he was wrong.

CHAPTER TWO

Watching the Northman devour his food like a hungry bear, Venaro sipped his cooling wine and thought carefully on his words. Bandur and two others had appeared with a bowl of stew, some jerky and several hard biscuits. As the barbarian assaulted the food, which was the only word Venaro could think to describe the way the other man ate, he bade the others to leave. Bandur hadn't been happy about this and had stormed out, his hand on his sword hilt. Now, the merchant watched his guest eat and pondered the situation.

The blonde Northman was huge, well over six feet and the merchant would guess approaching seven. Bandur, who was considered tall in these lands, was perhaps six feet in height, while Venaro himself was near that height himself. The barbarian was heavily muscled and bore battle scars, most notably on his arms and shoulders. He wore a leather jerkin studded with bronze discs that left his arms bare, and leather bracers upon his forearms completed his armor. His clothing was rough spun cloth and his boots were of worn elk leather, unless Venaro missed his guess, which did not happen often.

What troubled Venaro the most was the other man's age. While his great size and obvious prowess showed the man was a warrior, he was much younger than the merchant would have originally guessed. He wore no beard or facial hair but had a crop of stubble growing there. The merchant decided it was the barbarian's face that betrayed his youth. The man's pale skin, common from the northern climes, still looked unlined and save for the scars that he bore certainly had seen no more than twenty years in Venaro's estimation.

"Why do you stare at me so?" The barbarian asked, his voice a dangerous growl. He looked at Venaro with storm-gray eyes and set his bowl down. Everything about the barbarian was primal and savage. His hair was all of a length, hacked short at the shoulders but not in the manner of a court dandy that spent time on it. It seemed that the youth simply chopped it off, perhaps with a knife when it annoyed him.

His voice calm and measured, Venaro replied. "Where I hail from, it is impolite to ask questions of a guest while they eat."

The answer seemed pleasing to the Northman and he nodded. "It is the same in my country." His accent was thick and he spoke with a strange cadence. Yet for all that he seemed to speak the trade tongue that was so common in these lands easy enough. Venaro paused to thank his ancestors that it was so, for he was quite sure that none of his men knew the Northman's language any more than he, himself did.

The merchant could not help but notice the look that flashed across the barbarians face as he spoke of his homeland. Sorrow and grief were mingled with rage in the youth's eyes. Venaro considered his next words very carefully then.

"Is the food to your liking?" The merchant said, still desiring to speak of simple things.

A shrug of great shoulders. "It was filling." Was his simple reply.

Venaro nodded. "That is good." He smiled then. "Shall I get you more?"

The Northman shook his head. "It was not poisoned, I think but no."

With a start, Venaro replied, "I would not poison a guest!" The barbarian's direct manner of speaking was something the cultured merchant would have to get used to, he could see.

"No." The other man said, still evaluating his host with those strange eyes. "I do not think that you would."

Ever curious, the merchant couldn't help asking, "If you thought the food was poisoned, then why would you eat it?"

"I did *not* think it was poisoned." The barbarian answered pointedly, as if talking to a simpleton or a child. "Besides I was hungry and I heard you tell the other man you could have left me to die or killed me easily enough."

Venaro was struck again by the directness of the Northman, as well as his casual reference to how easily he could have just died. The other man didn't seem discomfited or uneasy about it but rather more alert speaking of violence of any kind.

Deciding that simple and direct was how the man preferred speech, Venaro answered. "It's true, we could have left you to die or killed you but that was not my desire." Despite his calm manner, Venaro was a bit unsettled by the predatory way the man smiled at the statement. "You disagree? You think you would have survived the elements?"

Another eloquent shrug and then the barbarian yawned, stretching his massive arms wide. "If it were my time to die, I'd have died on that beach."

Venaro felt a change of topic would be for the best. "I am sorry; I must ask you to forgive my manners." He said, smiling. "I have not introduced myself. My name is Venaro, merchant and traveler." He waited then, not wanting to press for the others name.

"I am Tanoc." The barbarian said simply, without offer of any more information.

"It is a pleasure to meet you, Tanoc." The merchant replied smoothly. "I saw your ship go down in the storm. It's how we found you." Venaro asked his next words cautiously. "Might I ask where you were coming from?"

Scowling, though whether at the memory of the ship sinking or the question itself, the merchant couldn't say, Tanoc was silent for several moments. "We were...leaving our home." He said, his voice thick with emotion.

Feeling that it was unwise to ask where the youth's home might be or why he left it, Venaro instead asked, "Where were you going?"

A long pause followed before Tanoc finally responded. "South." He answered simply. The merchant said nothing and simply waited. The barbarian muttered then, "We knew of settlements down this way."

"HA!" Came a cry from Bandur, who had obviously been listening outside the tent flap and now bulled his way inside. "I told you he was a savage, Venaro! He all but admits to raiding villages and towns here!"

The barbarian hadn't moved or stood when Bandur came in but Venaro rose slowly and just as slowly interposed himself between the other two. "That is not what he said." The merchant spoke calmly and quietly. "You need to step back outside, Bandur."

The ex-soldier ground his teeth. "He's a murdering brute that needs to be put down!" His voice rose and his hand was on the pommel of his sword. "I've heard enough!"

"So have I." Tanoc said rising smoothly and standing. "Do not threaten me, fish-belly and think you are safe because your master stands between us!" The barbarian hadn't raised his voice but the challenge and threat were as obvious as bared steel.

Venaro, sensing how rapidly the situation could all spiral out of control, put a hand on his guard's chest. "Step away, Bandur!" He put all the authority he could muster into his voice then. "*Right...Now!*"

It might have gone differently if the barbarian was an older and wiser man but then again, perhaps it was in his violent nature to be confrontational in all he did but he smiled a wolfish smile at Bandur and then laughed. "Your master has spoken, cur!"

Bandur took a step back and with a curse ripped his sword out. "I'll kill you, you murdering filth!"

The merchant raised his hand and pointed at his subordinate.

"Get out, Bandur!" He held up a hand back toward the barbarian. "He is unarmed and he is my guest! I'll not have you spill his blood in my tent!" Venaro half turned then and saw the barbarian had stalked forward.

"I need no steel to deal with this one!" Tanoc thundered then. "I will take his sword and feed him his own guts!" Not just anger but a savage exultation colored the youth's words and he was still smiling, his teeth bared like a snarling animal's.

It occurred to Venaro then that he might be in real danger. "Will the two of you fight in my own tent, where you've taken food as a guest?"

The question gave the Northman pause then. It was clear that his customs were, in this regard, similar to those of many lands. He had broken bread and accepted the gift of the merchant's hospitality. Venaro could see in the other man's eyes that he had gotten through to him and for a moment he thought he could still calm this situation down.

Those hopes were dashed when Bandur growled, "Outside then, you savage!" The former soldier stalked out through the flap but over his shoulder added, "Unless you're a coward like every other Northman I've ever met!"

Tanoc's face flushed an ugly red and he clenched his fists. The merchant knew it was a lost cause then but still tried. "Please, my friend, let me go and talk to him!"

The barbarian said nothing else and walked past the merchant.

Outside, it was still raining but it had died down to a drizzle now. Bandur was waiting there in a circle of the others. The other men, for the most part, looked troubled at the situation but a few, Callum included, were jeering the barbarian and slapping the guard on the back.

With a flourish of his sword, Bandur held his arms wide, the sword glinting in the light of the torches. "The savage has no weapon." His voice was mocking and Venaro, who'd come to the tent flap could see that there was nothing he could do. Blood would be spilled this night. He instantly thought of the sabre he kept in his chest but as he did, someone else intervened and one of Bandur's men threw a short sword down in the slush and mud near the barbarian.

"Pick it up!" Bandur said grandly. It was clear he was going to attack as soon as Tanoc reached for the blade. Only a few paces separated them. He looked at the men around him and arrogantly began, "I'm going to…"

The man never finished the sentence. Before he could finish it, Tanoc rushed him, moving with incredible speed. Venaro had known many warriors but he'd never seen a man close to that size move nearly so fast.

It was to his credit that Bandur realized what was happening and tried to bring his sword around but he was too slow. The barbarian caught the former soldiers forearm in an iron grasp and with his other hand snatched him up by the throat. It was almost horrifying to watch the huge Northman shake Bandur savagely as a dog would a rat. Then, Tanoc twisted his opponent's wrist and there was an audible pop.

Bandur screamed hoarsely as his wrist broke, though it came out as a choked gargle, since the vice-like fingers of the barbarian still held his throat. The guard's sword fell from his incapacitated hand onto the cold ground.

There was a stunned silence as Tanoc threw the injured man to the ground as if he were a bundle of sticks. Then he clouted Bandur on the side of the head with his immense fist. The former soldier was knocked back to the feet of his friends without a sound and lay there completely unconscious.

Tanoc roared like a beast and pointed at the others. "*The next man to threaten me dies!*" The barbarian seethed with rage but was hardly breathing from the short-lived bout with Bandur. His teeth were bared in a snarl and several of the men took a step back. It was clear he was ready to pick up Bandur's fallen blade and commence the slaughter.

"No one is threatening you." Venaro said flatly.

Tanoc half-turned; lowering his hand and unclenching his fist. He didn't say more but let out a breath like the snort of a horse.

Venaro walked out to stand next to the Northman. "I know that Bandur is your friend and I know you don't trust Tanoc here." He spoke his words as if he were discussing the weather or the price of a horse. "However, you all know the situation we're in here and I want to point out that Bandur started this altercation and refused to listen to me."

The men standing around said nothing but it was clear from their expressions that they agreed. They all knew Bandur for a hot-head and more than one of them had been forced to back down or face a beating from the big guard. Venaro guessed that more than a few of them were happy to see the proud ex-soldier taught a lesson, though he was just as sure that they still didn't trust the barbarian. The truth was that the merchant wasn't sure he could trust Tanoc either but it was a moot point. They were in desperate straits.

"I want you to all remember what happened when the orcs attacked." Venaro spoke in that same calm voice and watched the fear descend on his men. "Maybe you've forgotten why we're still up here, running out of food and fearing every day that they'll attack again but I have *not* forgotten."

The merchant could see them thinking about it now. They'd been fooling themselves for the most part. They'd run from the orc attack and most of the real fighting men, Bandur's comrades for the most part, had died on that day. They'd been hiding up here, praying to the gods that the savage monsters wouldn't find them.

Venaro's calm voice was warm and reassuring. "Now I believe that Tanoc can help us." He knew quite well that before the demonstration of the barbarian's prowess they might have argued or questioned him but it was hard to do so with the toughest of them unconscious and drooling into the mud. Although Venaro had been angry with the ex-soldier for instigating this, he couldn't find it his heart to still feel that way, as now the men looked at the Tanoc with fear and awe. "Get Bandur to one of the wagons and see to his wounds." He said then.

As they moved to obey him, he saw Callum shoot both he and the Northman a dark look. Shaking his head, he looked at Tanoc. "That one could still prove a problem." He said ruefully.

The barbarian spat in the mud to show what he thought of such a worry. He then looked hard at the merchant. "Orcs?" He queried, his voice flat.

Venaro knew then that his hunch had been right. The green-skinned monsters were as hated by the men of the north as they were men anywhere. He had hoped against hope that he'd find survivors willing to trade their fighting prowess for food and shelter. At first, he'd been dismayed to only find one survivor but like his earlier hunch, the merchant guessed that he'd found a warrior who stood out even among his own kind.

The shrewd merchant said none of this to the barbarian but simply clapped him on the shoulder and gesturing back toward his tent, said, "We need to talk."

For a long moment, the Northman looked at Venaro, then, startling the merchant, laughed out loud. As his laughter rang through the trees, Venaro couldn't help but cringe inwardly. He hoped none of Bandur's friends thought they were laughing at the man's plight. With a half-smile, the merchant nodded and headed toward the tent, wondering if he'd made a mistake.

The cell was damp and cold. There was light but it was of the feeble variety, given off by lit torches and one old lantern set on a rickety table. There were other cells in the line but these were mostly empty. There were only three prisoners held presently. The first was an old drunk, snoring gently in the sixth and last cell in the line. The second was a young man with a runny nose, scabbed hands and the coarse, patched garb of a peasant. He had been brought in for stealing but as the guards knew it was only bread he'd taken to feed his family, they'd been relatively gentle.

The third inhabitant of the jail was the object of the guards' scrutiny and conversation. They knew little of this prisoner. The fact that there was a woman in the cells and a stranger at that would be cause for comment on any day. There were two guards on duty and they stood close together near the table, which was a half dozen paces from any of the cells, talking in low tones. Though they looked similar enough in their leather armor and gray tunics roughly embroidered with the symbol of the town of Wend, a badger surrounded by sheaves of wheat on a background of green. However, upon closer inspection, the similarities ended.

The larger of the two was also the younger. He had the look of a farmhand with broad shoulders and rough hands. There was stubble on his cheeks, showing that he was trying to grunt forth a beard with doubtful results. His skin was ruddy and his coarse hair the color of old straw. He kept looking at the cell that held the woman, the newest addition to the jail, from time to time.

The shorter man was a solid, blocky man with a well-developed paunch, a balding head and graying hair. For all that, there was something in his eyes that spoke of experience and his movements and actions were sure and certain. No doubt a veteran of some war or border skirmish that had moved to an out of the way place to forget and try to move on. It was obvious from his bloodshot eyes that he was using alcohol to hasten the process.

"Who do you think she is?" The younger guard queried, his gaze straying to the woman's cell again. His voice was higher pitched than his size would suggest and he seemed nervous and excited, like a young calf.

The older man shook his head and snapped, "It don't matter." He studiously had avoided looking at the cell for any length of time and he continued to do so now. "She's a law-breaker and that's all we need to know." Though he seemed sure of himself, it was obvious to his comrade that he was uneasy.

"What's wrong with you, Hedolf?" He asked wonderingly. The

young man had seen the other guard remain cool under pressure, whether from an angry superior or when breaking up a fight in the tavern. "Do you know her?" He added, his gaze moving again toward the cell.

"No, I don't know her!" The guard named Hedolf hissed. "She can hear us y'know!" His irritation was plain as the rather bulbous nose on his face but there was something else that even his admittedly dim colleague couldn't help but notice.

"Well, what's wrong with you?" The youth said, now turning to look directly at the cell. "She's just a woman, right?" He scratched at a pimple at the edge of his mouth. "I mean, she's dressed strange and doesn't seem scared at all…" The young man's mused, his voice betraying wonderment. "And she looks different than any of the girls around here…"

The older guard grabbed the younger by the elbow and whirled him around then. His lined face showed fury warring with concern. "Listen, you idiot, she's no tavern wench or farm maid you can brag and tell lies too!" The young man wore an expression of surprise but his gaze still strayed toward the cell despite himself. Hedolf's voice was deadly serious and he poked the other man in the chest hard. "Are you listening to me, Gren?!"

"Hey!" The young man looked irritated and surprised. He pulled back a step and his face flushed. "Get your hands off me!" It was obvious that he was angry as well as embarrassed. The latter truth seemed to infuriate Hedolf.

"Stop making eyes at her, you great fool!" The older guard barked.

"You can't just shout at me, Hedolf!" Gren replied in a loud voice.

"Oh yes I can or have you forgotten my rank?!" Hedolf snapped back, pointing to his shoulder which bore a single crimson stripe on the green field behind the snarling badger.

Now Gren bore a wounded look. "I was just looking." He said, his voice defensive like that of a surly child. It was clear that he didn't understand why his friend and drinking companion would suddenly pull rank like this.

"Well, stop looking!" Hedolf growled, clearly unwilling to let it go. "That woman isn't some floozy whose bottom you can pinch and whisper sweet nothings to!" Gren's face flushed an even deeper red now, betraying the fact that he'd been thinking of just such things. "She's dangerous!" The older guard nearly shouted.

"C'mon, Hedolf." Gren scoffed then. "She's only a woman!" It was clear that the young man had a low opinion of the feminine gender and obvious that he believed they had limited uses. "Look at her!" He said, gesturing toward the cell. "She's dressed strange, I'll grant you and she is a real beauty but she's just…different…" His voice became softer. "She looks like a courtesan maybe or a dancer…yeah I bet she's a dancer like they have in the great cities…"

Hedolf looked ready to strangle the younger guard then. "Listen to me, you fool! She's no dancer or high class doxy, she's dangerous!"

"Who's dangerous?" The woman spoke then, her voice breathy and low.

With a start, the two guards looked at the cell's occupant, Gren with open admiration and Hedolf grudgingly. The woman standing on the other side of the bars was taller than Hedolf and striking. Her face was angular yet somehow beauteous. Her eyes were a light brown and to the older guard seemed mocking and cold. Gren didn't seem to notice as he was drinking the sight of the woman's form in. He was right in that she had the figure of a dancer, graceful and slim. It was hard to determine her age, as she looked neither old nor young and her dark hair framed a face that was as inscrutable as the moon.

Where Gren saw an exotic beauty though, Hedolf saw danger. He could see the strength in her limbs and figure. She was no willowy, weak damsel and he was certain that she was stronger than a lot of men. He was doubly certain that she was quicker than anyone he knew. It was her eyes, though that unnerved Hedolf. He was no coward but he'd seen eyes like that before and they were always, invariably eyes that belonged to killers.

Seeing that Hedolf wasn't going to answer, Gren took the initiative. "I don't think you're dangerous at all." He said, a warm smile on his face.

The older guard cuffed the younger on the shoulder as he cut in. "Pardon's ma'am but we're not to talk to the prisoners." Hedolf gave Gren a glance that clearly told him to keep his mouth shut.

"I'm not dangerous." The woman answered playfully. "This is all a misunderstanding."

"I'm sure that…" Gren began but whatever he'd been about to say was lost as Hedolf cut in.

"That's for the magistrate to decide ma'am." Hedolf answered neutrally.

"You're very polite." The prisoner said then and smiled, her teeth white and lips full. She looked at Gren, her smile growing wider. "And you're very handsome." She said boldly.

Though Hedolf wouldn't have believed it, Gren flushed even more and before he could say anything, he grabbed the young guard by the elbow and shoved him toward a set of stone stairs on the far side of the room. "Upstairs now." The older guard grated. Protesting and spluttering, Gren led himself be pushed halfway up the stairs.

Finally, Gren stopped and turned to Hedolf angrily. "You can't push me around like this!"

"One more word and you're on report!" The older guard snapped. "There's enough to worry about without you losing your head over a woman!"

"What's to worry about?" Gren asked furiously. He was embarrassed to be treated so in front of the prisoner and it showed.

Hedolf's expression was incredulous. "What's to worry about?" He looked ready to tear what little hair he had left out. "Bandits, orcs and other monsters prowl outside our very walls and you want to know what's to worry about?!" It was obvious that Hedolf was worried and not just angry. "There's been talk of strange figures about town at night and the disappearances and don't forget the strange symbols and markings we've been finding!"

If either man had been paying attention at that moment, they'd have seen the woman's expression grow thoughtful. However, they were both focused on each other at the moment. "He's right, Gren." She said from her cell, her smile now gone. "You should be careful, there are dangerous things out there."

Before Gren could say a word, Hedolf spun on the stairs and growled, "Shut your mouth, prisoner!"

"Or what?" The woman asked, almost purring playfully. Her smile was back but those cold eyes never wavered.

"Or I'll shut you up!" Hedolf said in an ugly voice.

"Oh, dear." She replied mockingly. "I wonder what Oled would think of your brutish treatment of helpless prisoners."

Hedolf grew pale and he murmured, "How do you know my wife's name?"

"I know a lot about this town, Hedolf." The mocking voice floated up to him. "Just as I know you owe more on that little hovel than sweet Oled realizes."

With a start, Hedolf shook himself and stalked back down the stairs. "Are you a sorceress then, to read my thoughts?" His hand strayed toward the cudgel at his belt.

Mocking laughter met him at the bottom of the stairs. "I am someone who knows that it pays to find out all she can."

Gren had followed Hedolf down the stairs and put a hand on his shoulder but the older man shook it off. "Then I'm sure you know they're going to hang you." Hedolf growled.

The laughter became a breathy chuckle and the woman's eyes flashed. "Oh, I've no intention of hanging." She said and leaned forward against the bars. "You're a good man, Hedolf. I know you've been passed over for promotion and I know the captain of the guard is a fool and a coward that just happens to be related to the right people on the town council."

Hedolf recoiled then. "Derku save us!" He said, his hand

making a warding sign as he called on the deity.

Her husky laughter sounded again. "I already told you, I'm no sorcerer or wizard. I'm simply well informed." Her smile was wry now. "Though I suppose in this backwater town intelligence might seem like wizardry."

"SILENCE!" Hedolf roared, waking the drunk and causing the bread thief to recoil to the back of his cell.

The woman merely laughed again. "Just let me out of here, why don't you. It's clear you know that things aren't right in this town." Her smile waned and a serious look took its place then. "I don't intend to be here much longer."

Angrily, Hedolf drew his cudgel and rapped the bars sharply then, causing her to draw back slightly. "That's enough out of you!" He said shakily. "Don't make me come in there!"

"I am unarmed." The woman said simply. "Why don't you come in here and beat me, then." She spread her arms wide. "Perhaps you like to beat women?" She asked sweetly. "I wonder if dear Oled knows."

Speechless, Hedolf looked at Gren, who wore a bemused expression. It was clear that neither guard knew what to make of the woman.

"Very well, I'll keep silent." She finally shrugged and turned away from them.

Mollified, Hedolf put his club away and stomped away from the cell. In doing so, he didn't see the woman slightly turn her head and smile at Gren nor did he see the faltering smile that Gren returned her after a moment.

CHAPTER THREE

For the first time in days there was no rain or sleet. The clouds did not entirely disappear and the sun shone only fitfully through them but for Venaro and his men were pleased nonetheless. They'd had their fill of bleak, sunless days during their stay up in the cold hills and if the sun gave its light, however briefly, it was a blessing.

After having laid Bandur low the night before, Venaro and Tanoc had spoken long into the night. The merchant had asked questions about the ship that had gone down and those who had been on it but Tanoc had said little. Whether this was because he didn't know all that much about his fellow passengers or because he didn't want to say was a mystery to the merchant. They had also spoken of the orcs that prowled the land and the situation that the merchant and his men found themselves in, cut off from civilization at they were. Eventually, they'd grown tired and after showing the barbarian a pile of furs and blankets he could sleep on, Venaro turned in, hoping that he'd been right and that he'd wake in the morning without his throat cut.

The merchant's faith was justified and he'd awoken to the heavy snoring of the Northman who lay under the furs across the tent like a slumbering bear. Venaro had risen to find that the storm had finally passed and checked on his men. They were well, although many were still nervous about the stranger in their midst. He'd done what he could to quell their fears and had then gone to check on Bandur. He'd found the ex-soldier nursing a broken arm, a sore head and wounded pride. Callum hadn't been far and while the man hadn't said much, it was clear that he still wanted to see the barbarian dead. Bandur had also offered little in the way of conversation but the big man didn't seem as venomous as his friend, despite his injuries.

Venaro had been checking on the horses when Tanoc stepped out of the tent. The barbarian strode to the edge of the camp and began relieving himself while whistling. The drovers looked at each other nervously and watched the merchant but otherwise went about the business.

A few moments later, the Northman strode over, wiping his hands on his tunic. "Is there any food?" He asked rather cheerfully.

The trader nodded. "One of the lads is cooking oats now." He looked at the barbarian and added. "We're running low on supplies."

The only answer that the towering Northman gave was a quizzical look that seemed to ask why such a thing was his concern. Part of Venaro wanted to shout at the man or point out that he'd be dead if it weren't for them but he knew it was futile. The barbarian saw the world differently, he was starting to realize. He didn't seem to show any worry or fear at his situation, shipwrecked and bereft of his countryman, nor did he show and remorse or grief.

Deciding to try a different tack, the trader asked, "What are your plans, Tanoc?" Venaro kept his voice calm and his demeanor light.

Tanoc looked around at the camp and without hesitation said, "I need to return to the shipwreck."

"The beach where your ship ran aground?" Venaro asked cautiously. "I assure you, my friend, we searched for other survivors and found none."

With an impatient shake of his pale mane that reminded the

merchant of lions in the southlands, the barbarian replied, "You misunderstand." Gesturing to the empty sheathe at his side, he added, "I need to find my sword if I can."

"Ah!" Said Venaro. "I understand. Well we have swords that you can use." The merchant walked over to a crate that held the stockpile of extra weapons that his men had and grabbed a scabbarded sword. Returning to the other man, he held it out to him.

For a long moment, Tanoc looked at the offered blade. He then took the sword and looked at it. It was an iron long sword with a hilt and pommel of bronze. The Northman unsheathed it and Venaro felt, rather than saw, the drovers nervously watching on. It was clear they weren't happy about the barbarian being armed but they said nothing, which pleased the merchant. For his part, Tanoc looked rather underwhelmed. In fact, he looked at the blade as if it were something unpleasant he'd pulled from under his boot.

The Northman hefted the sword and took a couple of swipes with it. He grimaced and muttered, "The balance is terrible and the cursed thing feels like it is going to break just holding it."

Venaro had to admit that the sword looked awfully flimsy clutched as it was in the bearlike paw of the barbarian. Apologetically, he offered, "It's one of the bigger swords that we have."

Another shake of that mane. "I need to go to the shipwreck." The barbarian reiterated. "I need to find my sword…" He trailed off and an unexpectedly sad look crossed his face. "Or one like it."

The merchant couldn't help himself. "My friend, we've spoken of the orcs and other dangers that haunt this bleak coast." He tried and failed to sound as if he weren't pleading. "Perhaps you could look through our armaments…"

The Northman was having none of it. "I need to go to the shipwreck." He said emphatically. His storm-gray eyes flashed as he looked at Venaro now.

With a heavy sigh, the merchant acquiesced. "As you say,

Tanoc." He motioned at the drovers. "Prepare the horses!" His voice was rueful, despite his best efforts. "We're going back to the shipwreck."

A short time later they were riding back toward the coast. Callum led the way, still glancing back at the barbarian with undisguised hatred from time to time. Venaro had debated within himself whether or not he should bring the man but had decided it was better to have him here where he could keep an eye on him.

Tanoc had noticed the vicious stares as well. "That man wants to kill me." He said matter-of-factly.

Venaro gave a start at the barbarian's nonchalant manner of speaking about someone wanting him dead. "Well, he and Bandur are friends." He said noncommittally.

"I did not slay his friend." Tanoc replied with indifference. "I could have but I honored your hospitality."

"And for that I am grateful." Venaro said, meaning every word. He still couldn't help but wish that the barbarian hadn't broken the other man's arm.

"If the fool ahead does not stop staring at me so, I will deal with him as I did his fool of a friend last night." The Northman said conversationally.

Rather than argue or defend the fool in question, Venaro changed the subject. "I wonder, Tanoc what you've decided to do once you've found your sword." The young warrior pulled a sour face that proved to Venaro that the other man really didn't think he'd be able to find it at all. When he said nothing, the merchant continued, "As I explained to you last night, my men and I are in a dilemma. We are far from any safe haven and the orcs we spoke of are between us and any settlements."

With a shrug of his thick shoulders, the Northman offered, "You should have more warriors when you travel."

Irritation warred with good sense within Venaro before he finally replied. "When we headed north I had over a dozen guards. We lost a few to skirmishes on the way but I thought we could hire more when we reached our destination for the return trip." The barbarian raised a questioning eyebrow but said nothing more, so the merchant continued speaking. "When we got to our northernmost destination, the town of Rudden, we found it destroyed." His voice was bleak as he remembered the destroyed settlement. "There were no survivors."

"Orcs?" The barbarian asked, his curiosity piqued now.

"I don't think so..." Venaro answered hesitantly. He knew what he and several among his men thought but he was loathe to say it out loud.

"It weren't orcs what destroyed Rudden!" An old drover riding nearby spat. "It were the *Pallid* or I'm a gnome!"

Looking at the gnarled old animal handler who, though short, was clearly not a gnome, Venaro replied, "We don't know that for certain." He turned back to Tanoc, continuing blithely, "All we know for certain..." He trailed off then, seeing the Northman go pale, and something approaching fear enter his eyes. "Tanoc?"

The barbarian looked away, refusing to speak. His fists were clenched where they held the reins of the horse he rode, his knuckles white.

"All we know for certain, is that the town was sacked." Venaro finished his sentence lamely. It was strange to see the seemingly fearless warrior so unnerved.

"Sacked?!" The old drover replied incredulously. "It were the strangest sack I ever heard tell of!"

Struggling to remember the man's name and failing, Venaro cut in. "We don't know for sure what happened." His voice sounded false and insecure even to his own ears.

"What else could it have been?" The older man continued. "Barely any of their belongings looted, all the children and old people slaughtered and the adults just gone!" His voice had an edge of hysteria to it. "I tell you it were the Pallid what came for 'em!"

"That's enough!" Venaro snapped, his voice commanding and the old drover finally fell silent. The last thing he needed was for the men to panic now. Remembering how close they'd come to doing just that as they rode through the eerie massacre at Rudden, the merchant suppressed a shiver.

The beach was deserted save for the gulls, who were feasting among the dead washed up there. It was clear that the storm had dredged up more bodies and they lay here and there among the debris of the ship. The sun was behind the clouds again from time to time was peeking through. As the group of men rode down the path from the cliffs, the gulls began squawking indignantly only flapping away when any of the horses rode too close for comfort and soon dropping back down in their wake.

Tanoc dismounted and at a signal from Venaro, the others did so as well. The young barbarian handed the reins to a nearby drover and set off among the detritus, his gaze roving here and there through the wreckage. The merchant and his men followed at a distance, leading their equally reluctant mounts. The crabs and birds had been at many of the bodies and it was not a pretty sight.

If any of it disturbed the Northman, he didn't show it but instead seemed perturbed as he searched. Once, he stopped and knelt, rising with something in his hand that turned out to be a dagger. He looked angry enough to toss it aside but looked at it and then stuck it in his wide belt.

The drovers were quiet and nervous. It seemed madness to come here among the dead searching for a lost sword, they muttered amongst themselves. Venaro silently agreed but felt it best to humor the young warrior for now. Watching the youth hunt among the corpses of his countrymen with such a casual manner made him question what he'd seen when the old drover spoke of Rudden. The trader wondered if he should speak to the Northman but he didn't know what to say. He had questions of his own and they couldn't stay long. With the break in the weather other things than themselves would be moving about.

"Look there!" One of the drovers hissed. Venaro and the others looked in the direction of the man's pointing finger and saw figures moving down the cliffs up the beach. As if summoned by his dire thoughts, orcs had found them!

Drawing his sabre, the merchant calmly spoke. "Don't let the horses bolt but don't get in the saddle." He knew that none of his men were trained to fight from horseback and that even though he was a fair enough combatant in the saddle, they were too close to the surf and it would be easy to be thrown here. They obeyed and drew their own weapons facing their opponents.

The orcs had clearly spotted them and were gesturing and brandishing their crude weapons. Their pale, olive-green skin was daubed with war-paint where it showed beneath their hide armor. The orcs bared their tusks as they swarmed down the beach like savage dogs let loose from a leash. So eager were they to get at the humans that they slammed into each other as they came and one was knocked from its feet.

Venaro's face was grim. There were more than a half dozen of the savage creatures and he'd brought only five men, thinking it best not to leave the camp unguarded. He cursed himself inwardly but knew that, with Bandur down, the remaining men would be hard pressed to defend the camp. "Get ready." He said sternly.

Then, like a flash, Tanoc rushed past the knot of men facing the orcs. The barbarian had the sword Venaro had given him in one hand and the dagger he'd found in his off hand. He hit the mob of orcs like a thunderbolt, stalling their charge.

The lead orc had seen the barbarian coming and had swung its crude axe round but the man deflected the blow away and with a counter-thrust ran the monster through. The second orc rushed forward and swung down with a spiked war-club but Tanoc leapt back and bellowing a war-cry hacked into the green-skin's arm. When the orc howled and dropped the club, the barbarian deftly stepped in and buried his dagger in the beasts' throat.

"Forward!" Venaro urged his men and they rushed up behind

him. They weren't eager to face the orcs but the barbarians charge had bolstered their courage and they shouted and hollered as they followed him. The merchant knew that the orcs could surround the barbarian if they didn't support him. As they closed, he saw an orc with a spear moving to do just that, his arm raised to cast the missile. Venaro lunged and stabbed the orc in the side. As the monster screeched and recoiled, it dropped its weapon and the trader's blade found its heart.

The drovers rushed into their foes in a frenzy born of equal parts hate and fear. They weren't well trained and it showed but they were strong men, used to hard work and they hacked and stabbed, giving and receiving terrible wounds from the orcs.

His war-cry almost a song of joy, the barbarian had side-stepped the orc he'd stabbed in the throat, leaving the dagger buried there. Tanoc saw the largest of the orcs bearing down on him, bearing a large, crudely fashioned axe. As the monster came on, the Northman rushed to meet it. The brutish green-skin swung the axe down in an arc that would have slain an ox but it only met sand, as Tanoc dodged to the side and lashed out, slicing the orcs shoulder deeply. As black orc blood began to flow, the young barbarian grinned like a wolf and said something in the orcs own tongue.

Hearing the orc language come from a human was a shock and Venaro could see that the monster was taken aback as well as it hissed something in reply. He could not, however, pay much attention as another of the savages swung a club at his head. The trader brought his blade up to block but his arm went numb from the force of the blow and he fell back a step. The orc slavered like a fiend as it rushed forward but was caught in the side by a drover's axe. When the thing stumbled, Venaro and the other man were on it hacking and slashing until it fell. The merchant looked up to see the bearded face of Callum, as the other man pulled his axe out of the orcs side.

"My thanks." The merchant gasped, realizing he probably owed the man his life. Callum merely nodded and went to aid another drover as Venaro thought to himself that he was going to give the man a bonus if they lived through this.

Enraged, the big orc swung his axe from left to right, seeking to disembowel his foe. His injured shoulder weakened and slowed him and the human dodged his strike. However, this orc was a cunning veteran and immediately twisted, driving the axe back the way it had just come, using the strength of his uninjured arm. The barbarian didn't have time or room to dodge and threw his sword up to block the strike. The heavy axe hit the sword several inches up from the hilt and snapped it.

In disgust, the Northman hurled the broken blade at the orc. When the green-skin ducked, he rushed in, grabbing the handle of the axe. Stunned, the orc fell back a step. Most humans would do anything to stay out of reach of an orc but this one showed no fear! The orc and human wrestled for possession of the axe among the melee that churned around them.

Nearby, the last of the orcs and men were slaughtering each other. The barbarian had killed two of the orcs in his initial charge and that had given the humans the edge. The merchant's calm orders also helped as he directed his men to deal with their opponents together whereas the orcs had no such direction with their leader tied up fighting the Northman.

Tanoc pulled his head back as the orc snapped its jaws forward, seeking his throat. When he did, the creature pulled hard on the axe and the warrior let go. The orc stumbled back and fell then. The barbarian did not press the attack but swept up a crude orc sword he'd spied in the sand, where its owner had dropped it. Meanwhile, the orc had regained its feet and seeing its enemy was armed, drew back to swing it. The Northman didn't give his opponent time to finish his move as he leapt forward and chopped down with the notched, curving orc sword. The blow split the orcs skull as it fell twitching.

The barbarian turned to find another foe, only to see they were all dead and gave a shout of victory. The exultant sound was chilling to the civilized drovers as they looked at the savage with nearly as much dread as they had the orcs.

Venaro walked over to the barbarian, who was stooping to pick up the broken blade the merchant had given him. "Thank you." He said simply.

"For what?" The barbarian asked in a puzzled tone.

Gesturing around him, Venaro answered bewildered. "The orcs. You stopped them, you killed their leader."

With a shrug that the merchant was getting to know very well indeed, the barbarian replied, "They were our enemies. We had common cause."

Venaro realized that it was as simple as that for the barbarian.

Tanoc handed him the broken sword. "I told you it felt like it was going to break." He said reproachfully.

The merchant couldn't help but chuckle then. "That you did." He looked up to see if the barbarian were angry but the man laughed out loud instead, his deep booming laughter echoing the sounds of the surf.

The barbarian walked off down the beach again and Callum and the others gathered around. The bearded man spoke. "Two dead and one injured."

Venaro nodded. "And we would probably all be dead if it weren't for him." He said, gesturing toward the Northman, who had knelt in the sand. The drovers all nodded in agreement, including Callum. There was no denying the barbarian's prowess.

The merchant walked down the sand toward the barbarian who was standing now, holding a great, double bitted battle-axe. A broad grin creased his face as he cleaned the muck and water from it.

"I see you've found a weapon to your liking?" The merchant asked.

Tanoc nodded and then contemptuously cast the orc sword out into the ocean an impressive distance. As the warrior hefted the axe for balance, Venaro spoke.

"I want to make you an offer, Tanoc." The trader said quietly.

The barbarian's gaze shifted from the axe to the merchant. "As you can see, these lands are very dangerous and my men are not warriors."

"Aye." The barbarian acknowledged thoughtfully, his eyes narrowing as he looked at Venaro. "Though you've skill with a blade."

Venaro gave a slight bow. "I was trained by skilled swordsmen it's true, though I'm far from one of them in ability." He met Tanoc's eyes steadily. "Help us get to civilization and I'll pay you well."

The barbarian looked at him for a few moments and then nodded in answer. He said no more but turned as Callum and the others came trudging through the surf. The drover bore a naked broadsword in one hand and a round shield in the other. Handing them both to the Northman, he said, "Don't know if it's yours or not." With a gesture to the sword.

The barbarians face fell for a moment and then his grin returned and he clapped Callum on the shoulder, jarring him. "Hah!" Tanoc laughed as he set the axe down to take the proffered weapon.

The broadsword was a robust weapon some three and a half feet long made of good steel. Its hilt and pommel were plain steel as well and the handle was wrapped in dark leather. Tanoc hefted the sword and his smile grew. "Not mine." He said simply. "But it will do." The barbarian took the shield in his left hand appreciatively. It was made of wood with a steel rim. After a moment, he slung the shield on his back, sheathed the sword at his side and then picked up the axe again.

As the drovers saw to readying the horses, Tanoc went to retrieve the dagger he'd found earlier. Pulling it from the dead orcs throat, he wiped it on the creatures hide armor and put it in his belt again.

"Tanoc." The merchant began cautiously. "I saw your face when the Pallid were mentioned. Have you seen them before?"

The barbarian froze for a moment and looked round at the

trader. His face was paler than usual again and he nodded.

"What happened?" Venaro asked lamely, trying and failing to phrase the question well.

Now, Tanoc merely shook his head and would say nothing. He stalked toward the horses and Venaro wisely let the matter drop.

By the time they rode away, the gulls had already gathered to feast greedily on the new items that had been so recently added to their banquet.

CHAPTER FOUR

It was silent in the forest. There was little in the way of wild game and even insects and birds seemed scarce. The barren trees had yet to put forth their first green shoots although some of the smaller bushes and plants had begun to do so. The damp, musty smell of decaying vegetation hung thick in the air and there was no breeze to disturb it. People only rarely came here for it was a desolate area where rocks heaved up from the ground and the tangled wood seemed to grow quickly.

The woodcutter moved as silently as he could, muttering softly to himself. It was an old habit and he'd developed it over the years as many people are wont to that must spend a lot of time alone. Though he was as comfortable in the wild as in any town, there was something about this place that set his nerves on edge.

"The trees don't seem right…" The man muttered to himself. He was feeling every bit of his fifty odd years at the moment, his knee twinging and his back griping like the wife he'd buried two winters earlier. Bending over, he groaned, as his back ached and picked up a fallen branch. Seeing that it was rotten and half hollow from insects, he tossed it away pulling a face. "Even the ones that still live seem rotten." He wheezed.

The bundle of sticks on his back wasn't very large at all and the woodcutter reflected that he hadn't been cutting much wood lately. He couldn't quite put his finger on it but as the woods had been cleared around town, forcing those like him to go further afield, he felt strange about felling trees or cutting larger logs. It wasn't that he feared to do so, he told himself, knowing it to be untrue. It was that he didn't feel like he wanted to draw attention to himself.

"That's just it." The woodcutter mumbled. "Never can tell who might hear ya." He continued to make his way through the woods, coming to a clearing. He'd not been to this part of the forest in some time. There had been a time when there were dangerous animals dwelling in these dense woods. Wolves foremost but also bears and great hunting cats would make their way down from the hills from time to time. He told himself that he was afraid of running into wild animals and that the axe he carried would do little good against such fierce beasts. "Yes, yes, wolves and cats used to abound in these parts…" The man said, his voice little more than a whisper. Again, he knew it wasn't true as most of the larger predators had been hunted and trapped out of the region a score of years ago. He couldn't really say what made him so fearful but the man felt better to lie to himself about it being wolves or hill cats. He hesitated at the edge of the clearing.

The terrain here was broken and seemed almost scarred. Great rocky outcrops thrust up from the ground like the blunt fingers of a titan. Moss and creepers clung to the sides of the rocks and here and there the trees grew atop them. There were spaces, great yawning overhangs beneath the rocks and the woodcutter well knew that some of them gave way to caves. In the bygone days of his youth, he and other men from his village had hunted bear in such places, luring them out and bringing them to bay with dogs before killing them with long spears. They had been fine hunts and part of him yearned for that time when he felt no fear beneath the boughs of the trees.

"It's strange now…." The woodcutter said then, his breath wheezing a bit. "Just seems different these days…" The clearing looked similar to many others but the woodcutter knew he'd come farther north than he had in years. So much of the wood seemed rotten and foul, he'd had little choice. The man wasn't just getting wood for today but he was looking for better stands of trees he could fell. He inwardly cursed himself for a fool. It was broad daylight and he'd seen no spoor to suggest there were wolves or anything else that could be a danger. He knew the warnings about orcs but the savages could be heard from a long way off and they always left an indelible imprint on the land when they were there. There were no axe strokes or crude symbols upon the trees. No totems hung to proclaim the superstitious orcs were anywhere near here. "Getting myself worked up for nothing." He muttered to himself. Yet he still wavered there at the verge of the clearing, afraid and not knowing why.

Unseen by the woodcutter, a trio of figures was watching him from an outcrop on the far side of the clearing. They weren't trying to hide but they were so still among the stunted trees that grew atop the rocky protrusion that they blended in easily.

"He's spotted us." A muted voice said. It was an almost shrill voice yet barely registered above a whisper.

In answer, another voice came, this one a woman's smooth and silky. "No, he is afraid." Satisfaction colored the speakers voice. "I can taste his fear from here."

A third voice, deeper sounded then. "We all can." There was boredom in this man's speech. "He doesn't know why but he fears to come closer."

The first voice spoke again. "We should show him what he's afraid of!" It came as a sibilant murmur. The excitement was clear.

"If you wish." The third speaker answered.

Down at the edge of the clearing, the old woodcutter was still battling nerves that he couldn't explain. "Need to head back." He said to himself, trying and failing to sound cheerful to himself, even as he lied. "Look another direction tomorrow."

The old man knew that he was fooling himself and he didn't care. He could not bring himself to enter the clearing. For the life of him, he couldn't have explained it but he was terrified and knew he was going to turn back. Still muttering to himself, he turned to see that he was not alone.

Three black-clad figures stood a mere twenty paces from him. The woodcutter shook and stuttered. "Tilva's Tresses, but you gave me a start!" He said naming the deity of the forest out of habit more than anything. "Didn't hear you come up on me!" He said nervously then, thinking that he'd forgotten there were also said to be bandits hiding in the deep forests. "My old ears must be failing me!"

Scrunching his thick gray eyebrows, the woodcutter squinted at the three facing him. They were a stranger lot than he'd ever seen. There were two men and a woman. Each was dressed in black clothing that even to his eyes was obviously of fine weave and cut. All three were very pale, like scribes or priests who spent all their time indoors, although they didn't seem frail at all. Their eyes were dark, almost uniformly so and they didn't seem to blink. Something about these people made the woodsman very uneasy.

"I...I'm just out looking for firewood." The old man stammered, gesturing at the bundle of sticks that he bore on his back. "Strange to see city folk all the way out here." He said in as cheerful a voice as he could muster. The woodcutter knew that there were no large cities within a hundred miles but he'd never seen anyone garbed like these people and guessed they must be from one.

The man in the center was very tall and he spoke, his voice a sonorous bass. "You are from Wend?" He asked simply. It was at once both a statement and a question and somehow also a command. This was a voice that was used to being obeyed. The speaker was broad shouldered and wore a black cloak of the same material as his clothes. His hair was black and close cropped.

The woodcutter nodded vigorously. "I...Yes I'm from Wend...well I live near there...outside the town..." He knew he was blathering on and could barely keep his teeth from chattering. Fear grew in his belly and writhed there like a cold serpent.

"Oh...he's afraid." The lady spoke then, her voice rich and inviting, yet somehow mocking at the same time. "He's *very* afraid."

She added, licking her lips.

The gesture was both sensuous and repellent and the man shivered making her smile. She was a beautiful woman with long, honey colored hair and a voluptuous figure yet she radiated danger in waves and the woodsman felt revulsion and terror clawing from within him. "I don't have any coin..." He began falteringly. What he said was the truth, he had spent what little he had earned to buy bread earlier in the week.

Laughter from the third individual cut him off. It was cruel, harsh laughter as was the voice that followed. "He thinks us Brigands!" This man stood a few strides closer than the other two. He was shorter than the other man and lean like a wolf in winter. His face would have been handsome but he bore a ragged scar that ran from cheekbone to jawline. "Can you believe it, Vok?" He said laughing again. "He thinks we're here to rob him!" His brown hair was long and caught in a tail that danced as he laughed.

The first man spoke. "Do you think that we're bandits?" His features seemed carved from granite and his voice held as little warmth.

"I...no I don't suppose..." The woodcutter mumbled as he tried to think of a response. "I didn't...I didn't mean to...to say that..." His teeth were chattering now as he looked at the forbidding trio before him.

Seeming to grow bored, the shorter man shook his head. "How tedious."

"I...please understand..." The old man said, his words a jumble. "I...I wasn't trying to...I didn't mean to...to accuse you of..."

The woman smiled then and even though she was the very picture of feminine beauty, the expression terrified the woodcutter. "Yes..." She said softly. "But just *taste* his fear." She said it as if she had bitten into something incredibly sweet.

The man with the pony tail glided closer to the woodsman. His expression was still humorous but his large, dark eyes were unnerving. "Yes but it is mingled with confusion." He looked back at the other two. "I don't care for the tang."

The woodsman knew he should run or perhaps try to pull his axe and defend himself but he was paralyzed with terror now. He couldn't say how he knew it but these three were the cause of the unease that he'd been sensing. "I…I'm so sorry…" He began. There was something he couldn't figure out about these people. Something that made nameless dread well up in him.

"What are you sorry for?" The blonde woman said mocking yet sweet.

"I…I'm not…I don't…" The old man couldn't help but stutter.

"This is getting boring." The shorter man said looking back at the taller.

The man named Vok spoke, his deep voice reverberating. "What would you have?" He was speaking to his fellows.

The woodcutter took a step back then, his fear finally causing his muscles to loosen. Something within him knew he was in deadly peril and the survival instinct within him screamed that he should run now while he had a chance.

The woman, her voice now pouty like that of a spoiled child, said, "You two always rush everything." And seemed to sigh.

That was when the old woodsman realized what had missed. The 'sigh' wasn't real. It was a motion, an affectation, a modeled behavior triggered by a memory. Granted, he couldn't have explained any of it aloud but now his mind finally registered what his instincts had been shouting the whole time. The 'wrongness' that he felt from these people, the fear that seeped into him from merely looking at them was well founded. None of them *breathed!*

As the old man took another step back, the scarred one spoke. "He's realized it now." He didn't move but watched the woodcutter. "You can see it on his face and the flavor is different."

"Yes…" The lady spoke then and 'sighed' again, watching revulsion, terror and dawning understanding on the woodcutter's face. "I like it."

A grimace from the man with the ponytail and he slightly shook his head.

Laughter from the woman came then, this time at her companion. "You were always so picky."

The woodsman fell back another step, ready to run for all he was worth. His shaking hands raised to the strap that held the bundle of sticks on his back.

"He's too old." The scarred one said matter-of-factly.

The woman nodded, her voice sad, yet still mocking. "It's true, dear, you're just too old to be one of us."

Confusion warred with terror and the woodsman couldn't even guess what they were talking about. His hands shook terribly as he fumbled with the buckle that would drop his bundle to the ground. He looked down and steadied himself by force of will.

When he looked up the woman was right next to him and he froze.

"He reminds me of someone." She mused.

This close the old man saw that she was as beautiful and pale as a snow-capped mountain. It was obvious now that she didn't breathe and he stammered, "Tilva forfend!"

A harsh laugh from the scarred man as he too moved closer.

"Your withered gods cannot help you!" He said then, a cruel light in his eyes.

The woman raised a hand and touched the woodcutter's face, lightly stroking his gray beard. She radiated a chill and he shook even harder, his hands falling useless at his sides. "He reminds me of my father." She said with satisfaction but no real warmth. There was perhaps a hint of something...sadness perhaps? Then the moment was gone.

"Would you remake him then?" Vok asked, still standing where the woodsman had first seen him, as motionless as a stone.

With an almost imperceptible shake of her head, the lady stepped away. "No." As if discussing a cloud in the sky, she added.

46

"He is too old to serve."

Nods from the two with her and Vok said, "He shall feed the *Dregs* then."

The woodcutter didn't know who or what the Dregs might be but he suddenly found his courage and dropped his bundle. With newfound resolve he pulled the axe from his side and held it forward. "S…Stay back!" He warned. "I'll n…not…hesitate to use it!"

The woman seemed lost in thought as she looked at him but the scarred man stepped closer. "I see you've regained your nerve." Spite and malice were stamped on his features. "Show me!" He said getting closer.

The woodsman swung his axe then, his terror giving him strength he hadn't known in years. What happened next was mystifying to him as the scarred man moved like a blur and simply *took* the axe away from him as if he were a child. The move was so smooth and powerful that it took the old man a moment to realize he no longer held the weapon.

"Pitiful." The scarred man said then.

"Wha…what do you…want from me?" The old woodcutter asked then, his voice pleading. "W…why are you…doing this?" He wept and stuttered, hating his weakness, despising the way he sounded.

It was not the scarred man or the woman who answered but the tall man they called Vok. "The world is changing." He said simply, as if giving a lecture. "Your time is done. There are those who will serve and be remade and there are those who can only serve as cattle."

"You…you're going to eat me?" The old man could barely speak the words so great was his terror.

"No." Vok replied. "We do not feed in the way you think."

Laughter from the other two cruel and mocking now. They seemed inhuman monsters and the woodcutter wondered how he'd ever thought they could be people at all.

"Still, the Dregs must be fed." The man called Vok said

cryptically. He nodded toward the scarred one as he said it and the other man drove the woodcutter's own axe into his calf.

As the old man fell screaming in agony, his tormentors stepped away from him.   The wound bled freely and he could not staunch the flow. Then he became aware of other figures around him. Misshapen horrors lurched and clambered from beneath the overhangs and ledges of rocks. They made slavering noises as they crossed the clearing and the woodsman moaned, trying to crawl away. He didn't make it far as the first of the Dregs were upon him. The woodcutter screamed as they bit and clawed into him, devouring him while he yet lived.

The old man's shrieks lasted awhile as the three figures watched, something akin to ecstasy on their features.

They hadn't had a difficult time in finding the orc camp. It was a noisy place and the smoke from their many fires was visible for miles. They'd been cautious in their approach but had spotted no outlying sentries as they had approached. From their vantage in the ascending hills above the valley where the orcs were encamped, they could see everything without being observed.

"The savages don't even have outliers." Bandur said, his voice full of disdain. It was clear that as a former soldier, he found it ridiculous that the orcs wouldn't have guards outside the bounds of their encampment.

Venaro nodded. "Yes but it is fortunate for us that they don't." The merchant's face was worried. He knew the orcs couldn't see the three men, screened as they were by the dense vegetation that they now crouched in but he still felt exposed.

"They're orcs." Tanoc rumbled, as if that statement explained everything.

Nursing his broken wrist, Bandur glared at the barbarian. "Aye, savage brutes who know nothing of tactics, eh?" The insult and insinuation that the Northman was little better than the monsters below was clear.

Tanoc didn't say anything but slightly turned to look at the other man. He then stared pointedly at the Bandur's injury, his insult just as clear.

"Enough of that!" Venaro hissed nervously. "We're not here to bicker amongst ourselves!"

The two warriors glanced at the merchant and then at each other. They knew he was right and while there was no love lost between them, they also recognized that they had to set their differences aside.

The look wasn't lost on the trader and he nodded in satisfaction. "Well?" He said with a slight gesture toward the monster's camp in the valley below.

Tanoc rubbed a hand on his jaw, the stubble making a rasping sound. "It's a large camp but I don't see as many orcs as I'd expected."

Bandur rolled his eyes. "It's daytime, barbarian." His tone extravagantly patient as though the Northman were feeble minded. "Orcs hate sunlight. They're mostly sleeping, I'd wager."

"You weren't at the beach." Tanoc replied. He didn't look over but kept his gaze on the valley below.

Venaro spoke then. "He's right." His voice was thoughtful. "Perhaps the overcast weather makes them more comfortable. After all, I don't think that the sunlight actually hurts orcs." His tone welcomed comment but neither warrior did. It was well known that orcs despised the bright of day and preferred to move at night. However, they had all seen that the green savages had been active in the day.

Now glancing down at the camp, Bandur was forced to agree. "Perhaps they've found better hunting during the day." His voice was more than a little skeptical though. Orcs loved the dark of night best.

"Or maybe..." The barbarian muttered cryptically then. "Maybe they've found something at night they would rather shun."

The other two men exchanged a long look then. It was clear from the bleak expression on the Northman's face that he wasn't just guessing at something.

Venaro cleared his throat. "Tanoc, is there something you know?"

The youth refused to look at either of them and his jaw bunched. "I'm not sure." It was all Tanoc would say.

Bandur glared again at the barbarian. "If you know something about why these orcs are acting so strange…" He began fiercely but then trailed off. Tanoc had looked at him with a look so forbidding that he thought better of saying more.

"It doesn't matter." The merchant said then, his voice rueful.

Venaro's expression was as exasperated Bandur's but he didn't want the two to squabble here and give away their position. "The orcs are here and we've got to deal with them."

"I'll say it again, why don't we try to go around?" Bandur asked for at least the tenth time. "We could avoid the whole area and they'd never even know we were here."

With exaggerated patience, Venaro replied. "We have to use the trails that the wagons can pass through, as I've already said." They'd already been through this line of conversation. "If the orcs tumble to the fact that we're near, they could catch us on the move and kill us all."

Tanoc nodded and Bandur bit his tongue. The ex-soldier actually agreed with Venaro's assessment but he couldn't see what else they could do. It seemed hopeless and with their supplies running low, they couldn't hide up in the hills forever. The only trails the wagons could use ran dangerously close to the orcs.

"We have to deal with the orcs." Tanoc said bluntly.

Bandur looked at the merchant and then at the barbarian. "Oh, so that's the plan, is it? We'll just *deal* with the orcs?" His voice rose a bit louder than he'd intended and the merchant hissed at him. Lowering his tone, the former soldier asked mockingly, "And how shall we deal with them?"

Ignoring the other man's sarcasm, the young Northman pointed at the encampment below. "We slay their chieftain." He said it as simply as if he'd told them they should gather wood for a fire.

Now it was Venaro's turn to ask doubtfully, "How can that be done?"

With more than a little disdain, Tanoc proudly said, "Anyone can be slain."

Bandur shook his head. "Are you a madman?" Tanoc looked at him flatly but the guard continued speaking. "How are we to get through that many orcs, find their chief and then kill him without being cut to pieces ourselves?"

"I am no berserk." The young barbarian said seriously then. "It can be done. We sneak in and kill their chief before they know we're there."

With elaborate slowness and infinite patience, Venaro hazarded the question. "How?" He was afraid he already knew the answer. "How can anyone sneak into such a place?"

The barbarian's wolfish grin was chilling. "We need a diversion."

CHAPTER FIVE

The riders were not pleased nor were they hopeful. Their mounts seemed as dejected as they were, their heads low as they rode slowly down the trail leading down from the hills. There was little sound, save for the occasional jingle of harness or a low snort from the horses. Even these small noises were alarming to the riders, each one causing them to look around wildly. Fear was a constant companion for each of them.

Venaro recognized how close to panic these men were. He had chosen them because of the abilities as riders more than anything else. The plan that he, Tanoc and Bandur had formulated called for a diversion and Venaro and these riders were it. They knew and understood what they were doing and why, but this knowledge helped very little. The merchant felt much the same as they did, though he didn't let it show. For the ruse to be successful, they had to not only get the orcs attention but get enough of the camp to pursue them that Tanoc and those with him could sneak in and kill the orc chieftain.

The plan sounded risky, to say the least. There were a hundred things that could go wrong and when they had laid their strategy out to the men, they were understandably skeptical. The merchant couldn't really blame them, as he himself, had more doubts than a miser's coins. However, when it seemed that the drovers might actually refuse, Tanoc had intervened. The barbarian had bluntly told them that he was more than willing to simply take his chances alone. He was confident, he had informed them, that he could make his way south with little problem and if they each wanted to do that, it was another option. This had shut them up rather handily, Venaro had noted. They weren't woodsman or trackers nor were they warriors or soldiers and each of them, to a man, knew that if they went their separate ways, they would most likely all die.

So it was that they had grudgingly agreed to the stratagem, each man hoping they would survive and most doubting that they would. Still, Venaro felt that it was a sound plan. There was risk of course but balanced against everyone dying, it seemed worth the risk.

The trail began to level out a bit ahead and the merchant, who was in the lead, knew that they weren't far from the orc camp now. He had, some time ago, realized how lucky that they'd been that the orcs hadn't found where they were hiding up in the hills by now. It wasn't for lack of trying, of course, but Venaro guessed that the orcs, who weren't known for planning or critical thinking, simply hadn't been able to coordinate their search. It was this lack of strategy that Venaro and the others had counted on, when laying their plans.

As the trail widened, the trader urged the men to spread out where they could. "Remember, it has to look like we stumbled on to their camp by accident." He hissed in a low voice. The riders mostly nodded and did as they were bid, though they seemed reluctant to do so and still bunched up more than Venaro would have liked. He sighed, not really blaming them. In spite of his years abroad, the merchant was as scared as any of them. This could all go very wrong and they might all very well be dead soon. His face showed none of these concerns though, as Venaro was a past master at masking his emotions. The men following him were astonished at his calm demeanor and it allayed their fears somewhat.

Venaro hoped that Tanoc was ready. He prayed to every god he knew and then tossed in a few more to ones that he'd only heard of. The merchant was not a devout man but believed it never hurt to try every angle. He prayed that the orcs would fall for the gambit.

In a small canyon not far from the edges of the orc encampment, there was a thick clump of bushes. The canyon was more of a defile, a crack that ran back into the rocky beginnings of the hills for perhaps a hundred feet before ending. There was little here save for rocks, bones, shrubs and the occasional tree but near the entrance of the canyon, where it was widest, the clump of bushes had grown to engulf a large area. It was there that Tanoc and a few others now crouched.

The men had crept down to this spot shortly before dawn. The Northman had spied it when he, Venaro and Bandur had reconnoitered the orc camp the day before. He had reckoned that it was about as close as they could get without being spotted. Now, as he sat in the thick bushes, Tanoc was glad of his choice. They'd come right before dawn, knowing that as the sun rose, the orcs would be at their most lax. The barbarian had led the others down to the canyon without incident as the green-skins, ever lovers of darkness sought refuge from the hateful orb of fire.

Now they waited. The Northman took his ease, sitting cross-legged near the edge of the brush. He was calm and the others sought to emulate him. They were only a handful and Tanoc hadn't really wanted to bring anyone else, doubting their ability to keep up but both Bandur and Venaro had assured him that these men were the toughest they had. Callum was among the group that followed Tanoc. His earlier dislike of the barbarian had all but evaporated now and he and the others knew their best chance of survival was to watch the Northman's back. Bandur had wanted to come with this group but Venaro had forbade it flatly. Tanoc hadn't wanted him to come either, knowing that he'd be a liability with his injury.

The barbarian smiled, remembering the acid look he'd garnered for pointing out this fact to Bandur. In the end, Venaro had left the former soldier with the others remaining at the camp. He had put Bandur in charge of making ready to leave, which would take some time. It was a necessary task but Bandur was a warrior and it galled him to stay behind. Though he didn't know it, he'd earned respect from Tanoc for this, though he doubted greatly that the other man would care.

Tanoc knew that the waiting was hardest, even for veteran warriors, which the men following him were not. He knew that they would fidget and whisper, if he didn't keep them in line. Therefore, he had inspired them before they left camp by saying, "I will break the jaw of the first man to speak." No one had spoken a word as they crept down out of the hills.

Dawn had come and gone by the time the riders came to the outskirts of the orc camp and the sun was shining brightly for the first time in days. Bandur had proven to be right as there were little in the way of guards on the outskirts of the encampment. Venaro didn't know whether the orcs were just lazy or they truly hated the sunshine this much. Remembering the gray day the orc raiders had attacked them on the beach, Venaro thanked all the gods he'd ever heard of that the sun was out.

As they came down into the valley proper, they began to see huts and smoke in the distance. The camp had no walls as such and the merchant realized that they could have galloped straight into the center of the place. He had no such intention of such a suicidal move, of course, as they now saw the first few orcs. These green-skins were sentries that dozed fitfully in what shade they could find, much as human guards might have done in the late watches of the night. Shockingly, they didn't seem to notice the human riders that were closing in on the first hide dwellings.

Realizing that he didn't want to get too close and noting the fearful expressions on his men's faces, Venaro held up a hand and the riders stopped a mere thirty strides from the nearest orc. The trader then gave a surprised shout and looked around at the men with him. They well knew that they'd better be ready to ride out quickly.

They didn't have long to wait as the nearby orcs snapped out of their stupor and stared dumbly at them for what seemed like an eternity but was only a few seconds. Then one of them roared and grabbed up its weapon. This seemed to break the illusion of stillness and the orc camp seemed to come alive like an angered nest of wasps. Starting with the outermost huts and tents and moving inward, there were grunts and bellows as orcs stumbled into the daylight blinking and squinting in the sunlight.

Once they spotted the humans who had seemingly blundered into their camp, they invariably snatched up weapons and came on the run. Toward the center of camp were the pens where the orcs kept a few of their mounts, great scarred, slavering mountain wolves that they rode. It was beyond human understanding how much cruelty it would take to break a savage wolf nearly the size of a horse but Venaro was thankful that they only had a handful of the wolves.

Not waiting for the camp to be fully mobilized and seeing that the nearest orcs were rushing toward them, Venaro wheeled his horse around. Seeing a couple of his men fumble at their weapons. "Leave off!" He yelled at them then, startling them. He was angry now as they'd carefully gone over what to do. As they looked blankly at him, he nearly screamed, "Vendru be merciful, we've got to get out of here!" He knew they weren't stupid but had rather succumbed to the instinct that bade all men to either fight or flee. Those men thinking to draw their steel and fight were obviously brave and their actions might have been commendable under other circumstances. However, with an entire orc camp rushing toward them, bawling for their blood, in their bestial tongue, it was madness.

"RIDE!!!" Venaro shouted at the top of his lungs.

Watching the orc encampment come alive, Tanoc was struck with the same thoughts as Venaro, though he couldn't have known it.

He thought of fierce stinging insects maddened and blood hungry. The men with him shifted in their positions but stilled at a look from the forbidding north-men. He said nothing but turned to watch the camp.

The barbarian knew they couldn't give away their position too soon or they'd be facing too many of the orcs. He watched as Venaro and his riders wheeled about and rode away from the camp. They'd discussed the direction they'd go and the riders took a trail headed south, away from both the orc camp and the hills as well.

He watched as more and more orcs poured forth from their dwellings to pursue the riders. They'd also discussed the odds of the orcs pursuing on foot and guessed that they would, knowing that on the overgrown trails the horses wouldn't be able to move as quickly. They had guessed correctly and Tanoc knew there was a very real chance the green-skins would be able to catch them if they moved quickly enough.

The Northman watched as orcs mounted the savage wolves they used for mounts. Those following him were fidgeting now, thinking of their comrades who were being pursued but still Tanoc waited.

When a truly massive orc strode from the largest hut near the center of the village, Tanoc knew the wait was over. The creature was the largest orc he'd ever seen and clad in armor of bone and hide. The orc's helm was a large horned skull and he bore a great axe of dark iron. The chieftain bellowed and directed the remaining orcs to move in pursuit.

Looking back at the men behind him, the barbarian offered a ghastly grin. "Time to slay and die!"

Cursing the thick vegetation that grew around the trail, Venaro led his men as fast as he could. He reasoned that if they'd fled at top speed they'd have soon outdistanced the orcs and the green-skins would have turned back, which would have been disastrous for Tanoc and the others. Still, such reasoning was cold comfort when orcs were in pursuit, howling for your blood.

Looking back, he could see the orcs running along the trail behind them. The horses were only able to move at a slow trot along the narrow path and the riders had to be careful to avoid fallen trees, low hanging limbs and other obstacles along the way. Orcs weren't the fastest runners but their endurance was legendary and they were perhaps a stones' throw away, which was far too close for comfort.

As if to illustrate this fact, one of the closest orcs hurled a javelin. The missile barely missed its' mark as the rearmost rider screamed when the javelin nearly hit him. The orcs gave a collective roar and Venaro could see more of them readying to throw projectiles.

The merchant leaned forward then, crouching low in the saddle, hoping his men would follow suit. There was little else they could do but ride as fast as they dared along the twisting trail and hope the orcs weren't very accurate on the run. A stone hatchet spun past, embedding itself in a tree and Venaro gritted his teeth.

"Ride!" He shouted then. "Don't look back!" Even as he gave the order, he knew they wouldn't listen. He himself couldn't help but glancing back over his shoulder and cursed himself for a fool. All it would take was for one of them to miss a branch or stone in the road and they could easily be unhorsed or one of the horses could lose their footing.

As more and more missiles were hurled by the orcs, Venaro forced himself to look back in front of him, again riding low in the saddle, trying to present as small a target as possible. Luckily, there were twists and turns in the path that meant many of the orcs were trying to hit them through a screen of trees.

However, this also meant that the riders had to slow for these bends in the trail and that allowed the orcs to get closer. Some of the savages were abandoning the trail altogether and bulling through the thick brush to try to get to the riders. Luckily, the undergrowth was so thick they were slowed even more, though they still hurled what missile weapons they had. One of these orcs, a brute that had gotten tangled in a thorn bush, screeched in rage and hurled a short spear that hit a rider near Venaro in the side. The man gasped in agony and fell from his horse.

The merchant looked back helplessly as the orcs in pursuit quickly caught up to the fallen rider. The first savage that ran up had a war club studded with bits of jagged bone. The orc brained the unfortunate man with a bellow, killing him instantly. Looking back in front of him, Venaro spurred his horse as fast as he dared.

"Ride on!" The merchant cried.

Erupting from the clump of bushes like a whirlwind, Tanoc rushed toward the orc camp. Behind him, the men following him scrambled out as well, their weapons clutched tightly and their faces bleak. Each one of them knew they might well not live to see nightfall but they were brave men who knew their best chance of survival lay with the seemingly fearless barbarian. They gave no war-cry or shout, following the example of Tanoc but ran forward, their gasps for air as they ran the only sound that they made.

They rushed past the outer ring of huts without incident as these were abandoned by now. Even moving inward toward the center of the camp, there were few orcs in the way as many had already left in pursuit of the mounted humans. They were a hundred paces from the chieftain's tent before they were spotted by an orc who had woken late and was staggering out of a nearby hide tent, spear in hand. The brute bellowed a warning and stepped to block the barbarian's way and Tanoc's axe sheared into his head for his trouble.

Several orcs nearby heard the commotion and turned to see the Northman wrench the axe out of the dead orcs skull. Not hesitating, Tanoc barreled forward into the nearest orc between him and the chief's tent some twenty feet away. The orc had a war club in hand and leapt to meet the man. The barbarian blocked his opponent's clumsy blow and with a short back-handed stroke to the neck felled him.

Several more orcs moved to intercept the Northman who was now joined by his comrades. Tanoc buried his axe in the chest of the first orc, lodging it firmly in the monster's breastbone.

As it fell back, he released it, seeing another orc rush in from his left. Leaping out of the way of the monster's stroke, Tanoc ripped his sword from his scabbard. Before he could do more, however, the orc fell to the axe of Callum who had rushed in. Favoring the other man with a fierce grin, the barbarian loped forward. The other orcs that had tried to block his path to their chieftain were engaged in combat with the other men and his path was clear. Tanoc pulled his shield from his back as he closed in.

The orc chief was a true monster, nearly seven feet tall and vastly muscled. The brutal creature's bone and hide armor made a clacking sound as it moved to stand before the Northman. The thing bared its tusk-like teeth in a feral challenge and growled something in its savage tongue. Tanoc grinned back as he jogged easily forward. His answer was a hoarse bellow of challenge as he came on and the orc sprang forward to meet him.

Tanoc blocked the side cut of the heavy iron axe, his left arm jarred from the impact. Lunging, he stabbed at the creature's torso, his blade skittering off the bone armor. When the orc reared back for another swing, the barbarian leapt back and let the axe whistle past, hacking down with his broadsword. This time, his aim was true and he laid the orcs right forearm open, just above its hide and bone bracer. Enraged, the chieftain reversed its stroke, seeking to hack into Tanoc's ribcage. The youth twisted and pivoted to his right to block the blow and nearly dropped his sword from the impact.

Grinning again, the barbarian spat, "Too slow, dog!" He back-pedaled and spared a glance behind him. His men were acquitting themselves well but there were more orcs, stragglers who hadn't responded quickly enough to pursue Venaro and his riders, coming out of the huts and tents now. Even as he watch a man went down with a crude spear in his back.

Tanoc knew if he didn't end this quickly, they'd all be slaughtered.

The forest trail opened up ahead and Venaro smiled. It was a rather grim smile for he knew what was next. Beyond a short stretch of field where only grass and short bushes grew the terrain changed. There the trail ran alongside a cliff that reared up. This was the very path that Venaro and his men had toiled along and it had been just wide enough for the wagons to negotiate, albeit carefully.

Hoping to lose the orcs giving chase, he looked to his men and shouted, "Ride hard now!" Snapping his reins and letting his horse stretch out and really run. As he galloped along, he risked another look back.

Another of the riders had been slain when his horse stumbled over a root. He'd urged the beast to regain its footing but in a flash one of the wolves had caught up. The orc on its back had hacked into the man's side with an axe and he'd gone done. Venaro knew he'd be haunted by the deaths of these men who'd trusted him but he rode on. Each man had known the risks and each had realized long ago that if they stayed much longer in their camp in the hills they risked a slow death from starvation. That or the orcs would have eventually found them anyway, the merchant thought grimly.

Now, as the horses really began to run, the humans pulled away from their monstrous pursuers. The orcs on foot fell behind but those mounted on their slavering wolves leapt ahead. While the orcs outnumbered their prey, it was only by a few and Venaro hoped to lose them on the treacherous footing of the cliff-side path.

The horses pulled ahead of the wolves slowly but surely and as they approached the cliff, Venaro paused at the side, waving his men forward. He guessed that while the horses were faster, the great northern dire wolves, known far and wide for their stamina could eventually run them down. He meant to even the odds. He and a few of the riders had crossbows and as the other riders swept past, they quickly launched bolts at their pursuers. Venaro and another man found their mark as the wolves dashed forward. The merchant's arrow took a wolf in the chest, while the other rider's arrow took an orc rider in the throat.

"Aim for the wolves." Venaro said calmly. He silently gave the other man credit for his aim but it was more critical to slow or kill the wolves than it was to hit the orcs. Realizing that they had time for only one more volley before they'd have to flee, Venaro spoke again. "I've got the one left of center." The other men called their targets and then they fired. Three wolves were struck, one fatally as an arrow took it in the eye. The other two stumbled as one was hit in the chest and the other in the foreleg. It would have to be enough. The merchant hoped it was enough.

"Let's go!" Venaro yelled then, wheeling his horse. The other men followed suit moving to join their comrades who were already riding along the treacherous path along the side of the cliff. One unfortunate soul was too slow and the closest wolf leapt on him, knocking him from the saddle. The merchant couldn't afford to watch the wolf tear the man's throat out, though he heard the wet sound, like that of damp shredding paper, as he had to ride for his life.

The wolves were close behind the merchant and the other archers but the horses proved more sure-footed than the wolves on the narrow path. While normally, a wolf might prove more capable in such terrain, orcs are not the best riders and they sawed at the reins of their mounts as they pursued and more than one wolf fell from the side of the cliff-side path that day.

Again, the horses pulled ahead and now Venaro could see the men who'd ridden past the archers waiting on the far side where the ground leveled out again. They had dismounted and were waiting with braced spears. There were only a few of them but between arrow fire and wolves losing their footing it was enough. The merchant and his archers rode past and the spearmen held their ground, impaling the wolves that ran in heedless of danger, at the urging of their orcs riders.

The trader and the other men then rode back past the spearmen, their swords now in hand. Alongside the drovers armed with spears, they made short work of the orcs and wolves who were scattered along the cliff-side. Superior tactics and planning had won over savagery and blind fury.

Not allowing his men time to gloat, Venaro barked orders as soon as the last orc fell. "Everyone back in the saddle!" In the distance, those orcs on foot were running for all they were worth to get to the cliff-side trail but the merchant could tell they had time to get away. "We'll head into the forest on the other side of the cliff, just as we planned!" He said, wiping sweat from his forehead. Though his men knew the plan, he felt it would bolster them to hear the next part again. "We'll lose the orcs on the trails there and double back!"

Venaro had no doubt that the next part of the plan would work. Past the cliff-side trail there were many trails as the terrain descended into the lowlands. It would be easy enough to get ahead of the orcs and follow a different path back. Then, they would head back toward their camp in the hills and wait for the group led by the barbarian.

'It's all up to Tanoc now.' The merchant thought, hoping the others were still alive.

Dodging a thrust from an orc with a spear, the barbarian shield-bashed his foe in the face. Hearing teeth break and the orc grunt in pain, Tanoc gave the chieftain a forbidding look. Twice, they had traded blows and while the Northman had opened a cut up on the orcs leg, the brutal chieftain had replied with a strike that had gashed into the leather armor on his chest. Tanoc realized the wound wasn't bad but it bled freely and he knew if he hadn't leapt back the blow would have killed him.

From behind him, Tanoc heard a cry of pain and turned to see Callum give ground as an orc hacked into his shoulder. The drover and his companions had fought bravely but there were only three of them now and they had huddled together slashing at their enemies while trying to protect the barbarians back.

Knowing that they were out of time, Tanoc threw himself on the offensive, his sword moving in swift arcs of glittering steel. The orc chief blocked the first, sidestepped the second then sought to counterstrike. The brute had missed the third strike however and the blow caught him on the neck.

While not fatal, the orc lurched back, one hand going up to staunch the flow of its dark blood. A cunning warrior, the orc swung its axe in front of it even as it gave ground. However, swinging the cumbersome weapon one-handed was slow and the Northman easily blocked the strike.

Feeling his shield splinter, Tanoc threw it down and sprang forward. Gripping his sword in both hands, he hammered down on the haft of the orc's axe and then drove forward. The point of his blade punctured the bone and hide breastplate and the orc toppled backward. Wasting no time, the barbarian, feeling rather than seeing that someone was behind him whirled to see the orc he'd shield-bashed lurching forward. His blade as swift as lightning, Tanoc clove the monster's skull. Spinning back to the fallen chieftain, he saw that the tough orc was trying to regain his feet. The Northman gave him no chance and brought his boot down hard on the hand that feebly tried to raise the axe in defense. Pitilessly, Tanoc brought his sword in a whistling side cut that half severed the orcs head. A quick stroke finished the job.

Stooping, Tanoc grabbed the horns of the slain chieftain's helm. The horned helm had a hide strap and so the severed head was still inside. Turning, the barbarian held up the grisly trophy and roared at the top of his lungs.

There were less than a dozen orcs left and they stopped short as the barbarian held aloft the severed head of their chieftain, who they'd until recently believed to be invincible. The indomitable barbarian bellowed more savagely than any orc and threw the head at the closest orc. It was too much for the superstitious savages, who worshipped the strength of their leaders next to that of their brutal gods. The orcs fled in terror before the grim barbarian, thinking that he must be something other than mortal.

Looking around, Tanoc saw that only Callum and another man had survived. Retrieving his shield, he strode over to the drovers and looked at them. With a glance at Callum he grinned. "Thought they killed you back there."

"Not yet, you bastard!" Callum retorted but for all his bluster, he grinned back. They'd have all died without Tanoc this day and he well knew it.

The Northman nodded and turned away from the carnage. "Leave them." He said to the drover who was trying to drag one of the bodies of his companions away. "There's no time."

"If we leave their bodies here, the orcs will come back and eat 'em!" The other man protested.

Tanoc stepped close and looked into the man's eyes until he looked away. "If we try to carry our dead away, it'll be us in the pot!" Seeing the other man hesitate, the barbarian shrugged and walked away, giving the matter no further concern.

As the Northman strode away from the orc camp, Callum walked over to the other drover, holding his injured shoulder. "He's right." He said, clearly not liking the situation any better than the other man. After a moment's hesitation, the two turned to follow the man they'd pulled from the sea.

CHAPTER SIX

Shaking his head slightly to ward off the drowsiness that
assailed him, the priest sat up straighter. It was very warm in the
room, the fireplace roaring to ward off the spring chill. Realizing that
it wasn't the first time he'd nearly succumbed to weariness, he chided
himself and looked around.

It was a nice office, built in one of the nicest homes in town.
Built of timber and fieldstone, the structure was very solid and warm,
unlike many of the nearby homes and businesses. The floors were
flagstone with thick rugs and the walls were of paneled oak.
Paintings and tapestries adorned the walls and wrought iron sconces
were placed at tasteful intervals. A large desk dominated the room,
solid and intricately carved. There were several bookshelves in the
room and the chairs, one of which the priest now sat in completed
the furnishings.

Thinking to himself that the headman of this town lived like a
lord, the priest rose and walked to a nearby window. Opening the
window a hands span to let in the cool air, he was a little startled at
the quality of the glass panes, knowing how expensive such
workmanship was. Breathing a sigh of relief, he walked back to sit in
the chair.

As he sat, the door to the office opened and a tall, pudgy man
in fine clothes entered. Walking over to where the priest sat, he

extended a hand in greeting. "Good day." The man said. "I am Edber, mayor of Wend." The headman seemed friendly enough but there was something in his eyes that wasn't overly welcoming.

Standing and taking the mayor's hand, the priest answered. "Well met, mayor." His voice was warm and almost jovial as he tried to put the official at ease. "I am brother Cenric of the Order of the Veiled Hammer." As he shook the other man's hand, the priest found it to be soft and pale, his grip feeble. Briefly, the priest mused that the mayor was one of those men who would have been strong had he not lived a life of ease and comfort.

The mayor was similarly sizing up the priest. Cenric was of middling height, stoutly built and clad in dark rough-spun clothing of dark brown trimmed with mustard yellow. Edber couldn't help but cringe, thinking that he would never have worn such colors or plain clothing. The priests' hands were thick and rough like a mason or field hands, his grip firm and his shoulders broad. A spreading paunch and a thinning fringe of gray hair showed that the priest was a bit older than the official and Edber would have guessed he'd seen at least fifty summers or more in his life. The priests face was round and kindly, as was his manner and Mayor Edber found himself relaxing a bit.

Waving toward one of the chairs in front of the large desk, the mayor walked around it. "Please, take a seat." He offered. He cursed under his breath and moved to the window, shutting it firmly. Turning back to his desk, the mayor shivered and sat down. "So, what brings you to our fair town?" He asked, striving to match the friendly tone of the cleric sitting across from him.

"I've been sent here by my order to investigate certain rumors." The priest said carefully. He well knew that officials like the mayor were seldom happy with anyone prying into their affairs.

"And what rumors are you speaking of?" The mayor asked haughtily. His air was that of someone who's heard news they half expected but still finds it offensive nonetheless.

Keeping his own voice as friendly as possible, Cenric

answered. "We've heard of the disappearances, stories of empty villages, strange markings on buildings." The priest was sure that the mayor knew exactly why he was here and exactly what rumors he was talking about.

Mayor Edber wasn't happy. "Wild exaggerations." He said flatly, all pretense of goodwill evaporated. "This region has always had problems, of course." He said, gesturing vaguely toward the window as if to encompass all the world outside it. "Orcs and other monsters have ever plagued this land."

"From what we've heard, these aren't orc attacks." Cenric retorted, a bit of the warmth slipping from his own voice. "Orcs burn and pillage. They leave a discernable footprint, if you will. From all we've heard, these settlements are empty and unspoiled, yet there is no trace of their inhabitants."

His face flushing an ugly crimson hue, the mayor snapped. "Children's tales!" He was glaring at the clergyman with open hostility now. "This isn't the first time I've heard such nonsense."

"So you have heard the rumors, then?" The priest replied. His face was bland and there was a hint of sarcasm in his voice. "Because it seemed to me that you weren't sure what I was talking about just a moment ago.

Gritting his teeth, Mayor Edber responded coldly. "There are always rumors that people tell each other." He shrugged and continued indifferently, "They are mostly poor people with nothing better to do than make up stories to scare each other." Leaning forward in his chair, he asked, "What is any of this to you? Why would a church send a priest here because of such tales?"

"My order is very old, founded during the wars." Cenric said slowly. He didn't need to clarify which war, as the realms of the north had been fighting for generations until they nearly destroyed each other. While the kingdom of Gurral had ultimately won the conflict, they were as decimated as the losers and anarchy had descended like a fat vulture. There was nothing approaching stable government and towns and villages had to become self-sufficient or perish. Most had become like Wend, a walled town who traded with other settlements but looked only to their own interests and concerns.

With apprehension in his voice, the mayor asked, "A militant order?" It was clear that he didn't want trouble with such an organization. Though such orders had no authority over a town, they were often powerful and their aims and goals difficult to understand.

The priest nodded. "Yes, though we did not fight in the wars."

Confusion clouded the official's features. "I don't understand." He was intrigued despite himself. "How can you be a militant order, yet not fight in battle?"

"Oh we do indeed fight." The cleric said. "However, my order does not combat our fellow man. We war against the dark forces who would destroy mankind itself."

Leaning back in his chair, the mayor paled. "Are you some witch-hunter then?" He all but snarled. "Come to burn old women at the stake because they look like crones?" Finding his courage then, Edber brought a clenched fist down on top of the desk. "I'll not allow you to harass the people of Wend!"

In a soothing voice, the priest held up both hands in a gesture of peace. "That is not what I do, mayor." Cenric's voice was smooth and calm. "Nor is persecuting herbalists and hedge wizards something I agree with. Neither I or my order condones such practices."

Somewhat mollified, the mayor sat back again. His voice was demanding then, as he asked. "Just what do you think is going on here?" He asked, fear and curiosity at war in every word. "Speak plainly."

"Very well." Cenric replied and leaned back himself, his voice becoming thoughtful. "The Order of the Veiled Hammer is, as I told you, a militant order. However, as I also said, we do not battle our fellow man but rather, for lack of a better term, the forces of darkness." The priest could have been lecturing in a hall as he continued. "As you know, the wars that have engulfed the known lands have all but destroyed higher government and left the people vulnerable."

The mayor gave a sniff at that. "Yes but we won in the end." There was an unmistakable air of patriotic pride about the man. "Gurral was victorious, as our cause was just and the gods were with us."

Cenric snorted at that. "The winning side always believes that their cause was just and the gods foreordained their victory." His face was gloomy as he added, "The losers feel their cause no less just but that the gods have abandoned them."

"That's a strange way for a militant cleric and Gurralite to speak." The mayor said, with a strange look.

The priest shrugged. "I've fought in many battles, mayor and they're nowhere near as glorious as the stories say."

"But you said that your order did not fight in the wars!" Mayor Edber protested.

With a sigh, Cenric retorted. "My order was founded over a hundred years ago. It was founded by knights and clerics who understood what was happening. They knew the wars that overtook the continent and then spread beyond would decimate the populace and leave *every* nation weakened." He looked intently at the mayor. "I never said that I'd never fought in battle. I only said that my order did not participate in the wars." There was regret in his voice as Cenric added. "I came to my calling later in life."

"Ah, so you were a soldier?" The mayor said approvingly. "What battles did you partake in?" There was real curiosity in the man's voice.

Despite his outward calm, Cenric's temper flared momentarily. The idea that this soft, money grubbing man was hungry for details of battles was offensive to him. He remembered all too clearly his last battle, the way the man, little more than a boy, had looked up beseechingly at him...

With a shake of his head, the priest practically spat. "I'm not here to discuss such things, mayor."

"Then what *are* you here for?" The other man replied flatly. "I asked you to speak plainly and you launched into a history lesson." It was clear that he thought he was being reasonable. "I asked a few details and you grow hostile."

Rubbing his balding pate, Cenric modulated his tone. "Please, forgive me." Inwardly, the priest berated himself for losing control, however briefly. "I've had a long journey and I'm tired." The mayor nodded but his expression remained neutral. Sighing again, the cleric decided it was time to be blunt. "As you know, there are much worse things than orcs or bandits in the world. These things are *not* children's stories or fables told by old people with nothing better to do." The priest's tone was firm now.

"There are wicked things that have stepped from the shadows to feast on the corpses of realms too weary and weakened to even realize what is happening." Cenric was trying to read the other man but the mayor was every bit a politician and his expression was neutral and guarded. "My order combats these creatures."

The mayor nodded then. "Of course I'm well aware that there are monstrous creatures that prey on men." His voice was conciliatory but the priest could tell the man was being condescending. "However, when a town has walls and vigilant guards..."

Cenric interrupted him bluntly. "I've seen towns just like Wend that were empty and lifeless. Their walls were still intact and their goods left for brigands to despoil." He finished in an emphatic tone, "Yet there was not a living soul to be found."

The mayor did not care at all for being interrupted and it showed. "Perhaps you speak of small villages, sir but I assure you that Wend can look after itself!"

The priest shook his head. He'd hoped that the mayor was simply pompous and greedy. Now, he was certain that the man was willful and stupid as well. His friendly look gone, Cenric stated, "And I can assure you, mayor, that Wend will suffer the same fate, if you aren't careful."

Lurching to his feet, Mayor Edber drew himself up fully to his not inconsiderable height. "I'll not have you rabble rousing and causing trouble here!" He all but shouted, pointing a finger at the priest. "I've been patient but I am warning you!"

Rising smoothly, the priest locked eyes with the mayor. "I am not here to cause trouble." He struggled to maintain his own temper. "I have already told you why I'm here." He couldn't keep the incredulity from his own voice.

"Wend does not need the help of your order." The mayor stated grandly. "We have looked out for ourselves for a long time now." There was self-satisfaction in his voice and manner.

"Do you truly mean to say that your pride would keep you from accepting help?" Cenric asked, anger and disbelief evident in every word.

Straightening his fine coat, the mayor snapped. "We don't need nosy outsiders causing people to panic and stirring up worry among the people." His voice was imperious. "I know what is best for my town, priest, not you."

Sadly, the cleric shook his head. "You are a fool, then."

"Silence!" The mayor shouted. "You'll not speak to me so in my own home!"

A voice came from outside the door then. "Is everything alright, mayor?"

"Everything's fine!" He stated in a register just below a roar. Then the mayor looked back to the priest. "I could simply have you thrown out by my guards out there. However, I do not wish to treat a man of the cloth so, even one who has acted so disrespectfully."

Cenric laughed out loud then. "I doubt that your guards would be up to the task." There was a dangerous glint in his eyes and the mayor's gaze strayed to the priests belongings, among which was a warhammer. Seeing where the other man was looking, he raised a hand. "I'm not here to fight with you or your guards. I've already told you I'm here to look into these rumors."

"Rumors of what?" The mayor shot back. "Missing people? Empty homes and villages? I already told you that I understand there are monsters and bad men out there."

"Then what harm is there in me investigating these things, mayor?" The cleric answered evenly. "There is more to it than missing people and I can't believe that you think it's simply orcs at work here." Now, he reverted to his lecturing voice, seeking balance in the conversation. "There are things that presage horrible events. Things that we call Emergences." Seeing the other man's uncomprehending look, Cenric continued. "Emergences are when things, evil things, begin to creep into the lands of men."

Unconvinced, the mayor shrugged. "And what makes you think that these things you're talking about are 'Emergences' as you put it?"

Leaning forward, Cenric answered. "Because all the signs are there." He hoped against hope that he could still get through to this man. "There are beings that feast not just on the flesh of men but their very feelings, even their souls. Worst among all of these are the Pallid."

"Enough!" The mayor hissed, shakily. "I'm not listening to any more of these ghoulish tales! We've plenty of problems without you causing a panic with these stories!" He gazed again at the priest's hammer propped against his pack. He half muttered, "I should have you escorted from the town."

"I am not here to cause you any trouble. I swear by the hammer." Cenric said fervently. He added the oath reflexively, knowing that the politician wouldn't have a clue what the vow meant or how serious it was. "I am not going to cause a panic or tell people what I'm doing. You can trust in my discretion." He knew how urgent the matter was and decided to add, "If you were to run me out of town, you should know that my order would take it as a grievous offense."

Sarcastically, the mayor replied, "But your order does not make war on their fellow man. Wasn't that what you told me?"

Gritting his teeth, Cenric nodded. "Yes and I spoke the truth. However, my order will not ignore harm done to one of its own." His voice was steely. "I am going to investigate these rumors and I will do so without causing you or your townsfolk any worry. You have my word."

The mayor hesitated before replying. The last thing that he wanted was a vendetta with a powerful order of professional warriors, however noble and lofty they claimed their goals were. "Very well, priest but I shall hold you to your word."

Cenric bowed slightly. "Farewell." He had nothing more to add and grabbed his things, heading toward the door. As he walked past the guard in the hall, he measured the other man up despite himself. Making his way out of the fine house, he reminded himself that the citizens of Wend were not his enemies. He was here to help them, despite the idiocy of their leader.

If the priest had realized that it wasn't simply stupidity at work, he would have looked more closely into the mayor. If he had known what was really going on, he would have crushed the man's skull right there in his own study. However, there was no way even so keen an investigator as Cenric could have realized what was really happening in the town of Wend at that point. He could never have guessed how little time was left.

So, Cenric, unconsciously whistling an old tune he'd learned from a soldier long ago, went to find lodging for the night.

For a long time after the priest left, Mayor Edber sat looking into the fire. He was angry and more than a little afraid. He felt sure that the cleric could see right through him and the feeling was unsettling. He simply sat and drank wine for a time.

Eventually, there was a knock at the door and he grunted, "Enter."

The door opened and a thin, sallow man walked in. He walked with a pronounced limp and made his way slowly to the other chair near the fire, sinking gratefully into it.

The mayor looked at his visitor and with a sour look, took another drink. The man looked more than half a beggar. His clothes were shabby and stained with food and wine. Stubble had staked a rather permanent claim on his features and not for the first time, the mayor wished he would either grow a proper beard or shave. The man's eyes were watery and squinting but there was unmistakable intelligence there.

"What did the priest want?" The visitor asked, his voice raspy and annoying.

Not for the first time, Edber cursed the day he'd met the other man. "Nothing." He said noncommittally. Then, seeing the other man look closely at him added, "He's new to the town and passing through."

"Don't lie to me!" The visitor hissed.

Shocked despite himself, the mayor leaned forward, his face flushing in anger. "Have you forgotten to whom you speak?!"

The shabby man countered. "Have you forgotten *for* whom I speak?"

The mayor recoiled and said nothing. Instead, he took another long pull from his cup, draining it.

With a low, satisfied tone, the mayor's visitor pressed. "Tell me, Edber, what did he want?"

Too shaken to bristle at the other man's ignoring his title, the mayor finally responded. "He's here to investigate the rumors." He glanced at the feeble little man not for the first time thinking how easy it would be to simply get rid of him. However, he shuddered to think of the consequences. "He mentioned the disappearances, the empty villages…"

"Hmph!" The shabby man said then. "You should have run him out of town!"

"Don't you think I didn't consider that?!" Edber replied. "He said he's from a militant order! There would be no end of trouble if I did that!"

"It doesn't matter." The other man mused. His expression was thoughtful and almost satisfied. It was troubling to the mayor.

"He...the priest mentioned...the Pallid." Edber said, his voice thick with dread.

"Bah!" The visitor scoffed. "Tales made up to frighten children!"

"That's what I told the cleric." The mayor said, rather uncertainly. "Yet, I wonder at what's happened since our deal with these strangers."

"What?!" The shabby man said derisively. "What are you saying? Do you honestly think they're somehow involved all that?" His tone was scornful. "Do you think our benefactors are undead come from the shadows to destroy us? Do you hear yourself?"

"Well..." Edber said timidly, hating the sound of his own voice. "It does sound far-fetched..."

"Ha!" The other man laughed jovially. "Of course it does!" Leaning in closely, he all but whispered. "Have you forgotten how much coin they've made us?"

Licking his lips, the mayor nodded nervously looking at the door.

The shabby man leaned back. "We stand to make a good deal more, mister mayor. You know that." He looked appraisingly at the leader of Wend. "Don't tell me that you want to back out now?"

"I don't know..." Edber said indecisively. "Maybe...maybe that's what I should do. What we both should do."

"Speak for yourself." The other man shot back. "I've been poor my whole life. I've never had anything and they've made me wealthier than I could have ever dreamed."

"But..." The mayor began fearfully. "Do you think...Is it possible they've had something to do with what's happening to the other settlements? When we began our dealings..."

"All we did was tell them things they could have found out on their own." The scruffy looking man interrupted then. "We just saved them some time." His tone grew appeasing then. "Look, they

76

have nothing to do with these disappearances and troubles. They're simply a consortium out to make money like the rest of us." Seeing that the mayor was nodding, the man continued. "You know these things are caused by orcs and bandits. Think how we can use the money we make from all this. You can make the town safer...stronger."

Edber continued to nod. "It's for the good of the town." He said, beginning to believe his own lie.

The shabbily dressed man nodded as well. "When Wend is the main hub of trade in the north, you'll see it was all for the best, my friend." He stood then and shuffled toward the door. "You'll keep an eye on this priest, won't you?"

The mayor paused in pouring himself another drink and nodded.

"Good." The shabby man replied and left. Not for the first time thinking he'd be glad when he no longer had to deal with the pompous idiot the town called a leader. Soon, he would be rewarded and not with simple coin. Soon, he would be remade.

CHAPTER SEVEN

Giving way more and more to level ground, the hills fell away behind the caravan. The forest trails had changed to wider paths before they became still larger cart paths. The wagons moved more smoothly along here and ahead, the paths became true roads.

Venaro smiled, thinking that they'd make good time once they'd reached the roads later that afternoon. He rode easily in the saddle, at the front of the line, glancing back occasionally to check on his caravan. Progress was slower now that they'd lost so many men and the wounded weighed the wagons down even more, the teams of horses working hard to toil ahead. Still, every man still alive knew that they could all just as easily have been dead.

The merchant looked at the barbarian riding alongside him, thinking that without him they'd never have survived. He knew that most of the men would have agreed, having seen the young giant in action. Most of the hard feelings and worries had faded, although Bandur still seemed surly around the barbarian. However, the ex-soldier's friend Callum had called him a fool after all that had happened and Venaro was pleased to see Bandur had acted more civilly toward the Northman.

Sensing the trader's gaze upon him, Tanoc turned to look at Venaro. "Something to say, merchant?" He asked in his deep voice.

Laughing despite himself, Venaro shook his head. "No, my

friend." He breathed in deeply the damp spring air. "Just…happy to be alive!"

Tanoc looked at the merchant for a long moment to make sure the other man wasn't somehow mocking him and then nodded. Then, the barbarian returned to scanning the forest that was receding around and behind them. Ahead the cart path wound down into true plains as the woods surrendered their hold on the land.

"You'll like Wend, I think." Venaro said then. He just felt like talking and also knew that he owed the barbarian his life. It wouldn't do to have him going into a civilized town and not understanding the rules. "It's a fine town with a great many amenities."

The Northman looked round again, his expression like carved stone. He didn't reply but simply stared hard at the merchant.

Realizing that perhaps the uncultured barbarian might not know what the word amenity meant but not foolish enough to try and teach him, Venaro hastily went on. "There are fine taverns and inns there and shops where you can buy most anything."

Tanoc's expression changed slightly and the trader could tell he had piqued the other mans' interest. He smiled, thinking that he was getting to know this grim warrior better as such a minor variation told him. Venaro had begun to realize that for the taciturn warrior, such changes in aspect spoke volumes to those who paid attention.

Realizing that he had the barbarian's attention, Venaro continued extolling the virtues of Wend and with it, civilization. "Towns like Wend are much larger than most of the other villages in this region. It's a center for trade and news of distant places can be found there."

"We have large settlements in my homeland as well." Tanoc grunted then. He seemed about to say more but then something stopped him and he looked away.

Venaro would have sworn that there was sadness and fear in that look but he wasn't suicidal enough to mention it. "Of course, I've heard of the great port of Rund."

Again, Tanoc looked at the merchant, this time in disbelief.

"You've been to Rund?"

The merchant replied, "No, I've never been there, I said I've heard of it." He hesitated, then asked, "Is that where you're from?"

"No." Tanoc said after a moment. The Northman's eyes were troubled and he murmured, "My village was west of Rund. We would go there sometimes, so my father could trade or to take to the ships…"

Realizing that Tanoc's mind was far away and not wishing to pry. Venaro grew silent. It was obvious to him that the barbarian didn't want to talk about whatever had caused him to leave his home. Venaro knew that when the north-men took to their ships it was most often to raid and pillage other lands. He didn't see either topic as productive and said nothing more.

After a time, Tanoc spoke. "What kind of place is this Wend?"

Venaro gave a slight start then. The Northman wasn't one to initiate conversation and he was surprised. Looking over at Tanoc, he guessed that the man was trying to figure out what kind of reception he could expect. It made sense, given that he was a Northman, whose people had always preyed on the settlements of other peoples.

"As a center for trade, Wend is open to all travelers." Venaro replied. Judging by Tanoc's nod, the merchant knew he'd guessed correctly. "Of course, you would perhaps have a rather chilly reception on your own, I would guess." Seeing the barbarian's jaw bunch, he went on hastily. "With us as companions, however, I don't foresee any problems."

Tanoc snorted in reply and shrugged. Venaro, again reading the man's gestures, estimated that the Northman was saying if there were any problems he wouldn't be the one to regret them.

"Of course, there are rules in Wend, as with any town." Venaro began carefully. "It would help if you understand the way things work. That is, if you plan on continuing to journey with us?"

Silence met him for a long while and they rode along. The barbarian didn't reply for a time and Venaro simply waited, listening to the sounds of the trail. The creaking wagons, the murmurs of the men around them, the jingle of the horses' harness, the buzz of insects and chirping of birds in the thinning trees. These were the sounds that the merchant knew so well and he felt more at home with them than he did in any house or tavern.

Just as Venaro was sure the barbarian was done talking, Tanoc spoke again. "I will go at least as far as this town with you." His voice was thoughtful. "After that…I don't know."

The merchant nodded then. He was happy to know the capable warrior would be with them to the city and the fact was he had begun to think of the Northman as a friend. Venaro wanted to at least help him acclimate to civilization a bit before they parted ways and was thinking of how best to phrase this when Tanoc spoke again.

"We have laws in my homeland." The barbarian said in stiff tones. "My people aren't savages."

"Ah…of course not." Venaro said cautiously. "I did not mean to imply…" He broke off then, seeing that Tanoc was grinning at him. The big barbarian had a strange sense of humor but at least he had one. Grinning back, Venaro quipped, "Of course, I'm sure laws are different there."

Tanoc nodded, still grinning. "Yes, we have a law that states any woman can throw any man out of her home for any reason, even a chieftain"

That took Venaro aback for a moment and he chuckled, blurting out, "You know, my friend, that's a good law!"

"You have no such law?" The barbarian questioned then.

With a shake of his head, Venaro explained. "I'm quite sure that neither Wend nor the villages in the kingdom of Gurral have such a law." He smiled broadly. "Of course I am not from this kingdom and my own country has different laws and customs."

Tanoc's look was appraising. "I thought you looked a bit different from the others." He said with a gesture back toward the men around them. "You are a stranger here like me then?"

Venaro hesitated before answering. "I am a foreigner to Gurral but not quite a stranger." He pondered how best to explain, then realizing that the Northman surely would understand the concept of trade. "As a merchant, I travel many lands. I've been doing this for a long time and I am rather well known in many places." With a conspiratorial wink, he added, "It is how I've made my coin."

The barbarian answered, almost thinking aloud. "So, they might not attack me immediately in this town?"

Venaro realized that this whole time the Northman had assumed he'd have to fight when they got to Wend. It came to him as well that Tanoc had been trying to figure out whether or not the merchant and his men would stand with him in such an event. Venaro knew then that Tanoc was quite intelligent, though he thought in a manner that might seem alien to civilized men. Violence was such a part of him, such an integral way of life that it was always an acceptable solution and one that he didn't fear but relished.

"No, Tanoc." Venaro said slowly, trying to think how best to explain. "They will be afraid or angry, at first. There are those who will think you are there ahead of more of your people, perhaps to spy out the land."

"Hah!" Tanoc broke in. "My people don't spy, we attack!"

Cringing inwardly, Venaro answered. "Yes, well as I say, there are those who will think that you mean harm to them, however, once they see that it isn't so…"

Again, the barbarian cut in. "How can they know if I mean them harm?" He asked with a puzzled expression. "I don't know if I will kill any of them." He shrugged. "I haven't met them yet."

A chill swept through the merchant at how casually the other man spoke of killing. "That's just it, Tanoc." He said firmly. "There are laws against killing in civilized towns."

Now the Northman's expression was amazement mixed with disgust. "What if someone insults me or draws steel?" His voice was incredulous as if he thought the merchant was jesting with him.

Keeping his voice calm, Venaro said, "There are guards in the town that will intervene. You can of course defend yourself if your life is threatened and at your trial that would be taken into account…"

Tanoc interrupted once more. "Are these people mad?"

"Don't you have trials in your homeland?" Venaro asked flatly. He knew that he was talking with a barbarian but at times the man's rudeness did offend even the unflappable merchant.

"Well…yes." The Northman replied, mystified. "But not because someone slew someone else in fair combat."

Again, the merchant found himself shaking his head. "That's what the trial would be about, don't you understand?" Trying a different tack, he said, "Listen, just don't kill anyone if you don't have to, alright?"

Another shrug of the thick shoulders. "I never kill anyone that I don't have too." Tanoc said as if he was talking to a simpleton.

Trying hard to keep frustration from his voice, Venaro said, "You can't kill someone because they insult you or because you don't like them."

Now the barbarian's only response was a look that said the merchant was a madman. He shook his wild mane and barked a laugh.

Patiently, the merchant continued. "If you have to defend yourself, then of course…"

"What of the right of challenge?" Tanoc interrupted. "What of the tradition of single combat to settle a dispute? Are you saying that this place doesn't recognize these things?"

"Well…not as such." The merchant began, ignoring the fact that he'd been interrupted yet again. "As I said, if you have to defend yourself…"

Once more, Tanoc interjected. "Madness!" He seemed agitated. "To think you people call us barbarians! If I…"

Now, it was Venaro's turn to interrupt. He knew it wasn't prudent or polite but he'd had enough. "Look, if you don't heed the laws of the land, you won't last long!" He hadn't realized it but they'd both reined in their mounts and were glaring at each other.

Before either of them could say more, they were both interrupted.

"Venaro." One of the drover's had ridden up to them, wearing a troubled look.

"What?!" The merchant snapped. He regretted his irritation almost instantly. The man was one of the outriders, tasked with riding ahead of the main caravan to keep lookout and warn them of danger. Venaro knew he was just doing his job. "What is it?" He said more evenly.

"There's something out there." The man said, pointing to a large clearing ahead. There was a large clearing there, beyond which were clumps of trees instead of true forest. They weren't far from the plains now.

Venaro looked where the man was pointing. "I see nothing."

"Not in the clearing, sir." The drover said nervously. "In the trees beyond."

"Orcs?" Tanoc asked with a growl, his hand moving toward his battle-axe.

"No." The man answered, his face pale. "Something else."

Silence ruled the cells. It had been some time since the other prisoners had left, the bread thief being let go with a warning and the drunk the same. A couple more malefactors had come and gone and still the strange woman languished in her cell. At least that was how Gren thought of it. It just didn't seem right for her to stay there. He wasn't sure what she'd done, although he'd heard there was murder somehow involved. Looking at her now as she lay in the bunk, he thought it preposterous.

"Hedolf said you'd taken a fancy to her." The other guard noted.

The observation drew a black look from the burly Gren. "Hedolf's a fool!" He snapped angrily.

The other individual was a slim man with a drooping mustache named Harman. The two got along good in most things as

Harman was young and considered himself something of a ladies man. Whether or not this was true was a matter for some debate as Gren and the others had seen Harman laughed at by as many girls as had given him the time of day. Still, the man was a fine archer and knew how to keep his mouth shut, Gren mused.

With a shrug, Harman replied, "Don't know if I'd say he's a fool." He chuckled at Gren's glower. "I'd say he just forgot what it was like to be young and unmarried." He said the last bit with a wink and then looked back at the cell and its shapely occupant. With a leer, he added. "I can see why she's got you all in a lather!"

"I'm not in a lather!" Gren said, raising his voice. "I don't need Hedolf or you sticking your nose in my business is all!"

"Ah!" The archer nodded sagely. "So she's your business now?"

Gren rose from the table the two had been sitting at. "What are you my mother?" He wasn't exactly angry at Harman, as the two were fairly good friends. They'd shared many a mug together as well as tales, often exaggerated as young men were wont to do. These tales were often of fights they'd had and women they'd bedded. "What's it to you, who I look at?" He added, looking back at the beauty in the cell. He simply couldn't seem to get her out of his mind.

"Gren." Harman said then, in a low voice. "Gren." He said again, more insistently.

The big guard looked round at his comrade. "What?"

"Listen, you've always been a good friend to me." Harman began slowly. "There was the time I got jumped in the alley outside the Winking Badger."

Laughing at that, Gren said, "Yeah, I remember that night! Those boys were about to crack your skull!"

Nodding, Harman rubbed the back of his head ruefully. "That's right and you were right there." His smile was vicious. "When we turned the tables on those yokels, they didn't like it much."

Now Gren nodded. "Remember how the one screamed like a girl when I broke his arm with my cudgel?"

"Yes, I do." Harman knew he had to break in or Gren would start reminiscing for an hour or more. "Remember the time that barmaid, Jenet wouldn't give me the time of day?"

With a grin, the other man replied, "I told her you'd been injured in battle defending a farm a few months before." He chuckled again.

"Her father was a farmer." Harman recollected. "Once she thought I was some kind of hero looking out for people like him, it didn't take long to get her attention." Seeing Gren's attention wandering again, as it so often did, the guardsman said, "So I want to be a good friend, too."

"Eh?" Gren mumbled not looking away from the cell. "What do you mean?"

"I mean," Harman began, standing and stretching. "You can't get her out of your mind, right?" At the other man's answering nod, he continued. "Maybe you just need some time to...you know...get to know her."

Now, the big guard did look around. "Here?" He half hissed, acting like a child afraid he's going to get in trouble.

"Sure." The archer shrugged. "Look, I'm gonna head upstairs and get something to eat, stretch my legs for a bit." He looked meaningfully at the cell.

Gren flushed despite himself. "I don't know...I couldn't just..."

"Hey, I'm not saying force yourself on her." Harman said then. "Just talk to her without anyone else around, right?" His voice was reasonable and soothing. "You know how criminals can be." Lowering his register to a conspiratorial tone, he continued. "She's probably scared and lonely. I think she's facing the noose or at least some years in jail. Maybe she needs some comfort, eh?"

"Hedolf said she's dangerous." Gren mumbled then.

Harman laughed at his friend then. "I never thought I'd see

the day that big Gren was afraid and of a woman at that!" Seeing the other guard's ugly look. "Listen, if you're too scared to talk to a girl, then that's your problem my friend!" He half turned from the table and then turned back. Putting the ring of keys down, he shoved them across the table toward Gren. "If not..."

As Harman walked away, Gren couldn't help but think that the man was a good friend. He wasn't sure what to do, though as he was conflicted. He could lose his job and be brought up on charges. On the other hand, as Harman had pointed out, she was a prisoner, facing a long time in jail or worse. She might welcome some company...

His mind was made up when the woman spoke from the cell.

"I am lonely, you know." Her voice was low and breathy. She was leaning against the bars of the cell and smiling at Gren.

The young guards' breath caught and he turned to look at her. There was something about her. She was so exotic...so different. Thinking that Hedolf was a fool, Gren almost unconsciously picked up the ring of keys from the table. He took a couple of steps toward the cell and hesitated, torn between his lust and his fear.

"Your friend was right." The prisoner said softly. "I'm scared to think what might happen..." She shivered, the movement somehow enticing. "If I'm to die or go to prison I'd like to at least know some...comfort...before." As the woman spoke, she looked directly at the youth, her intentions plain.

Gren flushed excitedly and stepped toward the cell. "What...What's your name?" He asked lamely. Instantly, he felt a fool but he somehow wanted to know more about this mysterious woman.

"You want to know my name?" She asked. "Why?" She was looking boldly into the guards eyes now, as if searching for something there. The effect was almost hypnotic.

"I...I don't know." Gren replied, feeling foolish, knowing he was blushing like a lad talking to a maid for the first time. He couldn't help it. There was just something about her. "I just...want..." He began haltingly then. "I just want to get to know you."

"Well, that's easy enough." The woman said then, stepping away from the bars and looking at him through her long dark lashes. "Why don't you come in here and we'll get to know each other a bit better."

Gren was instantly fumbling with the keys, trying to find the right one. He glanced guiltily between the stairs that led up and the beauteous creature before him. Finding the right key, he opened the cell door and stepped in. "You won't..." He began, his voice husky. "You won't tell anyone?" Absently, the guard closed the door behind him, which locked with a click.

Her only reply was a shake of her head that set her dark tresses to dancing. She ran her hands through her hair and stretched.

It was all the invitation the besotted guard needed and, dropping the keys, stumbled forward to take her in his arms. She felt exactly as he thought she would, he thought, leaning in to kiss her.

The guard hadn't seen the prisoner's hands run back to a certain point in her hair where she'd hidden a sharpened bone longer than her hand. She had slowly ground it to a needle sharp point over the last few days after finding it in a corner of the cell. As he leaned in, she whipped her left elbow forward, catching him in the throat and knocking him back. In one fluid movement, the woman spun, lashing out with her foot in a precise kick that found her would be paramours' knee, dropping him like a stone.

Gren could only wheeze in pain as he could barely breathe. His eyes were watering and he choked, trying to form words. His hand went for the club at his side but he was stopped short as the woman held the sharpened bone to his throat like a dagger. She moved like a viper, her movements fluid and faster than anything the guard had ever seen.

"I wouldn't do that." She said, her voice still that same soft husky register. The woman stepped around him and took the cudgel, flinging it out of the cell. The sharp point never left Gren's throat as she knelt to retrieve the ring of keys from the stone floor. There was a calculating look in her eyes as she stood. "Now, I'm leaving, dear Gren." Her attention never wavered, though his eyes flicked toward the stairs. Almost reading his thoughts, she smiled. "Your friend, Harman said he would give you time to get to know me, remember?" Her voice grew cold and mocking now.

The big guard tried to say something but all that came out was a croak, not dissimilar to that of a frog.

Her smile broadened sweetly. "You won't be able to talk for a bit. Just wait there on the cot and they'll find you soon enough." She cocked her head to one side, her smile fading. "Don't try anything." She said simply and stepped away, backing toward the cell door.

They both knew that she'd have to turn and use the keys to open the door. Gren looked at the floor, breathing heavily, his breath coming in gasps. He could hear her footsteps as she got to the cell. He was hurt and she had a weapon but he was a big man and the thought of facing the jeers of his comrades and the punishment that would follow was too much to bear.

Gren lurched to his feet, his injured knee making the effort slow and awkward. He lunged toward the woman, who'd found the key quickly, having obviously watched to see which one he'd used. The guard sought to pin her up against the bars, where he could bring his greater strength and bulk to bear. It was a good enough plan but Gren hadn't reckoned with her speed.

Stepping smoothly to the side, she never missed a beat as the big guard slammed full force into the bars with bone crunching force. He groaned and fell, his forehead bleeding and one arm injured. Before he could even look up, she had stepped in and driven the sharpened point of the bone into his ear with unerring accuracy and brutal force.

The man dropped like a stone to the ground, instantly dead.

The woman knelt smoothly and with a wrench, snapped the

length of bone off that was sticking out of the dead man's ear. "Not smart, Gren, she murmured." She threw the remnant of bone out into the main area where it landed beneath the detritus under the table. "I would've let you live, for all that you're a pig."

Standing, she unlocked the cell and let herself out. Turning back to the, she locked the door and with a grin, tossed the keys inside where they landed on the far side of the cell. Glancing down, she regarded the corpse for a moment, her smile growing cold.

"The name's Whisper." She said to the dead man and then she was gone.

CHAPTER EIGHT

Something stirred in the clump of trees. The underbrush swayed and moved jerkily, a clear sign that something was coming. The movement was erratic and not in straight lines judging by the way the bushes moved.

Looking at his men, Venaro saw that they were ready. Although they hadn't had time or even the space to bring the wagons into a circle, they were fanned out in front of the lead wagon, weapons held ready. There were a few guards at the rear in case the scout had been wrong and this was, in fact, some orc trick. Toward the front of the men stood the barbarian, his axe in hand. In that lead group of men were Bandur and Callum as well. On either side, the merchant had placed those men with bows and crossbows, ready to launch deadly missiles as soon as they knew what was coming. Inwardly, Venaro hoped there were enough of them to withstand whatever was coming. He mused that it was strange that none of them thought for a second that it could be a group of people coming toward them through the trees. The movement was all wrong and there were strange sounds coming from the woods.

They saw the first of them break through the brush and at first, the trader thought he'd been wrong. The thing walking toward them certainly looked like a man, albeit a man with strangely pale skin. It wore ragged clothing that looked rotted. It had a head and two arms and then he realized that it lurched forward on three legs. Not three complete legs, though. It looked like somewhere below the knee of the left leg, another calf sprouted from the first going down into its own foot, which seemed different. Then, the horrified merchant realized what was different. The front foot looked like that of a horse, complete with a hoof!

The men around him gasped in disbelief as more and more of the creatures staggered out of the bush. Some looked for all the world like normal men and women, save for their pale skin and slack features. Others, however bore strange deformities, although they seemed not to be deformities at all. They were more like additions that had been added and not chaotically but with intent.

Here, a woman stalked out of some shrubs, her dress torn in a dozen places. From her right shoulder was a regular arm that looked mangled and torn. However, from that same shoulder, another arm sprouted, this one appeared to have belonged to an orc, its green skin pale and torn. The arm flexed and moved as if it was natural to the creature.

There, a man limped forward on normal seeming legs, normal arms swinging at its side. He almost seemed whole, save for the fact that he had no head!

An ugly stump of a neck with a wound showing that at some point, the creatures head had been severed. It wasn't blind, however, and walked unerringly toward the line of men on the far side of the clearing. Then, as it got closer, they realized that there were eyes in the monsters' chest! They were large, round, moist eyes, like a cows' eyes and somehow the most horrifying thing was when they blinked slowly.

There were worse abominations in the group of slobbering, moaning things. Difficult to look at or contemplate and Venaro knew he'd be haunted by the images of what he saw there and he looked away, shuddering. After a moment, he realized that his men were doing the same and it dawned on him that the things were closing on them!

The thought galvanized the merchant and fear coursed through him like a drug. He saw that the monsters were deceptively quick and they'd already halved the distance between them and the horrified men.

"Don't just stand there!" The merchant bellowed, his voice sounding strange to his own ears, laced as it was with terror. "Shoot!"

As their employer shouted at them, the archers among the group shook themselves and launched arrows and bolts at the oncoming creatures. Their aim was far from accurate and most of the missiles flew wide.

Realizing that it was hard for them to shoot at things they didn't even want to look at, Venaro practically screamed. "Aim!" He walked over to the closest archer, who was fumbling with an arrow and yelled right in his face. "If we can't hit them, they'll be on top of us!"

That seemed to register and not just with the man Venaro was yelling at. Recognizing that if they couldn't stop the horrid things at a distance, they'd be able to close with them, the archers all reloaded and this time they aimed. Their aim was true and as the wretched horrors were struck the men gave a cheer.

It was short lived, though, as not one was stopped and the cheer died. Arrows and bolts sprouted from limbs, torsos and even heads and still the monsters kept coming. They were within fifty paces when the men launched another volley and the results were the same.

Those men with melee weapons at the ready were all but panicking looking shakily from the men around them to the oncoming horrors. Then Bandur stepped forward, a shield strapped to his injured arm and a sword in his other hand. "Make ready!" The former soldier bellowed, his voice a commanding bellow. It seemed to steady the drovers. Looking at the oncoming monsters, Bandur raised his sword and yelled. "All together!"

The men listening weren't soldiers or guards but they'd been in more than a few fights in their lives, though none, including the recent battle with the orcs seemed as dire. They were heartened by the command voice of the ex-soldier and rallied around him in a wedge.

Venaro breathed a sigh of relief and drew his sabre, trying not to think of the arrows that the creatures ignored. He stepped to join the others that were readying themselves for the onslaught and then then noticed a lone man a dozen strides away, not gathering into the group.

It was Tanoc. The Northman's face was pale, his form rigid and an expression of terror stamped there. His axe hung forgotten in his hand as the nightmarish things closed. His teeth were gritted and his lips peeled back in an animalistic snarl.

Before, the merchant could say or do anything, Bandur held his sword aloft. "Forward!" He roared and ran toward the creatures, most of the men behind him. There were a few that stood rooted to the spot, however, their fear overmastering them and their expressions much like the barbarians'.

As the men charged forward, the shambling things sped up and met them. It was instant chaos as men hacked and stabbed in a frenzy of fear and hate. The monstrous things swung their fists or grabbed at their opponents, seeking to bear them down.

Bandur blocked a blow from a heavy fist, wincing as his broken wrist throbbed. Ignoring the pain, he thrust the thing through the chest, seeking its heart. The creature, which looked like a fat man with only one arm and a stub for its' right arm didn't even slow down. The caravan guard backed away in horror, knowing that his strike was true and he'd stabbed it in the heart.

Nearby, another of the freakish things didn't even stumble as a man hacked into its shoulder with an axe. The weapon caught in the bone and flesh and the monster grabbed the man by his vest with its other arm. The drover hollered and tried clutched at the cold hand, only to find the skin sloughing off so that he couldn't get a grip. The man screamed as the thing drew him close and ignoring the weapon lodged in its shoulder bit him in the throat. The screams became a gurgle as the man sank to the leaf strewn ground, his blood painting it like some insane mosaic. The monster didn't let go but kept biting and biting and biting…

All around them, the horrific things were ignoring blows that would have killed a man. They reeked with the stench of death and it was clear that they were dealing with the storied undead. Many of them had heard such tales and they knew that they were not dealing with living foes. The terror was like a living thing among them as it oozed and roiled in their hearts.

"Zombies!" One man screeched and buried a hatchet in his foes head. As the skull cleft and blood and brains oozed, he yelled, "Ya have to get 'em in the head!" However, his theory was short lived, as his opponent, a vile creature with one paw that looked suspiciously like a bear, clawed into his face. The man fell back, screaming in agony and the monstrosities other hand clutched him drawing him close. The things teeth, strangely sharp like that of a forest predator snapped into the drover's face and his screams intensified.

Venaro backed away as a hideous thing with a strangely distorted face closed with him. It looked like, at some point, the creature had been disemboweled and he could still see rotting entrails as it shuffled forward. Its head was caved in, as if by a heavy blow but like all those around it, the thing seemed to ignore the ghastly wounds. The merchant recoiled as it made a swipe at him with gnarled hands. His training and instincts kicked in and he lunged quickly forward, the point of his saber pierced the monsters throat. Clotted blood fell out in globs, rather than flowed but the creature kept coming. It tried to grab him again and Venaro leapt back, narrowly avoiding its grasp.

Looking desperately around, he spotted Tanoc, still standing rooted to the ground like a tree. The barbarian's eyes were glazed and the merchant realized he wasn't seeing what was going on right now but was reliving some traumatic event. There was a thing that looked like a woman with four arms, one of which hung limply like a dead snake coming toward him.

"TANOC!!!" The merchant thundered as loud as he could, his deep voice reverberating through the clearing.

The Northman seemed to come to himself and he flinched as if he'd been struck. He looked wildly over at Venaro, who was still backing away before the horrific creature that tried to seize him in its rotting hands. All semblance of inaction gone, the barbarian leapt toward the merchants' attacker like a hunting cat. Bounding toward the creature, Tanoc swept his battle-axe in a great arc low at its legs. The axe sheared clean through the rotting limb and the monster fell over.

Whirling, Tanoc faced the many-armed horror fast approaching. As it reached for him, the barbarian stepped to one side and hacked the arm off. The arm on that side seemed to be grafted on beneath the things armpit and when it too tried to grasp Tanoc, it was lopped off. Not waiting, the barbarian chopped into the monsters leg below the knee and it fell. In a frenzy now, the Northman began hacking the creature apart and before long there were nothing but body parts.

Venaro saw, to his horror that the severed limbs and body parts still twitched and moved but the barbarian's foe was neutralized.

Something grabbed at the merchant's ankle and he looked down in revulsion, seeing the thing that had tried to grab him had dragged itself close with its arms. Clutching at Venaro's leg, the creature was trying to drag itself close enough to bite into him. Shaking off his horror, the trader, remembering Tanoc's actions of a few moments ago, sliced down into the hand grasping him. Though it held on, his sabre sheared through the wrist and the merchant stepped away. The thing came on still, ignoring the fearful injury.

Stepping further back, Venaro shouted at the top of his lungs. "Go for their legs! Don't waste time trying to stab them!" So saying, he ran to help a nearby drover who'd speared one of the things in the chest. As it struggled to pull itself forward up the spear, the merchant sliced in low at the horror's calf, half shearing through it. It stumbled and tried to turn but the spearman held on and it couldn't. Venaro's saber darted in again and the thing fell.

Now, the men were banding together to deal with the undead. Wherever it seemed like they hadn't heard him, the merchant bellowed instructions. Many of the drovers weren't quick or strong enough and they were slain. However, the others were able to slowly turn the tide. As the last few of the gruesome things was cut down, Venaro walked over to where Tanoc was helping another man with one of the monsters.

As the Barbarian hacked off the things limbs, Venaro looked around, realizing that almost half his men were down. As he did this, he realized that every man that had fallen was dead. None were merely wounded. The monstrosities hadn't moved to new targets as a soldier would but wherever they'd pulled down their prey, they fed on the spot. The merchant grasped the grim truth then. If the creatures hadn't stopped to feast on those that fell, they'd have all most likely died or been forced to flee.

Looking back at the Northman, Venaro saw him watching the trees around them. The foul undead were all down and even now the merchant's men were hacking them apart. "What is it?" The merchant asked.

Tanoc shook his head and said nothing for a moment. Then, seeing several of the horrors still moaning and shuddering on the ground, he murmured, "Fire."

Venaro stepped close. "What did you say?"

"Fire." The barbarian reiterated. "You need to burn all the remains with fire." With haunted eyes, he stared at the merchant. "It's the only thing that will fully destroy them."

The merchant didn't hesitate, shouting to a few men standing nearby. "Get oil and torches!" Gesturing to the undulating carpet of body parts, he added, "We've got to burn them!"

With a sound of disgust, he felt something like a vise on his leg. Venaro's skin crawled as he looked down to see the dismembered hand still clenching his ankle as if it were still attached to the arm it had come off of. The trader used his saber to pry the hand off and shuddering, kicked it from him.

Looking back up, he saw that Tanoc was still watching the trees. "Do you see more of them?" He asked, scanning the foliage for himself and seeing nothing.

The barbarian's only answer was a slow shake of his head.

As the drovers came up with torches, one of them asked, "Will our own comrades rise against us?" There was fear on all their faces. Venaro didn't know and looked to Tanoc who ignored him.

One of the other men answered. "I've heard tell of zombies but I watched ole Nem sink his hatchet in one's skull and it didn't stop the thing!" There was panic in his voice. "What, in Derku's name, are they?!" They all stood there, some with torches in hand, huddled together for a while.

Then, Tanoc spoke. "They are Dregs." He said in a dead sounding voice. They looked at the barbarian who was still watching the trees, his axe still at the ready. "You need to pile them together and burn them." There was as much emotion in his voice as if he'd said they needed to gather firewood but his eyes were haunted.

"And what of our comrades?" Another man asked then.

The barbarian looked around at all of them and then nodded. He returned to watching the tree line and said no more.

"You heard the man!" Venaro shouted. He didn't want to give any of them a chance to ask why or refute what the Northman had said. He was willing to bet that Tanoc knew what he was talking about. "Burn them all!"

As the drovers began piling the bodies, Bandur came walking up, his eyes bleak. He looked angry and Venaro saw, with a shock that there were unshed tears in the man's eyes. In answer, the former soldier looked back toward the way he'd come where they were gathering the dead. "Callum didn't make it." He said softly.

"I'm sorry, my friend." Venaro said and gently patted the

other man's shoulder. When Bandur nodded and looked away, the merchant walked over to Tanoc, who hadn't moved an inch.

"What are you looking for?" Venaro asked. When the barbarian said nothing, he persisted. "I know you've dealt with these things before. You called them Dregs." His voice was hoarse from shouting. "What are they?" He asked, waving back at the things that had once been human.

Tanoc didn't answer but continued to stare at the woods. The hands that gripped his battle-axe were white knuckled, even though the danger was past.

A drover with a bow on his back paused in lifting a dismembered torso that still twitched. He looked over and saw it was the gnarled old drover who had fought the orcs with them at the beach. Venaro thought his name was Farn. The man dropped the corpse and looked at them. "He's watchin' to see if the Pallid are here with their minions." He hissed.

Irritation flashed through the merchant now. "The Pallid are nothing but old wives' tales!" It was hard to talk about fables and tales with undead all around them still twitching. "They're not real." He added, his voice sounding unconvincing even to his own ears.

"Not real?!" Came the bowman's scornful answer. "Yer lookin' at their handiwork right now!" The drover spat on the corpse of the thing he'd been hauling to the fire.

Venaro shook his head in disbelief. "I've never even heard of these...Dregs." He looked from Tanoc back to the old drover. "How do you know they have anything to do with the Pallid, who are said to be nothing but stories?"

"They are not just stories." Tanoc said then and the big warrior looked around at the drover calculatingly. "He's right." For a moment, he said no more but stood there with his jaw bunched and his eyes wild. "The Dregs are the minions of the Pallid. They are created by them and they answer to them."

Forgetting himself, Venaro asked quietly. "What happened Tanoc? How do you know about these things?"

The barbarian's eyes were sad and far away as he regarded the merchant. He shook his head and looked instead at the drover. "You know of the Pallid, old man?"

Farn nodded. "Aye." He spat again. "My brother was from a village far to the north-east. The whole place was overrun and he alone escaped." The drover's face was dark and his voice full of emotion. "When he told people what had happened, they called him a madman and a liar but I knew he was telling the truth!"

Venaro looked at the old drover. "They didn't believe him?"

"They was just like you, caravan master." Farn drawled. "They believed what they wanted to. My brother said it was the Pallid. He'd heard of 'em and described 'em and their Dregs." He shrugged angrily then. "But they said he was a lunatic and it had just been orcs or something else."

"What happened to him?" The merchant asked quietly.

"He died." Old Farn said sadly. "Died of his wounds, they said." He knelt to grab the body at his feet. "Tell ye what though." He said as he grunted with the effort of lifting the thing. "I think his mind couldn't take what he saw there. I think he up and died 'cause he didn't want to live with them memories!"

Looking back at the barbarian, Venaro thought that he understood. He wouldn't have thought the indomitable Tanoc afraid of anything yet he had stood nearly paralyzed today.

"Do you think they're watching?" Venaro asked softly, not wanting to panic anyone.

The old man snorted. "If they were here, they'd have already shown themselves and we'd most likely all be dead!" He said no more but stubbornly hauled on the twitching trunk until Venaro ordered a nearby man to help him.

Looking over at the barbarian, he could see Tanoc nodding in affirmation. Still, he couldn't help but ask. "You think the Pallid are here, Tanoc?"

The young giant didn't answer right away but he did finally turn from the forest. Looking at the corpses that the drovers were

pouring oil on for a bit, he finally answered. "The old man's right."
He stated simply. Then he added, "We should go soon."

The merchant ran a hand through his cropped hair in
frustration. "I don't have enough men to drive all my wagons."

"Then leave them." Tanoc said flatly.

"I can't do that." Venaro stated. He tried to think of the
men who'd just died but he was still a merchant.

"I'm not waiting around here." The Northman answered.

Venaro was disbelieving. "You'd abandon us here? After we
saved you?"

That eloquent shrug again. "I've saved your life several times
over now, merchant." Tanoc replied firmly. "I'd say we're even."

"But…" The trader began but floundered for more to say. It
seemed trivial now to think of money and goods lost with so many of
his men dead.

Relenting, Venaro said, "I could leave the less valuable goods
behind, I suppose." He said glumly. Nearby, Bandur and the others
were lighting the piles of twitching undead. They still moved in the
flames in an unsettling manner.

"I don't care what you do." Tanoc said harshly, breaking
Venaro's reverie. "I am leaving this place."

The merchant nodded and it was his turn to fall silent. He
couldn't really blame the barbarian. "Would our fallen have come
back as Dregs?" He asked finally.

Tanoc slowly nodded and almost whispered. "I have seen it
before."

By the time the wagons were ready and the surviving men
and animals prepared to move out, the fires were burning merrily and
the stench of roasting flesh filled the clearing. Little was said among
the men as they all shared the barbarians haste to be away from the
place. Eventually, the body parts stopped twitching, though there
was no one there to see.

Miles and miles away, three figures in night dark clothing watched hundreds of shambling things move south. Their scrutiny was intense and actually much more than that as they were directing the mass with their thoughts as shepherds would a flock with their voice.

"A group has been destroyed." Came the female's voice. "Away to the west. Not many but they've all been cut down and burned. I can sense they are gone." There was no emotion in her voice as she stated this.

The others nodded and the one called Vok spoke then. "It is of no import."

The scarred one looked away from the mass of Dregs, some of which began milling about. "Shall I go?"

Frowning, Vok looked at the other two. "No." He said simply. "It does not matter." With no direction, the Dregs milled about now like lost sheep. Some of them looked at each other, while others looked off at the trees or the sky above. Vok well knew that a single bird or animal that they saw would cause them all to lurch off in pursuit.

"They were on their way here." The woman's voice spoke. There was reproach there.

"It is unimportant." Their leader repeated. "There are others on their way to join us." He could taste their unhappiness now. He knew they wanted to investigate. The Pallid did have emotions they simply were much more muted than that of a human. "We have more than enough."

"What if we cross paths with those who destroyed the Dregs?" The scarred one asked. There was something akin to eagerness there.

Turning back to the milling Dregs, Vok replied. "We will extinguish them." He could perceive his companions' joy now, a slow, hateful thing. "What matters is our directive." The leader said, once more asserting his will. Those Dregs closest to him began to turn and face the right direction.

Obediently, the others joined him and soon the Dregs were

headed south again. Their delight bloomed like a sickly vine growing underground. They would soon be about their true work again. Soon, the reaping would come.

CHAPTER NINE

Ivy grew up the wall of the small house, giving it a charming look. The climbing vegetation could not detract from the dinginess of the domicile, however. It was an old house, no doubt among the earliest built. The place had the look of a village dwelling rather than a house in a large, walled town. It had been repainted many times and the current coat was a shabby, faded blue that was flaking, making the house look like a dog with mange. The windows lacked glass and were simply holes in the walls with shutters that closed them off. The front door was a battered thing that looked to be slowly rotting, despite the recent coat of thick, brown paint.

'*A decrepit place.*' Cenric thought, as he looked at the house. '*The mayor might be doing well but these people were not.*' Looking around at the houses nearby, which looked in roughly the same condition, he thought, '*And they weren't the only ones doing without.*'

His thoughts were interrupted by the rough voice of the guard that was his escort. "What god did you say you worshipped?" His voice and manner were belligerent and it was clear he didn't like the priest or his investigation.

"I didn't." The cleric murmured, stepping to look around the side of the house and the narrow alley there.

"What?" Came the guard's voice. "What did you say?"

With a sigh, Cenric turned to face the guard, whose name was

Dulwen of all things. "I never said what deity I worshipped." The man he was facing was a big, rough individual with greasy hair and rotting teeth. Whatever muscle he'd ever possessed was mostly run to fat now.

His manner surly, the guard said, "Well?" He put his thumbs in his belt and puffed out his chest, trying vainly to make it stick out further than his prodigious gut.

"Well, what?" The disinterested cleric asked, mimicking the other man's tone.

In exasperation, the guard snapped. "What god do you worship?!" His voice had risen to a register that was certainly louder than what should be used in polite conversation. "You are a priest aren't you?" Dulwen's second query sounded more like an insult.

Cenric looked at the guard for a long beat and finally, turning back to his contemplation of the house, replied, "It doesn't matter." Stepping into the alley, he considered the wall on this side, which looked even shabbier than the front.

"What kind of answer is that?!" Dulwen demanded, following the cleric into the alley. It was clear he was getting angry now and not just passing the time.

'He's used to bullying everyone to get his way.' Cenric mused. *'No doubt, he licks the boots of everyone who's more important and takes it out on anyone he can.'* Aloud, the priest said, "It's no kind of answer."

There was another man with the priest and the guard, a skinny young fellow with acne and teeth that a kind person might have called unfortunate. "Maybe he worships more than one." The youth said thoughtfully. His name was Juriel and he was the cleric's guide around the city for the duration. Cenric had tried to tell the mayor he didn't need the two of them or for that matter even one but the mayor had persisted. It was clear that when he'd said he would be keeping an eye on the priest, he had meant it.

The guard looked at Juriel for a moment and then back at the priest. "So, how about it?"

"How about what?" Cenric asked, trying to keep the irritation from his voice. He was finding it difficult to concentrate with this and he knew exactly what Dulwen was asking but some part of him wanted to needle the man. *'He doesn't realize yet that I'm someone he can't push around.'* The priest thought.

"Like the boy said," Dulwen barked, angrily waving a hand at Juriel. "Do you worship more than one god?"

Seeing that he was going to get no peace from the guard, who he'd begun to think of as Dullard, the priest turned around and favored the man with a smile. "I did not say who I worshipped because it is unimportant."

The guards eyes widened and he looked at the young man alongside him. "He says it's unimportant, Juriel." Shaking his head so hard it made his jowls jiggle, Dulwen said, "What kind of priest doesn't want to tell people about his god?" Folding his arms, he finished by saying, "Makes a person think you might be hiding something."

Cenric had had enough. "First of all, I don't tell people about my beliefs because I'm no missionary or evangelist, understand?" He stepped close to the guard then, trying and failing to ignore the man's breath. Though the other man was taller, the priest was a big man as well and he looked stronger, despite his age. "I am not trying to convert you or anyone else. That is why it's unimportant." Seeing that Dullard clearly wanted to argue, Cenric strode closer. "I don't have time to explain the beliefs of my order to you and you wouldn't care anyway, would you?"

Dulwen clearly didn't care for being talked to in such a fashion and he bristled. Glancing at Juriel, he raised his voice. "Now, see here!"

"No, my good man, I am afraid I'm going to have to ask you to see." The priest cut him off calmly but sternly. Cenric never raised his voice or shouted but the authority there was clear. "I have a job to do and you are a guard in this little town. A guard who's been ordered to help me." He could tell he'd been successful by the other man's body language. The guard had leaned back away from him.

"Now, if you don't want to help, then leave. Go back to your mayor and explain it to him." The cleric shrugged then. "If you want to interfere, you can also explain why a full contingent of my order will have to come and investigate instead of one man!"

The speech had brought the guard up short. It was clear he was out of his depth and just as obvious that he didn't want to get in trouble with the mayor. He looked over at Juriel, who was smart enough to look away, studiously gazing at a flock of birds overhead.

"Sorry sir." The guard mumbled.

The priest smiled broadly as if nothing had happened. "Not to worry." His expression was kind and jovial once again. *'They're all the same in these little provincial towns.'* The cleric thought as he continued his investigation.

The pair were quiet as the priest walked around the house, murmuring to himself occasionally and writing in a small, leather bound book as he did. From time to time, he would stop and look closely at some detail or another but neither of them could quite figure out what he was looking for. Eventually, they had worked their way completely around the dwelling, arriving back in the front. Cenric stood there for a while scribbling furiously in his notebook.

Greatly daring, young Juriel asked, "What are you looking for?" It was apparent that he was confused as he looked around. There was clearly nothing out of the ordinary. Even after a warning from Dulwen to keep quiet, he persisted. "Shouldn't we go inside?"

"Hmm…" It was all the cleric said for a few moments as he finished writing in his ledger. Then he cleaned his quill and capped his bottle of ink. Leaving the book open to dry in the spring air, he looked over at the duo, which he'd begun to think of as Dullard and the Boy and suppressed a sigh. "What do you see?" He asked of them both. Cenric doubted very much that either of them truly cared or could be taught anything but nonetheless they were his burden now. The priest believed in education in all its many forms and decided there and then to teach them a bit.

Of course, this would, as always be determined by the

prospective students. The sigh escaped him, despite his best efforts.

The two men looked first at each other and then at the priest. Then they looked at the front of the house and then finally back at the cleric again.

"Nobody's home?" Juriel ventured.

With a snort, Dulwen grated, "The place is a dung heap!"

Feeling a headache beginning behind his eyes, Cenric coached patience from his voice. "Yes." He nodded agreeably, as if stating the obvious was something to be applauded. "What else?" When neither of them answered, he gestured with his free hand. "Look behind the ivy."

Dullard refused, his expression stubborn but Juriel walked over and parted the thick ivy at roughly head height.

"Lower." The priest said patiently. "Around knee height."

The youth looked lower and as he twitched the vines aside, gave a low whistle. "You've got good eyes, sir!"

His curiosity getting the better of him, Dulwen strode over to where the boy stood and roughly shouldered him aside. When he saw what was drawn on the side of the house, his brow furrowed and he looked back at the cleric. "How could you see this?" The guard demanded, gesturing at the thick growth.

Cenric shook his head and walked closer. "I did not see it." He stated.

Mystified, Juriel whispered, "How did you know it was there?"

"I knew what I was looking for." Cenric answered. "You saw as well as I did that there was nothing out of the ordinary when we walked around the house didn't you?"

Again, Dullard and the Boy exchanged bewildered stares as if the priest was speaking in an unknown tongue or performing magic. Their only answer was the blank expression that Cenric associated with farm animals.

As another sigh escaped him, the cleric pointed to the strange symbol that was painted on the house. "I have seen this before."

The mark was a spidery thing roughly the size of a man's hand. It seemed to be painted on with a dark viscid substance that looked black, although on closer inspection, it was a very dark red.

"What is it?" Dulwen asked slowly. "What does it mean?"

"It is a glyph of some sort." Seeing that the two individuals accompanying him were unfamiliar with the word, the priest explained. "A glyph is an ancient form of symbolic carving. It conveys meaning or information nonverbally…" Realizing that the two had no idea what he was talking about, Cenric trailed off.

"But what does it mean?" The guard persisted.

The cleric shook his head. "I am not entirely sure." Cenric admitted. "It is a mark and in every similar case that I've seen, it's the same mark with the same results."

"Results?" Juriel almost whispered.

Nodding grimly, Cenric said, "Everywhere I've seen this glyph, there was a disappearance with no sign of a struggle. People gone from their homes without a trace." The cleric frowned, looking at the house. Seeing that his two pupils looked more afraid than enlightened, the priest closed his book with a snap. "Juriel is right."

"He is?" Dulwen asked.

"I am?" Juriel echoed, completely baffled.

"Yes." The priest affirmed. "He asked if we should go inside and we should." Cenric put his book in the bag he carried with him and walked up the steps to go inside. The door was unlocked and without looking back, he opened it and stepped in.

Dullard and the Boy hesitated at the steps, sharing a confused, frightened look for a moment. It was obvious that they didn't want to go inside. For all that it was midday and spring at that, there was still a lingering chill from winter. Of course, neither of them would ever admit that the chill they felt wasn't from the weather and they hesitated for several moments there.

Finally, with a disgusted sound, Dulwen muttered, "Not gonna let some priest show me up!" The big man hitched his belt up and stalked up the stairs, making an excessive amount of noise as he tromped along.

Juriel lingered for a moment more, looking around at the seemingly deserted part of town and hurriedly followed the guard inside.

Within, they found the priest standing in the front room of the little house. There were two doors in the room and a rickety set up stairs that led upwards. The man was looking around and frowning. *'No signs of a struggle and nothing out of place.'* Cenric thought. *'It's obvious they were poor.'* He mused, looking at the few, shabby furnishings. *'They were a tidy lot who had taken care of what little they did have.'*

As Dullard and the Boy finally came inside, Cenric walked over to the two doors leading from the small front room. Pushing first one open and then the other, he saw a kitchen and a bedroom.

Before the priest could enter either room, he was stopped by a questioning Dulwen. "What are we looking for in here?"

Rubbing at his temples, Cenric replied. "Anything out of the ordinary." He looked in the kitchen as he continued speaking. "Anything that might give us a clue as to what happened here."

"Well that's helpful." Dulwen growled.

Juriel scratched his head. "Think there'll be markings like what we found outside?"

Continuing to massage his temples, the priest thought, *'I'm definitely getting a headache.'* Aloud, he said, "There won't be any markings inside."

"How can you know that?" Dulwen asked in a surly voice as he opened the bedroom door. "You may have seen things like this before but how do you know this time isn't something different?"

Before Cenric could answer, Juriel spoke. "Maybe it's because that mark outside is a like a sign for someone else."

Now, the priest smiled at the boy. "Right, you are, Juriel." The young man's smile lit his face up, despite his crooked teeth. "I've come to the same conclusion, myself."

Dulwen looked at the priest and then at the lad. "So there's more than one person behind this!" He said triumphantly.

Cenric's smile faded. '*Apparently brawn is all that's needed to become a city guard.*' He thought sadly. '*They'd be much better off with a lad like Juriel than an oaf like Dullard. At least the boy is fairly bright.*' To Dulwen, the priest dryly said, "Apparently."

Juriel seemed emboldened by the priest's approval and said, "I'll check upstairs."

Having completed what the priest thought was a rather cursory search of the downstairs bedroom, Dulwen stepped out. "I'll go with you." It was clear that he didn't want to be here overlong.

The priest looked at them both and nodded. "Take your time and look thoroughly." The guard's expression showed that he didn't like being told what to do by a priest but Cenric was past caring.

The lad nodded seriously and Cenric looked at him. "See if there's any sign that anyone here was sick or infirm, Juriel." The boy nodded and headed up the stairs.

Dulwen paused and turned from the steps, then. "Why did you tell him to look for something like that?" His manner was belligerent again. "What do you know, priest? If you're hiding something…"

"I am not hiding anything." Cenric responded calmly, ignoring the now pounding headache. "I have already told you that I've investigated similar cases before."

"Yeah and I know that there's a lot of strange things that have been happening in town." Dulwen replied evenly. "Things that started happening around the time that you showed up."

Cenric laughed in the face of such a ludicrous accusation. "You can't believe that I'd be investigating things I was somehow behind." He could tell by the other man's countenance that it was exactly what he was thinking. "If that were the case, why would I even bother with coming here?"

Dulwen shrugged at that. "Maybe, you want to appear innocent."

Now it was the priest's turn to be amazed, at the sheer

ignorance on display. "Surely, you realize that if I were doing something like this, it would be easier to have never have spoken to your mayor?" Seeing that Dullard wasn't grasping his point, he persisted. "It makes no sense that I would even start such an investigation if I had something to do with it."

"Seems like your guesses are pretty lucky." The guard replied defensively.

"Then you believe that proper investigative techniques are either somehow mystical in origin or that I must have something to do with it?" Cenric said incredulously.

Dulwen struggled to understand the question the priest posed but was too stubborn to quit. "Well, there's more than these disappearances going on." Seeing the cleric's raised eyebrow, he went on. "There was that jailbreak that happened. Gren was killed and there's been no sign of the prisoner!"

"I doubt that had anything to do with this situation." Cenric said flatly.

"You don't know!" The guard said childishly. "There's talk around that the woman who escaped might have been a witch!"

The priest rubbed his sore head again and muttered, "Is everything you people can't explain linked somehow to magic?"

Defensively, Dulwen snarled "Magic's real!" His eyes narrowed then. "What kind of a priest doesn't believe in magic?"

With all the patience he could muster, Cenric answered. "Yes, magic is real and as a cleric I am well acquainted with it. However, I doubt that this escapee had to resort to magic or that it had anything to do with the disappearance of this family."

"What would you know about it?" The guard asked.

"I heard that the dead man was slain with a sharpened bone and left in the woman's cell." The priest snapped, his patience finally fraying. "That doesn't sound like magic in the least."

"Where did you hear that?" Dulwen demanded in a gruff voice.

Looking at the other man, Cenric raised his eyebrows. "Oh

come now!" He would have laughed but his head hurt too much. "Surely, you know how your comrades talk?" Dulwen's face showed that he did indeed know that the other guards talked and bragged about their jobs, he himself included. "What happened has been spread all over town."

"Well…" Dullard replied, stretching the word out, trying hard to think of a rebuttal.

'I doubt he even knows the word, rebuttal.' Cenric thought. Out of sheer spite, he offered his professional opinion. "From what I've heard, it sounds like she lured the lusty guardsman into her cell and stabbed him, using his keys to escape." He offered a sardonic smile. "Hardly witchcraft."

"Hey now, Gren was my friend!" The guard snapped. "I won't have you speak ill of him!"

The cleric slowly shook his head. "So out of my deduction, you gleaned an insult toward the dead guardsman?" Privately, he thought, 'These people are in trouble if these are their protectors.'

Before either man could say more, the argument was cut short by Juriel's excited voice from upstairs. "I found something!"

The guard and the priest turned toward the stairs where Juriel appeared, holding something in his hands. "You were right, Father Cenric!" He said eagerly.

"Don't call me father, lad." The priest corrected him absently. "It's not a title we use in my order."

"Oh, sorry." Juriel said as he walked down the stairs. He presented them with his discovery then. "I found it in the smallest room up there. It looked like a child's room." He was holding a cane and it was indeed sized for a child.

Dulwen looked at the priest and all irritation had vanished. "What does it mean?" He breathed.

The priest was silent for a long moment. "I'm not sure." He offered lamely. Dullard and the boy looked at him, the fact that neither man believed him writ large on their faces but the priest would say no more.

'No need to frighten them more.' Cenric thought. A chill worked up the priest's spine as he looked around at the empty house where everything was in place as if the family had just gone out for a stroll about town. *'If my fears are correct, they'll know soon enough.'*

Not far away, there was another abandoned house. If anyone in the town had cared to take notice, they would have noticed a rather alarming trend. However, the same person might have noticed that this house and others like it were different from the one that the Cleric and his doubtful duo were investigating. This house bore no strange marks and didn't look like the inhabitants had simply disappeared. This particular abode was a deserted wreck. If the aforementioned curious individual had looked into it, they'd have discovered the story of the family who had called the place home.

It was a simple tale, really and one that was very similar to many others in the land. It was the story of a father and eldest son recruited into an army to fight for greedy leaders. Those leaders spent their lives like cheap copper coins and father and son never returned from war. Meanwhile, a mother, daughter and youngest son were left to fend for themselves for over two years. The mother was a hard working woman who often had to leave her children alone. Eventually, however, she could no longer afford to pay for the quite modest home and they were evicted by the landlord. Without anywhere to go, they made their way to a boarding house. Sadly the woman and son were afflicted by disease soon and died, leaving the daughter the only sole survivor of the unfortunate family. She made a living working as a serving girl.

The pitiless landlord had plans to renovate the house but after the war fell on hard times like so many others. He had left the job half complete and eventually abandoned the place. It was ironic that he'd at least received some money from the mother who had tried so hard to keep her family together. It was perhaps equally ironic that he died of the same disease that had swept through the town and killed many others, including the mother and son.

Stories like this were the norm. War, disease and famine had reaped a bloody harvest in the kingdoms of man and the dead outnumbered the living. Monarchs and ruling bodies were too busy watching and plotting against each other to worry about the people they were supposed to be protecting. Times were bleak indeed and humanity seemed like a low burning candle, struggling to stay alight in the wind that seemed determined to blow it out.

The woman who entered the decrepit house cared nothing for such things. She was a survivor and like all survivors she had learned long ago to look out for herself. If she'd known the story of the aforementioned family, she likely would have shown as much emotion as she would have deciding what to eat for breakfast. Although Whisper didn't think of herself as cruel, she was pragmatic.

Looking around at the wreck of a house, Whisper quietly closed the door behind her and engaged the bolt she'd just jimmied open. She was clothed similarly to how she'd been when in the jail, save for a dark brown cloak that an onlooker might notice was dirty. This was because she'd tied her belongings up in the cloak and hidden it before she was captured. Those belongings consisted mostly of weapons a small pack and belt pouch. When she'd been captured by the guards she had simply held up her hands and let them take her.

Remembering that day, her expression twisted in anger. When she'd made her way to the master bedroom, it was supposed to have been abandoned, the merchant, one Sorvus, away on business. The hidden chamber where the merchant kept his wealth was cleverly hidden in the wall next to the bed. However, the merchant himself had been there, along with several armed servants. Murder had never been her intention and she would have simply slipped out of the house but the man was lying in wait for her in the darkened room.

Whisper knew that she'd been set up when Sorvus had said accusingly, 'So, she told me true! My enemies have stooped to hiring assassins!'

115

The 'she' in question could only have been Delia. Another merchant, Delia was a dealer in rare antiquities and the one who had actually hired Whisper to steal a particular item from Sorvus. Although Whisper had never worked for Delia before, the woman had contacted her through a mutual acquaintance about the job.

Although Whisper would have preferred to simply make her escape that night, it wasn't to be. Sorvus sent his three servants in to attack her and she'd defended herself. Two of them had died and the other was severely injured. She still would have left but the enraged merchant had chased her down the stairs with sword in hand. Her own blade proved the quicker by far and she'd left him dead there on the steps.

Outside there were lanterns and the shouts of the town guard. It was then that Whisper knew for sure she'd been set up and by whom. She had no doubt that Delia would simply swoop in and take what she desired once Sorvus was dead and Whisper was in jail or hanged. What she didn't know was why but she had determined right then and there that she'd find out.

Whisper had lit out the back door of Sorvus' manor house into the grounds. She knew that she might have escaped but that would have certainly meant leaving town and there were so many guards that she played the odds. Stashing her belongings in an old potting shed beneath a forgotten shelf, Whisper emerged and waited for the lights to get closer and let the guards take her.

Banishing the memory, she checked the ground floor, making certain that it was empty. Whisper then made her way up the rickety stairs. Like many of the houses built in Wend, there were a couple of bedrooms up here and downstairs sitting room was open the full two stories. She made her way into the room that she'd spotted from the street after making sure that the first room was abandoned as well. Within, the chamber was dusty and cobwebbed. She glided over to the boarded window and smiled as she looked out of it. The corner bedroom of the old house gave her a perfect view of what she'd come to see; Delia's manor house.

It was a smaller place than the manor of Sorvus but not by much. Looking intently at it, Whisper decided that it was the grounds that made the place smaller, not so much the house itself. The house she now stood in was along a back street and like many houses along said street was abandoned. This place sat near the corner of the high back wall of Delia's manor grounds. While the merchant's servants kept her grounds tended immaculately, it must have grated on her nerves that there were so many shabby houses nearby. Shabby houses with their overgrown hedges and untrimmed trees.

One such tree was right outside the window that Whisper looked out of, in fact. There, in the small backyard of the abandoned house stood a large, tough old oak with gnarled, spreading limbs that reached halfway across the street or more. The tree was budding with early green growth and would provide excellent cover in the night.

In better times, the inhabitants would have been responsible for keeping the tree trimmed. However, no one lived here now and with the owner gone and the town half empty, there was no one to do anything.

Humming a soft tune, Whisper pulled an abandoned table that the former occupants had left behind over near the window. She then left the room in search of something to sit on, returning a few minutes later with a stool she'd scavenged from another room. Sitting, she opened her pack and still humming softly, removed a small canvas bundle. With a satisfied sound, she unrolled the bundle and gazed fondly at her tools. Everything from small pry pars, picks and files to a little hammer had their place in canvas pockets. Whisper had made this kit herself.

Removing her cloak, she folded it and set it next to the tool kit. Then, she removed her rapier from her side and laid it there. It was an exquisite blade, with silver scrollwork on the blade and intricate filigree on the guard. It was the work of a master and had cost her a small fortune. Next to this, she put another sword, this one a short, stabbing blade. It was a rather ugly weapon next to the rapier, lacking ornamentation. However, it was well made and sturdy, with a deep blood groove, steel guard and pommel. Whisper left her many daggers in their sheaths as they wouldn't get in the way.

Selecting a small pry bar, Whisper turned her attentions to the window. She was confident that she wouldn't be disturbed and even if she was, she'd hear anyone coming through the boarded windows or creaky bolted door downstairs. The only other entrance to the house was the door that led off of the kitchen downstairs and it was boarded up as well. Carefully and quietly, she extracted the first nail from the first board. The only sound it gave was a small squeak as it came out and she set it soundlessly on the table next to her tools. Whisper never rushed or made excess noise and it was part of how she'd gained her name long ago, as much as for her tendency to speak quietly.

She was still smiling as she worked carefully on the next nail and the next. She was happy as she thought of her upcoming meeting with the merchant. The smile broadened as she knew Delia most likely thought she'd fled the town with the guards behind her every step of the way. The truth was that she'd laid low for several days after laying a false trail for the fools to follow out of Wend.

As the little pile of nails grew, the sun lowered in the west.

CHAPTER TEN

It was late afternoon and the sun was low in the sky. The guards on duty at the north gate of the town of Wend were paying more attention to keeping warm that cool spring day than anything else. Spring had arrived but here in the northern part of Gurral, it was still cold and the two men huddled near a brazier for warmth. They cursed the greedy mayor Edber, who had promised the guards they'd soon have shelter as they stood their post. First, the mayor had proposed a guard tower, then a stone outbuilding was spoken of and now finally plans for a wooden guard shack had been settled on. It was not lost on the guards that the mayor's house was of the best stone while they yet stood out in the cold in front of the gates year round.

So it was that the guards were shivering and cursing as the wind blew and so their mood was far from a good one. This was far from abnormal and in fact was why the guards hated this rotation at the gates. Often they'd diced to try and get out of the duty and one of the luckless men this day had lost at just such a gamble. The unfortunate man's name was Umfrey and he was none too happy.

"Bloody mayor." Umfrey grumbled "I swear to you I heard that he's talking of adding another addition to that damnable manor house!"

His partner, a taciturn individual called Oso shrugged. "What's yer point?"

"My point is we're out here freezing our parts off and he's building a bigger house!" Umfrey snapped. With a disbelieving look at the other guard, he asked, "Tell me you can see how wrong that is?"

Oso snorted and laughed. "Wrong?" With a look of disdain, he replied. "It's not right or wrong."

Umfrey was a fresh faced youth that was smaller than Oso but he bristled nonetheless. "Just what do you mean by that?" There was heat in his voice, if not his limbs. "You mean to say that it's alright that the mayor..."

"I mean to say..." Oso cut the other off, his humor fading now. "That it's not right or wrong." He shrugged again. "It just is." He knew that Umfrey was young still and didn't really understand the ways of the world or the ways of the town for that matter.

"But the mayor's been promising us for years..." Umfrey started to say but Oso cut him off again.

"What would you know about it?" The burly guard snapped. "I've been a guard since you was a pup and I've stood this watch many times. It's part of the job, Umfrey and you'd better get used to it and stop complainin'." By the end of his rebuke, Oso's tone had gone from irritated to conciliatory. He didn't want to be at odds with the lad, as they'd been working together awhile now and Umfrey was a decent enough sort. He just complained too much for the veteran guard's liking, as many of the younger generation did. The fact that Oso got a little extra coin on the side for informing to the mayor had nothing to do with it. At least that's what he told himself. He really didn't want to get Umfrey in trouble, the young guard just needed to learn how things worked.

Umfrey backed off a little then. He wasn't quite afraid of Oso but the older guard was an intimidating man. His scars spoke of the fights and battles he'd been in, not just with men but with orcs and other monsters they said. The young man had never worked up the nerve to ask about it but he was curious. "Sorry." He mumbled then.

Oso smiled a bit, the movement making his thick, drooping mustached dance. "It's alright lad." His smile grew rueful. "It is cold. I heard that by next year, the guard posts will be built and we won't have to stand out in the weather." He offered the last bit peaceably enough but Umfrey wasn't quite done complaining.

"I heard they're going to use wood." The young guard said sullenly. "Probably old wood so the town can save on coin. The wind will still cut through it."

A little exasperated now, Oso stubbornly said, "It'll still be better than bein' outside in it."

"Yeah but I still don't understand..." Umfrey started but was interrupted by Oso as he looked past him down the road.

"Looks like riders comin'." The stout guardsman said, squinting as he watched the distant figures coming toward the town. "Wagons too." Oso added thoughtfully. "Caravan maybe."

The two guards straightened their belts and sword scabbards and hefted their spears. Then they stepped from the brazier to stand before the gate and waited. It was still cold and they still shivered a bit, particularly Umfrey but neither man said a word as the wagons approached.

"What kind of name is Wend?" The barbarian asked brusquely. He'd been getting more and more out of sorts the closer they came to town and his manner was terse. Looking at the walls of the town as it loomed larger and larger, his scowl deepened.

Venaro thought about it for a long moment. "I am unsure." He finally admitted. "I've been traveling this region for years but the town of Wend is quite old." With a laugh, he added, "Much older than me I can assure you!" Seeing that the Northman did not share his laughter or even smile, the merchant ran a hand through his greying hair, thinking that he needed to get it cut soon. "I don't know if Wend is the name of someone or perhaps just a word used to describe it."

Mystified, Tanoc looked at the other man. He said nothing but raised an eyebrow in question.

"Wend?" Venaro said half in question. "Like the word, wend?" Seeing no change of expression on the barbarian, he added, "To travel? To direct your course?"

Nothing from the Northman. Now both eyebrows were raised alarmingly.

"It doesn't matter." The trader relented finally. "I don't even know if that's how the town came by its name."

"I do not know the word." Tanoc finally said. "It means travel?"

Nodding, Venaro replied, "Well, yes." Without thinking, he expounded further. "It means that the individual is proceeding on their way."

With a snort, the barbarian guffawed. "So the town is called travel?"

"Well...no." Venaro said slowly.

"You just said that it meant to travel, did you not, merchant?" Tanoc asked accusingly.

"Well I..." Flustered now and irritated at the Northman's relentless questions and even more annoyed that he was so dismissive when he tried to explain, the trader snapped, "I never said for certain that it was named for the word itself!" Venaro looked close at the other man and saw that Tanoc was grinning at him. The barbarian wasn't really serious in his questioning, the man just seemed to quarrel out of habit when he was bored or on edge. Imitating the emphatic way that Tanoc often spoke, the merchant schooled his voice to a flat, stoic tone. "It is called Wend because it is called Wend."

"Ha!" Tanoc laughed again. "I think I'm starting to like you, merchant."

Venaro sighed, seeing that they were getting close enough to the walls to see the north gate now. "You never use my name, why is that?"

The Northman turned those unsettling gray eyes on the merchant. "Names have power." His voice was flat. "They should not be used overmuch."

Now it was the trader's turn to laugh. "You must be joking!" He looked more closely at the barbarian and saw that he was deadly serious. "Oh, I see." He still couldn't suppress a chuckle and he didn't care. The barbarian laughed freely at everything that he found foolish about the culture of other people. "Well...Tanoc..." Venaro said, deliberately drawing out the other man's name. "I'll try to keep that in mind."

Grimacing, the barbarian growled something in his own language. Venaro was sure it wasn't complimentary. With a shaking of his head, Tanoc then said. "Well merchant, maybe I *don't* like you so much."

When the merchant only laughed louder, the barbarian frowned for another moment and then laughed despite himself, his mood changing like a swift storm. Venaro chortled for a few moments before he finally wheezed. "Well...I'm starting to like you too, Northman."

Tanoc smiled but it began to slip as they got closer to the gates. Venaro wondered if he'd ever seen such high walls made of stone or such a large town for that matter. The merchant didn't really know what to say as any reassurance he might have offered the stoic barbarian would have surely been rebuffed.

The Northman said little as they approached but just before they were within earshot of the guards, quipped, "It's a stupid name for a town."

The merchant had no time for a witty rejoinder but the statement made him smile. He was still smiling as they rode up to the gate. As the caravan neared the gate, one of the guardsman, a burly fellow with a drooping mustached raised a gloved hand. As the other guard, a younger man stood before the entrance to the town, the first guard eyed the line of wagons, men and horses. Venaro couldn't help but notice that he did a double take when he looked at Tanoc.

Still looking at the gigantic Northman, the man asked, "Who leads here?"

Seeing that Tanoc was already bristling under the guard's scrutiny, Venaro spoke up. "I do." The last thing he wanted was an altercation here at the city gates. "My name is Venaro."

Before he could say more, the younger guard asked, "What's your business in Wend?" It was clear the other guard was annoyed at the interruption. However, the man simply folded his arms, waiting for the answer.

"I am a merchant." He said simply, gesturing back toward the wagons. "These are my wares and I've buyers in town awaiting my arrival."

"Seems like I've heard that name before, Oso." The younger guard said.

With a grimace at the other guard, the man named Oso looked pointedly at Tanoc again. "Are all these men with you?"

Nodding, the merchant used his most charming voice. "Yes, they are my guards and they've kept the caravan safe through wild lands." He went on to add in a reassuring tone. "Everything is in order, of course. You're welcome to check the wagons, if you wish." He said it as if it weren't standard procedure but Venaro wanted these men to know that he viewed them searching his property as something he did at his own discretion.

"That we will." Oso replied. With a gesture at the younger guard, he said, "Check 'em, Umfrey." As the other man walked down the line of wagons, inspecting the contents of each one, Oso noticed the barbarian's gaze upon the archers atop the stone walls of Wend.

Venaro had noted Tanoc's examination as well and knew that it could easily seem like the Northman was sizing up the defenses of the town. "How does Wend fare?" He asked rather hurriedly. "Any news?"

"None worth tellin', really." Oso replied laconically, still eyeing the barbarian. "They say some villages up north have gone quiet and there's been trouble with orcs but that's rumors." He finally cocked his head to look up at Venaro, where he sat on his horse. "Where'd you say you was comin' from?"

The merchant, ever the diplomat, dismounted. He knew the guard might be more at ease if they could speak face to face. "We've come from the north coast, up near Rudden."

"Isn't that one of the villages we heard about Oso?" The guard called Umfrey asked.

"Aye, it is." The grizzled guard replied. "You know anything about Rudden?"

Venaro nodded slightly. "It was deserted when we got there." Seeing the guards' expressions, he explained. "I had business there, as it was one of the places I buy from but there was no one at all there."

"What happened?" Umfrey breathed. His face was pale as he asked, "Was it orcs?"

"I don't think so." The merchant replied. "I'm not really sure if I should go into all the details here." His gaze was intent as he looked at Oso. "I need to speak to Mayor Edber...about many things."

Oso hesitated then. He was well aware that trade was the lifeblood of places like Wend and he had indeed heard the name Venaro before. The man clearly knew the town and even knew the mayor by name. The guardsman was quite sure that harassing merchants was a good way to get demoted or even let go from the town guard. Still, it was obvious that he did not like the look of the barbarian one bit. "Does your...friend here know about our laws here in Wend?"

"Oh, for certain, Tanoc here understands the statutes of your fair town!" Venaro assured the guardsmen. He was well aware of what the barbarian had said to him about names but he was past caring. Even when the Northman turned to favor him with a scowl, he went blithely on. "He's my best guard and he has my complete trust. He'll cause you no trouble, good sir, I can assure you!" The merchant's tone was light and full of assurance.

"See that he doesn't!" Guard Oso growled, his stare as much as much a warning as his words. "We don't tolerate trouble-makers here in Wend!"

The Northman glared right back, his expression even more menacing. Before things could get any further out of hand, Venaro cut in.

"Thank you, my friend." The guard didn't look back at him for several moments and when he did, Venaro added, "We're just here briefly to trade and then I've other business away east once I'm done here. I do need to speak to the mayor, of course."

That seemed to set the guardsman's mind at ease. Let the mayor deal with this situation. If the Northman got out of hand or was a problem, they could deal with him then. Oso was no coward but he didn't fancy his chances with the hulking warrior, though he would have died before admitting it. With a nod, the guard stepped back. "Open the gates!" He bawled as he did so.

As the wagons moved forward, the barbarian finally stopped glaring at the guard, much to Venaro's relief. "Thank you." The merchant offered but Oso was still scowling.

Guard Umfrey, however said cheerily, "Welcome to Wend!" as they rode in.

"Stupid name for a town." The barbarian said, reiterating his earlier thoughts.

Venaro winced in spite of himself and hoped that the guards hadn't heard the insult. Even as he thought it, he knew they had just as surely as he knew the Northman had meant them to. It was going to be a rough stay.

There was a creak from the floor below, causing Whisper's head to cock ever so slightly. Her work on the window was finished and she'd moved her stool to the corner where she could watch the entire room. Sunset was imminent and she had carefully pried the window open, making sure that it would open easily when she needed to leave.

She waited for several minutes, not moving or making a sound, just listening. Over the past couple of hours, Whisper had attuned herself to the noises of the house and the neighborhood outside. Usually, she would take a bit longer to do this but time was of the essence. It didn't matter, however, the woman knew her craft and was certain she knew what sounds were ordinary sounds heard daily and what ones were new and different.

It was a skill that she'd mastered long ago and it never ceased to amaze her that most people knew nothing of it. It was as simple as listening, really listening, which was something Whisper knew the average person was simply incapable of. Like startled game, most people reacted to every noise and sight. The true hunter, whether of men or animals, knew the truth. Real stealth wasn't just about being quiet, it was about listening and watching everything.

Closing her eyes, as she knew there was nothing currently to see in the room itself, Whisper listened. There was the creaking of the house, still settling after all these years. In the distance the shouts and laughter of children could be heard. Closer than that was a dog barking, perhaps a street or so over. Then…there it was. The groan of an old board being stepped on. In her current state that was nearly a trance, Whisper was certain it was coming from the porch outside.

The woman weighed her options then. She could wait and see if whoever was out there came in. It would be easy enough for her to lurk out of sight and deal with them when they came into the room. However, she had business this night and could ill afford an interruption that could cost her time.

Quickly deciding, Whisper stood and like a wraith crossed the room to the door. She'd left it half open as was her wont and she peered around the doorframe. Down below, in the entryway, she saw a shadow. The woman didn't move or make a sound but watched. The shadow was cast from outside as someone stood there.

Still watching and waiting, Whisper heard the sound of low voices. Even with her keen hearing, she couldn't make out what they were saying and so she glided out into the hallway and half down the stairs. So stealthy was she that the only sound was her own breathing, a controlled thing that was barely louder than that of a cat. She was certain that whoever was out there hadn't heard her as she got near the bottom of the stairs. Crouching there, she listened and was rewarded with clarity as she was able to hear what they were saying now.

"I don't know if we should do it." Came a muffled voice. It was a young man's voice, nervous and excited.

A similar voice answered. "Yer always afraid, ain't ya?"

"Am not!" The first voice shot back in irritation.

"Hey!" The second young man hissed. "Quiet! This street's not completely deserted ya know!"

"That's what I'm sayin'." The first lad replied. "Someone might see us! It's still light out."

After a few moments, the second voice said, "Fine! We'll come back after dark and you better not be a coward then!"

Irritation could be heard as the first voice replied. "I'm not a coward!" Doubt was there as well. "What if we get caught this time? There wasn't even much worth stealing at the last place."

The voices were fading now as the pair moved away from the house. "Don't worry about that! I know what I'm doing." The second voice came again. "I heard that…"

They were too far away to hear now but it didn't really matter. Whisper knew now that they were petty thieves and young ones at that. She had no doubt that they'd spend hours talking and planning, bickering and arguing and daring each other. If they did come back, it would be after she was gone. Heading back up the stairs, Whisper thought it had been their lucky day. She would have killed them without a thought. She would bear no interruptions this night.

CHAPTER ELEVEN

The Crooked King wasn't the best inn that Venaro had ever stayed at, neither was it the worst. It was early evening by the time they'd made their way into the town, through the streets and finally to the inn. Despite himself, the merchant had breathed a little sigh of relief when they finally got there. They'd received a number of strange looks as they'd passed. Venaro supposed that any group of weary, wounded strangers with a small caravan of wagons would have been cause for notice. The fact that a towering barbarian rode with them elicited even more interest, the trader would have bet his boots on it.

When they'd arrived at the Crooked King, it looked much the same as Venaro remembered. It was a good sized building built of timber with a base of fieldstone. It was a rambling affair, having had additions added over the years and the final effect was something of a hodgepodge of building styles. The King as it was known by locals sat along the east wall of the town, almost slumped against it like a drunk, unsure whether he'll keep his feet or fall down entirely.

The merchant didn't care about the looks or the fact that the food wasn't great or the ale was at times sour. He didn't even care that occasionally, he'd had to run the mice out of his room when he'd stayed here before. What he did care about was that the owner was an old acquaintance and one who would know any news or gossip worth knowing. While not quite a friend, Jorun was someone

Venaro knew could be trusted to tell the truth and keep his mouth shut, as long as there was coin in it for him.

As they rode around the side toward the stables, Tanoc paused, looking up at the sign over the front door. The sign bore a painting of a fat red king with a yellow crown. While the king was painted with a rotund belly, there was something unsettling about how thin his face was, how cold his eyes were. The background of the sign was blue and green checks and though the paint was peeling a bit, it was clear that someone with some talent had painted the sign.

Riding near the Northman, Venaro said, "They call this place the Crooked King." When the barbarian rather predictably declined comment, the merchant explained. "Old Jorun, who owns this inn, hated the king with a passion." Venaro paused, remembering when Jorun himself had explained the meaning of the sign to him. "Jorun's son died in the last great war."

Now, he could see that he had the barbarian's attention. Tanoc asked curiously, "Why is it called that?" The Northman looked intently at him as he asked the question.

Venaro sighed then, not really wanting to talk about the war and all the horrors that went along with it. All he really wanted to do was get a room, get cleaned up and into clean clothes. Still, he felt obligated, on some level, to educate the barbarian about the land they were in. "It is called the last great war by people because all the nations were drawn into it." The merchant's voice was bleak. "Lacking the time to explain all the politics and military maneuvers, it's rather difficult to explain. I suppose you could say that it was also called the 'last great war' because when it was done, even the winners seemed like they'd lost."

Tanoc frowned but said nothing and the trader continued. "By the time the smoke cleared and the losses tallied, everyone from the greatest ruler to the most humble peasant realized that all the nations involved had lost more than they could afford." Venaro shuddered as he remembered those days. "The grand armies were no more and anarchy swept the land. Orcs and other monsters who had long hid and waited crept forth and took advantage of the chaos, while dispossessed men became bandits and mercenaries, preying on the weak."

"Who, then, won this great war?" Tanoc persisted.

"No one really won." Venaro said then. He could see that the barbarian didn't believe him. "You could say that the Grand Compact of Nations, as it was known, actually *won* the war. The country of Gurral, which we're now in, was part of that compact."

The barbarian snorted. "They either won or they didn't, merchant." He looked at Venaro with mild irritation.

"Ah, but that's really the whole point, isn't it?" Venaro replied. "Gurral was one of the victorious nations but it was broken, its strength shattered." He gestured vaguely around him. "Towns like Wend are rare islands in seas of lawlessness. Such places must fend for themselves and the only contact from higher leaders such as kings is when they send their tax collectors through."

The whole thing seemed to simply annoy the Northman. "Only you could make tales of battle sound boring, merchant."

Venaro didn't care. "They also called the last war, the War of Tyrants. Many called it the war of greed." He nodded toward the inn. "People like Jorun lost sons and brothers to a war that helped no one but the rich, who got richer."

Tanoc eyed the merchant speculatively. "You're a strange one, merchant." He scratched at the stubble on his face. "Is it not dangerous to speak so?"

The trader knew what the barbarian meant. Even though the reavers of the north were free men who spoke their minds, their rulers were fierce and quick to mete out punishment. Or at least he'd always heard it said.

Venaro yawned, tired beyond measure. Somehow talking of all this just made him all the more weary. "Not really." He finally answered. "As I said, this region is highly unstable now. The rulers of most lands these days are only rulers in name." He yawned again and grimaced. "It's as I told you, settlements like this one are on their own."

The barbarian said nothing more but nudged his horse toward the stables. He was clearly done with the conversation and that suited the weary merchant just fine. Venaro recognized that the Northman didn't care about the details of old wars in lands that his people had long preyed upon. The merchant vowed then and there that he was done trying to instruct the warrior further. Tanoc could figure it out on his own or he would learn the hard way. Venaro guessed it would be the latter.

Stable hands took care of their horses and unhitched from the wagons which now sat along the wall in the stable yard. A couple of unlucky caravan guards were assigned to watch the wagons, although the merchant assured them they'd be relieved soon. The rest of them headed to the inn.

Within, the Crooked King was a lively place. Music came from someone playing a flute as drunken patrons sang an old song. While not packed, the King had a lot of customers and they drank and argued, ate and gambled. Those nearest the door stopped to look at the newcomers briefly but Wend was a goodly sized town and people coming and going didn't elicit much comment. However, Venaro could see the stares that the Northman's presence brought.

Wasting no time, Venaro and the others headed lest toward the bar, where Jorun stood. The old man was losing a battle with his spreading paunch and his features told the tale of a man who often drank to excess. Still, the innkeeper seemed lucid enough as the merchant approached and recognized him instantly.

"Ah, Venaro!" Jorun said warmly. "You made it back, eh?"

Laughing despite all that had happened, the merchant nodded. "Barely, my friend!" He clasped hands with the innkeeper and couldn't help but smile. He'd always liked old Jorun. "My men and I are tired and hungry, Jorun. We'll need accommodations."

"Of course, my friend!" Jorun replied. "We've always got room for you!"

Venaro couldn't help but think this was because Jorun had made a good deal of money trading with him. He chided himself inwardly for his cynicism, wondering what was wrong with him. Of course, Jorun had made coin with the merchant and Venaro was known for doing just that.

Still, the old man had always treated him well and at times that was more than could be said for many of his countrymen. There were still those who viewed Venaro as a meddlesome foreigner who was taking coin out of their pockets. Jorun had always been friendly and respectful with the merchant. It was the whole sorry miserable trek that had soured his mood, Venaro told himself. The truth was that he had been shaken by the encounter with the Dregs than he would have thought possible.

Noticing that the innkeeper, like others nearby, was staring at the barbarian, Venaro raised his voice a bit so several of them could hear. "We pulled him from the wreckage of a ship." He said, nodding toward Tanoc. "He's fought with us against the orcs as we came back south and saved a lot of men." The merchant knew word would spread throughout the tavern and beyond and he hoped this information would at least quell and rumors or fears about the Northman.

Jorun nodded and smiled. "Of course, Venaro!" His eyes still strayed to the young giant. "You've always kept strange company but you always turn it into coin, don't you?" The innkeeper laughed but it didn't sound genuine.

A short time later, Venaro and his men were seated at a corner table with drinks in their hands and plates of mutton and potatoes set before them. While his drovers dug in, the merchant, barbarian and ex-soldier talked in low tones. Venaro couldn't help but notice that the other two men still ate, talking in between bites as they did.

"What's the plan?" Bandur asked around a mouthful of potatoes.

Venaro was hungry but he couldn't quite concentrate on food just yet. "I need to meet with my business associates here in Wend."

He was worried and it showed. "I cannot meet all of my contracts because of what we had to leave behind."

The former soldier shrugged. "It couldn't be helped, Venaro." He took a pull from his mug. "That's good ale!" He commented appreciatively and then said, "If they can't see the reasons we had to leave some of the wagons, then they're fools!"

Venaro shook his head slowly. He wasn't about to try to explain the finer points of commerce to someone like Bandur. Thinking of his conversation outside with Tanoc, he finally replied. "Yes, well, that's not how coin is made, unfortunately." He knew that would get Bandur's attention. "I've got customers who were expecting goods." The merchant picked at his food. "Hopefully, I can still sell what's left and make a deal for the next trip."

Bandur had stopped gorging and leaned across the table. "What of our pay?" He said, indicating himself and the drovers.

Sighing, the merchant's response was plain. "You'll get paid first, as always." Venaro had a standing deal with his employees; they got paid, whether he made a profit or no. It was part of why he was able to get the best men to work for him as well as why they were unusually loyal. Still, it wore at him at the moment to think that all Bandur and the others cared about was getting their coin. The ex-soldier had nodded, satisfied and returned to feasting.

Meanwhile, Tanoc had finished his food and two ales and was smiling appreciatively at the pretty young barmaid who was refilling his mug. She blushed at the northerner's frank admiration but smiled back as well.

Groaning inwardly, Venaro waited until the girl was gone and then hissed in a low voice to the Northman. "You need to watch yourself, Tanoc."

The barbarian looked around and merely raised an eyebrow, the smile still on his face.

"The last thing we need is trouble over a girl." The merchant said, trying to keep his voice as low as possible.

"What trouble?" The Northman said, smiling as he watched

the lass walk away. "She refilled my mug and smiled at me." Tanoc
stretched his mighty arms and looked back at Venaro.

"Yes but people can be strange about foreigners dallying with
their women, Tanoc." Venaro's voice was still pitched low but the
intensity of his warning was clear.

With the expressive shrug that the merchant had come to
know so well, Tanoc replied. "If smiling at a girl is dallying with her,
these people are bigger fools than I'd imagined." His smile had
slipped a bit but he purposely looked at the girl across the way now
and smiled all the more. She caught the smile and blushed again, as
she got another pitcher from the bar. Then she smiled back.

Sighing, Venaro looked at Bandur, who was finishing off his
ale. "Listen to me, Bandur." After a moment, the warrior looked at
him. "I have business to attend to and I need you to keep an eye on
things here." The merchant nodded at Tanoc. "I don't want things
to get out of hand."

"You want me to control him?!" Bandur asked and then
laughed out loud.

Even though everyone in the place was loud and no one was
paying them any mind, Venaro hissed in his low voice. "Yes!" He
was getting irritated. "You are in charge while I'm gone. I want you
to stay sober and keep an eye on things."

"Now wait just a minute!" Bandur protested. The man had
clearly wanted to relax and have a good time. His expression showed
that he was none too pleased by the merchant's orders. "I can't keep
the lads from carousing and you know I can't do anything about
him." He said the last, indicating the barbarian.

"I don't have time to argue with you!" Venaro snapped. "I
have to see my contacts and the mayor as well! Or have you
forgotten what happened on the road here?"

Bandur paled and it was clear that he had *not* forgotten their
experience with the monstrosities that had attacked them.

"You need to hold things together, Bandur and you can't do
that if you're drunk!" Venaro grated. Then, he realized how much

the former soldier had been through, how much they'd all been through. "Look, I just want you to keep things from getting out of control, alright? Keep them out of jail and try to make sure no one gets killed at least until they get paid."

At the mention of pay, Bandur's eyes gleamed and he nodded. "Suppose we can't drink too much 'til we've got a bit more coin in our pockets." He mumbled.

"Just so." Venaro said with satisfaction, vowing to himself that he'd leave instructions with Jorun that he wasn't paying for any more drinks until he returned. That would keep them from getting too out of hand, he hoped, as many of the drovers had little enough coin on them.

Rising from the table, the merchant said no more. He had business to attend to, not the least of which was to talk to the headman of Wend. Though he knew they were safe now behind the walls of the town, he couldn't get the apparition of the Dregs out of his mind.

As the merchant left the inn, most did not take note. One who did was an individual that sat alone, several tables away, eating quietly. He wore the garb of a priest and a warhammer was propped against the table. The priest's eyes flicked from the doorway the merchant had exited back to the men he'd sat with. He'd overheard much of the conversation and even as he ate, he pondered.

Gliding silently out onto the rooftop, Whisper crouched at the edge for a moment to regard the sky. She was satisfied to see that the crescent moon was swathed in clouds and she'd have plenty of darkness to work in. Looking around, she saw no one moving on the street or in the nearby yards and quick as a thought, leapt to the nearby branch of the tree. As soon as her feet touched the branch, Whisper lightly ran to the trunk of the tree. Her leap had carried her halfway across the branch where it was thicker, but she knew better than to trust to its strength overlong. Hugging the trunk, knowing its girth would mask her shadow, she stepped to another branch, the one that ran out into the street towards the manor she'd been observing.

Waiting, the woman silently watched and listened for a time. Though, she felt the urgency of her revenge, she ignored it, like a true professional and surveyed the approach. The branch that ran out toward the manor was long and spindly and she judged that she'd have to make the jump around the halfway point. It was not ideal but neither did she want to go by way of the street. The branch was only a few feet above the wall, after all and she should have no trouble as long as she judged the distance correctly. Whisper decided to leap next to one of the square, stone pillars that strengthened the wall every fifteen feet or so. It would give her immediate cover, as well as something to easily steady herself against. Still she waited, watching the street.

Before long, she was rewarded by first the sound and then the sight of lanterns bobbing up the lane. Whisper had found out the routines of the watch in the town and had known they'd be along soon. With the patience of a hunting cat, she didn't move a muscle and watched the small knot of guardsmen move down the street. The one thing the woman was glad of was that the novice thieves she'd heard earlier hadn't yet returned. It would not do to have the guards catch them and have the whole area roused. She waited as the guards walked down the street, checking to make sure all was in order in the area. Whisper continued to bide her time as the moved down the street and around the corner. She counted slowly to twenty once she could no longer see the lanterns before she made her move.

When the woman did move, it was with speed that would have shamed a viper, yet she was quiet as a field mouse. Whisper ran several steps down the branch and at exactly the point she'd decided earlier, made her jump. She leapt across the space between the tree and the high manor wall and landed effortlessly next to the stone column. The move was spectacular and had anyone been watching they would have been amazed at such a feat but there was no one to see. Her breathing only slightly faster, Whisper paused, using the stone pillar as cover, as she had the tree. Standing against the column, she was indistinguishable from its shadow. For several moments, she surveyed the manor grounds.

The grounds were a long rectangle with the manor house near the front. The sward was immaculately tended as were the trees that were planted at tasteful intervals. There were several smaller buildings on the property and these consumed the woman's immediate attention. There was a larger building near the back of the manor house that looked to be servants' quarters. Nearby, was a slightly smaller building that Whisper guessed was a stable, judging by its layout and location. Further back was what looked like a kennel that the woman vowed to keep a distance from. Closest to the back wall, where Whisper stood was a flower garden complete with a potting shed, quite similar to the one at the house of the late Sorvus. She smiled slightly, thinking her guess had been correct. Whoever had designed the grounds of these manors hadn't been overly imaginative.

Whisper climbed down the wall, rather that jumping. It was quite high and in the darkness, it would have been easy to turn an ankle or twist her knee. As soon as her feet hit the ground, she dashed to the back wall of the shed. Hugging the wall of the little building, she made her way around it and hesitated at its front corner. It was quiet, which was good. She hadn't seen any movement but her gaze sharpened on the kennel. As quiet as she could move, she didn't fancy her chances against the senses of hounds. Still, she was glad that there didn't seem to be any roaming the grounds freely.

Choosing her path carefully, Whisper kept low as she moved from the shed to the cover afforded by the flower garden. Keeping the garden between her and the kennel as long as possible, she waited again at its edge making sure she was still undetected. Satisfied, she then sprinted across the open space to the first tree some thirty paces away. When she got there, Whisper paused, waiting to hear barking or shouts. Hearing neither, she moved to the next tree in the same fashion. Quietly and cautiously, the woman moved like her name from cover to cover until she was closing on the manor house itself.

Resting by the tree nearest the stables, Whisper took stock of the area. The stables were between her and the servants' quarters, as she'd planned. While there were more trees that continued around the house, her attention was on the shrubs that decorated its perimeter. The shrubs were as flawlessly groomed and tended as everything else but more importantly to Whisper, gave her cover on her final approach to the manor. As she crouched at the base of the tree, she made sure no one was about. Other than the whicker of horses by the stables and more distantly, the murmur of voices from the servants' quarters, it was quiet. Picking a window where there was no light on the ground floor, Whisper wasted no time but sprinted to the shrubs beneath it. As soon as she got to the shrubs, she rolled under the pruned branches and wriggled under them. Crawling slowly and carefully, she didn't disturb the shrubs any more than a small bird might have.

Taking her time, she crawled until she was directly under the window that she'd chosen. Again, she waited, listening to make sure no one had seen her. After a few moments, she was satisfied and rose from the bushes to peer in the window. Heavy drapes obscured most of the room but she could see through where they were parted to a room beyond. She could make out little other than furniture but the room was dark save for a sliver of light under the door. Now, Whisper looked more closely at the window. The shutters weren't closed, as she'd noted earlier and that suited her just fine. There was a small wooden clasp that held the windows together and it was child's play to open it with a dagger. Carefully, she opened the windows, which parted inward like small double doors. There was a soft squeak but nothing more and the woman didn't dawdle this time to see if anyone heard it but leapt up and in.

Like a shadow, Whisper entered the room, parting the drapes. Her movements quick and quiet, she closed the window behind her but did not clasp them. She did pull the drapes close behind her and then paused, looking around the room. It was a bedroom, tastefully appointed but rather sterile and Whisper was certain it was a guestroom. There were no personal effects or decorations and it didn't look to have been used in some time. Moving around the bed and other furnishings, she crouched there by the door and listened, acclimating herself to the sounds of the house. It was silent except for low murmurs coming from nearby. Opening the door quietly, Whisper could see that the room she was in was at the end of a wide, long hallway. There were tasteful paintings hung on the wall between other doorways, all equally dark. Near the end of the hall was an archway, where she heard low voices. Stalking toward them, Whisper listened around the corner.

"...all I know is she's none too happy." Came the clipped voice of an older woman.

"Don't know why the mistress has to take it out on us." Came the surly reply of what sounded like a middle-aged man.

Clucking at him like a mother hen, the woman's voice was motherly yet chiding. "Now, now. You've been warned before, you know." The woman's voice was agreeable and warm. "It won't do to dwell on it. Just tread lightly around the mistress for a few days."

Whisper peered around the wall to see a large, formal dining room. There was a door off to one side and another archway that led to the front hall of the manor. Standing near the table was a brawny man with thinning hair. He was holding his hat in his hands and listened. The woman who was speaking was tall, rail-thin, and had gray hair. It was clear that she was in charge. The stood across the table from where Whisper crouched slightly to one side.

"Go and see to the horses, now." The woman said kindly. "The mistress will need the carriage in the morning."

"Yes ma'am." The man answered and turned to leave. As he did so, the woman also left, exiting through the doorway.

Whisper listened as the heavy tread of the man indicated that he'd left by the front door. After a moment, she glided across the dining room and listened at the door the woman had entered. She could hear the clink of dishes and pots and guessed it to be a kitchen. Moving past the door, she looked into the main hall seeing a huge, sumptuous room. Built to entertain, as well as impress, Whisper paid little attention to the room's fine furniture, exquisite oil paintings and detailed tapestries. What dominated her attention was the stairway that led to the upper floor.

Hesitating for a moment, Whisper pondered whether or not to deal with the old woman before heading upstairs. She didn't hear much noise coming from the rest of the ground floor and assumed that there weren't many servants allowed inside this time of night. Listening for a moment to the sounds from the kitchen, she decided that the servant would be busy for a while.

Her mind made up, the dark clad woman slipped through the great room to the stairs. Gliding up them, Whisper made no more sound than a ghost. She'd learned long ago how to walk up stairs silently, sticking to the outsides for the most part and stepping lightly and quickly. At the top of the staircase was another long, wide hall with doors on both sides. There were fine oil lamps mounted on the walls, turned low so that they only shed a soft glow. There were no lights from beneath any of the doors on the side of the hall. However, there was one door at the end that a bit of light shone underneath. This door was a finely carved, mahogany affair and Whisper knew it must be the door to her quarries room.

Though she'd met Delia, she'd never been here before, the merchant, rather wisely, choosing to meet her at a tavern within the town. It had, of course, been rather easy to find the home of the woman and find out information about the places defense and layout. Laughably, most of Delia's guards were stationed outside the manor house, predictably up front. However, Whisper wasn't taken in by the lack of guards inside or around the back. She smell a trap.

Softly as a breath, she stole down the hall to the first side door on the right. Lying on her belly, she looked under the crack in the door. There was little to see and Whisper grimaced. Rising to one

knee, she drew her short blade and tried the handle. Finding it
unlocked, she opened the door, her blade at the ready. No one leapt
at her or struck with a weapon. The room was empty.

Slipping inside, Whisper saw that the darkened room was a
study. There were walls of books and tubes with scrolls, maps and
charts. A map of the northern lands was hanging on one wall, drawn
in exquisite detail and showing the settlements and trade routes.
Ignoring it all, the woman strode across to the window on the far
side of the room. Pulling back the drapes slightly, she looked out.
Her view was the back of the manor grounds that she'd recently
traversed. Her present vantage was overlooking the stables, with the
servant's quarters off to the right. Looking down, she could see what
she'd spotted from the ground; a narrow ledge, no more than a few
fingers width ran below the window. It was decorative but made of
stone.

Whisper's grimace turned into a slight smile. The ledge wasn't
much and most who tried to use it would certainly fall but she wasn't
most people. Checking to see that the back of the grounds were still
deserted, she then raised the window and eased herself out onto the
ledge. She flattened herself against the wall and closed the window.
Her feet were turned to either side and in this way, she slowly inched
down the wall, her hands always sliding to find purchase. It wasn't
really difficult, as the manor was a combination of stone and timber
that gave plenty of hand holds.

Within a few minutes, she had passed the windows of the other
rooms on this side of the house. Glancing in each, she could see that
most were empty. However, a peek on the last window, revealed
dark figures within. Whisper's grin became fierce. It *was* a trap.
Continuing on her way, she crept to the last window, which belonged
to the room beyond the ornate door at the end of the hall. Heavy
drapes obscured her sight and the dark woman was forced to work
her way to the corner of the manor. There it was touch and go for a
moment, even for someone of Whisper's skill, as she negotiated the
corner. She was rewarded, however but a pair of windows that were

larger and dominated the whole side of the house.

Moving to the first window, Whisper saw a gap in the curtains and peered through. Her grin broadened at what she saw. The room was luxuriantly furnished, dominated by a massive four poster bed with heavy drapes around it. The rest of the furnishings were equally as intricate and expensive as the bed but what drew her attention were the room's occupants. Two heavily armed men stood near the door, weapons in hand. Nearby, a woman sat at in a regally upholstered chair that almost looked like a throne. It was Delia.

Whisper's lips drew back and her smile became a feral, silent, snarl. Delia was a handsome woman, who had once, perhaps been beautiful. There was a noble air to her features and bearing that made her almost look a queen. Her clothes were finely cut, yet not ostentatious, speaking of understated wealth. Her expression was severe yet worried. She, had no idea that the reason of her apprehension was right outside her window but she was about to find out.

CHAPTER TWELVE

The crescent moon was still swathed in banks of clouds as Venaro made his way to the home of Mayor Edber. It was a fine home and he'd been here before as he and the mayor had been involved in business dealings before. Thinking back to the meetings he'd had, the merchant recalled the man's avarice had worked in his favor. Now, he hoped that greed wouldn't be a problem.

There was a brass doorknocker in the shape of a boar's head in the center of the heavy wooden door and Venaro used it to strike three solid blows. Then, he took a step back from the entrance and waited. It was a bit of a wait before he heard footsteps heading toward the entrance but the merchant had half expected such a wait. While it wasn't overly late yet, he was quite sure that the mayor would not expect to be disturbed at night. He could hear someone fumbling with the locks and a moment later the door opened slightly.

On the other side was a rather harried looking serving girl, although it was perhaps a stretch to call her a girl, as she looked to be in her thirties at least. She was pretty in an unkempt, blowsy sort of way and she was holding a lantern. Looking at the merchant with a surprised expression that he thought might be her standard countenance, she drawled, "Whaddya want?"

"I am here to see mayor Edber, my dear." Venaro said in his most courtly voice, as if her were addressing a queen.

The woman's expression did change though it was still a rather vacant thing. A slight scowl of disapproval began to slip over her face like slowly drawn curtains. "It's late." She looked back inside the house behind her. "Don't think the mayor's expectin' company."

"Ah, my good woman but it's not that late and I'm an old friend of Edber's." She looked back at him, the scowl tumbling into a confused stare. The merchant guessed that she was one of those unfortunate souls that spent most of her life in a hazy, confused fog. Remembering what he knew of the mayor, he added, "I'm also a business associate of the mayor's." It was a stretch, as Venaro didn't really think the mayor convincing the local's to deal fairly with him for a small cut made them associates. However, he knew the man for the avaricious soul that he was and bet that his servants knew not to interfere with business.

Proving his guess correct, the serving girl opened the door wider and gestured for him to enter, mumbling as she did so "Wipe yer feet." She commanded as imperiously as if she were a queen. "Just cleaned the floors."

Venaro did as he was bid and then followed the woman. She led him through a front room where a couple of guards were sitting at a table playing cards. The men eyed him bleakly as he walked by. The merchant's responding grin did not warm their expressions. The serving girl then led him down a hall deeper into the house. For the most part, the place was darkened within. Apparently, the mayor did not like to spend more than he needed to light unused rooms, hence the lantern that the serving girl bore. Toward the end of the hall she turned left down a shorter passage and there knocked on a door.

"Yes?" A weary voice asked. Venaro knew the voice belonged to the mayor.

"You have a…" The woman began and then hesitated. "There's a…someone's here to see you."

"At this hour?" Irritation joined the weariness in the mayor's tone. There was the sound of another voice, pitched low and mayor replied, "It had better *not* be that bloody priest again!"

"Sir?" The serving girl asked hesitantly. "Should I…Do you want me to have him leave?"

Venaro felt badly for the woman then. He knew mayor Edber was the type of pompous official who would take out his displeasure on his subordinates, especially those he could bully. "It is Venaro, the merchant, lord Mayor." He said then, his voice deep and full of warmth.

After a moment, the mayor's voice came again. "Enter." He spoke as if his little office was a grand hall or cathedral.

The serving girl opened the door and Venaro smiled at her before entering. He really didn't want to cause her any trouble. She did not return the smile but once he was inside stepped back out, closing the door behind her.

The merchant looked across the mayor's office to see Edber and another man staring back at him. The mayor looked like a man ready to seek his bed and being kept from it. Standing near the desk where the mayor sat was another man, who looked perturbed but not weary. He was a weedy, poorly dressed, disheveled man with sallow features and a thin build. He was the type of person that one would normally not spare a second glance and in truth, most would try hard not to give a first glance. However, Venaro knew people and there was something…unsettling… about the man. He'd seen him a time or two before in town and often at the mayor's elbow. It wasn't all that strange, as powerful people often had sycophants at their sides. While this man fit all the criteria of someone who had attached himself to someone to better himself, there was something off here. Venaro struggled to remember the man's name.

"Ah, Venaro." Mayor Edber said without any real cordiality in his voice. "I trust there is a reason for you to come to my home this late?"

"It is good to see you again, mayor." Still struggling to remember the other man's name, the merchant crossed the room and sat in the chair facing the mayor. It was the same chair a certain priest had sat in recently and Venaro was about to have the same type of welcome. Deciding not to waste time dissembling, the trader got right to the point. "I wouldn't bother you at night if it was a simple business matter." The mayor's only response was to raise an eyebrow and Venaro continued. "The town of Wend is in danger." He stated it plainly as a fact, not letting any panic or fear into his voice.

"Really?" Edber asked drily. "From what?"

It was clear from the monosyllabic way that the mayor was responding that he wasn't taking the merchant seriously. Keeping his annoyance from his voice, Venaro answered flatly. "From the Pallid."

"The Pallid?" The shabby man asked incredulously. "Surely you don't believe in such children's stories and fables?"

Venaro looked at the thin man in irritation and the name came to him then in a flash as the merchant heard his voice. "They aren't fables, Malken." He turned back to the mayor. "I have seen them."

Now he had Edber's attention. "What?" His face paled. "You have seen these devils?"

"Impossible!" Malken breathed and then laughed. "According to the tales, if you had seen them, you wouldn't have lived to tell of it!"

Venaro remembered now that he didn't like the shabby, little man. "I did not see the Pallid themselves." Before either of them could comment, he added, "But I saw their creatures, the nightmare things known as Dregs."

Malken's eyes narrowed as he stared at the merchant but the man's eyes were on the mayor, else he would have seen a look of venomous hatred that was startling. The shabby man quickly veiled the look behind a smirk, glancing over to make sure the mayor hadn't noticed.

He needn't have worried as the mayor's attention was on the merchant. "What are you talking about?" Worry and confusion warred in his face and form.

"Dregs are servants of the Pallid." Venaro said patiently. "They are like hounds that obediently follow them and they are very hard to kill."

"You slew them?" Malken asked skeptically, then.

Venaro nodded. "My men and I, along with a warrior who travels with us fought them." His voice was bleak. "We lost some good men but we stopped the creatures and burned them, which is the only way to truly finish them." Now his speech grew urgent. "But I think there must be more of them out there, mayor and where the dogs are, the masters cannot be far behind."

Malken's voice was scornful. "You think?"

The merchant turned to face the other man and nodded. Before he could say more, the shabby man asked, "Did you see these...Pallid?"

Venaro shook his head after a moment, "No, however..."

Malken cut him off. "However...you think...perhaps." He looked at Mayor Edber then, "I think this fellow is perhaps seeking to start a panic, mister mayor." The mayor looked doubtful for a moment and then Malken added, "Like that priest was. Maybe they know each other."

Edber's expression became a grimace. "Is that true? Do you know that meddlesome priest?"

Mystified, Venaro's said, "I don't know any priest's around here or anywhere for that matter." He didn't know what was happening but he sensed the mood had turned against him. "I'm not a very religious man, mayor." He glared at Malken then, "However, I know what I saw...what we fought against."

"It was probably orcs." Malken said, looking at the mayor, who nodded in reply.

"It was *not* orcs." Venaro realized with growing horror that this was what he must have sounded like to the old drover, Farn. "I know what orcs look like and I've fought them many times. Believe me, these creatures are Dregs, the servants of the Pallid." Even as he said it, he could see that neither man believed him. Malken and Edber shared a look that said they'd heard enough.

"Thank you for your...warning." The mayor said then.

The merchant rose slowly, feeling like he was in a dream or rather a nightmare. These men had no idea what horrors were even now lurking in the darkness. They felt secure in their fine houses behind their walls and thought nothing could touch them. He murmured something in response but later, could never remember what he'd even said. One thing was certain, these people were all in danger.

Venaro took a few steps toward the door and then half turned. "You said something about a priest?"

With a snort, the mayor replied. "Aye, a trouble maker if I ever saw one." Mayor Edber was staring at Venaro and his expression was that he was looking at another trouble maker. "I had to warn him of the penalties he would face if he caused a panic in town."

That the statement was a threat only slightly veiled, barely registered on Venaro's consciousness. "What was his name?" He asked.

Malken stepped from around the desk and hissed, "His name is trouble and apparently, he has a twin!" He glanced back at the mayor for support then and when the town leader nodded, he continued, emboldened. "We don't want people worrying and panicking here. We don't need rabble rousers in Wend!"

Venaro looked at the man as he would have a particularly loathsome insect. If he had time, he might have had further words with both of them. If he had time, he might have pointed out several facts or explained things better. However, the merchant had begun to feel like he was running out of time. These men would never believe him and act. The truth was a large part of Venaro hoped that he was wrong, that he was worrying over nothing. Somehow, though, he knew that he wasn't. These men were foolish and clueless and he decided to leave them to their delusion. The merchant left the mayor's home without another word.

What Venaro could not have known was that one of them knew quite a lot about the events taking place. One of them, in fact, knew a bit more than the merchant could ever have dreamed.

Watching the merchant go, a smile crawled over Malken's face. The smile was so sickly that the mayor felt revulsion when he saw it. He was glad when the other man said he had business out of town and would be gone for a few days. The smile was still on the shabby man's face when he left the mayor's house not long after the merchant had. It was still there a short time later as he was heading out of the gates.

The girl was no longer blushing as she looked into the storm-gray eyes of the huge Northman. Lilli had never seen such a man in all her young life and while she had originally been a little apprehensive at the sight of him, she had felt a thrill of something…curiosity perhaps? Whatever it was, she felt drawn to the man, who had smiled so broadly and was handsome, in a brooding sort of way. Add to all these traits was the fact that for all that her countrymen called him a barbarian, the blonde warrior hadn't pawed at her or spoken coarsely to her, like so many of them. In fact, he hadn't said or done anything unseemly, apart from his frank admiration of her.

For his part, Tanoc hadn't seen a woman in some time and Lilli would have been surprised to know that he found her as equally exotic. The barbarian had known women in his time but they were the women of his people; tall, fierce and powerful. This was not to say that they weren't beauties in their own right but the barmaid was something different. She was a slender, willowy thing, almost fragile with large brown eyes and dark tresses.

From across the room, Bandur scowled again at the two, where they stood near the bar. Then his gaze traveled back to the group of men who were also watching the pair. The former soldier knew trouble when he spotted it and just as Venaro had predicted, these men looked none too happy. The last thing the caravan guard wanted was a brawl or worse, particularly as he wasn't overly fond of the barbarian. Still, he had his orders from the merchant and the fact was, Tanoc wasn't doing anything wrong or unseemly. Bandur had seen half a dozen men offer worse to the maids who worked at the Crooked King and not an eyebrow was raised. Still, Tanoc was a foreigner and worse, a Northman. The irony of how recently he'd felt the same as these men wasn't lost on him but he shrugged it off. Bandur was pragmatic and he knew that no good was going to come of this.

Another set of eyes watched the Northman and the barmaid. Cenric could see that the mood was turning ugly and that more than half a dozen men were now beginning to loudly speak of unwashed barbarians, filthy north-men and foreign devils. He had assessed the man in question and had no doubts that the powerful warrior could handle himself but he knew that a brawl here could quickly mean the guard would be involved. The priest was well traveled and he guessed that the savage Northman would be loath to surrender to authorities and bloodshed would be all but inevitable.

The barmaid laughed and blushed as the barbarian said something and smiled down at her, reaching out to touch a wayward lock of her hair. That was all it took for the miscreants to stand to their feet, barstools and chairs making a scraping sound as they were pushed back. By now there were ten or so of them and the other patrons hastily got out of their way. The fact that these men had offered worse treatment to Lilli and the other barmaids was never even a thought in the minds of these men. All they saw was a hated Northman, an enemy, trying to steal one of their women.

With a groan, Bandur got to his feet. He looked back at the table he sat at with the other drovers and cursed. There were only a few of them left, the others having gone off to seek other entertainments or sleep. The few that were here were more than a little drunk and would be no help. While there was no love lost between him and the barbarian, he had his orders. Still, his wrist wasn't fully healed and he didn't fancy their chances against nearly a dozen men.

Grimly, the onetime sergeant thought that it wouldn't take much for others to join these men and then they'd have a real problem on their hands. Thinking how unfair it was that he had to side against his own countrymen with a man that until recently, he'd rather have seen dead, Bandur moved toward the bar.

Nearby, Cenric also stood quietly and gathered his belongings. He watched the burly caravan guard begin walking toward the bar and after a moment, headed the same direction. The priest made sure not to follow directly behind the other man, as he didn't want him to think he might be sneaking up on him.

Lilli's eyes widened as she looked past her admirer to the group of men who were now gathering around them in a semi-circle. Seeing her expression, the Northman half turned.

One of the men spoke. "We don't want your kind in our town!" He was a heavyset man with a pot belly and thick jowls. Even though he was a known drunk and had been overly free with his hands when it came to women, the men around him acted as if he were a pious clergyman. "Get away from him, Lilli!"

"Don't tell me what to do, Haron!" Her voice was terse as she snapped back at the fat man. "We're just talking and it's none of your business what we do! You're just jealous because I've fended off your advances you pig!"

Tanoc's gaze was like ice as it fell on the portly man called Haron. The townsman froze and his mouthed opened and closed. It was clear that he wanted to say something but fear stole his tongue as he looked up at the huge Northman. For a moment, nothing was said and it might have ended then and there but another man, perhaps emboldened by the fact that he was further away from the gigantic barbarian hissed, "Filthy whore!"

The barbarian turned completely to face the rabble before him then, looking for the one who'd spoken. None could meet his eyes but glanced from one to another, searching for courage among their numbers. Then, Haron snapped, "He's a murdering barbarian!" He'd found his tongue when the awful gaze of the forbidding warrior was no longer on him. "How many of our kin have died at the hands of such reavers?" At this statement, the men around Haron growled and now faced the barbarian. Several more men at other tables stood then, perhaps thinking of lost loved ones.

Jorun, the innkeeper had been working behind the bar and seeing the way things were going, tried to intervene. "I don't want any fighting in my place." He didn't shout but his voice was loud enough to be heard. The innkeeper understood why these men, most of them simple tradesmen and farmers, hated the sight of a Northman in their midst.

However, the barbarian had done nothing wrong and was with Venaro, who Jorun counted as a friend. "Everyone calm down…" Jorun began reasonably but was interrupted by Haron, who seemed to be the leader of the impromptu group that looked to be well on its way to becoming a mob.

"You're going to take his side?!" Haron spluttered, his jowls quivering. "After all the coin we've all spent in this place?!" Outrage was painted on his face but it was a false thing. Haron was the type that reveled in causing trouble for others and beneath the veneer of false indignation on his expression was an ugly sort of glee.

Cenric noted the expression as he walked up to the group at the bar. He exchanged glances with Jorun, who had lapsed into silence. The owner of the Crooked King said nothing but his eyes told the tale. The man clearly didn't like what was happening and while he had several bouncers for handling drunks and the like, this was clearly more than they could deal with. He noted the caravan guard had also walked up to the back of the group.

Haron was talking louder and louder now, practically shouting. "I say we run this filth out of town!" He said gesturing toward the barbarian. "I say we whip him like the beast he is! I say…"

"You talk a good fight, fat man!" Tanoc roared, his stentorian voice, the roar of a lion. The barbarian glowered as he took a step toward Haron.

Sensing the eyes upon him, Haron didn't back down, though he was sweating now and leaned back. It was clear that he didn't want to try his luck with the barbarian but he had no intention of doing that. Bellowing even louder, he said to his comrades, "Now, he threatens us, lads!" No one pointed out that the Northman hadn't threatened anyone or that he was speaking directly to Haron and not the group.

Bandur tensed, his soldier's training telling him that violence was imminent. His mind raced as he tried to think of something to say that could stop this but he knew nothing was going to work. These men were full of liquid courage and fired up by Haron's words. The pudgy man was just the kind that real fighting men loathed, pompous and full of words but slow to action.

The priest, likewise, was thinking of how to defuse the situation and although he was a great deal more eloquent than the ex-soldier, he too was at a loss. Cenric knew that these men were in no mood to listen and if he spoke, he needed to make sure he chose the right words.

Whatever anyone might have said to stop the whole thing became a moot point as Haron looked past the Northman to Lilli and in a vicious tone spat, "Vile slattern, we'll deal with you after we..."

Haron was interrupted again but this time it wasn't by words. Tanoc's right fist connected with the fat man's jaw, breaking it like a wishbone at the end of a feast. The pudgy townsman flew backward several feet to land on his back, his eyes rolling up in his head.

For a heartbeat, all was still and again, it might have all ended there but a man's voice came from somewhere in the mob of now more than a dozen men.

"Get him!" The voice cried and the crowd surged forward.

CHAPTER THIRTEEN

The slight clicking sound might normally have captured the attention of the room's three occupants. However, it was timed so that it came right when one of the guards was talking. Though he spoke in a low register, it was just enough to mask the sound of the window's lock being sprung.

Whisper wasted no time but lunged forward as the windows parted. She leapt from the window sill toward the back of the man nearest her. It was a credit to his skill that he had begun to turn as the window opened. He bore a sword in his right hand but the cunning intruder had come in on his left. By the time he realized his mistake, her blade had cut his throat.

Wasting no time, she leapt back as the other guard, a left-handed warrior, swung a mace that would have crushed her skull had she been there. Whisper was too skilled to try and block the heavy, iron weapon with the slender blade of her rapier but gave ground slightly, then, seeing that the merchant, Delia was headed toward the door, hurled a dagger with incredible precision. The other woman sank to the ground with a sob of pain, the dagger buried in her thigh.

The guard with the mace half turned, no doubt fearing that his employer was dead and that he'd failed in his charge. It was the merest of movements, a slight turning, a quick glance. It was all the opening his opponent needed. Whisper lunged forward and the guard brought his mace up to block. The whip-like blade bounced off his weapon but with a deft roll of her wrist, she turned the force to her advantage and point sank into his left arm.

Again, the guard showed his worth as he quickly leapt back, almost tripping over the merchant, who was trying to regain her feet. He quickly switched the mace to his off hand and was bringing it into a guard position as a dagger came flying at him. Even fighting with his off-hand, the guard was able to lurch to one side and the dagger narrowly missed him. However, the dagger had been a ruse and now he was off balance. Whisper had stepped forward and drove her blade into the man's forearm.

With a grunt of pain, the thick-set man dropped his mace. Still, he had some fight in him and rather than give ground, he rushed forward, seeking to knock his lighter opponent off her feet. Whisper was simply too fast, however and spun out of the way. As she did so, she pulled another dagger and rammed it into the man's side.

As her opponent fell like a stone with a wet sounding gasp, Whisper stalked toward Delia, who was crawling toward the door. Sheathing her rapier, she kicked the other woman hard in the side. The merchant couldn't even scream as her tormenter dragged her back to the chair she'd been sitting on and flung her into it.

With a glance toward the door, Whisper assured herself that it was still locked and barred from the inside. The very thing that the merchant had counted on keeping her safe would mean that it would take time for any rescuers to get to her. Looking back at the merchant, she could see that the other woman was trying to steady her breathing, though she shuddered with pain.

"You're tougher than I guessed, Delia." Whisper's voice was low and friendly and full of warmth. The merchant gave a look that was shocked and Whisper chuckled. "I'm not angry with you." She said as if discussing weather or fashion. "Not yet." She let the statement hang there for a moment between them."

Delia licked her lips and swallowed hard. Her gaze flickered toward the door and then back to Whisper. She didn't try to move beyond breathing as she knew there was no chance. Her mind raced as she weighed her chances of survival, as she might have weighed profits from a business venture.

Whisper saw the look and knew it well. She couldn't count how many times she'd seen it before. Her hearing, much more keen than the soft woman seated in front of her, detected a stirring from the floor below. A door shut and distant footsteps. She knew she didn't have long. She held the bloody dagger before the merchant's face. "I want answers, Delia." She turned the knife so the other woman could see the glint of the lamplight on the steel, the slow drip of coagulating blood that bathed it. "I don't have time for lies *or* for mercy." She waited a beat and let her prisoner consider her words. "I'm sure that you have a reason for setting me up and you're going to tell me. Don't lie to me."

"How...how would you know if I was lying or telling the truth?" Delia asked. It was the first time she'd spoken and her voice was steady, though her breathing was quick.

Again, Whisper chuckled that breathy chuckle. She found that she felt a grudging respect for the merchants poise and grit in the face of death. "Convince me." She made the statement simply but there was that in her voice that was more threatening that the bloody dagger.

"Alright." Delia said. "It wasn't personal, I can tell you that." She looked in the flat eyes of her captor and saw not a flicker of emotion. She nodded and continued. "It was business."

"How was framing me for the murder of Sorvus business?" Whisper asked menacingly, the dagger moving closer to accentuate her question.

"That was..." Delia hesitated, loathe to continue. She wasn't sure what was more menacing, the dagger or those eyes. "It was a side benefit."

"What are you talking about?" Whisper asked ominously. She thought she heard soft footsteps in the hall and was wondering that she hadn't heard an alarm raised yet or at least someone asking if

Delia was alright. "You have seconds to tell me the truth and no stalling or I'll kill you and find out from someone else." Her voice was a savage hiss as she grabbed the other woman by the hair and brought the dagger up to her throat.

Delia didn't struggle or try to move. She'd seen Whisper in action and knew she had no chance if she tried to escape. Trying not to look at the blade or those cold eyes, she answered. "There is a bounty on your head."

This took the Whisper aback and for a moment her eyes widened, though the dagger never moved in her steady hands. "What bounty?"

"I found out about it not long after you'd come to town." Delia admitted. She saw no reason to dissemble and every second she gained by talking was another moment of precious life.

"I didn't know you were interested in collecting bounties, Delia." Whisper's voice was cold.

"I'm not." The merchant replied. "I hired you for the job but then when I found out about the bounty, I decided to set you up."

"Why?" Whisper questioned. "Why would you risk it? You had to know that I'd come for you."

"Yes, I knew that was a risk." Delia admitted. "However, I thought the bounty hunters would be in town by then. I didn't think you'd escape."

Whisper grinned like a shark. "Your mistake." She frowned then. She'd heard movement outside in the hall for sure that time. "You still haven't told me why you would try to set me up. I think you're trying to stall me." Delia's eyes went wide and then flickered toward the door. "I think you left that old grey hair orders that if anything suspicious happened, she was to get the other guards together quietly and not raise the alarm." Delia's crestfallen expression said that Whisper was right. "You have seconds to live if you don't tell me everything." The dagger at her throat pressed against the merchant's throat and a little blood flowed as the skin broke.

"Sorvus was trying to push all of us merchants here in Wend out!" The words tumbled forth now as Delia spoke in a panic. "It was a matter of time before he had a monopoly here and none of us could stop him. When I learned about the bounty, I hired you to break in and then tipped him off." Now that the merchant was talking, she couldn't seem to stop. "I hoped that you'd kill him for me…"

"…And get killed or captured myself in the meantime, leaving you to collect on the bounty as well as cleaning Sorvus out after he was dead." Whisper interrupted.

"I…you getting killed wasn't my concern." Delia admitted. "It didn't matter to me, really. For all I knew you would escape and that would have worked just as well."

"Except that then, you'd miss out on the bounty." With an appraising look, she asked, "How much was it?"

Delia hesitated and the dagger pressed harder. She leaned back involuntarily and Whisper grabbed her by the hair so she couldn't move further. "Ten thousand Crowns." She said finally.

Now it was Whisper's turn to be taken off guard. "Ten thousand?" She looked at Delia again. With wonderment in her voice, she nodded. "No wonder you decided to set me up."

"I told you it was business." Delia replied.

There was movement at the door and Whisper cocked her head. She knew she didn't have long. "Yes you did." She murmured. Her hand was a blur as she struck.

A few minutes later, the door was broken open and nearly a dozen guards swarmed in, the matronly figure of Delia's head servant behind them. The window was open to the night and the bodies of the two guards lay still. Quickly, the old woman moved to where her mistress lay and was relieved to see that Delia still lived, though there was a bruise on her temple and her leg was bleeding heavily.

One of the guards had gone to the window and looked out. "There's nothing…I can't see anyone out there." The others had moved into the room and were searching through all the closets and wardrobes.

"Stop that." The gray haired servant snapped. "The mistress is alive and whoever did this is gone." They snapped to attention as if she were general of an army. "We need to get her downstairs and guard her round the clock until she wakes." As the guards moved to obey, the head servant watched to make sure they were gentle as they moved her. She shivered and looked out at the night beyond. "Someone close that window."

The barbarian met the first opponent with a stiff left jab that brought the oncoming combatant to an abrupt halt. The second came in from his right and threw a wild punch that the towering warrior blocked easily. He had no time to do more though as a third crowded in with a stool in his hand. Quickly, Tanoc stepped in and shouldered him so hard he fell to the ground, his improvised bludgeon clattering out of his grasp.

Bandur groaned as he stood indecisively for a moment near the back of the press. It hadn't been that long ago that he had counted the Northman a foe himself. It went against the grain to fight against his countrymen and he had half a mind to let them beat the barbarian bloody. Then again, he well knew that the murdering savage might well kill some of them and he had his orders.

The ex-soldier's decision was made for him when one of the men near the back turned to see him standing there. With a cry of "This one's with him!" the man threw a punch. Bandur's training took over and he stepped back and the blow missed. Then, he threw a punch of his own that sent his opponent reeling back.

Cenric looked across the bar at old Jorun. "You need to stop this." The priest said tersely.

The old man looked at the brawl with a resigned look and shook his head. "No stopping it now." He said sadly and gestured for his bouncers to back away. There were more of the bars patrons joining the men who had initially confronted the barbarian.

Tanoc laughed and kicked an onrushing tough in the chest. The would-be assailant, a weedy looking young man with bad teeth, flew back into his companions. Wasting no time, the barbarian waded into the throng, laying about him with his fists. Bones were broken and teeth lost but still they came on and with the advantage of numbers began to hem the Northman in.

Bandur blocked a blow with his injured arm and gritted his teeth at the pain. Savagely, he struck his opponent a solid blow in the face that dropped him to the floor. Looking back at his table he shouted, "Help me out here, you fools!" The few of the drovers and guards that were still left were mostly drunk and the one of them that managed to rise from his chair was swaying as he stood there.

As the mass of men pushed in close, they grabbed hold of the barbarian and punched and kicked and gouged. Many of these strikes were made ineffective by the fact that they were packed in so tightly that they were unable to get a clean hit. Others were so wild that they accidentally struck their comrades. A few did get through, however but the wild barbarian simply laughed aloud as he was punched in the head, kneed in the side and someone tried to fishhook his eye, missed and got a finger in his mouth.

Tanoc bit down hard and nearly severed the index finger of the unfortunate man who let go with a scream. Snapping his head forward, he head-butted another combatant in the face. As that assailant dropped like a stone, he reached out and snatched the man who had kneed him by the throat and threw him into several others. The warrior then cleared a space with his fists and elbows.

The men of Wend fell back breathing heavily now. There were more than a few that had joined Haron on the ground and there were fewer joining their fight now, having seen the huge Northman in action. One of the toughs produced a knife with an unpleasant smile.

The barbarian answered with a ghastly grin of his own. His battle-axe, shield and helmet were back at the table but his broadsword and dagger were sheathed at his side. Tanoc's hands were a blur as he pulled steel and the sound of the blades clearing the sheaths rang out in the stillness that had settled upon the Crooked King. Everyone there knew that it was far more serious now that blood would be spilled.

"That is enough." A powerful voice echoed through the tavern then. All eyes turned to see the priest had walked into the semi-circle ranged around the barbarian. "There need not be bloodshed."

"He started it." One of the men whined as he got painfully from the floor.

"That is debatable." Said the priest. His kindly look was gone and his voice grew stern. "I saw the entire thing and while it is true that the warrior did indeed throw the first punch, he was clearly provoked." A murmur ran through the crowd and the statement garnered some ugly looks but the cleric was nonplussed. As if giving a sermon, he continued. "It was obvious that you were all going to jump him eventually anyhow." Cenric had always been a good speaker and his voice now rang with authority. "As of now, this is a little dust-up that I'm sure we can all agree was regrettable but something everyone can walk away from." With a glance back at the barbarian, he added, "However, if this goes any further, someone is going to get killed."

"Yeah, he is." Said the bravo with the knife. His words were boastful but his eyes were full of dread as he looked at the weapons in the hands of the barbarous killer. It was clear that he didn't like his chances now but didn't want to back down in front of the audience in the tavern.

"Perhaps." Cenric allowed. The Northman chuckled bleakly and the priest knew he was a breath away from carving his way through the townsmen of Wend. "Perhaps, it would be the Northman's blood that stains the floors of Jorun's fine establishment this night." His gaze bored into the man with the dagger.

"Or perhaps it would be yours." When the man looked away

after a moment, he looked to another and then another. "However, no one has to die and no one has to go to the cells at this point." At this last, he looked back again at the barbarian.

After a moment, Tanoc lowered his weapons, still looking at the men gathered around him. It was obvious that he wasn't going to sheathe them until they backed off. His gaze was cool as he measured his foes. It was like the regard of a wolf, Cenric thought.

Looking back at the others, Cenric added, "I'm sure the town guard will be here soon." Several of them looked toward the door. "Let's not make this any worse than it already is."

The mention of the guard seemed to work and the men seemed to relax and breathe. Several stepped back and the semi-circle became a ragged thing. The man with the knife too stepped back and put the blade away. So too, did Tanoc and Cenric allowed himself a smile. Then he heard the sound of heavy boots as the town guard entered the tavern. Thinking that trouble seemed to follow the Northman, it was a bit of a struggle to keep the smile on his face as he turned to face them. Then, however, he spotted a familiar face and the smile broadened. *'Dulwen...not Dullard...'* The priest thought to himself. This might be easier than he'd thought.

It was late as the group walked on and more than a few of them had tripped in the darkness, cursing and grumbling as they did. It wasn't just irritation, however, that had their tempers fraying and their nerves fraying; they were afraid. From time to time, they looked at each other, trying perhaps to gain some measure of comfort from the presence of other people. Unfortunately, it didn't seem to help any of them much as the individuals gathered here were a rather desperate lot, each wearing their own troubles like shrouds.

The moon had finally shown itself, gliding from behind the clouds like a graceful dancer. It was a crescent moon and loomed so large that it was nearly as bright as day when the group exited the thick forest behind them. They had been steadily climbing in elevation, though it was such a gradual change, many hadn't even noticed it. Now, they were upon a broad expanse of heath. The terrain here was desolate, short grass and bushes broken by clumps of large rocks here and there. There was something about some of the formations of stone that spoke of design. Certainly, some of them were simply rocks thrusting out of the earth but others looked suspiciously like they had been carved and set in peculiar patterns. There was something about it that seemed old, something that made the milling cluster of people feel like intruders here.

Pausing near a stone finger that was at least twenty feet in height, Malken caught his breath. He'd never been in good physical shape and he'd always explained his physical problems at length to anyone who would listen. There was a deeper truth that his mother had always known and pointed out whenever he would 'take to whining' as she charmingly put it. Malken was lazy. He thought about it for a moment as he looked back at the people who had followed him out from Wend. He'd always hated when she'd told him that his problems began and ended with him. How he shouldn't blame everyone else for his troubles and take charge of his own life. With fierceness that would have surprised most who knew him, he thought how glad he was that she was dead and gone. The woman had terrified him, though he was loathe to admit it.

A cough sounded from the group and he saw a woman put her arm around her son. The boy was very sick and had coughed the whole trip. Often, the others had carried him when he was too weak to walk. Of course, Malken hadn't carried him or even offered. Malken looked out for himself, first, foremost and always and the walk had left him wearier than he could remember feeling in a long time. As he gazed upon his fellow citizens of Wend, he felt nothing but contempt. They were sick and worn, most of them poor and all of them desperate. There were some among them who were whole but these had come to get help for their loved ones. Here a father carried a daughter who could not walk for herself while there a woman guided her half blind husband up the slope, murmuring encouragement the whole way.

Malken hated the whole lot of them. That he was sickly and weak and similar to many of them only made him hate them more. He felt no sympathy, no kinship for any of them. They could have all been loathsome insects scurrying around in the dark based on the revulsion he felt for them. None of them mattered one bit to the shabby little man.

"Sour." Said a disapproving voice from behind him.

Malken nearly jumped out of his skin and whirled to see someone was leaning against the side of the stone, shrouded in darkness. Nervously, he stammered, "What?"

"It's a sour thing." Came the other man's hard, cynical voice again. "Your loathing and dread."

For several moments, Malken was flummoxed and too afraid to speak. Just as he was trying to think of more to say, the mocking voice sounded again.

"You were expected earlier." There was a note of derision there, laced with some dark humor that the shabby man couldn't fathom.

"We…It was difficult getting here." Malken stammered. "Many of them are sick and weak."

"Sick and weak…" The other mused. His voice grew mocking then. "You're a fine judge of such qualities aren't you Malken?"

Shame and rage coursed through Malken like a potent narcotic and he clenched his fists. He couldn't think of anything to say, his still present fear warring with the other emotions.

"A strange mix." The disparaging voice noted and with a start, the shabby man realized that somehow the other man could sense his emotions. "You'd kill me if you had the chance." Dark amusement tinged the voice. "You'd kill anyone if it got you what you wanted." There was something else there as well in that speech unless Malken was mistaken. Admiration, perhaps?

Malken still couldn't say anything despite himself and was

almost grateful when an interruption came. From behind him someone coughed and he turned to see the group from Wend had moved closer and the woman and her ill son were a few paces away.

"Who are you talking to?" The woman asked.

Malken couldn't remember her name and, in truth did not care. He didn't care about any of them. They were a means to an end and nothing more, despite the fact that they all came from the same town. He'd always been an outsider.

When Malken hesitated in answering, the voice near the rock pillar replied instead. "He is talking to me." Stepping out from the shadows on the side of the rock and into the moonlight, the man's movements were so fluid it was almost as if he were floating. He was of middling height and whipcord lean, though dressed all in black, it was difficult to tell much of his build. His pale face seemed to hover above his body in the darkness. It was a handsome face but wore a cruel, mocking expression. The smile was disdainful and seemed a permanent fixture.

The people of Wend seemed to recoil from the man's appearance. They seemed as unable to speak as Malken, although they looked around at each other. None of them could have said precisely what it was about him that bothered them so but each felt unnerved by his presence.

This didn't seem to bother the man at all as he walked closer. Bathed in the moonlight, they could see him more clearly. He looked younger than he first seemed and now they could see a jagged scar on the side of his face. With a smile, the man bowed, the movement causing his long tail of hair to fall forward. "Welcome." He said without any warmth. "I am Kast." He said simply. "If you will follow me." He then turned and walked up the slope.

The people of Wend followed after looking at each other for a moment. Hope and fear were at war in their hearts and on their faces. A few tried to talk, to make comment or ask questions but they soon fell silent as if afraid for their voices to be heard.

Malken quickstepped up to walk near Kast. He was as afraid

as any but as always, the shabby man's ambition was greater than anything else. "I thought Vok would be here." He had meant to venture the question boldly and hated how fearful his voice sounded.

With grim mirth, the other replied. "Vok is here." He didn't turn to look at Malken. "That is where I am taking you."

"I...oh." The shabby man replied lamely. He couldn't think of anything else to say and soon was struggling to keep up with the pace set by the other man. For a time, they walked in silence. After a while, Malken realized that the man called Kast had slowed his steps so as not to lose those who followed him.

"Is this all of them?" Kast asked turning to look back at the people struggling up the slope. They were having a rough time of it as many were sick and had to be helped. It was painfully slow going as they were forced to move around rocks formations and thick clumps of thorn bushes.

Gasping for breath, Malken finally answered. "All that gathered have followed me here." Seeing the other man's flat stare settle on him, he added, "There were a few more but they changed their minds or were unsure and we could wait no longer."

A curt nod was Kast's only reply. He surveyed the people like a rancher inspecting a newly purchased herd. The expression on his visage was unsettling and Malken look away. They stood there for a few moments and finally, the shabby man asked, "Where is Vok?"

"Patience." The scarred one replied. "You will see Vok soon. He's waiting for you." His smile was predatory as he looked at Malken. "They're all waiting."

The shabby man shivered in the moonlight as he tried and failed for the thousandth time to master his fear.

CHAPTER FOURTEEN

The house was as bright as a festival with every room lit by lamps and candles and the exterior much the same save with larger lamps and torches rather than candles. There was no darkness out to fifty feet and it was dimly lit at double that range. Figures moved about within and for all that it was the middle of the night, it could have been midday for all the bustle and activity.

Venaro paused near the front gate, thinking hard. He wasn't entirely sure what was going on or if it would be profitable. It was clear there had been some sort of upheaval and without knowing what was happening, it could be problematic to simply stick his nose in. However, as he pondered the dilemma, one of the guards inside the gate spotted him in the street.

"You there!" Came the guards' gruff voice. "What's your business here?!" There were several guards standing there and they were well armed. "Step forward into the lights! No quick movements now, we've a bowman watching you!"

The merchant slowly stepped forward and raised his hands to show he was unarmed. Whatever this was, he knew that his instincts were correct. This was trouble and it wasn't his trouble. Meekly, he offered, "I was just passing by and paused to get my bearings, friend."

In a decidedly unfriendly voice, the guard snapped, "I saw

you standing there and looking at the manor!" The gate creaked open and two men with drawn swords stepped out. The torchlight glimmered off the naked steel and Venaro thought how cosmically foolish it would be for him to die here, having survived so many dangers in his lifetime. "I'll ask again, what is your business here." The guard who had been speaking was a big, brawny man and he stepped out as well. His sword was in its' sheathe but his hand rested on the pommel. The archer eyed the merchant from within the manor walls, an arrow nocked.

Deciding that it would be folly to dissemble, Venaro spoke. "I am a traveling merchant. My name is Venaro and I have had business dealings with your mistress in the past." Watching the expressions on their hard faces, the merchant wondered what was going on here. "If this is a bad time, I can take my leave."

"I don't think so." The guard said. "Search him." One of the swordsman sheathed his weapon and moved to comply as the other held his blade at the ready. The merchant didn't move as he was searched and was glad he'd decided to leave his sabre back with his belongings at the inn. He'd known he had business associates to see as well as the mayor and hadn't seen the sense of going about armed. Still, he thought that it was certainly not his day for receiving welcome.

"Nothing but a money pouch." Said the guard who had patted him down. He briefly opened it to ascertain that it held nothing but coin and then closed it up. He didn't take the coin or even try to filch one and Venaro's estimation of the quality of the guards here raised a notch.

"Right." The man in charge nodded. "Inside then." He added, gesturing toward the gate. It was clear from the way they all stood that it was not an invitation the merchant could refuse.

"If you could just tell me what this is all about, perhaps I could…" Venaro began but was cut short.

"Quiet!" The gate guard snapped. Pointing to the archer and one of the swordsman, he ordered, "You two stay at the gate and I'll

169

get this one sorted out."

As they moved within the walls, Venaro said nothing more. It was clear that he wasn't going to get anything more from these men as well as the fact that they were on edge. Walking up the crushed stone path that led from the main gate toward the house, the merchant could see it looked like the whole manor was alive. Guards and servants moved everywhere and they all seemed as agitated as his escort.

Arriving at the palatial front of the manor, the gate guard spoke with another man who was wearing armor and bore a heavy axe in one hand. The axe made Venaro think of Tanoc incongruously, though this man was not the warrior that the Northman was, he'd wager. The two men turned to look at him and the new guard, who seemed to be in charge sent the others back to their post at the gate. "I am Mauk." He said it without adding title or other designation but it was clear that he was in charge. "Follow me." He added simply and then walked into the manor.

Following the other man, Venaro looked around for some clue as to what had transpired here but saw nothing. Mauk led him past through a dining room into a large kitchen where a woman stood at a stove where she was heating water. She was tall and thin and had gray hair gathered neatly into a bun. She stood straight as a rail with posture that many soldiers would have envied.

"They found this one skulking near the gate." Mauk said.

Venaro couldn't help but protest now. "I wasn't *skulking* anywhere." He said, mimicking the other mans' tone.

The woman turned from the stove and Venaro recognized her then. He couldn't remember her name for a moment but she was the governess who ran the estate. He could tell that she remembered him as well and he doubted that despite her age, she ever forgot a detail.

"Master Venaro." The woman said kindly. "So good to see you." Her voice was warm until she shot a look at Mauk and then it chilled. "I trust you are well?" It was clear to both men that her question was directed toward both men. It was obvious that she wanted to make sure that neither Mauk nor the other guards had been rough in their treatment of him.

"I am well madam Amice." Venaro said, her name coming to him in a flash. "Apparently I have come at a bad time?"

"Nonsense!" Amice replied, her smile making her wrinkled face light up. He remembered that she had always treated him well and that she considered him a 'gentleman of means and wisdom', if he remembered it correctly. "The mistress will be happy to see an old friend and acquaintance." She looked pointedly at Mauk as she said it and the man's jaw clenched as he seemed at a loss for words.

Venaro remembered now that Amice was quite a formidable woman who ran the manor with an iron fist. Generals and tacticians would be jealous of her acumen and poise as well as her mind, which was clearly brilliant. He remembered that her employer trusted her implicitly. "Mauk and the other guards were quite friendly and were merely showing me the way, madam", the merchant said magnanimously.

Mauk shot him a look that said he wasn't sure if he was being insolent or not. However, Amice made a shooing sound and the big man left the kitchen like a child that had been scolded.

"He's a good man but he is a bit too serious at times." Amice said, her eyes twinkling. She turned back to the stove, where she had the boiling water. "So, master Venaro," she said, ever correctly polite, "What brings you here?"

"I need to speak with your mistress." He could see that the old woman was making a poultice on the table. A variety of bottles and jars were on the table and most had nothing to do with cooking. "I know that you said it was not a bad time, however..." He let the half-question hang there for a moment.

Amice shook her head briskly. "As I said, I'm sure that she'll be happy to see you." The woman took several small towels and using tongs dipped them entirely in the steaming water. When she finished, she took them out again and placed them in a bowl.

Gesturing toward the bowl, she gathered the poultice and a few other things and headed toward the opposite door.

Thinking again what an authoritative woman she was, Venaro took the bowl and followed her out of the kitchen. Beyond the door was another hall and he followed her down the hall past several doors until she stopped before one.

"Ouch!" A voice snapped from behind the door. "Be careful you butcher!"

A grim smile flitted across Amice's face. "Mistress, I've brought the towels and the poultice." The smile grew as she elbowed the door open. "And there's someone to see you."

"Gods above that hurts!" The voice practically shrieked. "I don't want any visitors! I told you…"

Venaro came into the room behind Amice. It was a guestroom, a small one that had no windows and he knew the manor boasted much finer rooms than this. It was an odd detail but he ignored the stray thought and smiled his winningest smile. "Delia, it's good to see you." He said warmly.

The merchant Delia was propped up on a small bed in a nightgown, which was pushed up so that the open wound on her thigh could be ministered too. It was a narrow wound but it was deep, judging by the welling blood. Clearly, she'd had a bit to drink, judging by the bottle of wine and the empty cup next to the bed on a stand, but it was obviously for the pain and her speech was not slurred nor her eyes dimmed.

Showing no thought for propriety, Delia managed a wan smile. Weakly she quipped, "It is good to see you too, Venaro." With a look down at her leg, she added, "Though you're hardly catching me at my best here."

The merchant laughed in spite of the situation and Delia weakly joined in. "What happened?" Venaro asked then. "Are you alright?" He'd always like Delia, despite her somewhat predatory business practices and for a time the two had been intimately involved but that had been years ago. Still, they had remained friends and business associates, occasionally rivals, but always on good terms.

"I'll tell you...Ouch!" She practically spat at the man who was cleaning her wound. "Leave off for a moment!" The man sat back and looked reproachfully at Venaro's intrusion but ceased his ministrations. "I'll tell you what happened!" Delia began again. "*Whisper* happened!"

The doctor, if that euphemism could be accepted, looked mystified, as did Amice but Venaro's gaze sharpened. "Whisper?"

"Yes!" Delia said insistently. "She nearly killed me!" Leaning back weakly on her pillow, the merchant shook her head.

"Delia." Venaro said gently. When she looked at him again, he stepped closer, pouring his old friend another cup of wine. Keeping his voice low and calm, he handed her the cup. "Tell me everything."

"...so as you can see no weapons were used and no blood spilled." Cenric said genially. He'd been explaining the situation and allowed himself to hope the trio of guards would see reason and leave it as a brawl that was now ended and over. He didn't think for a second that the huge barbarian was going to meekly submit to being arrested. For all that he wasn't overly fond of the guardsmen of Wend he still thought it would be a shame to see their blood decorating the floor.

"Looks like a little blood got spilled." Dulwen drawled laconically, sizing up the Northman as he did. The guards had entered quickly and upon seeing many of the patrons injured had the instinct to blame the foreigner.

"Yes but what blood was spilled was not the product of steel." Cenric insisted. "Surely you can see that."

Dulwen and the other two were still looking at the menacing barbarian doubtfully. "They said he started it." He added with a gesture toward the assembled men who had been brawling with

Tanoc. It was obvious that even though they had outnumbered him, they looked the worse for wear.

"That's a lie!" All were surprised to hear the voice of Bandur, including himself. "They were just angry because he was flirting with the barmaid." The ex-soldier glared at the guards. "Last I heard, there was no law against talking to a girl."

"Don't matter." Dulwen, who seemed to be in charge, said lazily, his thumbs hooked in his sword belt. "They said he broke poor Haron's jaw and that's what started the ruckus."

Cenric could see that Dullard wanted to blame the Northman. It was evident that this was motivated by many things and more evident to an observant man, like the priest, that the guardsman probably didn't even know why. The truth that Cenric knew and that the guard would never admit to was that he was afraid of Tanoc. This was also why he hadn't simply tried to take the Northman into custody. He hadn't taken his eyes off him or moved his hand away from his sword since entering and neither had the other guards.

"It actually does matter, I'm afraid." Cenric said insistently.

Dullard looked sideways at him, loathe to move his gaze from the dangerous barbarian. "And why's that?"

The priest sighed. "It matters because there are witnesses, myself included that can attest to the fact that the man was provoked." His gaze was steely as he continued. "It matters because there were more than a dozen of them that attacked the Northman. Finally, it matters because his assailants drew steel first." He pointed a finger at the man who'd produced the dagger earlier. "If you want to arrest someone, your own laws say that you should start with him."

"That's a lie!" The man with the knife shouted. Then, realizing that the man he was calling a liar was a priest as well as the fact that the dagger was sheathed at his side, he amended his statement lamely. "Well...I pulled my knife but I had to!"

"Because you were losing, you mean!" Bandur interjected.

Cenric sighed again. He knew that the caravan guard was trying to help but he was the sort of man who added to conflict, not reduced it. "The how and why's are unimportant really and I'm sure that we can all agree that no real damage was done, can't we?"

Dullard, proving he was worthy of the nickname, looked around doubtfully and then took a step toward the barbarian. "I'm thinking you should spend a night or two in the cells."

Tanoc turned squarely to face the guardsman and smiled chillingly. Though Dulwen was a big man, he was soft and the barbarian was larger and clearly much stronger. No one in the tavern had a doubt who would win in a contest between them even if the other guards backed Dulwen, possibly even if the rowdy mob from earlier got involved.

Seeing Dulwen hesitate, Cenric quickly said, "You know that is neither legal nor is it fair." The guard looked round at him and the priest pointed to old Jorun. "If anyone wishes to bring charges here, it should be the owner of the establishment." It was a gamble, Cenric knew but he had a feeling Jorun wouldn't want to press charges and make trouble for himself with Venaro. At least, that's what he hoped.

The guard looked at Jorun, who looked miserable. Shooting the priest a venomous glare, the owner shook his head slowly. "What's done is done." He shrugged and added, "Everyone's alright, I reckon."

He was still staring at Cenric and the priest couldn't really blame him. These people were regular customers and he was sure they wouldn't be happy. Still, the innkeeper had a reputation as a fair man and he'd seen the whole thing. Looking at Dullard, Cenric knew that the guard was hesitating because he didn't want to lose face. He'd known a lot of pompous fools just like Dulwen and he knew what was needed to bring this business to a close.

"Looks like you've done your job here." The priest began in a conspiratorial tone. Then, more loudly, he added, "They'll all think twice, I'm sure before causing any more trouble!" He gestured broadly at them all, finishing with the barbarian. Everyone knew that the guards hadn't really settled anything but now they could feel like they'd done their duty.

Dulwen looked doubtfully at Cenric and then at Tanoc. "Just so long as there's no more trouble." He said forcefully to the barbarian who merely answered with that cold grin. Looking back at the priest, he asked, "Do you know him?"

Cenric shook his head then. "No sir, I do not." Just so he was sure that the guard would let it go, he replied, "But I know your good mayor and I'm sure that he'd agree there's no reason for further problems this fine evening." Cenric hated to name the mayor but he was sure reminding the guards that Edber had given the priest authority within the town was no bad thing.

Without another word, Dulwen grunted and turned to leave, the other two guards following in his wake. The group around the Northman began to disperse as Jorun's bouncers moved among them. Meanwhile, Tanoc looked around for Lilli and saw that she'd disappeared. His expression was like that of a child denied something and it made Cenric realize he was younger than he'd first thought.

"Looks like I owe you a drink." A voice said. "The name's Bandur, I'm the head guard for Venaro's caravans."

Cenric nodded. "That sounds good." Gesturing toward the forlorn Northman, he replied, "I need to speak with both of you, if you can collect your friend."

Bandur simply nodded in reply.

"And let's make it two drinks." Cenric added. "I'm sure we've a good deal to talk about."

The former soldier guffawed then. "I think you're my kind of priest!" He was laughing as he went to get Tanoc before the warrior could go off in search of the girl.

Cenric wondered if he'd be laughing once he heard what the priest had to say. *"Perhaps more than two drinks."* He thought to himself glumly.

Venaro listened patiently as Delia spoke, her voice raspy and pain filled. He did not interrupt with questioned but simply nodded in the appropriate places and kept a sympathetic expression on his face.

"...Then she left as quickly as she'd come!" Delia finished. Her face was flushed and she looked exhausted. The 'healer' had finished his ministrations and left some time before. Amice, too had left, having other business to attend to and the two merchants were left to speak in private.

"She never said why she wanted to kill you?" Venaro asked gently. Something was bothering him about Delia's tale, several something's, in fact. However, he sensed that he'd need to handle the other merchant delicately to find out the whole truth.

"She said something about Sorvus..." Delia ventured cagily. "...I think she thought...maybe that he set her up...perhaps she thought I was in on it somehow..." It was clear as she went along that Delia was struggling with her narrative.

Venaro arched an eyebrow eloquently. "Ah, I see," was all he offered in comment. Normally, Delia was a master bargainer, shrewd and cunning and a much better liar. He could understand, given her trauma and her wound but was glad it was working to his advantage.

Proving that she wasn't so far gone as not to notice his sarcasm, the woman made an exasperated sound. "What difference does it make?!" Her voice was shrill. "She's a murdering whore who should be strung up!"

Moving away from the wall where he'd been leaning, Venaro sat in the chair that the 'doctor' had recently vacated. Pulling it closer to Delia, he spoke in low, calm tones, such as one would use with a frightened animal or child. "It could make a very large difference, my dear." Seeing the confusion in her eyes, he continued. "You see, I don't think that Whisper wanted to kill you. I think if she wanted you dead, you would indeed be dead."

Delia looked away then and he saw the truth of it. Venaro had hit the mark squarely and there was more that she wasn't saying. Before he could ask more, however the door opened and Amice bustled in with clean clothes and fresh bedding.

"Here we are." The governess said briskly. "Master Venaro, I'm going to have to ask you to step outside…"

"Not now Amice!" Delia cut in sharply. "Can't you see we're busy?!"

That earned them both a rather severe look from Amice, especially Venaro, who was favored with a glance that told him he'd better have a care. "Very well." She said frostily. "I'll leave you too it." Setting her bundle on the side table, Amice headed toward the door. Pausing, she looked back. "I trust that you will not wear milady out with excess talk, Master Venaro?" It was crystal clear to the merchant that Amice was saying it would be bad for him to do so.

Shaking his head, the merchant replied. "I wouldn't dream of it, madam." Seeing her frown, he added, "We're almost finished and then I'll let her rest."

With a sniff, Amice said, "See that you do." With that she was gone. Venaro reckoned that he would no longer be a favorite with the forbidding governess but it couldn't be helped.

When the door closed, Delia hissed, "What do you mean, if she wanted me dead, I'd be dead?" Her voice was low but urgent. "Do you know her?" When Venaro answered with a slow nod, she grated, "I might have known. After all, you know everyone don't you, *master Venaro*?" Now, her voice was colored with sarcasm.

"I have met her before." Venaro answered after a beat. Seeing the acid expression on his colleague's face, he shook his head. "No, I didn't hire her, Delia. Surely you know me well enough to know I'd never have someone assassinated?"

With a rather wounded look, the other merchant gritted her teeth. "I don't think I know much of anything these days, it seems."

Venaro wasn't fooled. "I doubt that very much." When Delia's expression smoothed, he knew that he'd again hit the mark. "In fact, I think you don't want to tell me what you've done to draw Whisper's wrath." Still no response and Venaro had to give her credit. Delia was a remarkable woman and he'd always admired her poise and intelligence. "I can help you…if you'll let me."

With a snort, the merchant woman shot back, "What makes you think I need your help?"

Sighing, Venaro replied. "Because the only reason that she didn't kill you is she wants time to think." Seeing that she wouldn't look him in the eye, he went on firmly. "If she decides you're still a threat or know more, she'll be back. She'll kill you the next time, Delia."

The noble lady paled and she finally looked up at her old friend. "How could you help me?"

Venaro smiled then. "Whisper knows me, perhaps not well but she and I have mutual acquaintances and I think she would at least speak with me." Smiling, he added, "Hopefully without putting a dagger or two in me."

With a sour look, Delia's narrowed her eyes. "Don't joke about it Venaro!"

His gaze was steady. "I'm not joking, my dear." His voice grew more serious. "I can't say that I know Whisper well enough to guarantee that she won't cut my throat but it's a chance I'm willing to take."

Shrewdly, Delia regarded him from beneath her long lashes. "Why?"

Again, Venaro sighed. For all that he was fond of the other merchant, she was an adept conversationalist and a cunning adversary when she wished to be. "I'll admit that it's not just for you." He said slowly. Seeing her smug look of satisfaction, he shrugged. "There's more at stake here than one life. This whole town is in danger."

Now Delia's brows raised in question. "Really?" Her voice was imperious now. "What is this danger?"

"Oh no!" Venaro said a little more loudly than he intended.

"I've told you quite a bit and you've given me nothing whatsoever." He was getting tired of the game. "Tell me exactly what happened between you and Whisper and why she came here or I'll walk out that door and you can hope your guards are up to the task of protecting you!"

"Venaro, dear!" Delia said with mock outrage. "I can't believe you would leave me here to die in this helpless condition." She fluttered those eyelashes at him and smiled. "After all we've been through together?"

His breath caught for a moment and the merchant had to admit to himself that he was still attracted to Delia, even though he didn't trust her. After a moment, he chuckled. "I have never thought of you as helpless, my lady." He took her hand after a moment, fully expecting her to pull away. When she didn't, he spoke urgently. "Let me help you, Delia!"

She looked at their hands for a moment and the smiled a very sweet and genuine smile. "Very well." She looked into his eyes and then pulled her hand away. "I'll tell you everything but *NO* lectures!" It was an old issue between them. Delia was rather more cutthroat about her business dealings that Venaro and it had always been a point of contention. When he nodded, she paused, thinking how best to continue. "I'll tell you as quickly and simply as I can."

When she still paused, Venaro, knowing that this was hard for her, nodded and said, "Go on," in a gentle voice.

When Delia began to speak again, it all came out in a rush. "It all started when I found out that Sorvus had worked out a deal with the mayor." Her voice was seething. "Those bastards were going to push the rest of us merchants out of town and Sorvus was going to control everything!" Venaro's eyes widened and his jaw bunched. Such practices between merchants and corrupt officials weren't uncommon but this was indeed bold. Seeing the look on his face, Delia continued. "When I discovered that a well-known thief and assassin had come to town, I decided I wasn't going to stand for this. Sorvus wasn't going to drive me from my home!"

Venaro nodded. "So you hired Whisper."

"Yes, I met with her and she agreed to deal with Sorvus." Here, once again, Delia hesitated.

"But something went wrong?" Venaro pressed mildly.

Delia's eyes were far away, remembering. "I...I found out about the bounty." Venaro said nothing and waited. Finally, the woman continued. "There is a bounty on Whisper's head for ten thousand gold crowns."

"Oh Delia..." Venaro said in disappointment.

"I told you, no lectures!" She snapped back. "Business has been bad here in Wend! We don't all have your contacts and resources, Venaro!"

"And we don't all have such fine estates." He shot back drily. Then, realizing how unproductive such an argument would be, Venaro moved them back on topic. "So, you decided to collect on the bounty."

"Yes." Delia looked back at him earnestly, pleading with her eyes for him to understand. "I didn't hire Whisper to kill Sorvus." Venaro's expression remained neutral and she sighed. "Although, I'd be lying if I said I didn't plan for her to kill him." She continued to explain forlornly, now seeming ashamed. "I'd heard that Whisper no longer accepted contracts for assassinations but was available for other things. I hired her to break in and steal something from Sorvus' hidden vault."

"But things didn't go to plan?" Venaro guessed.

"Up to a certain point, everything went to plan." Delia said and shrugged. "I set her up." She was studiously avoiding Venaro's gaze now. "I hired her to rob Sorvus, then I discreetly let him know that she was coming. I didn't even want anything from the vault but I figured that she would kill him and escape or she would wind up dead or both." Her voice was almost pleading for him to understand. "Either way, it was good for me and for the town. If Sorvus died, then the rest of us could stay and prosper. If Whisper died, I could claim the bounty, as no one else knew about it and I had heard bounty killers were looking for her."

Venaro nodded sagely, having pieced the rest together from hearing of local events. "However, Whisper killed Sorvus and was taken by the guard. Now, though she's escaped. Thus, her visit."

Delia nodded, obviously shaken. "Now I don't know what to do." It was obviously difficult for the capable woman to admit it and Venaro couldn't blame her. Still, it was a dangerous game she'd played and he wondered if she still felt justified.

"Well, sitting locked up in a room with no windows surrounded by guards is a start I suppose." Venaro said wryly. "However, as long term plans go, I don't think it'll work forever. You have to realize that eventually, she'll get to you."

Stubbornly, the woman squared her shoulders. "Not If I can wait her out." She glared at Venaro. "Eventually, the bounty hunters will come and she'll have other problems that me to deal with!"

Venaro ran a hand through his thinning hair and sighed once more. "I don't think any of us have that kind of time, Delia." Her eyes asked a question that he wasn't ready to answer. "The town is in danger and I can't go into it all right now. You wouldn't believe me if I told you and I don't have the time."

"Try me." Delia said stubbornly.

"Very well, the Pallid and their minions are destroying settlements here in the north and Wend is next!" Venaro said, the words tumbling out quickly. Seeing her incredulous expression, the merchant continued, "I don't have time to convince you, Delia but you've got this place buttoned up tightly and that's a good thing because they're coming whether any of you believe it or not." He forged ahead. "Of course, it won't matter to you, if Whisper gets to you first."

Reluctantly, Delia asked, "Will you help me, Venaro?"

The merchant nodded. "I'll try, Delia." Inwardly, he cursed himself for a fool. Still, he knew himself too well to think he could just turn his back on her. They'd long been friends and once much more and he was still fond of her, despite it all. So he found himself saying, "I'll get word out that I need to speak with Whisper." He looked at his fellow merchant. "You do the same. She'll be keeping a close eye on you, so it shouldn't be difficult. Make sure she doesn't think it's some kind of a trap."

"You know she'll think that no matter what, don't you?" Delia replied.

"Yes, of course!" Venaro returned brusquely. "Let's just hope she lets me try to convince her otherwise." He didn't see the need to state the obvious; if Whisper thought it was a set-up he wouldn't live to tell the tale.

CHAPTER FIFTEEN

Their murmuring had grown more and more in the past few days until it was like the incessant whisper of insects. When busy, such noises could be easily ignored, drowned out by the hustle and bustle of the day. However, when night fell and it was quiet, it was all that could be heard.

In one way, Malken could hardly blame them. They had started this journey fearful and that fear had grown and blossomed into full grown terror. He knew this because his own fear was like a caged beast, barely kept behind bars. The shabby, little man felt as if at any moment he might scream or let out mad, braying laughter.

In another way, the little man hated the group that had followed him from Wend. True, they'd done nothing to him but even here, he felt an outsider. Where the others leaned on one another for support or spoke quietly to each other, he was left alone. Granted, he kept to himself, as always but even in that he found a way to fault the others rather than realize that he remained alone because he wanted to be. There had been a time, years ago, that the shabby man had nearly had an epiphany about himself. He'd been in a short-lived relationship with a woman and had felt something that some might have called love. Malken had never been sure about it because she had professed love for him and he'd reciprocated but even then it had been more to placate her than anything. Sadly, however, he had never really trusted her and she, sensing it, had left him. Indeed, she had left the town, at least, that is what everyone else had believed. The truth was that when she had left him, he'd followed her for days and when she wasn't looking, Malken had dragged her into an alleyway and cut her throat.

Looking at the pathetic group before him, a savage desire to do the same to all of them welled up in him. He could almost see himself doing it, feel the blade and the hot blood. Of course, he was no warrior nor was he brave enough to even attack one of them head on. Still, he felt something like hunger when he thought of bleeding one of them, watching their eyes grow dark.

"Interesting." A feminine voice chimed near him.

Malken bit back a curse, as he spun to see a woman standing to one side, just slightly behind him. She was tall and blonde, with the face and figure of a goddess yet there was something about her that the shabby man, ever fearful, sensed; an aura of cold malice and danger. She was looking at him with dark eyes that at first looked like a very dark brown but if one looked closer were black as pitch. They were like the eyes of a shark or some other predator that had never felt pity or fear or compassion. The little man could not meet those eyes for long and turned away like a cur, shame coursing through him.

"You loathe them so much." When the woman spoke again, he noticed that she had the voice of an angel as well. He had no doubt that many men saw her and thought that she was exactly that but Malken was not fooled. He had a heightened sense for menace and this woman radiated it as surely as any wolf or bear. The shabby man still could not find his voice as he was so unnerved by her. In a way, she was worse than Kast or Vok. Perhaps it was her beauty that made her somehow seem more terrible.

There was curiosity in her voice now. "Is it because you aren't really one of them?"

Now, something else filled Malken and it took him a moment to realize the emotion. It was gratitude. The thought that someone could understand him so easily, especially someone that he'd just met, was intoxicating and he found himself drawn to her in a way that her physical beauty had been unable to evoke. Of course, the little man couldn't have known that these creatures not only feed on strong emotions but they had a way of pulling them out, of provoking them, like a card sharp who knows how to coax the right cards from the hands of other players.

Malken gave a quick, sharp nod in answer, somehow still speechless before her but it seemed to satisfy the woman. She gave an answering nod of her own and even that simple movement seemed graceful.

As she regarded the group of people from Wend, she murmured, "My name is Fina." For a time, neither of them said anything and none of the group noticed her presence, as they stood a fair distance away from them. Malken had taken to sheltering in a small stand of trees while the group had waited these past several days and the others had taken shelter near a rocky overhang. The fact was, he'd barely spoken to any of them and they'd said little to him either. "Have any of them died?" She asked in a clinical sort of way.

Nodding slowly, he answered shakily. "Two of them." It wasn't that he mourned those who had died, it was that he feared there would somehow be consequences because of it. "One succumbed to her sickness and another, the old man with the bad leg, tripped on the last slope and broke something." There was a sneer in his voice then. "The others carried him here but he died last night."

"Only two then." Her cool voice carried some satisfaction in it now and Malken realized that he needn't have worried.

Greatly daring, the shabby man asked, "Is Vok close?" Pursing her lips as she studied the group much as her comrade, Kast, had done, Fina nodded slightly in answer.

After a few moments, Malken's curiosity and irritation won out over his trepidation and he couldn't help himself. "Why have we come all the way out here and waited so long?" He tried to keep the annoyance and fear from his voice but he failed.

Turning to regard him with her large, dark eyes, Fina smiled. "So there *is* something to you besides fear and hatred." Folding her arms, she studied him like a child would an insect, in equal parts curiosity and revulsion. Finally, she answered his question. "The moon was not ready." She stated mysteriously.

Looking up at the moon, which loomed large, fat and round in the night sky, Malken shook his head. "We've been waiting...for the moon to be full?"

Her laughter was bright and trilling. "We are children of the night, children of the moon, Malken." There was a joy and pride in her voice and countenance as she too, regarded the full moon. "There is power to be had in the sight of her unveiled face."

It was all a mystery to Malken and he felt baffled and afraid all over again. This was no woman, as he'd known all along. When he'd first met with Vok and first taken him to different homes within Wend, he'd felt then that he was not a man, not truly. When he'd watched Vok make the strange marks on the homes, he'd felt like he was watching something horrifying. As he'd stood by while the tall, forbidding stranger had spoken to the sick, downtrodden and dispossessed of the town, the shabby man knew that there was something terrible at work. The truth was that he didn't care. They had promised him power and strength and everlasting life and that had overridden all his fears. That grasping urge did the same for him now.

The others had noticed the woman now and many had stood. They didn't approach her though but looked at each other and talked quietly, no doubt their conversation much the same as it had been the past few days. Some had wanted to turn back and most had begun to doubt the wisdom of their choices. They were all afraid and that fear had only grown. Still, they'd consoled themselves as Kast had led them to this place where food and shelter waited. Many of them had eaten better from the crates and casks they'd found than they had in a long time. They were still uneasy though and they had given Malken dark looks and angry questions. His answers had been vague and general as he knew little more than they did.

Fina stood there for a while, her shadowy gaze taking in the group for a time. She seemed to be assessing each of them and Malken took a little comfort when he realized that none of them could meet her stare for long. A few of the braver among them were able to lock eyes with her defiantly and these made her smile. The last to do so was the mother of the sickly, coughing boy and Fina seemed pleased. "It is time."

"Time for what?" The shabby man finally asked uneasily.

Turning her regard back to him again, Fina's face was as inscrutable as the luminescent moon above them. "You will see." It was a cryptic answer but it was all she said.

Malken looked away from her again, telling himself not to be afraid, that he'd made a deal with them and that they would reward him as they'd promised. However, it seemed hollow to himself and doubt and panic were clawing away in his stomach like starving rats. He looked up at the moon, as if to diving something, some answer from her face but it only made him more uneasy.

A scream tore his attention back to his surroundings and he saw that there were figures standing at points equidistant from where he and Fina now stood. The group of people from Wend were in the middle. '*Like fish in a net.*' Malken thought and then shivered. The figures walked closer and in the brightness of the full moon, their features were easily distinguished. Kast sauntered up like a youth at a country fair with coins in his pocket. He smiled at the townsfolk but said nothing.

From the other direction came Vok and the sight of him filled Malken with dread and he could tell from the expressions on the faces of the townsfolk that he was what had inspired their fear as well as the scream from one of them. Whereas Kast and Fina were dangerous and fearsome, Vok was worse. It was as if the tall, forbidding man wore dread like a garment. When he spoke, his voice was deep and powerful. "You have come to us for help." The statement was simple and elicited no sense of hope or warmth. "And there is aid…for some of you." Vok let the pronouncement hang there as the townsfolk looked at one another uneasily.

With a start, Malken noticed other figures moving to ring the group in where they stood near the rocky outcrop where they'd been sheltering. The others noticed the figures as well and they stared quietly for a few moments but only until the first of the Dregs came into the moonlight. More screams erupted as they saw the grotesque monstrosities. The shabby little man felt like screaming himself as he saw them shuffling closer. Figures with too many limbs or too few, awful things with animal parts instead of human and all of them with those dark, dead eyes.

"You have brought us your sick and infirm." Vok said without humor or cruelty, without any emotion whatsoever. "I told you that there was a cure for them; that we could give them life and so we shall."

"Malken, you bastard!" The mother of the coughing boy said fiercely, stepping in front of her son. The others snarled and yelled up at him angrily as they looked up at him as well. He had no doubt that if they could lay hands on him, he would be a dead man. Now, however, the creatures of the Pallid had moved closer and were between him and them.

Kast laughed and it was a hollow, unpleasant sound. "Don't blame him, you all believed what you wanted to!"

Far from feeling grateful, the shabby man felt like running off into the night but knew there was no escape. He supposed it was something that the Dregs hadn't paid him any heed at all but were focused on the townsfolk in the center. He'd never seen the monstrosities before but had heard of them and the control the Pallid had over them. Watching them now, he had no doubt that without the three controlling them, the monsters would rip the townsfolk, himself included, apart.

Vok was speaking again, as dolorous and grim as a tomb. "Some of you may have the strength of body, mind and spirit to survive the *ritual of remaking*." This surprised Malken, as he'd thought only he would have such a chance. "The others, will nourish the Dregs."

"What are you talking about?" One of the burlier men asked fiercely. He was standing near his wife, a painfully thin woman who was dying with a wasting disease. Malken knew the man was a tough individual who worked for a local merchant. "I brought my wife here to be healed of her condition!" He stared straight at Vok with fists clenched. "You came to my home and you promised you would help her!"

Facing the irate man, Vok nodded. "And help her, I shall." He took them all in with his gaze then. "The sickly shall know a life free from sickness and pain, doubt and fear."

"As one of them?!" A middle aged man asked, pointing at the Dregs in horror. He walked with a cane and his limp had been terrible since being injured while riding a horse. "I'd rather stay the way I am right now or die a clean death!"

Now, Vok shook his head. Almost like a father correcting a child, he answered. "It is too late for that." His black eyes were large as he spread his arms wide, seemingly growing larger, unless it were a trick of the darkness or moonlight playing with their senses. "Those who run will be eaten by the Dregs, whether whole or not." As he said it, the misshapen creatures howled and snarled, slobbered and drooled. Then, though there had been no visible signal from any of the black clad trio, the ring tightened, as the monsters came lurching forward.

Some could not bear it and ran screaming. True to Vok's word, these were run down by the Dregs and born to the ground. Their screams did not stop, as the hideous creatures began feasting while they were alive. A few, seeing gaps in the lines of the monsters forming as their fellow townsfolk were pulled down, tried to get through. These were however, stopped by the Pallid themselves, who moved with blinding speed and impossible strength.

Nearby, Fina flowed away from Malken, who nearly shrieked

aloud. She saw a woman trying to run through the press. She'd been fighting a disease for years now, as Malken well knew and was dying but still sought to escape. Seeing a space open up when several of the Dregs pulled down a couple who had tried to run before her, she fled as fast as she could. Fina was suddenly there, a thin sword of a strange greenish metal in her hand. She struck so quickly that Malken couldn't even see where she'd hit the fleeing woman until he saw her sink to the ground sobbing as she held her bleeding leg. The Dregs closed in, their malformed limbs thumping along and her screams added to the tumult.

In the distance, Kast casually disemboweled the big, brawny man with the sick wife from Wend, with a longsword of the same greenish metal. The man's movements and form were perfect, like a great swordsman but again, inhumanly quick. The man's wife sank to her knees next to him, weeping as the Dregs rushed in.

Through it all, Vok barely moved. He surveyed the carnage as a conductor would an orchestra. It was all over very quickly and with many of the Dregs still feeding, the dark trio moved closer to those who had stood still, too afraid to flee. They began separating the townsfolk then, some of their decisions surprising.

When Kast made to move one of the stronger looking men away, Vok shook his head. "He is too fearful." His gaze was bleak. "He will never survive the remaking."

Doubtful, the other Pallid looked at the victim and then back to Vok. Finally, he pointed back toward Malken with his sword. "And he will?" The question made the shabby man shiver. "I can feel his terror from here as plainly as any of the others. At least this one is strong."

Gliding up to the man in question, Fina laid a hand on his shoulder. "Strength isn't everything, dear Kast, as you well know." A look of annoyance passed over his face, quickly gone, and she continued. "Were you the strongest of your brothers in arms that day?"

Kast shook his head. "No, you know that I wasn't."

"What made me choose you wasn't the strength of your sword arm but the strength of your will," Fina said tranquilly.

Again, Malken was surprised as Fina looked the youngest of the three but apparently it wasn't easy to tell their age. Fina had apparently chosen Kast for this ritual that they were speaking of. This was the ritual that Malken had sold his fellow man and possibly his soul for if one was to believe the priests that spoke of such things.

As if reading his thoughts, Fina pointed toward Malken. "*His* will to live is strong." A bit of humor was in her voice now. "His will for revenge is even stronger. Yes, there is fear within him but his ambition and hunger is greater still." She cocked her head at Kast then. "Can you not feel it? Are your senses still so dull?"

"Fina is correct." Vok said then and Kast bowed to them both. Something passed between the three but whatever it was, it was something Malken and the others could neither see nor hear.

Turning back toward the trembling man who he'd once thought strong enough to survive being remade, Kast's sword moved like lighting. With a scream, the man fell to the ground, holding his leg and Malken realized in that moment, the Pallid hobbled humans as men would livestock that had run too often.

Vok walked closer to the mother who stood between them and her son defiantly. The boy was sobbing and coughing and bared her teeth like a cornered lioness. "You cannot have him!" She said ferociously.

This caused Vok to smile broadly. It was unsettling, so many white teeth in such an impossibly large smile. "*This* is one whose will and body are strong enough to survive the ritual." There was something approaching emotion in his voice. Satisfaction was evident as he continued. "She will almost certainly survive."

"You...you'll have to kill me, first!" The mother spat fiercely. "You lied to us!" She looked over at Malken to include him in her venomous gaze. "You lied to us all!"

"You may choose to look at it in that way." Vok said, rather absently, his pale face seemed almost flushed as his eyes half closed.

"Can you taste it?" He said to the other two. "Her fear and rage, her despair and anguish mixed even now with determination?" He sighed then. "It is exquisite." He stepped close to the woman, who still kept her child behind her. "What is your name?" When she refused to answer, he looked over at Malken. "What is her name?"

Like a dutiful hound, he answered, "Muriel." This earned him another murderous stare from the woman.

"Muriel." Vok said in satisfaction, almost savoring the name. "You will be splendid as one of us."

"Never!" She screamed and wept freely now. "Leave us alone! My son..." She stopped then, hope dawning in her eyes. "Let my son go and I will join you! I will become whatever you want! Just let him go, please!"

Laughter sounded as Kast stepped past her and wrenched the sickly boy from his mother. "We have no need to bargain with you."

"No!" The woman shrieked and stumbled forward after the boy. "Please *nooo*!"

Fina sauntered back up to where Malken stood, shivering in the moonlight as Kast took the boy away. "Are you ready?" She asked the terrified man.

Malken licked his lips and quickly nodded in answer, not trusting his voice.

A little ways away, the mother struggled in Vok's implacable grasp reaching vainly for her son. Her wails and shrieks, rending the air like a knife, louder than the feasting of the Dregs or the moans and cries of those few townsfolk still living.

"The others will be eaten and those who are able will be changed to serve." Fina said matter-of-factly.

Finding his voice, Malken asked hoarsely, "The...the remaking, Vok spoke of?"

That bright trilling laughter came from Fina again, as if they said at tea in a garden somewhere. "No, silly Malken!" She smiled at him as if he were a foolish child. "They will be added to the ranks of the Dregs." Her voice was still cheerful and light. "Some will be slain and their body parts added to damaged Dregs, while some of the stronger will be made entirely new Dregs. It is a very different magic that creates them, you know."

"And...and...me?" Malken asked nervously, half fearing that she would laugh in his face and tell him that he too would be devoured by the monsters who were even now feasting on the unfortunates of Wend.

"Why, you will undergo the ritual, as we all did." Fina said putting an arm around him.

The shabby man knew he should feel better then but he still felt wretched. Empty and hollow at the betrayal of his fellow townsfolk and yet sickened by his will to gain everlasting life and the power that these immortal creatures possessed. He looked up into her terrible eyes then, steeling himself. "I...I am ready..." Malken stammered.

"Good." Fina said cheerily and led him down toward Vok. In a conspiratorial whisper, she spoke in his ear. "It is quite painful, you know." When he looked up with panic in his eyes, she nodded as though she was concerned but there was a playful, wicked malice there, just beneath the surface. "You may not survive."

It was too late, even if Malken wanted to back out and he well knew it. He focused on his own selfish desires as he and the others were brought near the shadowy trio. He remembered all the rage and pain he'd ever known. He wanted this, he reminded himself over and over as it began.

As fresh screams began, the moon looked down, serenely gliding across the sky bearing silent witness to it all.

It was well past midnight by the time Venaro arrived back at the Crooked King. His mind was whirling with his conversation with Delia, the situation with the assassin, Whisper and the dark threat of the Pallid and their minions. He recognized his exhaustion and forced himself to think only of the bed that awaited him and sleep.

He was thinking of sleep as he entered the common room of the 'king'. Normally, Jorun would have locked up for the night after the last patrons had left but Venaro had informed him that he would be late and the old innkeeper had made provision for this. There was a young man waiting just inside the doorway, a lad in Jorun's employ, who nodded to him and then secured the door behind him. The merchant nodded in reply and made to walk toward the stairs that led up to the rooms when the lad cleared his throat.

Looking back, Venaro asked wearily, "Yes?"

"They've been waiting for you." The young man said simply, looking toward the taproom. Following his gaze, the merchant saw three men seated at a table near the center of the room. Venaro recognized two of them instantly as Bandur and Tanoc, although the third man was a stranger to him. "Master Jorun said I was to lock up and you'd be responsible for making sure it stayed that way." Venaro simply nodded in reply but the lad wasn't done. "He also wanted you to know that he's trusting you to keep an account of any drinks you have."

Venaro couldn't help but chuckle at that. With the whole world in chaos, you could always count on an innkeeper to keep track of who owed what. Seeing the serious look on the youth's face, Venaro replied. "Tell master Jorun, I'll keep an exact account." He smiled as he said it and then walked over to the bar and stepped behind it. Finding a ratty sheaf of parchment papers, he then found a stub of the hard charcoal that the old man favored. Flipping through the parchment, he found the one with his name at the top. Whistling at the total, he realized his men had been very free with their drinks tonight indeed. The merchant made four more marks and then poured four mugs of ale from the tap, setting them each on one of the trays on the counter.

Seemingly satisfied, the young man went off in search of his own bed as the merchant carried the tray toward the trio that hadn't said a word the whole time. Venaro recognized their serious expressions and knew that he wasn't going to get a lot of sleep tonight.

As the merchant walked up, Bandur rose. "Good to see you sir." He looked rumpled and his hands were swollen, like he'd been fighting.

Venaro looked at Tanoc, who looked much the same only much surlier. Turning back to the caravan guard, he asked mildly, "Trouble?" He half feared that the two had gotten into another brawl.

No doubt, Bandur intuited what the merchant had been thinking for his first words were, "We didn't start it, sir." The 'we' in question was obviously meant to mean himself and the barbarian as well as showing that they had been allies in whatever had transpired.

Setting the drinks down, the merchant rubbed his temples. "Didn't start what, exactly?"

Tanoc said nothing, looking at the merchant for a moment with a fierce stare and then staring off at nothing. Bandur seemed in a quandary as to where to begin and was mumbling something inaudible.

The third man spoke then. "What he says is true. They didn't start the altercation." The man was of an age with Venaro, perhaps a bit older. He was a short, stout man in the robes of a priest and bore a warhammer which was propped against the table next to him. His head was balding and he only had a fringe of grey and white hair like a halo around the sides and back. Though he had a bit of a paunch, it did not fool the merchant, who could tell a fighting man when he saw one. His hands and his forearms, his demeanor and most of all his eyes gave it away.

"I don't believe we've met." Venaro said smoothly extending his hand.

The priest shook his hand firmly and the merchant felt the strength there and knew he'd been correct. "Cenric." He said simply.

"Always good to meet a man of the cloth." Venaro said and then slid the others a mug of ale and held one out toward the priest. "Unless your order is one that forbids strong drink?"

With a laugh, Cenric took the mug and drank deeply. "Bah! My order has more important things to worry about than telling the brethren what to drink." He smiled then. "Although, of course, drunkenness if frowned upon."

Seeing that Bandur had taken a drink and Tanoc hadn't deigned to notice the mug the merchant had slid in front of him, Venaro asked, "And what order would that be?"

"Ah, right to the point!" The priest said in satisfied tones. "I like that!"

Taking a drink and realizing that he'd needed one, Venaro waited.

"I am a priest of the order of the Veiled Hammer." Cenric said simply.

The merchant nodded then. "I have heard of your order." He sipped at his ale and considered all the implications. "It is said that you do good works."

Cenric smiled. "So, you've heard of us. That's good." Then, rather cryptically he added, "That will save time."

Venaro looked at the barbarian and the leader of his caravan guards. "Since neither of these two wants to explain to me what's happened or how you made their acquaintance, I assume you wouldn't mind?"

The priest chuckled. "It's not all that complicated, really." He pointed at Tanoc. "This strapping Northman was making time with one of the tavern wenches and some of the locals took offense. It was only words until one of them insulted the girl"

Venaro groaned. "And then?"

Laughing harder, Cenric replied, "Then the lad knocks the offending man out with one punch!" Seeing the merchant's pained look, the priest got on with it. "It got a little out of hand then. "With a nod toward Bandur, he continued. "This one steps in and tried to stop it all and then helped when they wouldn't back off. It was turning into a fine brawl until one of them pulled a dagger."

The merchant's breath caught then and he looked at the

barbarian.

"Don't worry, it didn't come to that." The priest said.

Bandur took up the narrative then. "Cenric here stepped in and talked 'em down, Venaro." The ex-soldier shook his head. "He's a shrewd talker. In fact, sir, he's a lot like you."

The merchant shook his head but the priest spoke then. "Don't be modest, sir, for I've heard the name of Venaro a time or two in my travel's" Venaro looked askance and the Cenric chuckled again. "The silver tongued southern merchant who is a hard bargainer but a fair man and never one to be backed into a corner." With a shrewd stare, the cleric asked, "Is it true what they say? That you're as quick with your saber as you are with your words?"

Now it was Venaro's turn to laugh and he did so heartily, finding that he rather liked the priest. "I assume I have you to thank then, for neither of these men being dead or in a cell?" When Cenric gave a negligent shrug, the merchant asked, "And the guards?"

"I explained the situation to them." The priest said in an offhanded way, as if he'd really done very little. "They were willing to see reason." With a wry glance toward the hulking barbarian, he added, "Besides, I really don't think they wanted to try and subdue this one!"

"What is wrong with him?" Venaro asked of the others, seeing that Tanoc had said nothing at all and didn't even look their way.

"It's the girl, sir…" Bandur began but then stopped as Tanoc's head whipped around alarmingly. The murderous glare in the Northman's eyes stilled his tongue.

However, Cenric seemed to feel no fear. "Ah, it would seem that the object of his affections wanted little to do with him after the scuffle." Venaro couldn't help but grin as he doubted anything Tanoc was involved with could be called simply a scuffle. "Apparently, one of the men he injured was a cousin of hers."

Now Tanoc turned his enraged eyes on the priest but Cenric merely smiled back. Then the barbarian looked around at the others and finally looked down at the table. Finally, he spoke. "I wouldn't have hit him so hard if I'd known it was her kinsman."

To hear the savage slayer say something in such sheepish tones was just too much and Venaro burst out laughing and the others joined in. Tanoc's head jerked as he looked up and for a moment he looked like he wanted to gut them all. Then, perhaps seeing how foolish it really was, he joined in himself. Of course, there was really no telling what went on in the mind of a merciless warrior like Tanoc, whose mood could change like a spring storm.

Shaking his head, Venaro looked at Cenric, who had stopped laughing and was looking at him seriously. "I assume there's a reason that you've waited here to speak with me." He took another drink of his ale. "Just like I must assume there's a reason that you helped out these two in the first place."

Now it was Bandur's turn to look around in surprise. He'd still been chuckling at the barbarian's situation with the barmaid. Now, thinking on what his employer had just said, he stared at Cenric. It was clear that he'd never even questioned why the priest would get involved in the whole mess.

Without hesitation, the priest calmly returned their regard. "I need to speak with you about the Pallid."

CHAPTER SIXTEEN

Pain...terrible and unending...waves of pain...continually
rolling like the waves of the
ocean...unyielding...implacable....merciless...

Malken had lost track of time, of place, even of himself. He
only dimly thought of himself as a person anymore. There was only
the stark majesty of the pain that ruled his every fiber. In the
beginning, it had left him breathless but now if he'd been able of
coherent thought, he would have done anything to return to the
beginning, when the pain had come and gone. Now, it was ever
present ruling his very being like a horrific god, angry and vengeful
and uncaring.

When they had brought him and the few others in close,
they'd given them no clue as to what would happen. The dark trio
had ruthlessly dragged the few from the town that they thought
might survive the process, commenting on their various qualities as a
farmer might look at a horse or cow. The others had looked at him
with revulsion and hatred but had all been too terrified and dejected
to try and harm him.

The shabby man hadn't known what to expect. He'd been
told of the ritual that the Pallid used to create more of their kind but
they had been sparing of the details. All he knew was that it was
called the *Ritual of Remaking* and that Fina had told him it was painful

and that he might not survive. Even with the fear of what it would be like roiling in the pit of his stomach, Malken knew he couldn't back out now. There was nothing for him back in Wend. If he could have somehow escape and go back there, they'd behead him if they ever found out what he'd done. Besides, he knew that Wend was done for, destined to be just another empty town with not even corpses to show the carnage that had transpired.

So, Malken had waited with the others, shivering in the light of the full moon, listening to the Dregs feed and then turning away as the horrid monstrosities fused parts of the victims with their own necrotic flesh. It was not only horrific, it was impossible. Watching from the corner of his eyes, Malken knew in his heart that there was no way these creatures should be able to exist. They were aberrant, a complete abomination against nature and yet there they were. The shabby man began to realize that whatever magic or power made such a thing possible was powerful beyond reckoning. Whatever his other failings, Malken was intelligent and he began to understand that it was a power that might well reshape the entire world.

The trio did not wait for the Dregs to finish their feeding and assimilation but soon had the 'candidates' formed into a rough knot. The others stood as far as they could from Malken, which suited him fine. He still wasn't sure if one of them would try and stick a dagger in his ribs. Muriel, the mother of the coughing boy, in particular had stared at him several times, a murderous gleam in her eyes.

However, they didn't have long to wait, as Vok approached. He was holding a stoppered bottle made of a type pale stone that the shabby man had never seen before. Without preamble or ceremony, he approached the closest man, removing the stopper. A slight, green mist and a strong, noxious smell wafted from the container. The man, a strong young farmer from the outskirts of Wend who'd brought his ailing mother to this blighted place hoping for a miracles, looked terrified. The farmer shrank from the towering apparition that was Vok but the Pallid grabbed the youth by the throat with one hand, his movement a blur. As the man began to gasp, Vok poured a small draught down his throat and then released him. The youth fell to the ground, gasping and choking but Malken noticed that he seemed unable to spit any of it out. His violent struggles did not cease but continued as he kicked and shuddered like a dying fish.

One by one, the others were subjected to a drink from the bottle and the effects on them all were the same. A detached part of Malken's terrified mind noted that the other Pallid stood near, as if to step in if any tried to struggle overmuch but it was unnecessary. The speed and strength of Vok was truly incredible and if the other Pallid were to a normal human as an adult was to a child, he was perhaps that much more powerful than they were.

Finally, the tall, massive figure of Vok stepped before the shabby man, his frame blocking the moon before him. He was a shrouded figure of darkness limned by the moon's glow behind him. He didn't grab or force Malken as he had the others but paused for a moment, looking down on him in silent regard.

"You have been a faithful servant." Vok intoned without emotion. "Having seen the beginning of the ritual, you may turn aside from it."

Confused, Malken hesitated before replying. "I…I don't want to be a Dreg." He said, hating the way his terror and disgust was so clearly evident.

A movement from the shadow made the terrified man realize that Vok was shaking his head. "There are those who continue to serve us as humans." He said in the same deep monotone. "They remain what they are and we reward them beyond measure for their works."

Licking his lips, Malken looked around at the other Pallid. They offered neither comment nor expression, their faces like stone as they watched. "I am the only one that you offered this too?" He asked, gesturing toward the others who seemingly were suffering from death spasms.

"You have been our servant this whole time." Vok said in affirmation. "You could continue to serve us thus still."

"But...I would still...still be human?" The shabby man asked. "I'd still be...this?"

A shadowy nod was Vok's only response and the trio simply watched him for a time. They seemed in no hurry and didn't prod or rush him. This, in itself, Malken realized was a type of honor, for the Pallid cared no more for humans than men did for livestock, perhaps not even that much.

Finally, Malken shook his head. "I...I don't want..." He struggled to speak clearly but in some perverse way, he felt that he could be more honest with these...creatures...than he ever could be with his fellow man. "I don't want to be this way anymore!" He said all in a rush.

Vok stepped forward then and nodded. Closer, Malken was able to see that there was an expression upon the cold marble of the Pallid's face now. Something akin to compassion or mercy flitted there for a moment. Perhaps the shabby man only thought he saw it or imagined it there but he felt that Vok somehow understood him.

"You will know pain such as you never thought possible." The towering Pallid warned him. "It is worse than mortals were ever meant to endure. You will wish for death." Vok paused then and locked eyes with Malken. "And death will court you like a lover."

The shabby man licked his lips again and nodded quickly. He was terrified still but something more drove him on. Ambition? Greed? He would be hard pressed to say aloud what had driven him to this point but it didn't matter. Looking up at this powerful being before him, Malken knew at that point, he wanted to be the same.

Vok opened the bottle again and this close, Malken could see the otherworldly essence as a wispy, ghostly fume. He could smell its potent, noxious vapor, so strong it made him gasp. "To be remade, you must spurn death's embrace." Vok said. When he saw the little man's expression, he said more. "We Pallid do not worship death as many have speculated. It is our yearning to escape it that drives us to seek the remaking." His voice for a moment seemed far away and held some semblance of emotion, if not warmth. "It has ever been thus…" The Pallid trailed off for a moment, lost in memory.

"I want…I want to be remade!" Malken said haltingly, yet full of certainty. He wanted to throw off mortality and rise as something powerful and glorious. The thought of being a creature like Vok was intoxicating to him. No longer would he bow and scrape to those stronger or richer than he. No longer would he live in fear of what others thought, forced to hide who he truly was. The shabby man realized that he wanted this more than he'd ever wanted anything. He'd lied and killed and betrayed his own people for this and nothing would stop him now!

The Pallid held the bottle forward. "Then drink." He intoned, once more as inscrutable as the face of the moon.

Malken opened his mouth as Vok poured from the ancient bottle. As soon as it touched his tongue, he knew that he'd been mistaken. It was like a thousand needles stabbing him at once. He felt numb as he swallowed the foul draft but not truly for the pain blossomed through him like nothing he'd ever known.

As he began to thrash on the ground, Vok leaned down and spoke. Malken fought to seize on the words like a drowning sailor to a piece of flotsam that might save him. "You must hold to that which brought you here." The Pallid said. "Death will seem like a reprieve and it would be. Yet whatever desires have driven you to this point will see you through if you hold to them."

Whatever else the Pallid might have said was lost on the shabby man as he sank into an ocean of pain. However, he'd heard Vok's words and realized that something more than a desire for power or immortality had driven him beneath it all and it was that thing that he grasped for now and held tightly to. Above all else, Malken wanted one thing. He wanted revenge!

It might have shocked the inhabitants of Wend to know that the scrawny, sickly Malken hated them so much. They would have never believed that he could hold such endless reservoirs of loathing but it was true. With a miser's greed, the shabby man had held close and calculated every sneering rejection, every mean comment, and every single time they'd pushed him around and bullied him from childhood to manhood. From the men who had physically threatened and dominated him to the women who had controlled him even as they spurned his advances once he'd grown up. He even hated the children, who had ever mocked him and sang spiteful songs about him. He despised them all with a passion that had eclipsed every other emotion he'd ever known.

They would have told a very different tale, the townsfolk of Wend. A tale of a man who saw every kind word as a twisted joke, every offer of friendship as something to be mistrusted. To be certain, there had been those who had been cruel to the man known as Malken. However, the fact was that there had been those, such as the woman who had the misfortune of trying to love him that found that Malken thrived on being an outcast. He understood spite and hatred, malice and cruelty. Love and acceptance were things that even when offered freely were beyond his reckoning. Even if he'd thought any of those offers had been real, something within him would never allow him to accept them as such.

As the shabby man sank into that dreadful sea of suffering, he thought of what it would be like to return to that hateful town and have the power to hurt them, to inflict fear and pain and it warmed him. He thought of standing over each and every one of them in dark triumph and it fuelled him. Even as the pain reached his very core and hammered into him unendingly, Malken held to one darkly luminescent thought, one thing that brought savage joy to his quailing soul; *REVENGE!*

No one said a word after the priest had spoken. Bandur's face betrayed fear and he looked from Venaro to Cenric. Tanoc looked away, his teeth gritted and his jaw bunched. The merchant's demeanor was calm and he nodded slowly.

Not waiting for a response, Cenric spoke. "I've heard that you came from the north near Rudden." His voice was neutral and friendly but his eyes were sharp and hawkish.

Venaro spoke evenly. "It is true, we've recently returned from up that way. I have many business contacts." He wasn't exactly evasive but he didn't know how much he should tell the cleric.

The priest, it seemed, was in no mood for dissembling. "I've heard that Rudden hasn't been heard from and that people say it was orcs. I've heard others say that it wasn't looted and burned which is what orcs would have done." Cenric leaned forward intently. "I saw you when you came in the tavern earlier. You all looked strung out and tired from the road but there was more too it. You looked haunted." Seeing that Venaro was still not saying anything, he added, "Then you spoke of what your men had been through and they all acted like they'd seen a ghost."

"So eavesdropping is within the purview of the clergy now?" Venaro said dryly but without any real spirit.

"It is when my order believes a menace like the Pallid are on the rise." The priest said firmly. "I will do what is necessary to stop these creatures and I believe that you know what I speak of from experience."

Bandur interjected then. "How can you know all this?" He seemed truly mystified. "I remember what Venaro said and he never mentioned *them*." He refrained from naming the Pallid and the priest had noted how when he mentioned them, all three men shifted uneasily in their seats.

Venaro, however, was the one who answered. "He's no ordinary priest and his order is no ordinary group of clerics, spreading their particular brand of religion."

Cenric nodded and then laughed. "Well...." He mimicked Venaro's dry tone. "That's one way of putting it."

The merchant warmed a bit to the topic. "I was told that the Order of the Veiled Hammer was responsible for the destruction of the Cult of Serenity."

The priest's humor completely evaporated. "A foul

business." His brow furrowed and he took another drink. "The bastards were sacrificing people to the sea."

"It's said they had some sort of monster that served them." Venaro added, gauging the priest's reaction. "A creature of the deep ocean that could survive on land and devoured their enemies."

"That abomination was no ordinary animal!" Cenric spat. "It was the product of vile sorceries and conjuring! It slew half a dozen of my brethren before we brought it down but we destroyed it with steel and with fire!"

Venaro nodded in approval and noticed that Bandur was enthralled. Even Tanoc was looking at the cleric with grim appreciation now. Quietly, the merchant spoke. "I'm sorry to hear of their loss. I've heard that the cult was even sacrificing children."

The priest nodded after a moment, still obviously reliving memories. "That is true." His eyes had a haunted look. "We put those murdering devils to the sword, every last one of them."

"So it's true what they say about your order." Venaro said approvingly. "You do kill monsters."

Cenric looked around and after taking another drink, answered. "Yes." He nearly whispered. "We've killed our share of monsters." Then his voice grew stronger. "I still think the people who worshipped the ancient things beneath the waves were worse monsters than that scaly demon we destroyed." He made to take another drink and stopped when he realized the mug was empty.

Rising from the table, Venaro went to the bar and filled four more mugs. "I've heard other tales of the Order of the Veiled Hammer." He was careful in choosing his words. "Stories that don't paint them as heroes but as oppressors."

The priest laughed then. "There are always those who are quick to judge someone who will stand and fight against the darkness." He locked eyes again with Venaro as the merchant returned to the table. "There are also those who would stand aside and do nothing or worse, flee from such darkness when it shows itself."

Venaro sighed. "And you wish to know which kind of people we are."

Looking at the two men, Bandur felt like a child listening to adults speak. "What do you mean?" He looked back and forth between the priest and the merchant. "What difference does it make what kind of people we are?"

Not waiting for the cleric to explain, Venaro smiled at the Bandur. "Cenric here wants to recruit us."

The ex-soldier's head whipped around to look at the priest who smiled as well. "You're a perceptive man, Venaro." Cenric said finally.

Sliding the priest another mug. "And as I said earlier, you're no ordinary priest, Cenric." Both men took a drink and then Venaro explained to the others. "Cenric here is a type of investigator for his order. I don't know the title they use but they send him out to find out whether their presence is warranted or not." He looked back at the priest then. "Is that about right?"

"More or less." The priest said, looking at the mug of ale and then taking a sip. "My actual title is Investigative Ceptor, though it's not important."

Seeing Bandur's confusion, Venaro intervened. "He's a sort of ecclesial detective." Then, realizing further definition would be needed, he simply said, "He investigates things that his order might need to deal with in advance of them getting involved."

His face blushing, Bandur growled, "I'm not a simpleton."

"Of course you aren't." Cenric soothed. "However, you can't be faulted for not being as educated as Venaro here. You were a soldier after all, weren't you?" In answer, Bandur sat straighter and the priest looked at the trader. "You don't miss much yourself, do you Venaro?"

In answer, Venaro took a drink from his mug, exaggerated and slow. Tanoc finally took a drink but still said nothing and for a few moments the priest and the merchant simply stared at each other.

"You said that he wanted to recruit us." Bandur said in troubled tones. It was clear that he didn't like the idea. "We're not priests. Hells I haven't been to a temple in years, Tanoc there's a heathen and I've never known Venaro to be a religious man." He looked at Cenric suspiciously then. "Why would you want to hire us…and for what?"

The priest answered the ex-soldier but he was looking at the merchant. "As you said, I am sent to discern troubles in an area and ascertain whether or not the order should intervene." He held the mug now but did not drink. "I come to find out whether or not troubles that we here of are emergences."

"What exactly is that?" Venaro asked. He had a fairly good notion of what the priest was getting at but wanted to be certain.

"Monsters exist in our world." Cenric said, his voice taking a lecturing tone. "From orcs to giants, there are things inimical to human life. However, there are things that have a will and an ability to actively try and exterminate men as though we were insects." The others felt a chill as they listened. "When such a malevolence coalesces, we call it an emergence."

Now, Bandur asked, "How is one monster different from another?"

Cenric looked at him closely then. "How is a soldier different from a murderer?" When the man bristled, the priest held up a hand. "I mean no offense for I too was once a soldier but the question remains and is one that has long baffled philosophers."

"A soldier is doing his duty!" The caravan guard said hotly. "A murderer is a sick thug who does so for money or pleasure!"

"True…true…" The priest allowed. "Yet the end result is the same, is it not?" He looked at Venaro and Tanoc, taking them all in. "A life is lost, cut short by violence."

Venaro looked shrewdly at the cleric then. "Are you a pacifist, priest?" He frowned. "I had not heard that your order was a peaceful one."

Sighing, the cleric shook his head. "No, alas my brethren and I are not peaceful men, it is true." He looked at the angry former soldier seated next to him. "We are mostly men like Bandur. Soldiers, knights, warriors…men who have made death their trade." He looked sad. "We must battle the darkness and peaceful men cannot do so."

"Then why are you saying that soldiers and murderers are the same thing?!" Bandur said vehemently.

"That is *NOT* what I said." Cenric said with authority ringing in his voice. "I asked how they are different. The point I am making is that men kill one another in wars and yet the survivors return home to live lives of peace among one another."

"It's not all that easy for some." Bandur said painfully.

Cenric nodded. "It's true that some have difficulty adjusting but that is not my point. The point is that their fellow men do not look at them as murderers, even though they may have taken more lives than such a criminal could have."

"It's not the same thing!" The former soldier said defensively.

"No, it isn't," Cenric said in agreement. "However, it is hard sometimes to live with the memories, isn't it?" When Bandur looked at him, he added, "I told you I'd been a soldier in my day as well."

"Look, we can debate the necessity and moral implications of the war and all that it entails for hours." Venaro said with an edge to his voice. "You said yourself that philosophers have debated this endlessly but you were talking about these emergences?"

The priest answered calmly. "The distinction that I'm trying to explain here is not a moral one but a practical one." He well knew that he'd lost Bandur and possibly Tanoc, although the barbarian was giving him a shrewd look. "Both a soldier and a murderer kill but societally one is acceptable as one does so for patriotic reasons. A man fights for his country and we deem it is just."

Despite himself, Venaro was getting irritable. It wasn't that he didn't understand what the man was saying but he'd never been a soldier or a believer. He had been the victim of a senseless war, seen his entire family butchered and while he was no pacifist, he abhorred war. A realist, he saw that at times it was inevitable but the way some gloried in warfare made him ill. He said none of these things but looked at the priest and said levelly, "Get to the point."

Perhaps, divining that he'd struck a nerve with the merchant, Cenric smiled apologetically. "Very well. Imagine the brutality of monsters such as orcs or ogres." He let them think on it. "Such creatures aren't men and will kill and devour them if they can. Their tribes can grow large enough to be true threats against villages and towns." The other men nodded as he was saying things that every child knew. "Yet, these monsters do so to eat or for territory, things that we can easily understand. As brutal as these fiends may seem, we can understand their motives." He let them think on that for a moment. "It is not so with the Pallid."

Now, the other men nodded, finally seeing his point. They had seen the Dregs firsthand and heard stories of their masters. Tanoc looked pale as he remembered the horrors of his homeland.

"The Pallid seek nothing less than the extinction of mankind." Cenric said grimly. "They do not want anything that we hold or create, they don't want our goods or our towns. They want to remake the entire world in a deathless image that is an affront to nature herself." The priest did not relent as he explained. "They cannot be bargained with and feel nothing. No concept of mercy or coexistence exist within them. We are nothing more to them than cattle that they will feed upon and use."

The others said nothing but Venaro asked, "Why the term 'emergence'?"

Cenric took a drink finally. "When a group like the Cult of Serenity or a band of monsters attacks a settlement, it is something we will deal with." His hands shook for a moment. "When something like what is happening here in the north occurs, we call it an emergence." He looked at the other men bleakly. "When darkness no longer shrinks from the light but emerges fully to conquer, you see?"

Venaro was shaken despite himself. "These aren't random

attacks." It was a statement, not a question.

Now, the priest looked at the barbarian. "Why don't you ask your friend here?" Tanoc gave a start but Cenric forged ahead. "Ask him what has happened in his homeland."

"How do you know about that?!" Tanoc growled.

"My order has eyes in many lands." Cenric said simply. "The point is that this isn't happening in one town or one land. These aren't isolated incidents. This is an emergence."

With something like panic in his voice, Bandur asked, "And you want to recruit us?" He looked around at the others. "For what?!"

The priest looked at each of them. "To fight."

Put so baldly, the statement elicited silence and the other men retreated into their own thoughts for a few moments. Finally, it was Bandur who spoke.

"Why us?" His voice was unsteady. "What about your brother hammers or whatever, why don't they come here and stop these things?!" His voice was close to panic as he remembered the Dregs they'd encountered on the road.

It was Tanoc who answered him. In a dull voice, he said, "Because there is no time."

Venaro looked at the Northman, startled. Then, he regarded the priest. "He's right isn't he?"

Cenric nodded sadly. "I came here to ascertain how serious things were in the northlands. My order is stretched rather thin these days and we are under orders to approach the authorities for aid."

With a bitter laugh, Venaro interjected, "That's a waste of time, here in Wend!"

"I take it you've spoken to the mayor as well, then?" Cenric asked.

"That buffoon only cares for his money and his comforts." Venaro said bitterly. "He practically threw me out when I tried to warn him. He won't believe that it's anything other than orcs no matter what I told him."

"Unfortunately, the situation in Wend is rather commonplace."

Cenric noted sadly. "Corruption is rife and people are unable to look beyond their own walls and their own situations." He sighed. "We believe that the Pallid waited for the wars we fought amongst ourselves to decimate the population and leave us weak before they struck."

"Then why aren't they attacking in force?" Bandur asked, ever the soldier.

"It's a fair question." The priest allowed. "But you must understand that these creatures do not think in terms of warfare as we would. They spread out and take villages and towns, farms and settlements here and there. Like a virus infecting its host, they take over gradually."

"By the time anyone realizes what is happening, it is too late." Tanoc whispered.

It was then that Venaro began to understand what the Northman had been through. What he must have seen happen to his own country was beginning to happen here. The thought was chilling.

Cenric gave the barbarian a sympathetic look, which was ignored. "It is true. I'm afraid by the time any one country rallies an army, they'll be vastly outnumbered by the Pallid and their Dregs."

"What can we do, then?" Bandur asked, fighting rising panic. "What can anyone do against such darkness? We're no army, we can't defeat them!"

"We can stand." The priest said. "Here and now, those of us willing and able to fight can stand against the Pallid and defeat them." Venaro looked frightened and Tanoc numb while Bandur looked aghast at the statement. "It's true." Cenric said firmly. "They aren't forming armies yet and we're dealing with a few Pallid commanding some Dregs. The mayor won't do anything but the soldiers might rally to us if we stand and fight them here and now."

Bandur was a brave warrior but it was clear that he'd been all but unmanned by his experience with the Dregs. "It's impossible!" He looked at Venaro. "We should flee!"

"Where will you run?" Cenric asked. "You may escape the fate of Wend and survive for months or perhaps even years but eventually, the Pallid will cover the whole continent and then move on to other lands." There was righteous fervor in his voice now. "They'll darken the whole world if brave men do not withstand them!"

Venaro breathed shakily. He didn't want to admit it, even to himself but his plan had been to alert the authorities and then get out of this area as fast as possible. He was no soldier and had never had any intention of playing the hero. He looked up at Cenric and could see that the priest understood.

"It is not the time or place that any of us would choose." The priest said quietly. "It never is."

The merchant looked at the priest like a man in a fever dream. "Can we win?" His voice sounded like that of a stranger to his own ears, terse and nervous. "Can they be beaten?"

In answer, Cenric looked at the barbarian, who had been staring down at the table, his fists clenched. It was silent for a time until Tanoc looked up to see them staring at him. The war between fear and courage was written plainly on his face. Finally, the Northman answered. "It can be done."

Bandur broke in then. "I thought your home had been destroyed and you fled?"

Tanoc looked across the table with the expression of a man who might shed blood at any moment. "My homeland fell." He said painfully after a few moments. Then he continued. "But toward the end, some rallied and joined together to fight." His voice was almost a whisper. "If we had all stood together, we could have won."

Cenric's voice was strong. "If we stand together here, we can win." Looking at the three men, he stated the truth plainly. "The mayor is corrupt and there is no one with the strength and will to fight unless we give it to them." His gaze, like iron, pierced each one of them. "The question is, will you stand?"

CHAPTER SEVENTEEN

The paint on the sign was peeling and in many ways that could be thought of as a blessing for the 'artist' who'd painted it must have been blind or drunk or both. There was just enough of the shoddy, faded paint to see the painting of a buxom wench laughing as she held two jugs of ale out invitingly. However, one could tell that even when new, it was a terrible rendition unless the woman in the painting was ridiculously proportioned with an improbable bosom and lips so massive, she'd have been a monster in real life rather than a comely woman.

Whisper slipped into the Laughing Maid taproom and looked cagily around. It was fairly busy as it always was. The tavern wasn't an inn or a hostel and its business was serving alcohol, which it did. The 'Maid' sold cheap ale, mead and wine for cheap prices that brought customers into the place in droves. They weren't discerning in their tastes or anything else for that matter. People did not come to the Laughing maid for the ambience.

There was one other thing about the Laughing Maid that a few people knew as well. Its owner, a disheveled fellow by the name of Geoff, had ties to the underground and was once a member of the thieves' guild. While he now ran a 'respectable' business', If a person could think of the Laughing Maid as such, the 'Maid' had always been the perfect place to get information, make illicit deals or just find out what was going on beneath it all.

A few people looked up as Whisper entered but not for long. People here knew to keep to their own business and more than one foolish individual had been carried out the back with a dagger between their ribs. The few that took even passing notice didn't see much to comment on. A tall woman wearing the baggy clothes common among locals here. Her hair was tied in a tail and she wore a broad brimmed brown felt hat that so many of the folks from town here favored. Her face was smeared with just the right amount of dirt that would make her look like a laborer or a cleaner. On closer inspection, it would have been obvious that she wasn't from Wend but there would be no such inspection.

Without hesitation, the tall woman strode to the bar. There were a few other women in the place, including the tavern maids and these were, like the men, a rough lot. Their hands were calloused from years of hard work and their faces seamed and tanned from working out in the elements. Ordering an ale, Whisper looked around and caught sight of the man she was looking for near the back. After paying for the drink, she took a long pull from the mug, masking a grimace. The ale was terrible swill but she needed to blend in. Forcing a lopsided grin, Whisper belched and lurched away from the bar.

Threading her way through the crowd, Whisper made her way toward the back of the taproom. There, at a small table, just big enough for two, sat her quarry. She took her time on the approach, as was her wont, surveying the scene and the man she was to meet with.

Hugh was a slender man with a pocked face and an oft broken nose. Dressed in ragged clothes, he had a nervous air and his movements were quick like a bird or rodent. Whisper knew the type. Not overly strong, he was no doubt fast on his feet and quick with his hands. Probably not smart enough to rise far, men like Hugh did well enough for themselves until age slowed them just enough for the guard to catch them or an enemy's blade to find them.

Looking up sharply as the woman got closer, Hugh asked, "You her?"

In answer, Whisper pulled out the chair across from him and sat down lithely. Nodding, she looked slowly around to see if anyone had taken undue notice of her. Seeing that they hadn't, she turned her gaze back to Hugh. "I was told you have something to tell me?"

The thin man nodded quickly, reinforcing the similarity to a rat. "Someone wants to meet with you." Leaning forward, Hugh whispered conspiratorially, "Someone who knows who you really are!"

Her expression never changing, Whisper asked drily, "Who am I?" As she asked it, she knew his answer would determine whether he lived or died, though she doubted that he realized it.

"You're the woman what escaped from the cells and it's said tried to kill some rich merchant lady!" The scrawny man hissed and then lowered his voice at a severe look from Whisper. "They say you're a dangerous one."

Watching his eyes, Whisper felt satisfied that the man didn't know exactly who she was and that spared his life. She knew that there were people in town who knew she was, knew the name of Whisper but they all knew better than to let it be common knowledge. If someone like the nervous, bony specimen in front of her knew, it would have meant that someone had talked and only a handful of people knew that. Of course, it was entirely possible that Delia, the merchant might have spread the word about her but she'd seen little evidence of such a thing. Whisper thought the merchant was too intelligent to do that. She could have killed Delia and in not doing so, she was fairly certain that the wealthy woman would understand to go to the authorities or talk too much would bring Whisper right back to her door.

"Do you think I'm dangerous?" Whisper asked the little man, her eyes glinting.

"I don't rightly know." Hugh said. "I don't want to find out, either." He stated emphatically, looking directly at her.

Whisper was forced to amend her earlier opinion of the man. He was brighter than she'd originally thought and in these backwaters, a lot of men saw a woman and dismissed her out of hand. It made some things easier and others more difficult. At least now she wouldn't be forced to make an example of him.

"So…" She asked him lazily, as if it wasn't all that important. "Who wants to meet with me?"

Hugh shook his head. "Oh no!" He whispered fiercely. "I don't work for free! You wanna know that you'll have to pay to find out!"

Leaning back in the chair, the very picture of disinterest, she took her time in answering. "And I'm supposed to believe that you weren't paid to deliver this message already?" Though her voice and posture was laconic, her eyes were flinty, staring through the man.

Fidgeting nervously, Hugh finally responded. "None of your concern what somebody else mighta paid me." He shrugged. "Way I see it, you think it's important, you'll be plenty willing to pay."

"How much?" Whisper asked. Playing with the brim of her hat, she leaned forward before Hugh could answer. "Keep in mind that if you make up some ridiculous amount because you mistakenly think I'm desperate, I may just bleed you in an alley after making you tell me." He right hand, which had been under the table shot out in a blur to Hugh's shoulder to flick a bit of soot from his coat. The movement was so fast that had it been an attack, his throat would have been cut before he could have done more than blink and he knew it.

Gulping nervously, Hugh blanched as he looked at the woman across the table. He'd been told that she was very dangerous and he shouldn't antagonize her. He'd thought it had been his good fortune that he'd been the one to meet with her. Now, he was starting to think that some of the others were too afraid and had sent him rather than face her himself. Still, greed was second nature to him, so he blurted. "Ten crowns!" She didn't speak but pursed her lips and her eyes narrowed. "I…I mean…Five crowns?" He made it a question now, not a demand.

Shaking her head slowly. "Five crowns?" She made a clucking sound. "That's a lot of money for a name. Especially when all you have to do is meet for a drink in a public place..." She let it hang for a moment and then added, "Where you'll feel safe." Whisper leaned forward and took one of his hands lightly. The movement was quick but gentle and to an onlooker they might look like two people sharing an intimate moment. "Do you feel safe?" She asked him softly.

For a moment, all he could do was make a strange, half-strangled sound. When he did speak, his words came out in a torrent. "Two, I meant! Yeah...two crowns seems fair!" Too afraid to pull his hand back, although his expression evinced an overwhelming desire to do just that, he rambled on. "Unless...unless that's too much?" He had lowered his voice incrementally as he talked. "Maybe a single crown? That might be the right amount? What do you think?"

Whisper smiled at him and rather than that putting him at ease, it was if a hunting cat had just bared its fangs and he squirmed all the more. "I think a crown is a goodly sum." She said softly. "It is a sum a man might live to spend on drinks and women and thank the gods for his health."

Hugh's face went completely white and he gulped, his mouth opening and closing. His hand was limp in hers and she could see the fear in his eyes. The skinny man nodded vigorously.

Letting his hand go, Whisper's smile broadened. "Good." She locked eyes with him, which was difficult as he didn't seem to want to look her in the eyes. Once again, she had to change her mind about Hugh. He was quick and smart but a coward. She hadn't even had to openly threaten him or show steel and she would have settled on four or five crowns if he'd bargained. If he wasn't careful he'd never survive. Her voice was friendly as she said, "I'm going to get your crown from my pouch Hugh." She'd told him so he didn't think she was reaching for a weapon and run away.

Nodding, the little man snatched his hand back like he'd been burned. He found that he couldn't look away from her eyes now, where before he'd been afraid to meet them. He was sure that she was going to kill him in front of all these people and walk away. When she produced the gold coin with the image of Gurral's ninth king stamped on it, he drank in the sight. Suddenly, that crown was much more than money, it had become a symbol his continued health. Hugh had never been so happy to see a coin and that was saying something.

Sliding the coin across the table, Whisper watched the man take it in trembling hands. "I hope that you understand that you should keep quiet about our little meeting?"

Hugh froze. "I…I'm supposed to take back word that you've agreed to meet with him." It was clear that he didn't want to risk her displeasure but just as clear that he had money riding on completing this task.

With as much patience as she could muster, Whisper couldn't help rolling her eyes before she answered. "I mean don't tell anyone else, Hugh." She used his name and it had a calming effect on him. "Of course, you'll need to tell him that I'll meet." She now knew it was a man and this meant that Delia wasn't trying to personally meet with her. She'd half expected that and that such a meeting would be a trap. "Now, you've taken my coin, tell me, who is it that seeks me out?"

The scrawny man tucked the coin away before answering. "His name is Venaro."

"If we do this…If we stand…what can we do?" Venaro's voice was hoarse and sounded strange to his own ears. He'd been known as the merchant with the silver tongue but now he doubted that he could sell a fine meal to a starving man for a single coin.

The priest looked at all three men seriously. "First, we can warn those who might listen." He saw the look on the merchants face and grimaced. "I know, we've both been to see the mayor and we know that he isn't worth a second try. However, there are always good men, brave men as well as greedy cowards." His voice was firm and strong and he could see they doubted. "Perhaps some of the guards, those who really care for their town and their families. At the very least, we can tell them what is coming."

"And then what?" Bandur asked, incredulous that his employer was even considering this madness. "We stand on the walls of Wend with the guards and give our lives for the town?" He looked at the merchant, priest and barbarian with wide eyes. "This *isn't* my home! I've no family here! Why should I die for this town?!"

"That is exactly what these creatures count on." Cenric said sternly. "For men to refuse to stand and fight unless they personally stand to lose something." His voice was scornful. "I suppose that as long as something bad doesn't befall you, then it doesn't matter, is that it?"

Bandur shook his head. "No!" He clenched his uninjured fist. "That is not what I meant." He said more quietly.

Pointing to the Northman, the cleric said relentlessly, "He just told you that if his people had stood together, things would have gone differently!"

"He's a red-handed savage!" The ex-soldier said vehemently, his voice rising.

Tanoc bared his teeth like a wolf and practically growled. The barbarian looked ready to come over the table at the other man.

Venaro intervened. "Easy, Bandur." Then he faced Cenric. "You cannot guilt people into fighting your war, priest."

"My war?" Now it was the priest's turn to be incredulous. "Have you heard nothing I've said? This isn't just a problem for Wend, the Pallid mean to darken all the realms of men with their blight!" He shook his head and asked the merchant, "Have I misjudged you then, merchant, is all you care for coin? Will you flee and leave these people to their fates?"

His voice pleading, as though the cleric was his judge and jury, Bandur interjected. "I'm no coward…"

Cenric was having none of it and cut him off. "But you're going to run, which is what cowards do!"

The caravan guard's face turned an ugly red and he surged to his feet. "Now, see here, priest! No one talks to me that way!"

Rising from his seat just as quickly, Cenric's response was ferocious. "Don't threaten me!" His blocky hands clenched and unclenched. "You seek to flee this doomed place, swearing you're not a coward and you take umbrage?!" He brought a meaty fist down on the table so hard that it shook and the mugs jumped and danced on the table.

The merchant stood as well. "Enough, the both of you!" He hadn't expected to see this side of Cenric. The man was like no priest he'd ever seen. Smoothing his voice, he tried to speak in a civil tone. "You ask for our help and insult us. Surely, you can see how unreasonable that is?"

"*Unreasonable*?!" Cenric said, mimicking the merchant's tone at a higher volume. "Unreasonable is coming to men who have seen the face of this evil and thinking they will stand and fight only to find they lack the spine!"

Despite all his years of dealing with difficult people and being a past master at the art of negotiation, Venaro realized the man was getting to him. He could feel his temper, normally a chained thing under his control, straining to get loose. In the back of his mind, lurked the ugly notion that the real reason the priest was able to unsettle him so was that he was right. "I am listening to you but you must understand what it is that you are asking." The merchant said firmly but calmly. "You expect us to risk our lives for a town whose leader won't even hear us. For a place so corrupt that they will look the other way at practically anything."

The priest calmed himself with an effort. He fought to control his breathing and lower his voice. "I am asking you to help me." He looked at all three of them. Venaro faced him across the table, his face a mask, while Bandur still looked angry enough to throw a punch and part of Cenric dearly desired the fool to try. Then, he looked at the Northman, still seated, his hands clasped and his eyes far away. "I am asking you to help me save lives." His voice was impassioned as he plead with them. "The town's officials may be corrupt and so might some of those who are sworn to protect her but they are not all that there is to Wend. There are mothers and fathers, *children*..." He let that sink in for a moment. "Innocents who will be devoured by these foul monsters." His voice was rich and powerful and it was as if he preached to lost souls, which in a way, he knew he was. "I will fight and I may die but I *WILL* stand between those innocents and this darkness." He looked at each of them, then. "I will do it, even if I must stand alone."

Tanoc lurched to his feet then. His gaze locked on the priest like a dying man granted a reprieve. "You will not stand alone!" The mighty barbarian said fervently. "I will stand with you!"

Bandur looked to the Northman, a foreigner who'd been shown precious little welcome and had less reason than any of them to risk his life for this place and these people. He knew shame so deep that it burned him. "I too, will fight with you!" He growled and looked at the barbarian, a challenge in his eyes.

Venaro couldn't help himself and laughed aloud. As the others turned shocked gazes on him, the merchant clapped slow and loud. "My, dear Cenric, I have bought and sold and traded among all types of people for most of my life." His voice was wry but appreciative. "I thought I was a master salesman but *YOU*." He shook his head, truly impressed. "You could have made a fortune as a merchant!" He sighed helplessly then. "I will stand with you as well, my friend."

Cenric smiled at each of them. "Good." He said simply.

"I assume that you have some sort of plan?" The merchant asked sardonically.

The priest nodded. "I do, although I must go somewhere first." His vague answer made the merchant raise an eyebrow. "You can tell those in the guard and any who will listen of what is coming upon this place."

"I'm afraid, I'll have to leave that to these two." Venaro said, indicating the other men. "I've other business that I must attend to first."

Now it was the priest's turn to raise an eyebrow but it was Bandur who spoke in a protesting voice. "You can't mean for me and....and *him* to..." He broke off, gesturing to the barbarian with a scowl.

The merchant nodded. "You'll have to do the talking, Bandur as our northern friend isn't much for conversation." He raised a hand to forestall further argument. "You need to talk to our men as well as the guards. We need to warn everyone."

"Why should I even bring him with me then?" The caravan guard asked rather sulkily.

"Because, you'll need someone to watch your back in case someone else doesn't like what you're saying, my dear Bandur." Venaro said with a smile.

Now the Northman laughed aloud and the priest smiled. Yawning, Cenric said, "It is late and we can do nothing more tonight." Seeing the effect his yawn had on the others, he nodded. "However, tomorrow, we must begin. I do not know how long we have but the full moon has just passed and I doubt we have much time." He said cryptically.

The others looked at each other but none asked what he meant, perhaps thinking that all priests must be at least a little mad. Tanoc said nothing more but began walking toward the stairs that led to the rooms above.

Bandur looked troubled and once the barbarian was out of earshot, mumbled, "I'm not much of a talker, sir." Looking at Venaro, he shrugged. "I'm not even sure what to say."

Stepping around the table, the merchant clapped the other man on the shoulder. "You're a good man, Bandur. You'll do fine."

Though he nodded, the caravan guard still looked troubled. As he walked away, they heard him murmur sarcastically, "Well that's encouraging."

"He will do fine." Cenric agreed as he walked over to the

merchant. "So, are you going to tell me what other important business you have to see to first?" His voice was jovial but derisive. "I trust, this isn't some last minute sale you have to see to."

Venaro looked shrewdly at the other man. "In a way, that's exactly what it is." Seeing the cleric's expression darken, he chuckled. "Look, I'll tell you what I've got to do, if you'll tell me what secret business you must be about."

Cenric frowned and then smiled, though it was half a grimace. "Fair enough." The priest finally allowed.

"There is someone I hope to enlist to our cause." Venaro said, carefully picking his words. "She is highly skilled and would be an asset in the coming fight."

The priest rubbed a thick hand across his stubbly jaw. "Yet, there's something you aren't sure of." His eyes were piercing. "Who is this woman?"

Venaro's jaw bunched as he realized this priest really didn't miss a thing. "She's a…she's a…" Finally, realizing Cenric was too canny to believe anything he might fabricate, he relented. "She is a former assassin and a thief that goes by the name of Whisper."

Cenric gave a low whistle. "I have heard of her."

Expecting the priest to protest, Venaro quickly said, "I know it sounds strange but she knows me and I am hoping…"

The priest nodded then and interrupted. "Do you think she'll help us?" He asked bluntly.

The merchant was surprised. He'd expected an argument or at least an objection but reminded himself that Cenric was no ordinary priest. "I hope so." He said, shrugging. "If not…well…"

The priest chuckled grimly. "If not, based on what I've heard of her, you may not make it back from meeting with her." Once more, he asked another question, in that same direct fashion. "How well do you know her?"

"Not all that well." Venaro admitted then. "I haven't seen her for years but she and I were involved in some business back then and we got along well enough." Seeing the cleric's appraising look, he raised his hands. "I didn't hire her to kill anyone, if that's what you're thinking."

"Of course not." Cenric said drily.

Irritated, the merchant pointed at the priest. "Alright, I've answered your question now you answer mine. Where are you off too with this bleak apocalypse about to descend on the town?"

"Why, I'm going to church." The priest said with laughter in his eyes. He smiled and began heading toward the door.

"That's not an answer!" Venaro said in vexation.

"But of course it is, my son." Cenric said as he reached the door and with wave was gone.

So used to getting the upper hand in conversation and in deals, the merchant found himself feeling like he'd just been fleeced like a rube in a city for the first time. Gritting his teeth, Venaro contemplated that he didn't like feeling this way at all. He made his way to the bar to make note of everything that they'd drank before retiring. After all, if by some miracle, Wend survived, Jorun still had a business to run.

CHAPTER EIGHTEEN

His eyes opened to a new world. Lying on his back, looking up, he saw the moon, no longer full but beginning to wane. He felt a kinship with it and rose to his feet, staring up. There was no pain or even memory of the agony that had been endured. Feeling something...some tug on his senses, he looked around and saw the others watching him. Where once he would have felt fear or admiration, he now felt little at all to speak of. It was then that he realized how sharp his vision was. He could make out the folds on Fina's dress, see with stark clarity the scar on Kast's face and every line on Vok's stern visage was as plain as a map to him. Beyond them, he could see the Dregs in the distance, no longer feeding but strangely enough, he could feel them...particularly their hunger.

"He survived." Kast said in as close an approximation of wonder as their kind could come. "I would not have thought it possible."

Vok simply nodded but Fina trilled a laugh. "I told you." She said and there was an element of smugness to her voice.

With a sense of dark wonder, he who had been Malken realized that the Pallid did feel things and possess something approaching emotions but they were murky, subdued things. He'd erroneously believed that they felt nothing, were incapable of feeling but now knew that such things were not so. The Pallid simply were different creatures with entirely different sensibilities. For example, he now felt no fear only a bizarre exultation that he could not have explained. Nor, strangely enough, did he feel the desire to explain himself as he had before he'd been changed.

"He begins to understand." Fina said, her satisfaction more evident than before.

Looking up at her, the man they had once called Malken realized he could almost...taste her emotion...the nuance of her blended contentment and humor. It was a thin thread of a thing but it was there. How it could be was beyond him but he could also sense the slight irritation and resignation from Kast. Vok, however, still seemed cloaked, though something...pride...came through. Was the leader of the three proud of him? It was strange but the remade Malken thought it was so, just as he divined that Vok had allowed him to feel it, it was so quickly shrouded again.

"Yes." Vok said then. "You will find that you can sense and taste the emotions of those around you, unless they have the ability to hide such things. Moreover, you will find that you require the sustenance that they provide." Sensing the newly remade Pallid's disbelief, Vok assured him. "It is true. We do not age nor do we feed as mortal's do. We require no earthly sustenance as our link to this world is a tenuous one." Looking up at the moon, he continued in that mysterious voice. "We are strangers here and the first of our kind were travelers from elsewhere."

"I don't understand." The one who had been Malken admitted.

Still looking at the moon, Vok replied. "It does not matter. Who and what you were no longer matters." Then he looked at the newly remade creature before him. "You are now one of us. You are now Pallid."

"We feed then...on feelings?" The newly remade Malken asked.

The others were strangely silent as Vok continued the instruction. "In a sense. You will find that the emotions and sensations of other beings, particularly humans, will maintain the link between you and this plane." Seeing that the student couldn't quite grasp it, the Pallid master waved a hand negligently. "It is of no import. You will understand in time. Both of you will."

It was then that he who had been Malken saw another figure rise from the gore streaked ground. Even though it was dark, he could see as the man he had been could have in the noonday sun. It was Muriel, the mother of the coughing boy. He could sense her bewilderment and it was understandable as she had not sought this as he had. She looked at him and then he could feel her loathing.

"This too will fade with time." Vok intoned. "She does not truly hate you and indeed, it is impossible for such as *we* to feel so strongly." Looking from one to the other, he added. "For now, you will both feel the retention of those things that belonged to the beings that you were."

The newly created Pallid stared at each other. He could feel her pulsing hatred and she his satisfaction. He had always despised everyone else from the town and cared nothing for her loss. She had lost her son and knew that she should feel it more deeply and was troubled that the loss felt like something that had happened to someone else.

"We should separate them, Vok." Fina said suddenly.

Nodding then, he answered. "Wise, Fina, as always." Vok's gaze was upon she who had lost a child. "It will take them time to forget all that they were and to work through the urges that remain from that time. In particular, her urge to destroy him will be strong for some time to come."

With faint surprise, the one who had been called Malken stared. "I thought that we were now immortal."

It was Kast who answered scornfully. "We do not age or suffer from disease but there are ways to destroy us as surely as any creeping thing in this world."

Fina stepped close. "Though we are no longer truly living, we are neither really dead." Her voice was clear and patient as she explained. "We are still of flesh and blood though our flesh is stronger and more resilient than that of any human's and our blood slows and eventually ceases to flow." Her eyes were luminous as she smiled. "Yet, we do not die. You will find that you are faster and stronger than mortals and your powers will only grow with time." Now, her mood became a serious, brooding thing that he could palpably feel and taste. "Nonetheless, there are things that can sever you from existence. Fire and silver can hurt us and iron is unpleasant."

"They will learn all these things in time." Vok spoke sharply then. "As we all learned them. For now, I will take her with me away east while you take him with you and Kast to see to Wend."

Fina nodded and it was clear that this course had already been planned. She asked, "Will you take any of the Dregs?"

Vok pondered it for a moment. "I had hoped for more than two who would survive the remaking." He said, looking at the newly remade before them. "It matters not, I will only take her. The Dregs will only get in my way." Thoughtfully then, he addressed them both. "You are no longer who you were and your old names matter not at all. You must choose new ones. Do you understand?"

They both nodded and found that they instinctively grasped what he meant. They were no longer human, no longer bound to who and what they had been. They were Pallid now. They remembered what they had been and perhaps would be shaped by it but they were entirely new creatures.

She who had been mother to a son spoke first then. "I am *Mourn*." She said and there was venom and spite in her voice and indeed, in her very being as if she radiated malice. "Pallid, I may be but I will forever mourn what was taken from me…and I will *never* forgive."

At her pronouncement, Vok and Fina seemed troubled, though Kast exuded amusement. Still, it was fitting and as she named herself, they all accepted it as who and what she now was.

The object of her ire did not care and spoke in an indifferent voice. "I shall be called *Null*." Even as he said it, the fledgling Pallid oozed satisfaction that the others could perceive. "I no longer care for the life that was or what *ANY* may think of me or what I have done."

His absolute negation of her venom struck Mourn and the others and she bristled and it was then they both knew that even Pallid be roused to something akin to fury. It was a torpid, ugly thing but it was clear she would dearly love to see what it would take to destroy him. He invited her to try with every fiber of his being, desiring to see what he could really do and having no doubt that he would be the winner of such a contest. Their shadowy, raw emotions were a powerful, vitriolic brew that was something analogous to two humans fighting to the death, screaming the whole while.

"*Enough.*" Vok uttered in command and so strong was his aura and being that Fina and Kast flinched, while Mourn and Null were driven to their knees by his power even so slightly unveiled. For a moment, all they could do was avert their eyes to the ground in obeisance. When they looked up, they sensed his permission to rise and the yoke of his control lightened. For all that they knew their new power, they recognized that they were as less than children before him.

"Mourn..." Vok mused, looking at her for a time. Then, he turned his regard to the other. "Null..." He said, mulling the names over and then, with a murky smile of approval pronounced, "It is so...and it is well..." Then he gestured and the two newly remade Pallid stepped away in answer to the command that hadn't needed to be spoken. The leash of his will was still there, a subtle thing but as real as the ground beneath their feet. They would not quarrel or clash with him before them.

To Fina and Kast, he spoke next. "When Wend has fallen, you will find me to the east."

They both bowed their heads in assent. Kast queried then, "Are we to bring more for remaking?"

"No." Their leader answered. "I will be a great distance away by then. Replenish the Dregs and renew them as needed. Then find me." They nodded their assent and he turned. Walking toward the other two, he paused before Null. "You are newly made and not invincible." It was a caution. "You will want to show your power in the town and gain petty vengeance. This is acceptable as long as you are not so carried away as to allow yourself to be destroyed."

Null's answering smile was a cruel thing as he thought of those he would get even with. They would know terror and pain before the end, he promised himself.

"Remember," Vok said sharply, "These things are unimportant and you will have a care. The humans are unimportant in the end, save as fodder for the Dregs or as potential candidates for the ritual." Turning back to Kast and Fina, he gestured toward Null. "Give him his will once you've reached the town. It is important that he learn and grow."

Then, he inclined his head to Null again. "You will find that such diversions as petty vengeance are reveling in your abilities will fade." This wasn't something the slender Pallid could readily accept and Vok smiled that impossibly huge smile. "You will learn…in time."

"We will have a large herd of Dregs now. Larger, once Wend is no more." Fina said. There was a sliver of doubt in her and Vok turned his smile to her.

"Your will is equal to the task." The towering Pallid included Kast in his gaze. "You are ready." Vok made no speeches or guarantees as a human leader might have. Instead, he simply unveiled his own will and sense of purpose, letting his faith in them permeate their consciousness. Then, he turned to Mourn, who had been silent the entire time. "Come." He bade her and walked away.

Hesitating for a seemingly interminable amount of time that was actually only a few moments, Mourn turned her venomous gaze on Null. "One day…" She whispered savagely.

Favoring her with a rictus grin, he replied. "I will be waiting."

Mourn whirled without another word and followed their

master away to the east.

Darkness shrouded the courtyard and was unrelieved by even a glimmer of moonlight for thick clouds covered her face. The buildings all around were deserted were already losing the battle to time and the elements. Creepers climbed the sides of the buildings, while weeds now dominated the flat ground, pushing up through the cobbled streets. This part of the town had long been deserted as it was outside the walls and no longer fell under the protection of the town guard, dubious though it was. It had once boasted a thriving open air market and a well-known bookseller as well as other homes, businesses and shops. That had been in a different time, a different era.

To Venaro, such days seemed like several lifetimes ago, though he remembered Wend as it was from more than a score of years as it was. The town had been an open, friendly place even during rough times and the merchant had always liked it here. Coin had flowed through trade as Wend had always been known as a fair place to do business and back then, many had believed it would grow into a true city. Now, looking at the deserted remains, Venaro felt sadness that ran deeper than nostalgia or fear for the future. The world had changed with the wars and he feared it would never again be the same. He felt his age.

Holding his lantern up before him, the merchant paused near a building. It was quite old built from fieldstone and timber. The roof had long ago caved in and at some point there had been a fire, though whether from vandals or an accident he could not tell. The shingle was gone, probably looted but he remembered this establishment well and could almost see it as it was. The inn had served the best dish of spiced mutton that he'd ever had and Venaro was no great lover of the cuisine here in the north. He stood there in the dark for a time, struggling and failing to remember the name of the place, his failure both angering and saddening him at the same time.

"So you *did* come alone." A silky voice noted from nearby.

Not turning, the merchant made a show of looking at the ruined inn and generally trying not to look startled though, despite himself, he most assuredly was. "I said that I would come alone." Venaro said calmly. His ears strained to hear movement or try to pinpoint where the voice was coming from but he knew it was folly. She wouldn't be seen until she wanted to be seen. The echo of her voice showed that she had picked her spot carefully.

The husky voice spoke again. "I was surprised to receive such a summons."

"Not a summons." Venaro corrected rather dryly, now looking around to see if he could spot the placard that had once hung above the door of the inn. Despite his situation, it still bothered him that he could not remember the name of the place. "More...an invitation."

Throaty laughter answered him then. "Ah Venaro, I'd forgotten how particular you are." The laughter seemed genuine and not mocking. "I haven't seen you in some time."

The merchant nodded, sure that she could see the movement in the light of the lantern. He knew that she was dragging things out just to make sure that he didn't have anyone following him that might show up late. She was cautious and very smart and he'd always respected her for that as much as for her other, more deadly abilities.

Playing along, the merchant slowly turned, still holding the lantern up so that his face was clearly visible. "Well, how do I look?" He felt a little strange addressing a dark and empty courtyard but he was quite sure that she could see him.

After a few moments, the voice came again, thoughtful and low. "Old."

Now it was Venaro's turn to laugh. "You wound me, lady." He laughed as he said it though for he knew he hadn't seen her in quite a few years.

"I didn't say that you looked bad." The voice whispered

coyly. They both knew he was trying to pinpoint her location even while he tried to appear as if he wasn't. "Let us say that you look older...perhaps not old."

The trader bowed to the empty darkened buildings around him. "You are too kind."

"And you are still too reckless." She said in a voice that somehow was chiding and mocking yet still not unkind.

Rising from his bow, Venaro was startled, despite his best efforts, when he saw her standing not fifty feet from him. He hadn't seen her step out and his bow hadn't been overly long but there she was, appeared as if by magic.

"It is good do see you, Whisper." The trader said, bowing again and lower.

A sardonic smile curled one side of her mouth. "Now that is not something I am used to hearing."

As he rose, Venaro shrugged. "I suppose that is true."

"It is good to see you as well, Venaro." Whisper said and there was actually warmth in her voice as she said it.

The merchant lowered his lantern and looked at the woman before him. She looked much the same as when he'd last seen her. Dressed in dark clothing with swords and daggers belted on, clearly visible now that she'd thrown her cloak back. Whisper looked a bit older perhaps. Not middle aged but no longer truly a young woman. She was, if anything, more beautiful than he remembered but that too had always been a weapon that she wielded as precisely as any of her blades.

"Well..." She said, mimicking his earlier tone and question, "How do I look?"

His smile was genuine as he answered. "You look well, my dear."

"My dear?" Whisper said, raising an eyebrow. "Surely you haven't grown that old, Venaro. You sound like an old man." Her eyes were not solely on him and had never stopped scanning the area.

"I feel old." The merchant wearily admitted. "I assure you, I have brought no one with me and no one followed me." He knew well that someone in her line of work hadn't survived by being overly trusting and raised his arms. "I came unarmed. You can search me, if that is your wish."

Whisper shook her head. "I don't need to search you." The statement wasn't so much about her trusting him as much as saying she wasn't worried.

"Follow me." She said and then turned and walked a dozen paces or more to the merchant's left. There, she slipped into a rent in the wall of a taller building. Once inside, the shadows cloaked her completely and she made no sound whatsoever. It was as if she had disappeared entirely.

It was to his credit that Venaro only hesitated for the briefest of moments. Chiding himself that if she'd wanted to kill him, she'd have done so already, he too walked through the hole in the wall. Once inside, he moved carefully, using his lantern to pick his way forward. It was hard to say what the building might once have been, as it had been so damaged but he would guess it had perhaps been a warehouse as the bottom floor was so large and for the most part devoid of inner walls. The roof was partly gone and there was a bit of moonlight starting to show through an opening in the clouds. Across the large room, he could see a set of stairs leading up to the upper floor that was half gone. She waited for him patiently at the top as he toiled his way through the detritus of broken crates, boxes and barrels, finally ascending the stairs.

"Keep to the right." She warned him, her movements suiting her words as she moved along the wall on the right side.

As he followed her, Venaro could hear the old floorboards groaning beneath his weight and he swallowed hard. It was at least a twelve feet drop as the old warehouse had high ceilings and he didn't fancy falling on whatever debris he would undoubtedly land on.

Whisper led him along the wall and to an area where more of the floor was intact. There were interior rooms here that had survived and she moved through a doorway. Following her inside after a moment, he saw that it was a spacious room with broken, dusty furniture. The roof was intact over this part of the building, however and the windows still had their shutters. He could see that at one of the windows, the shutters were pulled back fractionally. Near this opening was a table with a crossbow on it. There were two chairs at the table, the further chair pulled back as though someone had just been sitting there. Venaro had no doubt that this was where the woman had been waiting for him. From this vantage, he could see that she could see the approaches from several of the streets, including the one he'd taken and her voice could easily be distorted by the echoes of the buildings around it.

Throwing her cloak over the back of the chair, Whisper sat. As she did so, she deftly moved the loaded crossbow off the table with a grin. Unloading it, she gestured toward the empty chair.

Pausing to look out through the view offered by the window, the merchant mused. "I never could remember the name of that inn." He could see that she would have seen him plainly down there by the entrance of the place.

"I can't help you there." Whisper answered. "This part of Wend has been a ruin ever since I first came to this hole of a town."

Turning from the window, Venaro set his lantern on the table and took a seat. "It was a long time ago." He admitted sadly. "A lot has changed since then." Looking across the table at her, he smiled and looked around. "I've had meetings in worse places. You've thought of everything except wine." Then he laughed out loud as she produced a bottle and two clay cups. "I stand corrected."

As she poured them both a drink, she spoke. "I wish you no ill will, merchant." Sliding a cup across from him, she then took a drink from hers.

"I had hoped that was the case." The merchant said, still smiling and then taking a drink. He appreciated her showing him that the wine wasn't poisoned and once again reminded himself that if she wanted to kill him, she could have already done so.

"Still, I'm no fool." The shadowy woman warned. "I have no

doubt that you've come on Delia's behalf. I know the two of you are friends and have business dealings."

The merchant nodded and considered the complicated past he had with Delia. Looking at Whisper over the rim of his cup, he finally said. "I am not just here for her."

"I am in no mood for games." She warned flatly.

Taking another drink, Venaro set his cup down and just as pointedly answered. "Neither am I." He had racked his brain on how to convince the deadly woman before him to help and finally decided that blunt truth was the answer. "An army of evil creatures are about to descend on this town and wipe out every man, woman and child. I want you to help me stop them."

Despite her ice cool demeanor, Whisper looked startled. Venaro had never even heard of the assassin being flummoxed and vowed to remember the look on her face. Finally, she laughed in disbelief. "You must be jesting!" When he shook his head, she leaned across the table and looked in his eyes. "Orcs?" Again, he shook his head in negation. "Then what?"

"Pallid." He said simply and shivered as he said it. "They lead hundreds of their creatures that are called Dregs."

"Horse dung!" She refuted. "You come to me with fables?!"

He shook his head sadly. "I wish it were so but I have seen them." He thought and then amended his statement. "At least I have seen the Dregs. We were attacked by a large group of them on the road here and many of my men were killed. They are horrific, malformed monsters that aren't truly alive yet they move and kill and feed…"

His voice trailed off, as he remembered the horror of their attack. Venaro hadn't been able to get the images of the creatures out of his mind and he'd had nightmares ever since that day. He doubted that he'd ever forget it 'til his dying day.

Whisper's voice was serious as she brought him back to the present. "If this is true then we should be fleeing this place not talking about staying to fight." She looked at him as if he'd lost his mind.

"I…thought as you did at first." The merchant admitted. "It was my plan to warn the authorities…" When she made a rude sound, he nodded. "I knew that the mayor was corrupt but I had no idea how foolish and truly base he was."

"The guard is just as bad." The woman said grimly.

Venaro nodded, having heard of her capture and escape. "Yet, they can't all be so, can they?" He was asking seriously. "There must be some who will fight for this town or it would already have fallen."

Grudgingly, she spoke. "I'll allow that there are perhaps a few who take their oaths seriously." As she said it, she thought of Hedolf, the guard. The man had threatened her, certainly but he was one who took the defense of Wend seriously. Whisper always made a point to find out everything about the law in a town. It was how she'd known that the lad Gren was a lusty fool as well as the fact that Hedolf and a few others were not men who could be coerced. "What difference does it make if there are some of the guard who will stand and fight?" She asked, shaking her head. "If there are as many of these creatures as you say, it won't matter."

"I know it's bleak but I have my men as well and a barbarian from across the sea. He's a deadly warrior, perhaps even as dangerous as you." Venaro said in answer.

With a dismissive wave of her hand, she retorted. "And you think that he's mighty enough to turn the tide?"

"No." Venaro allowed, quickly. "What I am saying is that a few exceptional fighters can make a difference. We have a priest with us…"

"A priest?" She cut in derisively. "This sounds like a bad joke!" Her voice was mocking now. "A priest, a merchant and a barbarian walk into a tavern…"

Now Venaro cut her off. "I am not jesting!" He hadn't meant to raise his voice as she was not someone that a sane individual yelled at. "This priest has a plan and has called on us to stand for the people of this town."

"The people of this town can rot for all I care." Whisper said indifferently. "They would have hanged me if I hadn't escaped and you think I'll risk my life for them?" Her voice was incredulous.

"No." The merchant said then. "I think you'll risk your life for me."

She laughed in his face. "It *has* been a long time if you think I ever liked you that much, merchant!" Her eyes were flat and cold. "We were involved in one caper, years ago and you think I'd throw my life away for you? I barely know you?!" Her voice had risen as well.

Venaro shook his head. "That's not what I meant." He reached for the wine bottle and poured himself another cup. She shook her head when he offered to pour her another. "I know that we don't know each other well." He said drily and took a sip. "However, you know my reputation."

"Get to the point." The assassin said, her patience obviously wearing thin.

"Very well." He said. "I know about the price on your head."

"Looking to collect?" She said softly. Her voice was a soft whisper and he knew she was at her most dangerous when she talked so.

He shook his head pointedly. "Of course not."

"Oh?" She said, her voice that same husky timbre. "Your friend Delia thought she could."

"Delia was foolish." Venaro stated. "I am not." He took another drink, finding that his throat was very dry. "Nor am I involved in such business."

"That has not been your reputation." Whisper said, her voice gaining a little in volume and warmth.

A chill coursed through the merchant as he realized she had been most likely thinking of killing him on the spot just then. "I can help you." He said bluntly.

"What makes you think that I would need or want your help?" She asked acidly.

"Oh, come now!" Venaro said brusquely. "Let's dispense with the games as you said, shall we?"

"By all means, let us do so." Whisper said just as bluntly.

"Ten thousand crowns is a fortune by any standard." Venaro said. "Every thug with a blade will be looking to collect on that bounty. Everywhere from little backwaters to the great cities will be looking at that sum above your likeness."

She shrugged indifferently. "They will die." Her voice was confident, her manner unruffled and poised. Yet, there was a slight edge to her bearing that hadn't been there before and he knew he'd struck a nerve.

"I am quite sure that you will." Venaro said. "At least at the beginning." He tapped his cup thoughtfully. "However, what happens when they start coming at you in larger and larger groups? What happens when people approaching your talents and skills come calling?" His voice then was sad. "Can you really kill them all?"

It was evident that these were questions she'd been asking herself. "I may have to hide." She finally admitted.

"You know that will only work temporarily." He pointed out. "You know that they'll find you eventually. Perhaps it will take years but even at that, do you really want to spend the rest of your life running and hiding?"

He had to admire her poise as she wryly asked, "But you can help me?" She leaned back in her chair. "All my skills will not avail me but somehow, the wise and powerful Venaro can turn it all around?"

Clasping his hands, the merchant leaned forward. "I have connections that you do not." His voice was earnest. "I have people who trust me and will speak truth to me because they speak not out of fear but of respect."

"And because they know you pay well." Whisper said drily.

"Well…" Venaro said, smiling, "There is that." Urgently, he continued. "You must know that you need to find out who put this price on your head and why? Anyone offering that much gold will have the resources to hide their identity and motives. I can help you discover the truth."

"And for this help, you want me to fight against these monsters?" She asked. "I'm no soldier, Venaro."

"I know that." He answered. Running a hand through his graying hair, he now leaned back. "I am not sure how we can make a difference but this priest...he has something up his sleeve, I can tell."

"How well do you know this man, this priest?" Whisper asked suspiciously.

"Not well." Venaro readily admitted. "Yet...there's something about him." He shrugged then. "I can't explain it other than to say I believe that he's a good man who is going to fight for the lives of innocents." The merchant said raggedly as he sighed, "I cannot turn away from that and live with myself."

"You are a fool." Whisper stated in a not unfriendly voice. "But I believe you are telling me the truth." She rose then placed her hands on the table. "I will do my best to help you, as long as you agree to help me when this is done." She pointed a finger at him then. "Let's be clear, though." Her voice grew colder. "I am not dying for anyone. If things turn sour, I will leave this town and anyone foolish enough to stay too long to their death."

Venaro smiled and raised his hands in surrender. "That is all that I had hoped for." As the assassin gathered her things, he said mildly, "And you will leave Delia alone."

She paused in tying her cloak. "I should have cut her throat." She hissed.

"But you did not and I am asking that you continue to refrain." Venaro said. When her eyes narrowed, he held up a hand. "I can assure you that she has no plans to try and collect on this bounty. She is terrified for her life."

"She should be." Whisper said grimly.

Nodding, Venaro's voice was equally bleak. "She hasn't left her home and is holed up in an inner room with no windows, surrounded by a small army of guards." He was tired and he knew it showed.

"She is no threat to you." He looked her in the eye. "Do I have your word?"

For a moment, he thought her curt nod was all the reply he'd get but then she spoke. "As long as she stays away from me." Her voice was that low, calm tone again that he had no doubt was why she'd gained her namesake. "If she tries…"

"She will not." Venaro said. "I can guarantee that." Seeing that she was going to leave, he added, "We will need to gather at…"

"I know, the Crooked King." Whisper replied. "I found where you were roosting as soon as I received word you wanted to meet."

He wasn't even surprised. "We don't have much time." He said urgently. "You should come with me now."

"I'll be there when you need me." She answered. She stood there for a moment and when he looked down to get his lantern, she was gone with barely a rustle of her cloak.

CHAPTER NINETEEN

Long abandoned, the upper floor of the temple was strewn with wreckage. What pews were still present were smashed and rotted remnants and it was clear that the rest had long since been carted off for kindling or building material. The walls were mostly intact, as they were made from good stone but the mortar hadn't been seen to in some time and the locals had at some point been filching the stone for their own homes. The roof was almost completely gone and the whole interior of the church was open to the elements.

Cenric knew that many of his colleagues would have called the townsfolk wicked for their looting of the temple, saying that the people had turned from the gods. To him, though, the state of the church was evident truth that the clergy who had once been here had failed the people, not the other way around. Of course, there was no way of really knowing without speaking to residents who might remember or having an older relative who did. Unfortunately, such things were not his business this day nor did he have the luxury of the kind of time an inquiry like that would have taken.

The priest knew that his view on the state of a church like this was part of what made him so unpopular amongst his brethren. Nevertheless, Cenric truly believed that, although it was true that many had turned from the gods, greedy and lazy clergy were at least partially responsible. He'd long known that such views were part of

why he'd been sent out to work on his own but this was only part of
the reason. His abilities as an investigator and warrior outstripped
most and his faith was strong, whatever his detractors might have
said. The unpleasant truth was that theirs was a bleak world beset by
true evils. Unfortunately, many who bore the title of priest or holy
man were charlatans and fakes and had more concern for their own
comforts than for protecting people or fighting the encroaching
darkness. The fact that shocked most who got to know Cenric was
that he despised most clergymen more than most any spawn of evil.
For those priests were among the worst evils to walk the earth in his
opinion.

Walking up near the front of the temple where the lectern once
stood, the priest felt a wave of sadness wash over him. There was
only a stone dais here now, someone having long since destroyed the
lectern or stolen it to break the wood apart. Once, no doubt,
someone had taught the people of Wend of the ancient gods in this
very spot. Now, from what he could see, the people of this town
worshipped only coin. Shaking off his gloomy feelings, Cenric
headed toward a doorway at the back of the church. Stepping
through the archway, the door having long since been removed, he
saw what he'd expected to see; a series of chambers where the priests
had once lived. It was a small complex of no more than half a dozen
rooms, most of which were tiny cells.

Moving with a purpose, the cleric made his way toward one
chamber in particular. It was a dusty chamber, mostly empty, unlike
the others which were cluttered with debris and trash. This chamber
had been an inner cloister that looters probably thought of as a
strange empty hall. The fading frescos on the far wall were chipped
and fading but showed the priests of old going about their duties,
teaching the faithful and fighting against evil. Cenric realized that
this order, like so many in more untamed areas, must have been a
militant order, much like his own. This cloister, similar to those in
temples of his order, was used for quiet reflection and contemplation.
However, the priest was looking for something other than a place to

pray.

"Got to be around here somewhere." Cenric mused quietly.

He knew that he'd picked up the habit of talking to himself on occasion but had long shrugged it off as the price for long periods of solitude. While there were some that would say it was unhealthy to do so, Cenric laughed at such notions. He thought, *Let those priests and scribes who huddled together, safe behind tall walls, go out into the untamed lands, alone, as he had for so long. Then, see how they fared?* The cleric was woolgathering and chided himself mentally. Time was of the essence. Yet, he couldn't seem to find…there it was!

Near the far corner of the room, was one small flagstone that looked completely like any of the others that made up the floor. However, this one had a tiny mark that was so small and innocuous that it could have been a random scratch. It was what the priest had been looking for. Most priesthoods had their secrets and this one had been no exception. The mark, upon closer inspection, looked like nothing so much as a deep gouge, yet there was a tiny indent on one end pointing off at a right angle. Cenric had seen its' like before. Producing a small knife, he placed it at the corner that the indent pointed to. It took a moment before he'd found the exact right spot but when he did, he heard a click. Using the dagger as a lever, the cleric was able to get just enough lifted until he could use his hands to lift. This section of the floor was a cunningly concealed trapdoor just as he'd suspected!

As he opened the trapdoor, musty air wafted up from below and the priests grin quickly disappeared at the smell. Laying the trapdoor completely open, he could see that the inside had a handle and that the whole thing had been the work of master craftsman. There hadn't been any seem visible to the naked eye. Perhaps a master thief could have found the hidden door but Cenric doubted that Wend's underground had anyone with such skill. His hopes rose that what he sought below would still there.

It was dark beyond the trapdoor but the priest had come prepared. Tied to his pack was a small bundle of thick canvas.

Within were several torches. Opening his pack, he rummaged through it until he found his tinder box.

The metal box contained a chunk of flint rock and a small piece of steel lying on a bed of oil soaked wood shavings. Cenric struck the flint and steel together, just above the tinder, several times and finally a spark caught and the shavings began to burn. Carefully, the cleric held one of the torches, the head of which was wrapped with thick cloth and daubed with pitch, to the tinderbox. The torch caught and once it was blazing, the priest closed the top of the tinderbox causing the flames within it to die out.

Leaving the now hot box lying to cool on the stone floor, the priest gathered his pack and retied the bundle of torches to it. Hefting it over one shoulder and holding the torch before him, Cenric descended the stone steps that led down into darkness.

The stairs led down a narrow, claustrophobic passage for perhaps twenty feet or more before they ended at a rotting wooden door. With very little effort, the priest shouldered the door aside and stepped into a broad, circular room. The chamber was perhaps forty feet in diameter. It had been dug from the rocky earth and then supported by wooden beams and pillars of stone. The walls and floor had been inlaid with stone both for support and to keep burrowing creatures at bay. Cenric was glad to see it wasn't a simple barrow of earth and wood for such places were prone to collapse. There were niches dug into the sides of the walls and inlaid with stone as well. These niches still held the fallen faithful of the temple, wrapped in rotting funerary garb.

Two doorways were cut into the walls at opposite ends of the chamber, to the left and right of the stairs. These doors were rotted as well and the priest randomly chose the right to investigate. Opening it, the wood collapsed easily and Cenric could see a small passage. Moving down it, he saw more niches carved and more of the faithful at rest.

Eyes in the darkness of one of the niches startled him and he let out a gasp! Holding his torch forward he saw a thin rat was perched atop the skull of a dead believer. Exhaling, Cenric let out a most un-priestly curse and thrust the torch toward the vermin. The rat let out a screech and leapt from the moldering bones and scampered back down a tiny tunnel that it had dug into the niche.

Inwardly, the priest cursed himself for a fool, even as he grinned at the rush of fear coursing through him. It was times like this that he questioned his own sanity. *'I could be a senior brother or head of a church by now. I'm old enough and experienced enough.'* Even as he thought it, Cenric knew it was nonsense. He'd never be some cloistered priest who spent his days reading and praying endlessly. He'd always been a man on the move, a man of action. With a sigh, he mused, *'I'll likely die in a place like this.'*

Banishing such bleak thoughts from his mind, the cleric pressed on down the corridor he came to a stone archway. Beyond was another circular chamber, though smaller than the entry chamber.

The walls here, too held niches, holding the remains of the faithful. In the center of the room was a sarcophagus. The top of the lid of the stone coffin was carved with stylized, winged angels bearing swords. Judging by the markings, Cenric guessed that the sarcophagus contained either the founder of this church or one of its saints or heroes.

This chamber wasn't what he was looking for and the priest turned away from it. Heading back down the narrow corridor, he came out once again into the entry chamber. Traversing it, he went to the door on the other side of the room and forced his way past it, the rotting wood falling in easily. The passage ahead was similar to the other, save for the fact that it held no rat ready to startle him. At the far end was another archway and another circular chamber, roughly the same as the room that held the sarcophagus.

This room was different, however. For one thing, it contained no niches and the walls were covered with ancient plaster. Frescoes had been painted there and though cracked and peeled, scenes of the founding of the church and the perils and triumphs of the faithful were shown there. Ignoring the artwork, Cenric moved toward the center of the room. A smile split his face now and he breathed a sigh of relief for he'd found what he was looking for.

A carved stone pedestal stood waist height in the center of the room. The pedestal itself was a thing of beauty. It was carved all of one piece of dense gray stone and intricate angelic beings and robed clergy decorated it. The pedestal held his attention only briefly, as Cenric focused on what was placed atop it. A silver pitcher with fluted edges stood there. It too was a beautiful piece with delicate, intricate swirls etched into its entire surface, reminiscent of clouds. The pattern was almost hypnotic to behold. There was something about the vessel, something that transcended the mundane object that it was and Cenric knew he'd found what he'd been looking for. Looking within the pitcher, he saw clear water that looked fresh as if had been recently brought from a mountain stream. The water should have long since evaporated or at least be brackish and foul yet it looked cool and pure.

Going to one knee before the pedestal, Cenric prayed, murmuring the words earnestly. The man of faith thanked the gods for their mercy and their favor in allowing him to find this place. He emptied his mind of any thoughts save praising them for their beneficence and for a time was as still as a stone. Then, he rose, thanks still upon his lips. Reaching for the handle of the pitcher, he lifted it, surprised by its weight. Then, the priest drank deeply from the pitcher before upending it over his head. Doused in the refreshing water, the priest felt himself cleansed of doubt and fear, emboldened and renewed, energized with fresh purpose.

The stream of water from the pitcher did not cease and Cenric laughed aloud for pure joy. '*It is a reliquary!*' The thought warmed him, even as the fresh pure water continued to flow. '*We have hope! We are not abandoned!*'

Placing the pitcher atop the pedestal again, the cleric could see that it was as full as it was when he first looked in it, even though he'd emptied perhaps three times as much as it should have been able to hold. He felt invigorated now. The pitcher and the water within had been blessed by the ancient gods that so many believed had abandoned their benighted world. Such reliquaries were holy and proof of the deities enduring will. Of course, there were always those who would point and laugh at something as simple as a pitcher of water that never ran dry. Such scoffers would ask what practical use such a thing had when the lakes and rivers of the north were all around. Such people were doubters and fools, however, and Cenric had never paid them heed. The pitcher was a reliquary and the water it contained blessed by the gods of old. In the hands of one like Cenric, a true believer, who could pray and touch the very heavens with his fervor, it was much, much more than it appeared.

The priest went again down on one knee and began to seek the favor and will of the gods. Their blessing could turn the tide in the coming battle. For a long time, Cenric prayed and slowly, though he could not see it through his closed eyes, the water within the reliquary began to emit a soft, whitish blue glow.

Amid his fervent prayers, a thought held in the priest's mind; 'There is hope!'

Captain Fendrel was a gallant man of valor, taste and style, at least this was how he thought of himself. In truth, his view of himself was mirrored by most of those around him, from the ladies who nearly swooned when the handsome captain tipped his ridiculous hat, to them to many of the guards who served in his command, who desperately strove to emulate him. Fendrel was attractive and muscular, brave as well as suave and there were many in Wend who thought that he would one day be mayor himself.

On this particular day, though, the good captain was irritated and losing patience. The morning had started out fine. After an excellent meal, he'd made his way to the main barracks, his mind on many things but primarily a certain buxom lass who'd caught his eye. However, such lovely visions were banished when he arrived, as his subordinates told him he had visitors. Fendrel had several ideas who might have decided to pay him a visit, the aforementioned lady foremost in his mind but these hopes were dashed when he saw who awaited him in his modest yet tasteful office.

As he swept into the room, he saw two men within. One was seated and frowning, a burly man in the garb of a mercenary or caravan guard. The other was a massive man who could only be barbarian from across the sea, who was currently examining an orc axe that was hanging on the wall. Fendrel sensed trouble and his smile evaporated as he crossed the chamber to his desk and stood there eyeing the pair.

"My men said that you needed to see me?" Fendrel asked with little warmth.

The seated man rose, his frown deepening. "You are Captain Fendrel?" He asked, with doubt in his voice.

It was Fendrel's turn to frown. He knew he was one of the youngest guard captains in the history of Wend but the locals were accustomed to it. "Yes…I am." The captain said starkly, bristling a bit. "And you are?" He asked, glancing at the Northman as well.

"My name is Bandur." The man standing before him said.

Taking a seat, the captain gestured for the other man to do likewise. Then he asked, "And does your…*friend*…have a name?" Fendrel noticed the way Bandur grimaced when the captain called the barbarian his friend.

"This…is Tanoc." Bandur finally answered rather reluctantly.

The giant Northman turned away from the orc axe and looked at the captain speculatively. "Did you slay the owner?" He asked, jerking a thumb toward the weapon.

"I did." Captain Fendrel answered in clipped tones. "Why don't you tell me what you want here?" He said to Bandur, pointedly ignoring the barbarian.

The other man nodded and then swallowed. He looked at his comrade and then back at the captain. Then he looked around the room. It was clear that he'd come here for something but now wasn't quite sure how to say it.

Finally, the savage warrior snorted and said, "Just tell him!"

Twisting in his chair, Bandur growled, "I am!"

Rubbing his temples, the captain leaned forward. "I don't have time for nonsense. If you have something to say, then out with it." He'd said it as politely as he could but something within him still screamed that these two were trouble. Fendrel hadn't gotten to where he was simply by the strength of his sword arm or his smile. He was good at his job and that meant knowing people and how to deal with them. This pair looked like they'd just as soon kill each other and yet there was something else going on here.

"Right." Bandur said. "I work for a merchant named Venaro…" The man paused a bit at this point, having dropped the name. It was clear that he was used to people knowing his employer and wasn't disappointed this time as the captain nodded to show he'd heard the name. "We were returning from a trip north when we were… attacked by creatures…things that…it's hard to describe…"

Rubbing his eyes, the captain couldn't bear the ramshackle account any longer. "Orcs?" He couldn't manage to keep the sarcasm from his voice. He'd taken Bandur for a professional, maybe an ex-soldier, it was just something in his bearing and manner. Now, however, the man acted like a drunk.

Shaking his head, Bandur said, "Not orcs." His voice was strained. "Something else…"

It was difficult for Fendrel to contain his irritation now as he looked from Bandur to Tanoc. The huge Northman bore a similar expression to the one the man seated across from the captain. They both looked as though they'd seen a ghost.

"What? What…is….it?" The captain demanded slowly.

Bandur looked incapable of answering and it was the barbarian who answered in a dreadful whisper. "Dregs."

Looking from one man to the other, the captain leaned back in his chair. "What is that?"

"They're horrible…" Bandur said, his face pale.

Again, it was Tanoc who replied. "They are servants of the

Pallid."

This was something the captain had heard of and his face hardened. "The Pallid are nothing more than superstitious nonsense!" He could almost have laughed but it was clear that these men had seen something. "Now you might have seen some sort of creatures that were even possibly risen dead shambling about but to say you've seen Pallid…"

Bandur cut in, his voice raw as sandpaper. "We didn't say we saw the Pallid." He glanced at the barbarian. "But Tanoc said that the Dregs serve them."

In his very best calming voice, honed over years of settling squabbles and troubles within the town, Fendrel's response was typical. "So you saw something out in the wild. Something you'd never seen before and you can't explain. Perhaps it was a zombie or some other undead. The gods above and below know that such things are a blight on the land these days." His voice grew grim. "But to jump at shadows and say there are Pallid here?" He made the end of his rhetoric a question, to make them think.

"I *have* seen them before." Tanoc said acidly.

The captain glanced at the barbarian and mildly asked, "Where?"

Hesitating, the barbarian turned to look at the orc axe on the wall but it was clear that he wasn't really seeing it. Tanoc was remembering. His voice was distant. "They and their masters….they came to my home…" The barbarian said nothing more. His back was to them both and it grew quiet in the captain's office.

Then the door opened and another guard entered. Fendrel half jumped and swore at the newcomer. "Heralc's Blade! How many times have I told you to knock, Hedolf?!"

The man who had entered was short and stocky. He was older than any of the others, his lined face and fringe of gray hair betraying his years. Yet, he was a hale and hearty sort with a bluff manner and serious eyes. "Sorry sir." He began. "I was bringing you my report on the woman who escaped the cells and murdered poor Gren." His voice was flat as he spoke. "I believe that she's still in the town and I think it was she who tried to kill the merchant Delia."

Before the captain could say anything, Bandur spoke. "Hedolf?" When the man half-turned, he was sure. "Hedolf, you old bastard, it is you!" He roared, coming to his feet and a large smile banishing his frown.

Laughing, the guard known as Hedolf walked around the desk. "Sergeant Bandur!" There was real warmth in his voice as he looked at the other man. "How long has it been?"

"Years, my friend." The caravan guard said, stepping forward to clasp hands with his old friend. "Remember that time we were flanked by Duke Rhin's personal guard?"

Hedolf laughed and clapped Bandur on the shoulder. "Aye!" With a twinkle in his eye, he added, "I remember you nearly emptied your bowels when they charged!"

Bandur nodded and laughed even harder. "And as I remember it, you actually did!"

"I don't quite recall it that way." Hedolf replied, still chuckling. "How have you been? Last I heard…"

"All right, that'll be enough of that!" Captain Fendrel cut them both off, rolling his eyes. "Enough with touching reunion!"

Hedolf cleared his voice and turned back to his superior. "Sorry sir. Bandur here's an old friend."

"We were just telling your captain of a danger to the town…" Bandur began but was again interrupted by the captain.

"You were both just leaving, you mean." Fendrel said evenly.

"Captain, Bandur's one of the best soldiers I've ever known." Hedolf said, gesturing toward the other man. "If he says there's danger, we should listen."

"I *have* listened." The captain retorted. "And I have heard enough nonsense for one day."

Tanoc, who had turned at the two old soldiers greetings growled, "You are a fool!"

As the captain's face colored and Hedolf looked at the hulking warrior with some alarm, Bandur intervened. "He didn't mean that, captain." He glanced back over his shoulder. "He's just upset."

What either Tanoc or the good captain might have said next would never be known as again, the door opened and yet another guard entered. "Captain, the men are ready for..." This new guard, a large pudgy specimen with a vacant expression had walked in and then stopped short as he saw the barbarian.

"How many times have I told you men to knock before entering my office!?!" Fendrel practically screamed.

However, the guard wasn't paying much attention but pointed at Tanoc. "It's him!" His voice was half outrage and half disbelief as he tried to reason what the barbarian was doing in his captain's office.

"Dulwen, what are you talking about?" The captain snapped.

Looking around with his squinty eyes, Dulwen replied. "He's the one who started the ruckus at the 'king' last night!"

"I didn't *start* anything." The Northman grated dangerously. "I finished what those fools began."

Dulwen's locked eyes with the barbarian then but before he could say anything more, the captain interrupted. He didn't want a fight to break out in his own office and he certainly didn't like Dulwen's odds against the giant northerner.

"That's enough." Captain Fendrel's voice was flinty. "I've heard what you both had to say." He then pointed at Tanoc. "I heard about your display at the Crooked King and while the guards on the scene chose to let you walk free, I can assure you I'll tolerate no more nonsense out of you."

Bandur tried to speak then, "Sir, he didn't..."

Having none of it, the captain brusquely cut him off. "From my understanding there was a second man helping the savage." He looked at Dulwen. "Is this the other trouble maker?"

"Trouble maker?!" Bandur exclaimed. "Captain, we

didn't..."

Dulwen's smile was vicious as he chimed in. "Oh yessir, that's him alright. They was both busting up the place!"

"That's a damned lie!" Bandur snapped at the guardsman.

"*ENOUGH!*" Captain Fendrel boomed. "Now I don't want any more trouble out of either of you!" He looked at both men squarely. Bandur was angry but seemed resigned. However, the barbarian looked ready to brain Dulwen and rush him next. "I want you both out of here and if you cause any more trouble I'll have you in irons!"

Bandur shook his head. "Sir, if you would just listen..." He began.

At the same time, Tanoc took a step toward Dulwen, who visibly flinched. Groaning inwardly, Fendrel was glad to see Hedolf turn squarely to face the Northman. The captain reflected that while the man had certainly been a headache at times, Hedolf was someone who could be counted on.

"No more." The captain stated flatly. "Hedolf." When the guardsman turned to look at him, Fendrel looked at him and then the door. Pointedly, he said, "Escort your friend and his pet from the barracks right now."

With a heavy sigh, Hedolf looked at Bandur. "Let's go." He said simply. Bandur moved toward the door and then gestured at Tanoc.

As Hedolf, Dulwen and Captain Fendrel all watched unsure what he'd do, the mighty Northman looked back at each man right in their eyes. He was taking their measure and each of them knew it. It was if he wanted to settle this with steel right here and now, even though there were twenty guards within earshot. They waited, their nerves stretched and then just as the tension became unbearable...

"*HA!*" Tanoc laughed derisively and then, turning his back on them, walked out of the room. The insult that he found them beneath contempt was clear.

Bandur trailed after the barbarian without a word and Hedolf followed suit, after saluting. For a long time, Dulwen just stared at the empty doorway while the good captain ground his teeth.

Outside the barracks, Bandur turned to Hedolf and grinned bleakly. "I don't think he likes us."

Hedolf chuckled. "You ought to be used to people not liking you." He eyed the big northerner. "You might have actually found someone that people like even less than you!"

"I might have, at that." Bandur admitted but he didn't laugh. He couldn't as his fear roiled in his stomach. He'd hoped it would go better with the guardsmen, knowing what was coming. "Hedolf, death is coming to this town. You know I wouldn't make something like this up."

"I know that." The guard replied. He then looked at the receding form of the huge barbarian as he stalked away from them down the street, townsfolk giving him a wide berth. "Can it really be the Pallid?"

Now, Bandur did snicker. "You old dog! You were listening outside the captain's office!"

"Well...I did have that report to deliver." Hedolf admitted with a grin. "And I spotted you and that great lout enter the barracks and figured that I might have to intervene. I just waited for the right opportunity to make my entrance." He finished with a wink.

Bandur shook his head. "How is it that you aren't captain here?" He asked the question even as he thought he might already know the reason.

"You know how it is, my friend." Hedolf said with a shrug. "Fendrel's a local. He's young, handsome and related to some fairly influential people, some of 'em are even on the council." His grin widened. "And me?" He asked with a thumb to his own chest. "I'm just an ugly, old warhorse. A reminder of all that's been lost." He gestured helplessly at the town around them. "People want to forget the wars. They want to get on with their own lives. A man like

Fendrel's the future."

His voice sour, Bandur practically spat. "The man's a fool!"

"He's not so bad, really." Hedolf allowed. "To be honest, we've both served under worse men, Bandur." When the other man gave him a frank look of disbelief, he chuckled again. "I'm serious. Fendrel is a fair man, even if a vain one. He's a fighter too, Bandur. He's good with a blade and strong as an ox."

Bandur made a rude noise. "It takes more than that to command." His eyes were troubled. "Are all the guardsmen like the captain?"

"You mean, blind to everything and everyone outside of the walls of their own town?" Hedolf asked sarcastically. "Aye but there are some good ones among our ranks too. Even some of the more foolish ones will fight to defend their town."

"I hope it's enough, Hedolf." The ex-soldier practically whispered.

Looking sharply at Bandur, his old friend asked, "Is it that bad?"

His eyes haunted, Bandur nodded. "These creatures…these Dregs…they're terrifying and I don't mind admitting it."

"But you survived." Hedolf pressed. "You and that Northman lived through a battle with them."

"We did…" Bandur admitted sadly. "But some good men, some friends of mine, didn't."

"I'm sorry, Bandur." The guardsman said then. "They can be slain though?"

It took a few moments for Bandur to answer. "Destroyed is more like it." Was all he said then but when Hedolf looked at him pointedly, he nodded again. "You have to cut them to pieces and then burn them." Seeing his old friends look of disbelief, he went on forcefully. "I'm serious Bandur, they won't stop otherwise…" His voice was hoarse as he remembered that day they'd fought the Dregs, how they seemed to be unstoppable.

"What about…" Hedolf started to say and then lowered his voice, looking around to make sure none of the passerby on the streets were close enough to hear his words. "What about the Pallid?"

"We didn't see any of them." Bandur said almost dreamily, fighting to come back from the horrible memories. Finally, he got a grip on his thoughts. "Tanoc said if they'd been there, they would have attacked."

"How many?" The guardsman asked urgently then. He'd been unsure at first of Bandur's sincerity. He hadn't seen the man in a long time and the former sergeant had been known to drink. Seeing him now though, Hedolf was convinced, even if his captain was not. "How many of these creatures are there?"

"I don't know." Bandur answered with a shake of his head. "The group we fought were strays, I think."

"Strays?" Hedolf asked not understanding.

Bandur's voice was troubled. "Like sheep that get away from their shepherds." The dread was clear in his voice and fear began to slither into Hedolf's gut.

"What...What are they?" The guardsman finally asked, trying to keep his voice calm.

"I don't know." Bandur said. "They're some sort of...creature." He said lamely and when Hedolf's look showed he wasn't satisfied with the description, he burst out, "I'm not a wizard or a scholar, man!" His voice was pleading and urgent as he grabbed Hedolf's shirt. "They're some kind of undead...things...made from the parts of people and animals...and...and...I don't know how they came to be or why they can even move when the gods know they shouldn't be able to but they *do*!"

Seeing that his friend's voice had risen and people on the streets nearby were starting to take notice, Hedolf gently disengaged himself from Bandur's grip. "Easy, now." He said in calming tones. "Just rest easy, sergeant."

"You don't understand." Bandur said sadly. "But you will...soon enough."

His word's chilled the guardsman and Hedolf asked feebly,

"What will you do? Are you fleeing the town?"

Bandur shook his head in negation. "We're…Venaro and the priest think we should stay and help."

Hedolf didn't even ask what priest his friend was talking about. He did feel grateful to know that there were those who would stand and fight these things. He nodded thankfully at Bandur.

"I don't think your captain will let us man the walls with you." The caravan guard murmured. "At least not at first. He might change his mind after he sees them, though."

The whole thing felt unreal to Hedolf but he knew that Bandur believed what he was saying. He wished that he didn't believe his old comrade but with a sinking feeling realized that he did. The guardsman couldn't think of anything else to say or ask, even though he knew that he should. Finally, he asked "How long?"

"I don't know." Bandur admitted after a brief moment. "Tell everyone that you can to be ready." Bandur said, interrupting the other man's reverie. When his friend nodded, he turned to go. Walking a few paces, he turned back around and added, "And Hedolf? Make sure you have plenty of wood and oil."

As Bandur walked away from him, Hedolf rubbed his jaw and thought seriously about taking his wife and fleeing the city. He stood there thinking for quite some time.

CHAPTER TWENTY

Exultation filled Null's being as they made their way south. Every move that he made was effortless as he almost flowed along the ground. At first, he'd found it difficult as he adjusted to his newfound abilities. His early efforts were awkward and ugly yet with time and practice, he was able to move like the others if not nearly as graceful as they. It was a matter of his mind comprehending that with little effort, he could leap forward ten paces as simply as he would have taken a step before. He constantly misjudged the distances he could move and several times found himself lying on the ground. The others never laughed and he intuited that they understood this process as something they themselves had gone through.

"You will learn." Fina offered simply after he'd tried to leap atop a rock, misjudged the jump and flew over it to land on his face. When he'd shrieked his frustration, she added, "It takes time but soon you will unlearn all you have known and realize those limits are no longer yours."

Breathing in harshly, the new Pallid had said in frustration. "I don't understand."

"Of course you don't." Kast had said from his vantage atop the rock Null had leapt over. "It's why you're still mimicking what you did as a human."

"What do you mean?" Null asked, trying not to let his irritation show. He admired them their poise and their calm and though fear had left him, he still could only offer an imitation of their demeanor. It still grated him, though.

"Why are you breathing?" Kast asked simply.

"What...I..." Null sputtered and then stopped as he realized that breathing was a natural thing, a reflex that kept him alive. Yet now he realized that he no longer needed to breathe and wonder struck him anew.

Fina regarded him like an indulgent teacher will a student that she is pleased with. "You will relearn many things." She stated simply.

They'd said little more as they continued ever south toward the doomed town of Wend. One of the things that Null learned about himself was that he cared less and less for the fate of the town and its people. On his way to meet with the Pallid, when he'd still been a man named Malken, he'd wondered how he'd feel. He'd always known their plans for the town and out of spite hadn't cared. Then, he'd only cared for his own comfort and riches and now, as he looked out at the night sky, he realized how mundane and petty such mortal concerns were. He didn't need wealth any more than he needed to breathe and strange as the notion was, it pleased him.

They had traveled by night and day, though he'd noticed they covered less ground through the day. The Dregs needed rest no more than their Pallid masters but they all felt slower, more lethargic throughout the day. At night, Null felt more powerful and energized than he'd ever dreamed possible as a mortal and he knew the others were the same. He'd begun to learn to taste emotions and postures from them and he now understood that this was how the Pallid seemed to read each other's minds.

For example, he could tell that Fina was brooding and irritable on this night as they got ever closer to the town. He guessed that it was because Vok had put her in charge and she wanted to make sure that all went according to plan. Kast, on the other hand exuded an irreverent and impudent humor that grew as they went along. Null couldn't understand why until earlier in the day, Fina had snapped at Kast abruptly. It had been as they paused in a thick copse of trees and waited for the toiling Dregs to catch up. The trees gave some shade from the hated sun and the Dregs moved agonizingly slow.

"I will *not* fail." Fina had almost snarled, her cold eyes on Kast. Her fellow Pallid had answered not a word but his equally frosty smile never budged. Null had wisely said nothing. He'd begun to realize that there wasn't really animosity between the two so much as Kast's irritation at Fina's lead. This had dawned on Null as he realized he chafed at either of them being over him and wondered at it. For a human, especially one such as Null had been, there was always someone in charge, someone to answer to. Even great lords and kings who acted as though they were divine, had to make sure they did not alienate their subjects and face a rebellion. In recent years, a great many rulers heads had decorated spikes right along with common folk. This seemed different however. He knew that they could both destroy him and so he obeyed. They all knew that Vok was far greater than them and yet he knew instinctively that they all chafed beneath his rule.

Kast had looked at Null then. "It is like this for us all." It was still eerie despite everything that they could read his emotions so well. Again, it was as though they read his mind, though it wasn't strictly true. His feelings were simply as plain to them as an open book. "Is it not so, Fina?"

Grudgingly, she answered. "This is true, Null." Her voice was calm but her eyes were as cold as ever. "All Pallid revel in their power and all chafe at the yoke of another's control."

Taking up the lesson, Kast said wryly. "We have been told that it was not always like this." Null was surprised and the scarred Pallid grinned at him. "Yes, there was a time when we Pallid were free in this world and each one did as they chose. Some traveled in small groups but most were loners by choice."

It was obvious that Kast longed for such a time and Null looked at Fina. In answer to his unspoken question, she answered. "That time has passed." She said simply. Sensing his dissatisfaction with his answer, she continued. "Now, we are gathered together to prey upon the humans until only we remain." Now, she shook her head at his unasked query. "No, I do not know why nor do I know who rules us all. Vok is our master and this is all the truth that we must know."

Now, Null did voice a question. "And Vok?" He looked at both his fellow Pallid then. "Does he too, answer to a master?"

A pulse of unease from Fina was all he got in reply. "The Dregs are nearly here." She turned quickly from the others, gracefully almost floating out of the stand of trees. The Dregs moved to follow her as she appeared, like grotesque cattle. Like cattle they lowed as they saw her, yet it was a horrid cacophony of grunts, wheezes and strangled yells none of which were actual words.

Kast favored Null with a grim smile before they followed after her. "None of us know." His eyes were piercing. "I would not recommend asking Vok either." His voice and feeling displayed the fact that he thought it would be quite funny if Null did just that.

Now, it was again night and the Pallid were once more at ease. Fina had informed them that she'd timed their approach so that they would arrive at Wend in the dead of night. They and the Dregs would be at their peak and the humans would be at their most vulnerable. Chafing thoughts and feelings of another's rule over him were far from Null, as he looked at the waning moon. He felt dark excitement at the thought of their arrival and all that would take place. Even the annoyance of the excruciatingly slow pace of the Dregs didn't seem to matter. They would be there soon. One thing hadn't changed since he had become a Pallid. There were people he was going to visit when he got back to Wend. People who had belittled him, mocked him and lorded over him. His desire to make them sorry had not waned in the least.

Null's excitement and hunger reached out to the other Pallid like the scent of something delicious on the wind. They smiled like indulgent parents, remembering when they had been newly remade. They both knew that when he arrived back in Wend, they would likely not be able to control him. They also knew that he was still vulnerable and might possibly not survive. Their smiles remained in place. It was the way of such things among them.

They were nearly there.

Walking through the streets of Wend was like moving through a dream. All around Venaro, people talked and moved, bought and sold, laughed and cried. It was like a thousand other towns and villages the merchant had been to and yet there was one crucial difference. This settlement was about to be in a battle for its very survival and the ironic thing about it was the fact that they had no idea, despite the best efforts of those who had tried to warn it.

'*I should be headed south.*' The merchant thought to himself. '*It is pure madness to stay here.*' He reproached himself inwardly. '*Everyone who should care and should make a stand is oblivious.*' This justification seemingly refused to go away. Then there was the one that was like a throb in the back of his mind. '*This isn't my problem.*' These thoughts went round and round in his head as he headed back toward the Crooked King. Still, he knew that he couldn't turn away now. He was committed. One ironic thing strung him more than anything else. The fact that he'd never even really cared for the town of Wend all that much.

Nearby, two young lovers walked hand in hand. Venaro paused on his way to watch them from a distance. Their heads were close together and they were talking in that private way that people who are truly in love are wont to do. He looked to be a tradesman by his clothing and manner and she was perhaps a baker's apprentice, judging by her apron and dress. Two young people in love, no doubt talking of future plans and dreams.

Venaro felt his heart lurch as he remembered being young and in love. These were the real people of Wend. Not the fat mayor or inept guards or greedy shop owners. People like the ones before him like people the world over, seeking love and happiness. Inwardly, he couldn't help but laugh at himself. He'd always been something of a romantic and it only seemed to get worse the older he got. Still, he moved with a new purpose as he started back down the street that led to the Crooked King. He felt better about what they were doing and why they were doing it.

'*I must be getting old.*' He thought with a sigh. He was a merchant, not a hero. Yet his steps were sure and his mind was decided. He was going to do his best for these people. Thinking of the horror of the Dregs, he wondered how many people moving through their lives would soon be dead. He tried not to think about it but it persisted. '*Whisper would laugh at me. She would definitely agree that I'm getting old.*'

Not far away, Whisper surreptitiously watched the merchant as he made his way down the street. From her current vantage at the mouth of an alleyway, she saw him pause and watch the young couple walking hand in hand.

'*Old fool.*' She mused, not unkindly, watching him as he watched them. She'd no doubt that he was thinking some nonsense about young love and remembering a time when he was young. A smile curled across her face but it was sardonic. Whisper had known love, very real love once, so long ago that it seemed a lifetime. What she had learned was that the world was cruel and to love something was to risk having it taken from you. '*I'll never be that weak again.*' She thought savagely and the depth of the emotion surprised her more than a little. A face...*his* face...so handsome and kind...tried to surface in her mind. She ruthlessly banished the image as efficiently as she would kill an enemy. She hadn't thought about him in a long time and now was no time to start.

Venaro was moving again, heading purposefully down the street. Whisper turned and headed down the alley she had been standing in. It was momentarily going away from the merchant but just ahead another alley doglegged to the left. Taking it, she was moving more or less along the same direction as the merchant would be as he headed back toward the inn.

Whisper pondered for a moment the wisdom of her course but knew she really had no choice. She could easily flee the town but then she'd still have a price on her head. Venaro had spoken the truth. Even with all her skills, she'd have a difficult time surviving long enough to find who had placed such a high bounty on her head and why. The merchant had a long standing reputation as a man of honor and a man of his word. She would have to trust that he would help her as he promised.

'*Still*,' Whisper mused as she made her way down the twisting alley, '*I don't trust him enough not to tail him to make sure it's all not a trap.*' Even as she thought it, though, she knew the truth; old habits die hard and she was a survivor. The assassin didn't really believe that the merchant was trying to trap her. She thought he was too wise to try something like that. She just couldn't bring herself to trust anyone.

'*Besides*,' the woman thought with a wry little smirk, '*I'm sure the guards are still looking for me.*'

Cenric replaced the flagstone atop the trapdoor, pleased with how seamless it looked. The priest doubted that after all these years, anyone was going to come to the church but on the off chance that they did, they'd have to know what he did to gain access to the hidden stairs and the chambers below. Shouldering his pack, the cleric walked out of the church, pausing at the entrance and looking about. There was no one nearby. This area was less populated than others and most of the houses and business near the old temple were abandoned.

A sense of sadness swept over the cleric. '*Wend is a dying town.*' The thought came unbidden to his mind. '*Even if it survives this storm, mismanagement by its officials and poor planning will make it more and more vulnerable as time goes on.*' Cenric sighed, fighting the melancholy that he felt. He knew only too well the terrible things that he'd witnessed in his lifetime. Furthermore, he reflected that so often men do horrible things to each other without the need for any monster or creature to help him.

"Bah!" The priest harrumphed to himself. He knew that all settlements were like living beings. They were born, they grew, they aged and eventually they died. He was a bit of a scholar, though he would deny such claims and the priest knew of ancient texts that claimed that civilization was unnatural and couldn't be sustained. It was true that many civilizations and cultures had risen and fallen. '*Still,*' Cenric said to himself, '*Like spring after a long winter, new life springs up to replace death and decay.*' A practical man, the thought cheered the priest immensely. He hadn't come to save buildings and landmarks; he'd come to help the people of this town.

Breathing in deeply, Cenric smiled. It was a worthy cause and even if he died fighting the evil that loomed over this town, he didn't mind. It would be a good death, a worthy death. Patting the warhammer at his side, his smile deepened. '*If nothing else, I'll bring more than a few down.*' Then, he looked back at the abandoned temple and remembered what was hidden beneath it. '*Maybe more than a few.*'

The priest was smiling and whistling as he headed down the street away from the church.

Quiet reigned in the crooked king that afternoon. The crowd that would head in to begin carousing usually didn't arrive until near dusk or later. The few that were down in the taproom were those who were staying in rented rooms. Travelers and merchants for the most part, they kept to themselves. Here, a man in the robes of a scholar sat alone at a table reading from a scroll and sipping a glass of wine. Nearby, a merchant was quietly talking with a local tradesman. Further away, near the door, a bard strummed a lute and sang softly, her voice haunting and melodious. Near the center of the room, a few people were eating an early dinner.

Bandur was one of them. The big man picked at the mutton and vegetables on his plate. It wasn't that the meal was bad, he just wasn't hungry. Thinking of the fiasco at the barracks, he grimaced. Then, to have old Hedolf there only drove the point home to the ex-soldier. Wend was not ready for what was coming.

Like all soldiers who had fought in battle, Bandur was one who knew the waiting was the worst part. *'It's not just the waiting.'* He mused, spearing a spindly carrot on his fork and looking at it as though he'd never seen one before. *'What makes it all worse is that these fools won't listen!'* Forcing himself to take a bite, Bandur chewed the morsel mechanically. How many times had he been her before? When in the army, he'd known such moments. Times when his superiors made terrible decisions that cost good soldiers their lives. He'd seen pride and vanity kill more people than anything else when people wouldn't listen. The most frustrating thing was the sense of helplessness. *'There's nothing to be done for it.'* He thought for perhaps the hundredth time, yet then as with every other time, he knew it wasn't totally true. He could run. He could get out of this place and leave it to live or die on its own. Then he would invariably think of the priest and Venaro and what they'd say. He'd think of men like Hedolf. Good men who would never abandon their post.

The thing that plagued his thoughts the most was thinking of Tanoc, the barbarian. Bandur knew that the Northman had seen the Pallid and their minions destroy much of his homeland. The man wouldn't say much but he'd heard enough from Venaro to know the truth of it. Yet the barbarian showed no fear, only a stubborn, stoic resolve. Ever since they'd all spoken with the priest that night, Tanoc had been like a stone. What bothered Bandur was the fact that he was terrified and the barbarian was not. He'd rather die than let that savage watch him run away like a scared child.

So thinking, Bandur proceeded to dig into his supper. 'No sense letting it go to waste.' The caravan guard ate quietly for a few minutes before noticing someone coming down the stairs. As if summoned by his thoughts, Tanoc was there, his frame filling the stairwell. With a start, Bandur realized that he wasn't alone. Lilli was pressed up against the barbarian, her hair tousled and her dress rumpled. She stretched up to plant a kiss on the towering Northman who had to lean down to receive it.

'Apparently, they've made up.' Bandur thought sourly. 'At least there's no one here to pick a fight over it.' The ex-soldier mused, trying to cheer himself up. He put it out of his mind and focused on his dinner. Soon enough, he felt like he'd need his strength. His wrist was healing well but he knew he wasn't at his best.

Bandur finished his meal and pushed his plate back. Looking up, he saw Lilli coming to retrieve it. He shook his head when she asked if he wanted more or something to drink and she sauntered away. She passed near the bar on her way to the kitchen and smiled at Tanoc, who was leaning against it, a mug in his hand. He smiled back at her and then looked over at Bandur and raised his mug in salute. The caravan guard couldn't help but raise his cup and smile at the young giant.

'*Gods help me,*' Bandur mused, '*I think I'm actually starting to like him!*'

It was dark by the time that Venaro reached the Crooked King. The crowd had grown and as he entered, he was forced to push his way through. Stopping near the bar, he motioned to a harried Jorun, who grimaced. After taking a few drink orders, he had one of the barmaids take over and headed down to the end of the bar, where the merchant waited.

"I need to speak with you." The merchant said, raising his voice to be heard above the din. Old Jorun raised a bushy eyebrow in response and Venaro shook his head. "We need to talk in private."

Jorun looked around at his busy inn and then shrugged. Motioning for the merchant to follow him, he led the other man toward a side door off of the main taproom. These rooms were private meeting rooms that the innkeeper rented out for private parties or business that his customers didn't want to conduct out in the main taproom. Opening the door, ushered Venaro in. The room was dark and it took a few moments for the old man to light a candle. There was an oval table and half a dozen chairs dominating the center of the room. A single window was set in the far wall, the shutters closed against the evening chill.

"So...talk." Jorun said, his voice gruff.

Venaro stared at the merchant for a long moment. He could tell the man was being cold with him now. Earlier, he'd just assumed that Jorun was so busy he didn't really have time to talk but now, he was sure something was wrong. Divining what the problem was, the merchant said slowly, "I'm sorry about the troubles my men caused."

"Weren't them that caused it." Jorun said with a sniff as he lit another candle. "It was the barbarian. You never should have brought him here."

This was surprising to the merchant, who'd never known Jorun to judge a man based on his race. "Look, I know that the fight was bad but no one was killed." He tried hard to keep his voice calm but was more than a little annoyed. "From everything that I've been told, Tanoc didn't start it."

Now Jorun shook his head. "That's not the point, Venaro." He continued to move around the room, lighting candles. "It's one thing for a brawl to break out. Hell, it happens a few times a month."

"Then I don't..." Venaro began but was cut off by the old man. The merchant was a little shocked by how brusque the man's manner was. Jorun had always been unfailingly polite and the merchant had always gotten along well with him.

Jorun finished lighting the last candle in its wall sconce and blew out the bit of tinder he'd used. "That man is dangerous." He said flatly. "My lads weren't sure if they stepped in to break things up that he wouldn't start laying about with that sword or axe."

Now Venaro understood completely. Tanoc had this kind of effect on people. It wasn't just his obvious size and strength nor was it the weapons he bore or the fact that he clearly knew how to use them. There was something else about him, a primal way that he moved and spoke, as though he was a hunter and other men his prey. There was no hesitation and taking life seemed as natural to the barbarian as taking his next breath. The merchant realized that he'd slowly gotten used to the Northman.

"I understand." Venaro said then in soothing tones. "I'll make sure that nothing else happens, you have my word."

Jorun looked at him, his eyes sharp as flint. Finally he nodded. "I'll hold you to that."

The merchant nodded and yawned. He hadn't slept well after speaking with Whisper and he realized that he hadn't gotten much sleep for quite a while. He'd awoken earlier that day to go and speak with Delia but the woman had been sleeping. He knew he needed to warn her and had told her governess to leave word that he'd been by. *'When this is all over, I'm going someplace nice and I'll sleep for a week.'* Venaro promised himself.

"Will you be wanting the room the whole evening?" Jorun asked.

Venaro's brow rose in surprise. "I didn't say I wanted to rent a private room."

Shaking his head, the old man answered. "The priest told me you'd be needing it." He paused then, waiting for an answer.

"I haven't…seen him today." Venaro said slowly. "I suppose we'll need it for the evening then."

Briskly nodding, the innkeeper headed toward the door. "Good then, I'll add the cost to your tab."

"Jorun?" The merchant said, bringing the other man to a halt. "I need to tell you something. It's the main reason I asked to speak with you." He struggled with how to put it while the old man looked at him. "The town is in danger." Venaro finally said lamely.

The innkeeper raised an eyebrow. "Orcs?"

Venaro shook his head. "Worse than orcs."

Jorun folded his arms then. "Tell me."

The trader thought for several moments and then bluntly answered. "We were attacked by creatures known as Dregs on the way here. They are horrible things and they serve the Pallid."

It was quiet for what seemed like a long time then. Finally Jorun said, "Are you sure they're coming here?"

Venaro was more than a little surprised. He'd expected denial or derision or both. Then, he remembered that Jorun had seen a lot in his many years. "You don't seem surprised."

The innkeeper shrugged. "I've heard tales of the Pallid for a good many years. Towns and villages wiped out but their valuables left." He looked troubled but not disbelieving. "I've heard too many stories from too many people I know to be trustworthy to discount them all."

Despite the bleak situation, Venaro laughed. "If only the people in charge were as smart as you, my friend."

Jorun's answering chuckle was a rude thing. "I'm not rich enough to be in charge." He said with a wink. "Are you sure that these things are coming to Wend?" He asked flatly.

Venaro nodded. "I am quite sure."

"I assume you tried to warn our great moron of a mayor?" Jorun asked acidly. When Venaro nodded again in reply, the innkeeper snorted. "And he wouldn't listen, I take it?" Again, the merchant only nodded. "Well, I suppose I can warn folks as best I can. Mayhap I can get some of those on the guard ready, though that fool Fendrel won't listen any more than mayor Edber."

Venaro's voice was urgent as he spoke then. "You need to get ready to fight and warn as many as you can." Now it was Jorun's turn to nod. "The Dregs have to be cut to pieces and then burned to destroy them completely."

The old man didn't even blink at the instruction. He mused aloud, "I'll have to be careful, so as not to cause a panic Venaro."

The merchant agreed and realized that Jorun was warning him

not to cause a panic himself. "I'm done trying to make people listen, my friend." His voice was wry. "I probably should have come to you first."

Jorun shook his head. "I doubt most of 'em will listen to me either."

Both men knew the truth of that statement. Venaro smiled. "Should I settle my tab up now?"

Though Jorun's expression didn't change, his tone was ironic. "I reckon if we both survive what's coming, you can pay me then." His voice grew quieter. "If not...I suppose it don't really matter much."

"I suppose you're right." Venaro allowed. The merchant moved toward the door then. He had to get the others together. He hoped that the priest had a plan, although he could not, for the life of him, imagine what plan might help them all. He was stopped short by Jorun then.

"What of the Pallid?" The old man asked, his face pale. "Do you know how to stop them?"

Venaro's only response was a slow shake of his head. Finally he said, "I'll want some food and drinks in here, Jorun."

With a start, the old innkeeper nodded. "Right then!" He said briskly. They were both businessmen and while they were still alive, there was coin to be made and business to be done.

CHAPTER TWENTY-ONE

Sensations building and pouring over Null nearly made him stumble. It was very nearly sensory overload and the newly remade stopped and shook his head. He could sense and almost taste an overwhelming amount of emotions, feelings and moods to the south. He suddenly realized something that he hadn't noticed before; he was hungry. Like a starving man presented with a buffet, his mouth hung open, though he realized that he could no longer salivate. Null had no idea how long he stood there before the others noticed.

"Hungry?" Kast asked cavalierly. His expression had changed, Null noted. The cynical smile still remained but there was something…ravenous…there now as well.

Nodding dumbly, Null could think of nothing to say. He stared south, yearning for several moments. Then, he began to stumble that direction. Before he knew it, he was running, nearly flying as his feet spurned the earth. His appetite was all consuming in that moment.

He felt a powerful pulse of will and nearly turned. Ignoring it, he continued on his headlong flight. He'd never been so hungry in all his mortal life. Null now knew that this was real hunger, something almost alive within him. Not a craving of the stomach and the body, which were temporal and as fleeting as the mortal that he'd been. No, this was the hunger of an immortal, a dark god come stalking out of the night to prey on…

Null lost his footing and went flying through the air. For a moment, he didn't realize what had happened and then he slammed into the side of a tree. He expected agony but recognized that while such things could damage his body, he no longer felt pain like he once had. Looking up, he saw Fina standing there, looking as elegant as ever and then he realized that she must have caught up to him and knocked him aside. The fact that she had moved so quickly and was so powerful she could effortlessly manhandle him made him angry. However, this was nothing compared to the rage that bloomed in him when he thought she was trying to stop him from feeding. Something animalistic came snarling to the forefront of his being, banishing all rational thought. Baring his teeth, a guttural sound came from within Null as he leapt at Fina.

Suddenly, he found himself snatched out of the air and in Fina's grasp. The movement was so deft and strong that it was like a child catching a slow falling leaf as it fell. She then slammed him on the ground and that impact was much harder than when he'd hit the tree. If he'd had breath, it would surely have been knocked from him. As it was, Null realized that he could still feel pain. He could feel his very bones, hardened as they now were with the changes, creaking from the impact. His skin and flesh, much tougher than leather, had torn in places where he'd been driven into the rough ground. The back of his head had formed a small crater where it had hit and he knew if he'd still been a mortal man, he would be dead, his skull broken open and his brains spilled on the earth.

"Stop." Fina said simply. Her voice was as calm and sweet as ever, and there was no trace of anger as she looked at him. She held him with a hand on his throat as if he were a babe in arms.

For a few moments, Null struggled and growled like a beast. It was maddening. "I...am...*hungry!*" He flailed his limps and tried to move his head but it was all to no avail. He was stronger than he'd ever dreamed but he now saw how much more powerful she was than he.

"I know." She said and there was the faintest hint of

compassion there, he would have sworn. "We have all been there at the beginning. Now you start to realize that the hunger is a constant companion."

Kast had reached them and he noted, "We're far ahead of the Dregs." Fina looked back the way they'd came and eased her grip, allowing Null to look as well. They were several hundred yards ahead of the milling mass of the misshapen creatures.

"This won't do." Fina murmured. "We're very close and must keep a tight rein on them." She looked at Kast, who nodded in agreement. "If they spot meat, they'll be after it and we'll have to fight to restore control."

Kast's sardonic smile was turned on Null now. "They'd all charge off after a rabbit at this point." He looked back at the Dregs, who were starting to slow their pace. "Their hunger is greater than ours, though it is for flesh."

"Go back and get them moving again." Fina ordered. With a mocking bow, Kast whirled to go and do as he had been bidden. Looking down at Null, she spoke and there was a threat in her voice. "We are too close for this. You are newly remade but there is no time to teach you everything. Are you listening to me?" She asked it pleasantly but her grip tightened on his throat and he realized that Fina could literally tear his head from his shoulders if she so chose.

Nodding fractionally, as much as she was allowing him, Null squeaked, "Yes…" He tried to say more but couldn't. It was strange, for he knew he had no need to breathe but somehow, his new body required air to push through so he could speak just as it had when he was a living man. There were many mysteries to this new form but at the moment, survival was paramount for he could taste Fina's displeasure and her will. She would destroy him if he did not obey.

She smiled suddenly then, her teeth unnaturally white in the fading moon. Fina sensed that he understood. If he'd been a more mature Pallid, she would have left it at that but he was at the stage where words were still vital. "The town lies only a few leagues ahead now. We will arrive in the dead of night as I have planned and there is no time for your childish display." She loosened her grip fractionally. "I will let you up but do *not* test me further." Her actions followed suit and she released the fledgling Pallid.

Null struggled up from the ground. He did not cough or wheeze as a living man would have but he could feel every injury to his body. He did not wince as the pain was a minor thing, similar to a bruise that a mortal notices but shrugs off without complaint. Wisely, he bowed before her then. The shabby Pallid who had been Malken understood strength and even now there was an order. He knew this instinctively but swore that one day, *he* would rise above such as she and *he* would be in control!

"Caution and ambition." Fina noted. "You'll rise high and become powerful as your desire so plainly states." Then she added, "*IF*, you are not destroyed before you can mature." Fina pointed to the south. "Wend is close now and I cannot allow you to alert them that we are here before we are ready to attack." She then pointed back at the Dregs. "We must get them into position and let them see the town and the humans within. Their hunger will grow and we will hold them with our will until it is great. Only then do we release them upon the town." She looked at him then, her eyes piercing. "Do you understand?"

Nodding briskly, he answered. "Yes." Instinctively, as a man who suppresses his appetite, Null tamped down his lust for the things he sensed to the south. It was, perhaps easier for him than some. He'd grown up poor and knew what it was to go hungry. Then, he looked at Fina once more and opened his intentions to her. It was something that humans would not understand but the Pallid could sense emotions and will as surely as a mortal could read them from someone's face.

She smiled at him then. "You are a quick learner, Null." Fina sensed his hunger and ambition but also his pleasure. More than anything, the shabby creature that had been Malken desired to be equal with them. "It will come with time." She promised. "But you must take caution. You can be destroyed. There will be men upon those walls."

The thought of such men fighting against such as them seemed laughable to Null. They were mortals, cattle. How could they hope to stand against the dark majesty of the Pallid and their servants?

As clearly as if she'd read his mind, Fina divined the swirling mass of his emotions. "We are few, though our Dregs are many." She warned him. "They are our prey but if they stand united, they can be more difficult to take down. They can cut us apart and burn us with fire. They can stake us out in the sun until we are seared to oblivion by its hateful rays.

"But we can walk in the daylight!" Null said in surprise.

Looking back at the Dregs that were finally moving again, Fina replied. "Yes…we can move in the daylight but have you not noticed how difficult it can be?"

After thinking for a moment, Null nodded. He'd noticed how weary his body became when they moved through the day, how addled and sluggish his mind. "But, the sun can…kill…us?"

Fina was still watching the Dregs pensively. "Ordinarily no." She glanced back at him then, her expression and sentiment serious. "However, if we are staked out and our bodies cut open to let the sun burn us, we are burned from the inside out." Her revulsion for such a fate was clear and Null sensed that she had seen such a thing.

"You…you've seen it happen?" He asked, dread in his voice. He hadn't known that he could feel such an emotion but the thought of losing his new immortality to something like that was more than he could bear to think of.

"I have seen the aftermath." She said dolefully. "A Pallid staked with iron and cut open to the bone." Her tone grew instructional, even as she spoke of such a thing. "Our very blood, which ceases to flow, will burn and race through our bodies. Our organs, no longer used and inert as stones explode." Fina shook her head and turned to watch the progress of the Dregs. "Our skin cracks and sears as our flesh roasts. There is little left afterwards."

Null was horrified at the thought of such an end. "But how…who would even know how?"

"There are those who know how to slay our kind." Fina admitted. "Although, as we are no longer mortals, perhaps that is the wrong word. Nonetheless, certain mortals long ago learned our few weaknesses." She smiled at him then. "But their numbers are few and they have dwindled while we've grown strong. Humans are weak and greedy. Most of them would rather count coin and pursue their lusts rather than learn how to fight against us." Now there was a dark humor in her. "We have been careful for centuries, always cautious in our hunting, never gathering in numbers. Meanwhile, they've killed each other and grown weak and lazy in the aftermath. Now is our time." Her eyes glowed with pleasure. "Now we do not only hunt, we conquer!"

He was caught up in the fervor of her words and unveiled intent now. Looking at the hundreds of Dregs that followed them, Null felt flush with pride and power.

"Yet, we must be wise." Fina said then. "As we add to our numbers such hardy souls as yours that can endure the remaking and add to the numbers of Dregs as well, we must destroy all in our path." He looked at her and nodded. "When we attack, the Dregs will sweep through the town, killing and devouring all they see. We may feed on the fear and confusion but we must also continue to direct them. If we lose focus, resistance may form and the humans might turn the tide."

Disbelief radiated from Null. He was from Wend and he knew the people. There were a few that might stand and fight but most would simply run. He smiled unknowingly at the thought of them fleeing like squealing pigs only to be devoured by things out of nightmare. The fact that he was now one of those nightmares pleased him immensely.

Fina spoke again. "Even hunters and conquerors must take care that they themselves do not become prey, defeated by the blind notion that they are invincible." She put a hand on Null's shoulder and let her will flow through the contact. "You will have your revenge and you will feast on their sorrows." Her dominion over him was strong and he bowed before her again. "But you must heed my command."

Null swore that he would do so and let his intention to obey show. Yet deep in his heart, he knew he was going to pay a visit to certain individuals no matter what she demanded of him. He tried hard to cloak this and wasn't sure if it worked.

Turning away from him, Fina walked up a nearby hill, beckoning for him to follow. He did so as the Dregs, led by Kast came near to the base of the hill. Looking out over the vista beyond the hills and stunted trees, they could see scrubland and farmland and there, in the distance, twinkling lights.

They were nearly there.

"The time for dissembling is over." Venaro said, his voice grim. "We've all agreed to this course of action and we need to know exactly what your plan is, priest."

The others nodded in assent as they all looked to Cenric. Venaro, Bandur and Tanoc were seated around the table in the private room Jorun had rented them at the Crooked King. The debris of food and drink littered the table and they'd all talked quietly as they ate and drank, sharing what they'd done and learned. Venaro had told them of his visit with Whisper, while Bandur had explained how things had gone with the captain of the guard, his face bleak. Tanoc said nothing, devouring a whole chicken with gusto. The merchant had noticed that for once, the barbarian drank no ale and very little wine.

The priest looked thoughtful. "So the town guards know?"

"I told you, that fool captain wouldn't hear me!" Bandur replied heatedly.

"Yes, but they know." Cenric insisted. "You said that you told your friend Hedolf and you believe he'll tell others and ready them."

Helplessly, Bandur looked at the ceiling. "Yes, that is what I said." He replied, mimicking the cleric's tone. "But it won't be enough. Hedolf isn't the captain and he can't order them to do anything."

"It doesn't matter." The priest said, with a shake of his head. "He'll tell them and they'll have it in their mind. Is he smart enough to tell those he trusts first?" The ex-soldier looked at him grimly, as if trying to determine whether the cleric was insulting him, his friend or both. Finally, he nodded. "Good." Cenric said, seemingly satisfied. "That will have to do."

Venaro interjected. "How will that make any difference?" He could see Bandur's point. "This Hedolf won't be able to command his fellow guardsman to prepare or put more men on the walls."

Cenric explained patiently. "They'll be at least *thinking* about what Bandur has told them." Seeing their flat stares, he went on. "Look, what you must understand is that the Dregs are loud and clumsy. They cannot infiltrate the town." Their expressions showed that they remembered the Dregs better than they cared to. "At times, if there are enough Pallid, they themselves might do something like sneaking in and opening the gates but often, they have their hands full with directing the Dregs. At least until the creatures have a target."

"What if there are enough Pallid to do just that?" Bandur demanded, his voice somewhat hostile but the others could tell it was bluster. The man was fighting his fear, just as they all were.

Cenric shrugged. "I don't believe that there are."

Looking at the others, Bandur asked mockingly, "Can you believe that?" He raised his hands helplessly, his voice growing louder. "He doesn't believe there are!" He pointed accusingly at the priest. "Listen, you, we've seen these things up close!"

"As have I." Cenric replied mildly. The response quieted Bandur and the others stared at the cleric. He returned their regard for some time before speaking again. "We cannot afford to let our fear master us." His voice was tranquil and clear. "There will be plenty of people who let their terror control them, including many of the town guard, I'm quite sure. We must be steady."

"You still haven't answered Venaro." A sultry voice said from the window. They all spun to see that the shutters which had been shut and fastened from the inside had been opened and a woman leaned at the window. It had been accomplished so stealthily that they hadn't heard the slightest creak.

"Gentlemen," Venaro said drily, "Meet Whisper."

As the dark clad woman lithely leapt through the open window, the others had varying reactions. Bandur was instantly on edge, his hand creeping toward his sword hilt. Venaro smiled broadly, obviously happy to see her, while Cenric's expression was neutral, though he said hello. Meanwhile, Tanoc looked her up and down appraisingly, his smile even wider than the merchants, though for completely different reasons.

Standing before them, noting their reactions, yet ignoring them, Whisper was statuesque as she returned their regard. Finally, she quipped, "Is there anything left to drink?"

Still smiling, Venaro rose and pulled a chair out next to him for her as though she were a highborn lady. Then, he poured her a cup of wine. "Please, join us." He said.

The woman removed her cloak and tossed it over the back of the chair, ignoring the looks from the others. Bandur goggled at the number of weapons on the woman as he frowned at how close she was to his employer, while Tanoc continued his frank admiration. Cenric's expression never changed, even when she arched an eyebrow from over the rim of the cup and said, "You were going to explain this plan of yours, I believe?"

"So I was." Cenric replied. "It is actually quite simple but it requires a measure of faith from each of you."

Bandur looked from the woman to the priest in disbelief. "Is he serious?"

"I don't think any of us are true believers, priest." Venaro replied, his voice even.

Tanoc half turned and shook his head, while Whisper took a sip of the wine and said nothing. Her expression was flat as she looked at the cleric.

"Perhaps," The merchant began, his voice on edge, "You'd best tell us exactly what you have in mind."

Cenric smiled then. "Very well." None of them returned his smile and that actually gladdened him. He didn't believe in lying to people or setting them up. "We will not stand atop the walls with the defenders of Wend."

Bandur's eyes grew wide. "Then what the hell are we doing here?!"

"As you said earlier," The priest went on reminding Bandur of his report after speaking with Captain Fendrel, "The captain of the guard wouldn't listen and both Venaro and I can assure you that the mayor was no more tractable." Seeing that neither Tanoc nor Bandur knew the word, Cenric smoothly explained. "Willing to heed and act upon what we told him."

"Then what do you propose that we do?" Venaro said, his tone doubtful. "Bandur makes a good point. We stayed to try and save the town…"

"And save it we will." Cenric calmly interjected. "At least, if all goes according to plan."

"Then what *is* the plan?" Bandur asked tersely.

Cenric's brow furrowed angrily and he barked, "I will explain if you'll allow me to do so without further interruption!" It was times like this that he felt more a soldier than a priest.

Before Bandur could say anymore and precipitate further argument, Venaro held up a hand before his employee. "Please." He said in even tones. "Continue."

"Right then." The priest said, mollified. "What you must understand is that the Pallid and their minions will almost certainly breach the walls and overrun the town." He said it calmly but they all looked horrified, even the barbarian, though his expression was tinged with resignation. "What we must do is focus on saving what lives we can." He waited and seeing that there would be no further interruptions, continued. "There is a reliquary hidden beneath an abandoned temple, a blessed vessel of the gods. With it, I can hold the dark powers of the Pallid at bay and we can offer sanctuary to any who can flee there."

The priest paused, letting them take it all in. When he refrained from speaking and the merchant saw he was inviting comment, he spoke. "You're saying that a lot of people are going to die and we cannot stop it."

Nodding, Cenric's expression was sad. "That is correct." His voice wasn't quite pleading but it was close. "Believe me, I wish it were not so. If the mayor or the captain of the guard would have listened then perhaps it could have been different." His voice grew hard then. "However, they have made this choice and the unfortunate inhabitants of Wend must pay the price along with them."

Venaro nodded bleakly, knowing it was true. "What must we do?"

"We must defend the reliquary." Cenric replied. "I have prayed before it and the gods answered. The Pallid will feel its power and will seek to destroy it."

"If they can just walk up and destroy it, what use is it then?" Bandur asked dully.

Cenric leaned forward, his hands clasped. "Such reliquaries can keep evil things at bay and the Dregs will not willingly approach. The Pallid are stronger willed and though it will be painful to them, will push through and attack, likely along with whatever of their Dreg servants they can force to follow." He sighed then. "I will admit that it is no sure thing. It will mean that we'll have to hold out against them but my hope is that if we can do so, they'll give up and satisfy themselves with the remainder of those within the town."

Tanoc growled then, his deep voice surprising them all. "We just abandon the rest?"

The priest slowly nodded his head. "As many as will come will find safety within the grounds of the church if we can keep it clear of the Pallid and their minions." His mouth was downturned as he forced himself to finish his thought. "Anyone who cannot or will not come will almost certainly perish."

"What of the Pallid?" Venaro asked. "We slew the Dregs we encountered, though they weren't easy to stop. Can the Pallid be stopped?"

Cenric exhaled then. "They can be destroyed, though it is no easy task." He rubbed his head then. "I must confess that I have never faced one of them but in the annals of my order are examples and tales of how the Pallid may be defeated."

"Examples?" Bandur exclaimed.

"Tales?" Venaro said at almost the exact same time.

Whisper set her cup down still half full. "This sounds like suicide, priest." She locked eyes with the man of the cloth. "What do you suppose our chances of success are?"

"If a single Pallid comes to us with a band of Dregs, we may be able to defeat them." Cenric said slowly. "If there is more than one Pallid. Then I do not know..." He admitted this last and they could see it on his face. He doubted that they would survive such odds.

"Wonderful." The former soldier said. Looking at his employer, he shook his head. "Venaro, I don't think the rest of the lads will be up for it."

The merchant nodded. "You're right." He looked at Bandur seriously. "That's why they won't be there."

"What then?" Bandur said loyally. "Leave them to die with everyone else?"

"No." Venaro answered. Looking at the cleric, he said, "If there were determined points of resistance they could hold out against them, couldn't they?"

With a shrug, Cenric replied. "Perhaps, although they would be much safer at the temple."

"Yes but until we've dealt with whatever opposition gets thrown at us, that won't be any safer than anywhere else in the town."

Venaro argued. "I want the rest of my men to stay right here at the inn and help Jorun and his folk defend it. When we've dealt with the threat to this reliquary, we can send for them." He didn't say what they were all thinking; *IF* they dealt with the threat.

The priest nodded and then said carefully. "It could work but the Pallid will attack strongpoints so we've no guarantee where they'll strike as their creatures ravage the town."

It was enough for Venaro. "We'll tell them to make ready." He said, glancing at Bandur. "Jorun already knows so we'll put them at his disposal."

"How long?" Whisper asked then, her voice as quiet as her namesake. "How long can we hold out against them?"

It was Tanoc who answered then, his voice dull and faraway. "Dawn." He said simply.

As the others looked at the barbarian, Cenric spoke. "He is right." His voice was grim. "The Pallid will not fight on through the day as neither they nor their creatures are fond of the sun. They will leave with their spoils by sunrise." He looked at Tanoc, wondering at all the Northman must have seen happen to his homeland. "We must hold out until the next dawn whatever night they attack for they will surely strike in darkness."

"Spoils?" Bandur asked then. "What use could such monsters have for riches?"

Tanoc murmured, "People." He still would look at none of them. "They take people."

As the others looked at the barbarian with rising horror, Cenric said flatly. "Once their Dregs have consumed what flesh they will, the Pallid will swell their ranks with new Dregs or take survivors along as prisoners and do it elsewhere." His voice was hoarse and he drank from his cup. "Either way, it is a fate worse than death." He stood then and looked at the others. "Whatever happens," he intoned ominously, "I suggest you fight to your last breath."

It was quiet then in the room, each of them thinking gloomy thoughts.

"Should we…" Venaro began but none of the others ever knew what he'd been about to say for he was cut off by the not too distant peal of horns sounding.

"The tower guard has sounded their horns." Cenric said as they all stood in unison. "We are out of time."

CHAPTER TWENTY-TWO

Something moved in the darkness. Umfrey was sure of it. From his vantage atop the wall, he could see a long way off in normal conditions. There was little cover approaching the walls of Wend and that was by design. Now, however, the half-moon above was swathed in clouds and refrained from giving even that much of her light. Moon or no moon, though, the young guardsman was sure he'd seen something.

Looking at the next guard some fifteen feet over on the wall, Umfrey chewed his lip. If it was just an animal or some such, he'd look a fool and that wasn't an idea that he relished. Then again, if it was orcs or bandits or the like, he'd look more the fool if it came out that he'd seen something and kept quiet. Still, as he looked back out into the blackness, he felt a chill that had nothing to do with the crisp nighttime air. The chill ran up his spine and for some reason that he could not explain, he felt afraid.

Again, he looked over at the guard to his right, the closest man on the wall. He thought the man's name was Nigel or something. Umfrey wasn't wild about speaking with the man as he'd never been overly friendly. Looking at him now, the lad had a sinking suspicion that he was asleep. The brazier of coals between them didn't give off enough light to be certain but he was fairly certain. Something about the way the man hadn't moved much. He just stood there, wrapped

in his cloak, leaning on the wall. Umfrey's eyes narrowed as he
focused and he realized that the man was actually half sitting and his
cloak was pulled so far forward his face was barely visible. Then a
faint snore made him realize the other man was sleeping!

It was outrageous, of course, sleeping at your post of duty, atop
the very wall above the gates no less! Umfrey was of a mind to
report the other man but he was torn. Nigel was a drinking
companion and favorite of the captain and they'd known each other a
long time. Most of his superiors would side with the sleeping man
and most likely, it would be Umfrey who was punished. For the
thousandth time, he cursed himself for a fool for ever joining the
guard.

As Umfrey was dividing his attention between the darkness
beyond the wall and the sleeping guard, he didn't hear someone come
up the stairs behind him. The dark form was almost on top of him
before he heard the scrape of a boot that made him whirl, his heart in
his chest!

"Easy, lad." A firm, raspy voice said. "Don't skewer me with
that spear now."

"Oso!" Umfrey said, recognizing the voice. "I...I'm sorry..."
He didn't really know what to say. He'd leveled his spear without
thinking and he raised it again now. The older guard had always been
a tough man but he was, in the youth's humble opinion one of the
best the town had.

Stepping closer, Oso smiled to show there'd been no harm done.
"It's alright." Glancing around, he grimaced. "Nigel's fallen asleep
again?" Umfrey didn't answer but shuffled his feet. Oso shook his
head in disgust. "This never would have happened when I was
young in the guard." Looking at Umfrey, he growled, "We had a
proper captain back then."

Looking over at the dozing Nigel, Umfrey murmured. "What if
he's not really asleep?" The nervous youth lowered his voice even
further. "What if he tells the captain?"

"Tells him what?!" Oso snorted, his mustaches blowing like

curtains. "That I caught him sleepin' on duty and complained about the state of things?" His voice was rising rather than lowering. "It's shameful!" He looked at the sleeping Nigel, again. "He's probably drunk too! I ought to throw him over the wall!"

Fidgeting uncomfortably, Umfrey didn't say anything for a moment. He didn't really think Oso would do such a thing but the old soldier had a black temper at times and he was unpredictable to say the least. One time, he'd seen Oso knock another guards front teeth out when the man had commented about a girl who happened to be his niece.

"What's wrong with you?" Oso asked perceptively. "You're fidgeting like a whore in a temple." Umfrey automatically looked back out into the darkness and Oso followed his gaze. "You see somethin'?"

"No...I don't...I'm not sure." Umfrey stammered a bit hating the way it sounded. "I thought...I guess I just thought I saw something."

Stepping close, the older guard followed the younger man's gaze. "If you *think* you saw somethin', you might have actually seen it, lad." Oso replied not unkindly. Tugging at a corner of his long mustache, he asked, "Where did you think you saw it?"

"I thought..." Umfrey said, his eyes straining as he looked out into the dark. "It looked like something was moving by the hill up there." He pointed now. "Right where the road crests the top of the hill."

"Right where we were supposed to have that guard tower built a couple years ago." Oso observed. He might take the mayor's coin but that man could be a complete fool. The town had no outlying positions for guards to take. They couldn't see anything until they were right on top of them. The mayor pointed to the fact that they'd repelled orcs and mercenaries who had tried to sack the town but Oso knew the truth; those were small bands and not a determined force. "What did you think you saw?"

Umfrey didn't answer right away. "I'm not...sure." He said

reluctantly. "It must have been my eyes playing tricks on me." Oso turned to look at him, his eyes sharp. "Well…I thought…it was just a shape, really."

"A shape?" Oso echoed doubtfully.

The younger guardsman nodded. "At first I thought it was a man standing there but then the clouds move a little and I don't know, Oso, I swear it looked like he had too many legs." Umfrey shrugged then. "I blinked and it wasn't there." Looking sidelong at the older guard, he stopped talking. Oso had gone pale and stopped playing with his mustache, which was never a good sign. In the dim light of the brazier, Umfrey could see the man's jaw bunch.

"Too many legs?" Oso said and grabbed the younger man by the tunic. "Are you sure?!"

Umfrey exclaimed, "Hey!" He grabbed Oso's arms but the man wouldn't let go. "No, I told you I think I imagined it!"

Nearby, the drowsing Nigel had finally roused. "What are you two on about?!" He snapped crossly.

Oso started to turn, now thinking very seriously about throwing the idiot from the wall. It was at that exact moment that the clouds covering the moon parted and in the light of that baleful half-moon, he saw something that made his bowels loosen. There were figures out there just beyond the range of the torches and lanterns on the wall. Misshapen things that looked wrong even at this distance. "*Dregs!*" He breathed in dread.

"What's that?" Nigel said, standing up from his comfortable perch in the wall's crenellation. "You been talking to that daft Hedolf haven't you? I heard he was friends with that stranger who showed up in the captain's office." He was cross from having his nap disturbed as well as from the hangover he'd had from the night before. "Do you know he brought a northern savage here into Wend with him? Can you believe it? No good will come of it I tell you, we should run the lot of them right out of town!" He realized then that the other guards weren't paying attention to him, standing stock still and staring out into the night like they were touched in the head.

Walking toward them, Nigel was determined to give them both a piece of his mind. "Listen here, Oso..." He began but stopped when the other man moved.

Taking three quick steps, Oso reached Nigel and grabbing his shoulder, forcefully spun him around. "Look!" He snapped, pointing.

Before the other man could protest he saw the grotesque figures milling about. "By the gods!" Nigel breathed, his brain not believing what his eyes could see.

"There must be hundreds of them!" Umfrey said, his voice starting to rise in panic. Like Nigel, he'd heard that old Hedolf had been meeting with some of the guards, Oso included but he hadn't heard about what.

Oso's voice was grim. "Close to a thousand, I'd wager." Wasting no time, he grabbed the young guard by the arm. "Get to the tower and have them sound the horns."

Despite the situation, Umfrey was shocked and he hesitated. "The horns haven't been sounded in..."

His voice a growl, Oso shook the younger man. "Do you see *that*?!" As he said it, he pointed down at the twisted creatures. Without another word, he shoved Umfrey toward the tower some hundred paces down the wall and the lad took off, running hard.

"This can't be." Nigel said in disbelief.

Gritting his teeth, Oso replied. "They tried to warn us."

"Who?" Nigel asked, dumbfounded. "That fool and the savage? Old Hedolf?"

"All of them you idiot!" Oso said, his rage deepening. He knew the truth of it and shame and anger boiled in him. Greed ran the town of Wend. No one had wanted to hear warnings from strangers, even when one of their own had vouched for them. He could hear Hedolf's words ringing in his ears as the man had said his old friend was trustworthy. Even then, he hadn't wanted to hear it and had nodded and smiled. "We're the fools Nigel." He grated.

"What...what should we do?" The other man said fearfully.

Oso looked over at the guard, sensing his panic. "We fight." He said simply. "Luckily we're not all fools." He was thinking of Hedolf now and was thankful that they'd humored him to some extent. "Hedolf had us bring wood and oil into the towers. We didn't get that much but it'll be a start." Seeing Nigel's uncertain look, Oso smiled grimly. "He said they'd burn just fine."

Nigel looked ill and said nothing and for a time they just stood their positions at the wall. Then, after what seemed an age but was only a few minutes, the horns at the tower sounded. Oso's smile deepened. They'd be ready at least.

"They've seen us." Kast noted sardonically as horns sounded from the walls.

Fina didn't look over but her calm radiated in waves. "Of course they did." Her expression and manner were content. "The Dregs aren't made for stealth." Her ironic statement actually made the other Pallid chuckle.

Null was troubled, despite it all. It wasn't exactly fear but now that he knew he wasn't truly invincible, he was worried. "They'll be ready for us." He murmured. When Fina simply nodded, he tried to mask the frustration from his voice and feelings, knowing that he was failing even as he tried. "Shouldn't we attack now, before they're completely prepared?"

With a patient mother's tone, Fina explained. "As I told you before, we will keep the Dreg's leashed, their hunger growing." She looked at the walls contemptuously. "Let them gather all their warriors to the ramparts. It will not save them." Her voice was cold as she watched the men scrambling along the walls.

Not able to help himself, Null pressed. "How does it help us for them all to be on the walls?" He simply couldn't understand it. "Would it not be better for us to fight them in smaller groups?"

"We have nearly a thousand Dregs now." Kast said scornfully. "If they had every citizen in that town manning the walls, they cannot stop us." There was strain in his voice and in his sense. For a moment, Null didn't understand but as he pushed his senses, he realized that both of the other Pallid were having to fight to restrain the hungry Dregs. The creatures were grunting and hooting, salivating at the distant figures they saw on the walls. A newly remade such as Null could never have held even a single Dreg from its prey like this and he knew grudging respect for Fina and Kast, then.

Fina didn't look at him as she spoke. "We want them to gather on those walls." Now beginning to understand, Null nodded as she continued. "It allows the Dregs to have more targets before them. Once we release them, they will stampede forward and nothing will stop them." Despite the effort of holding the Dregs in check, a pretty smile curled the edges of her mouth. "They'll climb those walls and most of the guards will be dead before the rest of the town knows what is happening."

"Then the real fun begins." Kast said hungrily.

Null understood him perfectly. Even now, he could sense the confusion and terror from the men gathering on the walls in answer to the horns. It was intoxicating and he struggled not to lose control.

"This is not a battle." Fina's words caught his attention and he looked at her again. "We do not make war here. We are harvesting this place." They could all feel the Dregs hunger and lust for flesh mounting. Even Null with his senses, dull in comparison to the others, could now feel their blind hunger collectively. "Now, to the reaping."

As she said this last, Fina released her control upon the Dregs. Completely in sync with her, Kast let go only a second later. With the tether of their Pallid masters gone, the collective horde of Dreg's shuddered with anticipation and blood lust. The combined roar of bestial triumph and hunger seemed to shake the earth.

As one, the Dregs lurched forward to the feeding.

All over the sleepy town of Wend, people began to wake to the sound of the horns blowing in warning. They heard a strange sound like the bellowing of a titanic beast large such as had only walked the earth in legend. Then…the distant clash of combat followed by the terrible screams of dying men.

Mayor Edber came awake slowly, unsure what had woken him. He lay there in the darkness for several heartbeats and then he heard a distant sound. Struggling up out of the warmth of layers of blankets, he thought he heard a winding horn. Slowly, it dawned on his sleep addled mind that the warning horns of the tower had been sounded. Irritation coursed through him, then. Those fools had no doubt spotted a band of orcs or mercenaries and panicked!

Throwing the covers back, Edber cursed the cold and stood. Fumbling for a moment, he found his slippers and robe. Across the room, the fire was dying and before he did anything else, he shuffled over and put a chunk of wood on the fire. Warming his hands, he thought of how he and Fendrel were going to have a long talk. The very idea of his sleep being disturbed this way!

A knock at the door startled the mayor. A voice that he recognized as belonging to one of his guards spoke. "Sir?" There was some hesitancy but the voice was insistent. "Mayor, are you awake?"

"Yes, I'm awake!" The mayor snapped. "Come in!" Edber never kept his door locked, as he'd never seen the need when he had guards who lived in his home. These men were loyal to him and were a tough lot.

The man who entered was a stout warrior in boiled leather armor, a sword on his belt. "Sir, the horns have sounded." The guard said. He looked wide awake, as his was the night shift.

The mayor struggled and failed to remember the man's name. "I can hear them!" He said crossly. "Why do you think I'm up?!" The guard didn't say anything but stared at the town's leader. It made Edber all the angrier. "Wake the others." He said, forcing calmness into his voice.

"Sir, should we go to the wall?" The nameless guard asked.

"Of all the impudent…" The mayor spluttered in outrage. "Do not presume to think you know what is best! *I* am the mayor!"

The guard wasn't cowed. "It's just that if we're under attack sir…"

The mayor rudely interrupted the other man. "Nonsense!" His tone and manner showed how preposterous such a notion was. "It's orcs or brigands who have tried to sneak in or fired a few arrows at the walls. It's happened before, you know."

"Yes, sir." The guard said doubtfully. "But they wouldn't sound the horn for something like that."

Nodding so hard, his jowls quivered, the mayor answered. "Quite right!" He was annoyed by the cheek of this guard and vowed to fire him in the morning. Still, he'd been paid to do a job and he might as well have the man get on with it. "After you wake the others, you go to the wall and find out from Captain Fendrel what's going on." Then he added with a sniff, "Since you're so concerned."

The guard, whose name the mayor couldn't remember left the room when his employer turned away without another word. Edber looked back at the door with a venomous glare when it shut. '*The insolence of that man!*' He thought. '*I'm going to dock his pay for his unprofessional manner!*' The thought warmed the mayor more than the fire did.

As the Dregs surged forward, the horrified guards were numb with terror. They stood and watched them shambling on for several moments, doubting what they were seeing. Spears and bows were held in slack hands as each man fought rising fear. Then, a voice roared from atop the walls.

"*You spineless cowards! Loose those arrows! Get those spears up!*" It was Hedolf who was bellowing at them as he stalked among the lines.

One of the guards turned to look at the old soldier. "Where's the captain?" Then his voice turned accusing. "You're not in charge here, Hedolf! I…"

The man's voice was cut off as Hedolf struck him a backhand that nearly knocked him from the wall. The steel in his voice was shocking to those guards nearby. They'd all known of his time as a soldier but he'd never acted like this.

Grabbing the guard, who'd fallen back against the wall, Hedolf jerked him upright. "Here!" He snarled, shoving the man's spear back into his hands. "You dropped something!"

Dabbing at the blood that was leaking from his nose, the guardsman started to mumble, "You can't…" but was interrupted again.

Hedolf spun the protesting man around and pointed at the oncoming horrors. "*SHOOT THEM!*" Looking at all the other guards he roared at the top of his lungs. "*FIGHT, YOU SONS OF WHORES!!!*"

It was hardly a stirring speech and some of the men glowered but the veterans and real fighters among their ranks nodded and started getting the others in line. Hedolf had no rank but the fact was they knew the voice of command when they heard it and the captain was nowhere in sight.

One of the guards took a half step toward Hedolf and the archer he'd just shamed, his fists bunched. "He can't do that!" He said in an ugly voice. "That's a friend of mine!" Before he could go any further, a hand on his shoulder turned him back around.

"I don't think so, lad." Oso said calmly. "The enemy's out there." He said, gesturing out over the wall, as Hedolf had done. The young guard was bigger than him but soft looking, Oso thought his name was Dulwen. "We've got a job to do."

His eyes glanced the direction the older guard was pointing but danced away, not willing to focus on the onrushing horror. "I'm going to find the captain!" Dulwen said defiantly.

"You're going to do your job and man this wall." Oso said, his voice thick with menace. "Or I'll gut you where you stand." He didn't shout or bellow as Hedolf had done with the archer but his hand strayed to the sword at his belt. The move was that of a veteran as they were too close for the spears that both men now held.

Dulwen glared at the mustached guard, his face flushing. He was bigger and maybe stronger than the older man. Still, he knew that Oso had fought in real battle before and he'd seen him in action a time or two. There was something in the other man's tone that told him that Oso was not bluffing.

Seeing that Dulwen wasn't saying anything, Oso stepped back. He was no fool and didn't turn his back on the angry young guardsman but he doubted the big idiot had the guts. Then it didn't matter as the Dregs reached the wall.

The archers had been shooting and many arrows had found their mark but not one of the monsters fell. They ignored wounds that would have killed a man outright and weren't even slowed by them. The guards' faces blanched in horror and more than one thought of fleeing.

"*USE THE STONES AND OIL!*" Hedolf's voice rang across the battlements. Some of the guards leapt to grab the large stones that had been readied while others went for the buckets of heated oil and pitch. They hurled both over the walls and here and there along the walls, many of the monsters were hit.

Near Oso's position an abomination with several arms and the head of an old woman was crushed by a large stone. Further along the wall, a thin creature with the head of a hulking orc was doused with oil. Umfrey was there and threw a lighted torch down on the nightmarish thing and it began to blaze. Horribly, it continued its climb for several more feet before falling away, too damaged to continue.

"Good job lad!" Oso shouted in encouragement. Looking over the wall, though, he saw the stark truth; they weren't prepared for this. They hadn't really heeded Hedolf's warning and didn't have nearly the stones or pitch needed to keep the creatures from the walls. Their arrows were useless and more and more of the creatures were climbing up now. The monsters weren't even trying to get through the gates but were all scaling the wall, at times over the fallen bodies of their own.

Dulwen's voice was terrified. "It's not working!" He shook with fear and dropped his spear. "They're still coming!"

"Pick that up!" Oso barked but loathe as he was to admit it, he knew the oaf was right. The hideous things would soon be atop the wall. Here and there, some were brought down by heavy rocks, while others fell, wreathed in fire. But it wasn't enough. Hearing movement, the veteran turned to see Dulwen turn and run. "Get back here!" He shouted but it was too late. The pudgy guard was already too far away and nearing the stairs. Oso let him go. His kind were always the first to run. Loud and brash and soft. Gripping his spear tight, he looked down the wall where Umfrey stood at the ready with his weapon and smiled cheerily.

Though the young guardsman couldn't quite make himself return the smile, he saluted smartly. "We'll stop 'em!" He yelled to Oso, proud to stand at the side of such a warrior.

"You're soddin' right we will!" Oso shouted back, thinking *'We have to stop them. We're all there is.'*

As the Dregs reached the top of the walls, the guardsmen of Wend fought fiercely with them. With steel and fire, they strove with the creatures out of nightmare and there were acts of heroism and bravery that day, as well as base cowardice. One thing became increasingly clear to all involved, however; the defenders of the town were too few and not ready for such a foe. All along the north wall of the town, the monsters began to pour over the walls…and men began to die.

CHAPTER TWENTY-THREE

Screams and shouts could be heard in the distance. Strange bellows, like that of beasts mixed with the voices of men. The warning horns still sounded and beneath them, the growing sounds of combat were unmistakable. At the table in the private room of the Crooked King, the five seated there rose almost as one. None of them had a doubt as to what was happening. Even Whisper, who had never seen a Dreg, knew the town was being assaulted by the horrific deathless things. She could see it writ large on the faces of the men around the table.

"We must get to the Temple." The priest said and began gathering his things. As the others did so, he noted. "As I have already made contact with the reliquary, it is possible that the Pallid will sense it."

The barbarian and the ex-soldier were getting their weaponry together and then moved to the door. Venaro asked, "Where are you going?"

Tanoc did not stop and moved through the doorway but Bandur paused and looked back. "Armor." He said simply and then left.

Meanwhile, Whisper had stood and was waiting patiently with her arms folded. She glanced at the merchant and it was clear that she was ready. She'd put her cloak on as Venaro was now doing but otherwise, she was armed and ready.

Turning from the enigmatic woman, Venaro stepped closer to the priest. "I need to do something first."

Cenric looked up in surprise as he shouldered his pack and put his warhammer in the steel loop that held it at his side. "Where?" He said simply.

"I need to warn someone." The merchant said cagily.

"Who?" The cleric asked and then in exasperation noted, "I told you we have no time."

With a bleak chuckle, Whisper's voice was cold as she hissed, "Delia."

With a blank stare, Cenric looked between the two of them. "Who is Delia?"

"An old friend." Venaro said.

At the exact same time, Venaro spoke, Whisper interjected, "A murdering whore." There was venom there that neither man missed.

As the merchant turned to look at the woman, Cenric forestalled an argument between them. "We do not have time for this."

Not turning around, his gaze still on Whisper, Venaro replied. "I have to warn her." His next words were as much for the assassin as they were for the priest. "I will not simply leave her to die."

"Where is this woman?" Cenric asked in resignation. He could tell by tone in the merchant's voice he wasn't going to be able to sway him.

Now Venaro did turn to answer him. "Don't worry. It's not far."

Whisper rolled her eyes but had nothing more to say.

Outside the tumult rose.

Hedolf ducked as a monster with the torso of an orc and the spindly arms of an old woman lurched forward. The things legs were strange and the guardsman realized that it had an ungainly rhythm as it moved because they were from different creatures. One was the bandy leg of an orc, while the other was that of a man. The aforementioned arms looked weak but they were longer than a man's and that was when he realized what made them so long. From the shoulder to below the elbow, they were the arms of an orc but they were melded with a length of scrawny arms from above the elbow. The final effect was a long arm with two distinct elbows facing opposite directions, which allowed the arms to hinge either way, the effect unsettling. The creature flailed the arms back and forth in wide arcing swipes. The gnarled hands ended in what looked like six inch claws, possibly from a large hunting cat. The head of the mountain cat was atop the orc torso and its mouth was open, with its tongue lolling to one side.

The guard took all this information in on a subconscious level as he faced the thing before him. Looking at the abominations lifeless eyes, he felt a terror welling up in him like he'd never known when facing an enemy. The thing should not be. It was like some crazed taxidermists fever dream. Such a creature was an affront to nature and it was beyond reasoning that it could exist. Beyond just existing, it surely should not have been able to move, its melded parts running together like heated candle wax. Yet the horror did exist and it did move and every movement, every twitch was just…wrong. Though a veteran, Hedolf could feel panic clawing at his mind and terror in his chest so great that he thought his heart might burst. Even so, his training came to the fore as he kept his guard up.

Next to Hedolf, another guard leapt forward and drove a spear into the monsters chest. Ignoring the wound, the thing staggered forward and lashed into the man's face, half tearing it off with one of those flailing claws.

As the unfortunate man reeled back, clutching his ruined face, Hedolf threw down his spear and drew his sword. Seeing the creature lunge for the wounded guard, Hedolf brought his blade down on the foul thing's arm, half severing it. The thing made no sound or cry of pain, although a wheezing hiss like that of a cat trying to cough up a hairball issued from its throat.

Thrashing its other grotesque arm around, the hideous thing whirled in an ungainly side step. The monster was fast for all its awkwardness and though Hedolf tried to get out of the way but was caught in the right shoulder. He was glad for his chain mail that blunted the blow but gasped as the needle sharp claws stabbed through the links. The creature's hand clutched the guardsman's shoulder and began to pull him forward.

Desperately, Hedolf switched his sword to his off-hand, since he couldn't swing with his arm in the monster's clutches. The guard swung awkwardly at the monster's arm in a wild downward stroke. The sword connected but it was a glancing cut and the hideous thing dragged him closer to its face. The mountain cat's maw had begun snapping spasmodically and the vile Dreg bit its own lolling tongue off, shearing through it. Clotted blood like thick jelly fell from the wound but did not flow and Hedolf felt rising panic as he realized the thing was going to clamp those gruesome jaws on his head.

Then, another guardsman ran forward, a sword in one hand and a torch in the other. The young man was new to the guard but bravely rushed in, hacking at the creature's side. The Dreg didn't seem to mind the wound but did turn to face this new attacker, giving Hedolf a reprieve. Taking advantage, the older guard again swung his sword down on the arm that held him, this time chopping completely through the spindly thing. As he backpedaled, Hedolf marveled at the toughness of the Dreg's skin and bones, knowing that it should have much easier to sever the limb.

As the ungainly thing spun around, Hedolf shouted, "Burn it!"

The young guardsman thrust the torch at the back of the Dreg's head and the flames seemed to get its attention. It whirled back toward him, which was what Hedolf had been waiting for. He swung his blade in low, hacking at the bowed orc leg, half severing it. The monster toppled like a falling tree and as it fell, the two guardsmen were on it, hacking and slashing. Finally, Hedolf grabbed a bucket of pitch and dumped it on the writhing thing. He stepped back as the young guard burned the creature with his torch.

Breathing heavily, both men backed away from the horrific sight.

"They don't seem to like fire!" Hedolf remarked with grim humor.

"No sir!" The young man replied, his face flushed. "At least..."

Whatever he'd been about to say was cut short as a large, bony fist half again as large as a mans collided with the side of his head, crushing his skull. Even as the two had been talking, more Dregs had crawled up the wall. The thing now before the weary wounded Hedolf looked like normal man, save it only had one arm. However, this arm was that of a large orc, its fingers fused to its hand to it was a mace-like bludgeon.

Wearily, Hedolf brought his sword up, thinking, *'Three of us to bring one down and two of us dead. They're harder to kill and we're outnumbered.'* His next thought was a grim, hopeless one. *'We can't win.'* It was a credit to Hedolf's courage that he stood there, wincing in pain from his injured shoulder.

Captain Fendrel awoke from a stupor, ready to throttle whoever was winding that bloody horn. He'd had too much wine earlier and for a moment was completely flummoxed, not quite knowing where he was. Then, the woman next to him moaned and shifted and he remembered the tryst with the young seamstress and the drunken walk back to her rooms.

As the fog in his mind slowly lifted, Fendrel realized that the horns weren't ceasing. Listening more closely, he also recognized the timing of each blast as the horns were winded. This was the signal that there was an all-out attack on the town! He stood quickly then and cracked his head on the low beam of his paramour's ceiling. Cursing and groaning, he stepped away from her bed. He'd forgotten that the roof sloped down at the edges of the loft where the girl lived.

Stirring, the seamstress, he thought her name was Gerda or Gull or some other ridiculous thing, asked sleepily, "What's wrong?"

Though he'd found her shapely form and pretty face intoxicating earlier this night, the captain was out of sorts and his answer was curt. "It's nothing Gerda, go back to sleep!"

"It's Gwen." The young woman said in a hurt voice.

"Right." Fendrel said absently, casting his eyes frantically about the room, looking for his sword belt. Finally, he spotted it beneath the shift that he'd so recently helped her out of and snatching it up, headed toward the door.

Sitting up, as she finally realized that something was happening, there was unease in her voice. "Where are you going, Fendrel?" The man she had thought so dashing didn't reply as he reached the door. He never even glanced back as he roughly jerked the handle and opened the door. "Are you coming back?"

But he was gone without another word. She never saw him again.

"Can you sense it?" Fina asked as they stood atop the wall overlooking the gate. They had made sure to send an overwhelming number of Dregs here. It hadn't been difficult to get the creatures herded this way as there were so many guards defending the gate. Of course, it hadn't been for the normal, tactical reasons that a conventional force would have used. There were more men atop this section of the wall, which meant more meat for the Dregs. Those Dregs more suited for climbing had clambered up and wiped out the defenders here, losing a few of their own in the process.

Kast grimaced and didn't answer for a moment, his senses not as finely attuned as hers, though he would never admit it. "Yes…" He said slowly then and looked over at her. "What is it?" He had just returned from opening the gates, allowing those Dregs that weren't able to climb well easier access to the town.

Fina hesitated and looked over at Null to see if he too, could feel it but realized that he did not. The fledgling Pallid was overwhelmed with ecstasy as he sampled the flavors of the towns growing panic and terror. She couldn't really fault him. It was intoxicating to her as well and only her experience and strength of will kept her too from overindulging in the growing sensations.

"I am unsure." She finally admitted to Kast, watching as a fresh block of guardsman rushed from their barracks near the gates. The fools had finally realized that the gates were breached and these latecomers had rallied to try and retake it.

Kast had noticed it too and so had the Dregs, who grunted and bayed like hounds sighting their quarry, before rushing forward hungrily. "It feels...strange..." He said, absently watching the oncoming men. "Similar to...the sun at noonday....almost."

Fina nodded. "Yes. It is an unwelcome sensation." Now she was frowning as well. "Almost...Forbidding..." Gazing down to where the large contingent of the town guard was battling the Dregs. Inexorably, the men were being pushed back but she didn't like how long it was taking. "Deal with that." Fina commanded, nodding toward the battle below them.

Drawing his sword, Kast turned to go but hesitated. "And what of that?" He said gesturing toward the distant emanation they had both felt.

"I will decided momentarily." Fina replied in a sweet, mocking voice. "You go and play at swords while I think on it."

He glared at her and flashed his seething anger at being order about so but she met it with her unveiled humor and contempt for his petulance. It was so short an exchange that it was a mere glance but they understood each other perfectly. Such a dialogue between mortals would have taken ten minutes or more of back and forth conversation.

As Kast went to do as he was bidden, Fina looked toward the power that they sensed, her frown deepened. Though she wasn't sure what it was, she knew that she did not like it. Something would have to be done about it.

In the common room of the Crooked King, Jorun and his lads

looked like they were getting ready for a war. An impressive amount of weaponry covered the bar now. It was an eclectic collection, some of the older pieces from older eras and some looking newly forged. There were also a few shields, bows and quivers of arrows. Venaro had always knows that old Jorun never trusted anyone but he was impressed at the man's preparations.

As if to confirm the merchant's suspicions, Jorun rasped, "Can't trust the bloody guard to do anything!" Looking at Venaro, he pointed to the cache and added, "Take yer pick."

"Thank you, my friend but I've got my own weapon." The merchant said and then realized that he had yet to retrieve his sabre. Without another word, Venaro dashed up the stairs to his room. Unlocking it with the key, he crossed the room to the small table where his journal and ledgers were stacked, along with his weapon. The trader hesitated then. He'd hidden a small, locked coffer of coins under the bed and normally would never have left it. He shook his head with a snort and left then, though he did relock the door. *'I'll worry about money if I survive this mess.'*

Back downstairs, he saw that Bandur and Tanoc had rejoined the group. They were both wearing their armor now, the ex-soldier wearing his chainmail shirt and Tanoc his cuirass of leather and bronze. Bandur had retrieved his shield and held it awkwardly in his uninjured hand and his sword was sheathed at his belt. Tanoc too had retrieved the rest of his armaments, including a horned helm of the kind the barbarians favored. The helmet sat on the bar and Venaro mused that the Northman must have plucked it from the wreckage of his ship, though why he'd never worn it before now was a mystery.

Noticing the merchant's regard, Tanoc glanced at the helmet. "It was the first mates." He said in rare explanation. The barbarian was strapping on the rest of his weaponry now. Broadsword and dagger were sheathed at his belt, while his shield was strapped on his back. As the young giant buckled his bracers, he too looked at the helm. He murmured, "Almost didn't take it."

"Why not?" The merchant asked, curious despite everything else.

Tanoc shrugged. "Bad luck to take the helm from a dead man." He said it as if the merchant were a simpleton.

Venaro could not fathom why taking a dead man's helm was bad luck but it was fine to loot everything else. He remembered the matter of fact way the barbarian had pilfered weapons from the debris on the beach. The merchant shook his head, deciding not to ask for further explanation.

Near the entryway of the inn, the priest stood waiting for the group. "We must hurry." He said urgently.

Not far from the cleric, Whisper was leaning against the bar. She said and did nothing beyond watching the preparations with glittering eyes. Venaro was quite sure that she was ready, knowing all too well the weaponry the deadly woman carried with her at all times.

Unlike the merchant, Bandur couldn't seem to let the matter of the helmet drop. He walked over to inspect it with professional curiosity. It was well crafted of good steel with a leather lining. The open faced helm's great horns swept up to sharp tips that were capped with steel as well. "It's a fine helm." The ex-soldier noted, then looked at the barbarian. "You didn't wear it when we fought the orcs or the Dregs, why wear it now?"

Tanoc finished with his bracers and picked up the helm without looking at the caravan guard. Staring at it, he murmured, "It doesn't matter now."

The statement chilled Venaro as he realized the barbarian did not expect to survive the coming conflict. Watching the young Northman grimly place the helm atop his head and strap in on filled him with dread. If the mighty warrior doubted his own chances of survival, what were the rest of theirs? With the helm on and most of his face and head obscured, Tanoc's eyes seemed to flash from within the helm. His voice was hollow as he looked at Jorun and asked, "Where is Lilli?"

Shaking his head, the old man replied sadly. "She's gone home."

There was regret in his voice. "She said she needed to get to her mother and little brother as they've no one else to look after them."

Tanoc stormed forward and roared, "You let her go out there alone?!" Jorun's men reached for weapons but the old man made a gesture and they stopped.

The proprietor of the inn nodded slowly. "She wouldn't listen to reason lad."

The barbarian nodded, the motion exaggerated with the baleful looking helm on. He strode to where his axe lay and snatched the grim weapon up. Without preamble, the Northman headed toward the door and Venaro groaned inwardly.

Cenric, who was near the door interposed himself between it and the warrior. "Where are you going?" He asked in frustration. "We must get to the temple!"

"I have to find her." Tanoc growled. He seemed to think and must have realized that he did not know where the girl's home was. He looked back at the innkeeper then.

"Head south two streets and turn left." Jorun said, pointing. "Her mother's house is the third one down on the right hand side. It's got a roof of wood shingles and a front porch that's painted blue."

Turning back toward the door, Tanoc's voice was forbidding as death. "*Move.*" He said to the priest.

Cenric looked at Venaro, who shook his head. The merchant was shocked to see that the priest was actually thinking about it! Then, thankfully, the man stepped aside.

"Tanoc." The merchant said then.

The barbarian didn't look back. "I'll meet you at the temple." He intoned and stepped out into the night.

As Captain Fendrel led his remaining guardsman from the barracks, he could hear them whispering amongst themselves. These men were those who had been off duty in the barracks or at their homes and had only recently shown up, even as Fendrel himself had. Their whispers were of what they'd seen atop the distant walls as something, not mercenaries and certainly not orcs besieged the town. Like the others, Fendrel had come to retrieve his armor and weapons and now armed and armored, he felt confident.

"Stifle that!" He said as a nearby guard, a young recruit with big eyes murmured something about monsters. To the others, he snapped, "We're going to secure the north gate!" They said little else but they did follow their captain. Fendrel knew that the gate was critical as the reports he'd gotten from fleeing and wounded guardsmen spoke of the overwhelming assault from the north. Amid their moans and gasps of pain, they warned of hideous monsters that felt no pain and would not stop but the captain had no time to listen further. He knew the facts were brutally simple; an army of…something…he didn't know what had attacked the town and they had to stop it. He led his men out of the barracks and paused there in the courtyard.

The dashing captain certainly looked the part of a brave leader. Turning to address his guardsmen, he spoke, his voice ringing. "Wend is under attack!" His voice held no timbre of fear, no hint of doubt. "We are all that stands before our home and this threat! Who will stand with me?!" The roar of answering guardsmen was gratifying and it had certainly been a good speech as speeches went. Fendrel left the courtyard followed by his bolstered troops who could not wait to get to grips with the enemy. Then, they saw what awaited them before the north gate and they faltered.

The guardsmen could hardly be blamed. They'd been trained to deal with brigands and the occasional orc raid. They had never seen anything like the misshapen horde of drooling monstrosities that walked, crawled and hopped toward them like something out of a fever dream. Their mouths opened in stark amazement and weapons hung from limp hands like tools they'd forgotten how to use.

Brave Captain Fendrel broke the spell. "Forward!" He roared hoarsely. He was as shaken as any of them but for all his faults,

Fendrel was a brave man, a good warrior and not the worst leader the guardsmen of Wend had ever had. The captain stepped forward with his sword held high and the guards followed him into combat.

As they charged forward, the monsters who had attacked their fair town rushed toward them. The skill and resolve of the human warriors was tested against the ferocity and brute strength of the bizarre monsters that felt no pain. Time and again, the guards would think they had slain some awful, creeping thing only to have it rise and tear them apart. Some had remembered what old Hedolf had said and had brought what fire, oil or pitch they could lay hands on. These shouted instruction to the others and they began to burn and hack into the horrid creatures.

The captain pushed forward with a torch in one hand and his fine sword in another. He'd felt fear but now, seeing that these things could be stopped, he knew they could win. "Drive them back!" He shouted. The gate was near and if they could just push these creatures back, they could close it. "We must retake the gate!"

"I cannot allow that." Answered a cold voice and as the captain looked, he saw a man standing amid the misshapen horrors. Unlike them, he looked wholly human, save perhaps for his pale skin and luminous piercing eyes. The monsters around him seemed to defer to him and at a glance, halted. For a long moment, the swirling battle for the north gate ceased as the surviving guardsmen, breathing hard, looked at the snorting monsters that still stood between them and victory.

Captain Fendrel's face twisted in anger and confusion. "You are with them?" He didn't understand how it could be so. The man before him looked human, if dressed strangely in all black.

"No." The other man answered, smiling, the expression causing the scar on his face to writhe like a serpent. "They are with me." As he spoke, he drew a long sword of green metal.

The captain had never seen the like of that sword and despite the perilous situation was mystified. "Who are you?" Fendrel asked, gripping his own sword tightly.

The smile never left the black clad stranger's face. "I am Kast." He said simply and flowed forward like a cloud scudding across the face of the moon. So swift was his rush that he nearly ran the captain through, the other bringing his blade up to parry at the last moment.

The monsters charged forward then, as did the guardsmen of Wend. Cold steel met with warped flesh and bone. Fendrel took a step back and then lashed out with his own strike, testing his opponent's guard.

"Good." Kast said approvingly. "I haven't met a real swordsman in some time." There was real pleasure on his features now. He batted aside the captain's strike and rolled his wrist, thrusting forward with his strange sword.

Giving further ground, Fendrel barely threw his shield up before him. He swung his blade down at an angle toward his shield-less opponent's legs. Somehow, the dark warriors green blade was there, moving so fast it was a blur. "Why?" Fendrel rasped then. "Why are you attacking us?" Shifting his stance, he tried to stab upward. "Why are you helping them?" Two of his guardsman dashed past him, moving to flank his foe.

With astonishing speed, Kast sidestepped right and drove his sword into the chest of the guardsman there, who tried to block with his shield. The move was so slow and clumsy it looked like a child trying to combat a grown adult. "I told you," Kast said, still smiling as he dashed toward the guard on the left, "They are with me not the other way 'round."

The captain saw how quickly the warrior in black had killed the other guard and moved to help the other man but was too slow. This guardsman had a spear and he planted his feet firmly, trying to skewer the dark warrior. It was a good move and he executed it well but he was so overmatched it was pitiful. Flowing around the spear tip as if it were standing still rather than thrusting forward, Kast spun and chopped from right to left, slashing the guard's throat wide open.

Fendrel gritted his teeth as the guard fell, his lifeblood painting the cobbled street. For all his faults, and they were many, the captain was no coward and never thought of fleeing. "I'll kill you!" He barked hoarsely, hacking from right to left.

"Not likely." Kast replied, contemptuously parrying the stroke. "I'm not really alive." He added, with that rictus smile. Now, however, the smile was strained a bit. "Your form is slipping." The Pallid warrior chided.

"To hell with form, you bastard!" Captain Fendrel retorted. He realized that the darkly clad man had been toying with him. His movements when slaying the guardsmen had been swifter than when the two of them fought. The realization enraged him. "Fight me!"

Kast stood back for a moment. "Oh very well." He said then and surged forward so quickly that the captain was unprepared. Though he tried to interpose his shield between them, it seemed to his eyes that the dark warrior simply stepped past it. Then, the Pallid drove his green sword point into his right shoulder.

Fendrel felt the links of his mail part as the blade stabbed in. His armor had saved him from the sword going in further but the force of the blow was incredible. He fell back and weakly waved his sword before him.

Shaking his head, Kast murmured, "You could have survived the remaking, I think." Seeing the confused look on the captain's face, he drove his sword down on the other man's weapon with brutal force.

The captain's hand numbed as his sword clattered to the ground. Disarmed, he tried to turtle behind his shield.

"Come now." Kast said disapprovingly. "I thought you a swordsman not a ranker to cower behind a shield." Stepping forward, he grasped the rim of the triangular shield and tore it from the captain's grip.

Fendrel blinked in shock. He was completely without defense in the time it took to breathe deeply. He knew that he was accounted the best blade in the whole town and he'd been defeated so casually it was shaming.

"Yeees." Kast said sibilantly, his grin deepening. "Shame

and rage mixed with fear." His piercing eyes seemed half glazed as he feasted on the captain's raw, primal emotions. "The others never understand the flavor and sensation reaped during combat." A Dreg came near and he turned his head. The monster slunk away. Keeping his head turned, the Pallid waited while the captain fumbled with his dagger. "And hope, ah it adds a wondrous zing spiced to the rest."

The captain realized that somehow this thing was feeding on his very emotions. He'd thought the darkly clad warrior was a man but now he knew the truth; Kast was every bit the monster that the malformed things around him were, perhaps more so. He gripped his dagger and lunged forward, seeking his opponent's throat.

With contemptuous ease, Kast brought his sword down on the outstretched arm of the captain, severing his hand just above the wrist. As the man screamed, he stepped before him. "Now, we layer in pain." Closing his eyes, he savored it all. The Dregs were overwhelming the guardsmen and pushing them back from the gate. Yet a brave guard, seeing his captains' plight charged in with sword in hand.

Kast's expression never changed nor did his eyes open. In the tumult of battle with emotions so highly charged, he could taste where his opponents were and did not need sight. Letting the guard rush closer, he sidestepped him easily and then grabbed his sword arm. Slowly and casually, like a sadistic child pulling the legs from an insect, he drove his sword into the guard's forearm, the green blade, scraping along the bone. As the man screamed, Kast released his arm and grabbed him by the throat with his off-hand. Forcing him to his back before the captain.

Fendrel looked up then. He'd wrapped his fine cloak around his bleeding arm. Looking into Kast's eyes was like looking into the eyes of a demon.

"Now shock." The Pallid said. "Look around you, captain." He held the struggling guardsman by the throat as he casually spoke with his superior. "Look at the state of your men." As Fendrel looked around numbly, Kast's smile grew impossibly huge. "There it is." He loosened his grip on the guardsman so that he wouldn't pass out from lack of air.

The man's gasps drew the attention of the captain. "What do you want from us?" Fendrel asked in a small voice.

"We are taking what we want." Kast said simply. He was invigorated now, the sensations of the battle, particularly the game with the captain, had been exquisite. "You can see that your guards are broken and fleeing." As he said it, he felt the captain's feeble resignation. The meal was nearly done. "Look how my Dreg's feast on the fallen." Now the man's disgust and fear were peaking. "Your town is without defense and there is no one to stop us."

"Please…" The captain said lamely, hating the sound of his own voice.

"Ah!" Kast exclaimed as he savored this unexpected flavor. "The breaking of a brave man as fear overwhelms his notions of valor!" He wrenched the injured guard up so that the man was facing his captain. "I wasn't sure if you would break."

Fendrel wept openly in shame and fear, loathing himself the entire time. "I'll do anything." He sobbed, hoping for mercy. "Please, don't kill me!"

Cruel laughter answered the broken man now. "Hope lurches forth for a final time!" Kast crowed triumphantly. "Look at him." He said to Fendrel then, sensing that the man was soon to pass out from blood loss and shock. *"LOOK AT HIM!"* The Pallid grated savagely. "He is afraid, captain." His voice was darkly exultant. "Can you offer him solace and hope?" The Pallid cruelly forced the guardsman's head from side to side, forcing him to shake it like a marionette. The guard's struggles were feeble in the dark warrior's. "No…I think not."

"Please…" Fendrel said, avoiding the stare of the guard in the Pallid's clutches.

"Now…" Kast said, forcing the guards head more and more until he finally snapped his neck. "…for…" The guardsman died

316

without a scream but the captain gave a start. "...abject..." The Pallid continued twisting and twisting then until he tore the guards head clean off. "...Horror..." He smiled grimly as he presented the grisly trophy to the once dashing Captain Fendrel, who fell back screaming.

Rising, Kast tossed the head aside feeling refreshed and full. "That was delicious." He released the leash of his will on the two Dregs who had crawled toward the fallen captain while the drama unfolded. They'd busied themselves with other carcasses but the prospect of the one living human left was tantalizing to them. As they rushed in to devour the screaming captain, Kast sighed. It was a fine end to a fine meal.

CHAPTER TWENTY-FOUR

"I assure you, I am not jesting." Venaro's voice was insistent and serious and Delia's forced laughter died on her lips. "These creatures are attacking the town and are not easily destroyed."

Looking deep into his eyes, the merchant woman nodded slowly. "And these...Dregs...can they be stopped?" Her eyes strayed to Amice, her governess, whose expression was equal parts doubt and fear, though she masked it well.

"Yes, though not easily." The merchant said. "They must be chopped apart and burned." Venaro spoke bluntly as he neither had the time or the patience for pretense. "Any part of these monsters not burned up with still try to kill you." His voice was full of the memory of their encounter with the Dregs on the road. "I have seen them ignore wounds that would slay any living creatures out of hand."

"Very well." Delia said briskly then. "Amice, inform the men to prepare for an attack on the grounds." The old woman opened her mouth and then closed it, seemingly lacking any words. Explain to them what Venaro just told us and tell them they will need wood and oil for fires and plenty of torches."

As Amice walked out as if in a dream, Venaro said, "I have to go."

"Go?" Delia echoed. "Go where?"

The merchant had known all along that she would ask him this question and still hadn't found a decent explanation. He offered the best one that he'd been able to think of. "Some others and I are going to try and stop these things."

Delia made a very unladylike sound then. "Are you mad?" She asked in derision but there was concern in her voice as well. "Stay here with us, Venaro." She urged. "Stay with me."

Gently, he sat on the bed and took her hand. Looking into Delia's eyes, a flood of memories came, unbidden to the merchant's mind. "I cannot stay." He told her, thinking how he'd once loved her, how part of him loved her still.

"Why?" She asked pleadingly. "You're no hero, you're not a young man, by the gods, Venaro you're not a guard pledged to defend this town!" Delia's voice had grown angry and insistent as it always did when she was not getting her own way.

Rising from the bed, the merchant leaned forward and kissed Delia's forehead. "Be safe." He said softly.

"I don't understand." She said then. "What can you possibly do?"

The merchant knew that there was no explanation that he could give her that she would like. He wasn't about to try and explain the priest's plan, which he wasn't overly confident in. Neither was Venaro going to tell Delia that Whisper was among those with him. Thinking of the assassin, Venaro said, "You won't have to worry about Whisper anymore."

Delia's eyes narrowed. "You already told me of the Pallid and their creatures, Venaro." Speaking of his earlier visit. "Why did you really come back?"

"I wanted to make sure that you'd heeded my warning." The merchant replied defensively.

Leaning forward, Delia looked into his eyes again, her gaze shrewd. "Don't lie, my sweet." Her voice was gentle. "You never could fool me."

"I never tried." Venaro countered, smiling.

"You came back to tell me Whisper wasn't going to try and kill me." She marveled.

"I didn't want you to be worried about that on top of everything else." Venaro shrugged.

Delia's voice was urgent. "Stay with me."

Letting go of her hand, Venaro kissed her again, this time gently on the mouth. "I cannot." He said, after the kiss and moved toward the door. "Goodbye, Delia." As she murmured her farewell, he closed the door behind him on the woman he'd once tried to love and wondered if he was the biggest fool who'd ever lived.

Near the gates to Delia's manor, Bandur, Cenric and Whisper waited for the merchant to return. He'd neither asked them to wait nor to go but they'd stayed by unspoken agreement. When Bandur had made to follow him, Venaro had shaken his head and told him to stay with the others. Now, the trio stood outside the gates under the watchful eyes of the guards, just inside the light offered by the lanterns there.

"I don't like the way they're looking at us." Bandur growled, rubbing his injured wrist.

"They're not looking at you." Whisper offered cryptically, smiling expansively at the guards on the other side of the manor gates.

"Oh?" The former soldier said. "Who are they looking at?"

"They're looking at me." She answered sweetly, her gaze not leaving that of the guards.

Bandur snorted rudely. "I hardly think they've got women on their minds right now!"

Cenric intruded into the conversation then. "I think she's referring to the fact that they've been given a description of the woman who tried to kill their mistress." He nodded toward the guards. "They're trying to ascertain whether or not this is she."

As Bandur made a spluttering noise, Whisper turned her smile

320

on Cenric. "Very good, priest." She quipped. "There's just one thing you've gotten wrong, though."

"Oh?" The priest asked absently. From time to time, Cenric looked out into the darkened streets. From time to time, they could hear distant shouts and screams. It seemed like they were getting closer. "What's that?"

"I didn't *try* to kill her." Whisper stated huskily. "I had my blade to her throat and could have done it as easily as blinking."

"Shh!" Bandur hissed, looking at the guards nearby.

Whisper laughed almost seductively. "They're not sure it's me and I think they've orders not to open the gates for anyone."

"They let Venaro in." The caravan guard pointed out.

She nodded then and mused, "Yes...they did, didn't they?"

"What's wrong with your arm?" Cenric asked Bandur then.

The ex-soldier shrugged. "Broke my wrist." He said noncommittally. Bandur wasn't about to admit that Tanoc had broken it after easily disarming him.

The priest stepped close. "Let me see it."

Like a child, Bandur drew it back. "It's fine." He said in a surly voice. "It's healing alright."

"Don't be foolish!" Cenric snapped. "You'll need your strength!"

Automatically obeying the voice of command there, Bandur gingerly let the cleric examine his inured arm. He winced as Cenric felt the wrist, wondering why every healer or doctor he'd ever known wanted to press at the area that you'd just told them was hurting.

"This won't do." The priest said. "At least it was a clean break." Looking up into the other man's eyes, he ordered, "Hold still." Then, Cenric closed his eyes and laid a hand on the injured area, murmuring something softly that neither of the others understood.

Bandur started at the warmth that he felt spreading through his injured wrist and swore that he saw a faint golden, white glow coming from the priest's hands. Whisper saw it too and gave a low whistle. "True divine healing." She noted wryly. "I didn't think there were any left that could work such magic."

Cenric's eyes opened and the glow faded. "There are few enough of us left with the faith." He admitted, looking at Bandur.

The former sergeant flexed his hand and moved his wrist slowly, a smile growing on his face. "I'll be buggered!" He exclaimed. "It's completely healed!" Drawing his sword, he swiped at the air. "It's like it was never injured!"

Whisper smiled wryly and with a gesture at the guards on the other side of the gates, said, "Looks like they don't approve of you drawing steel."

"The hell with them!" Bandur said and then, remembering that those men were armed with bows as well as swords and spears, sheathed his sword. Throwing his shield on his back, he then adjusted his sword belt so that his scabbard rode on his left side as it should. He smiled with pleasure that at least he wouldn't have to fight left handed.

Staring at the priest, who was looking off into the dark city, Whisper asked, "This plan of yours, wasn't it about saving people?" Her voice was cynical and caused him to turn around to face her. "Now that there isn't time to warn them, won't it just be us at this temple?"

Sighing, Cenric said, "I will admit I'd hoped that we would have more time." He was pensive as he moodily stared back out at the town. "However, if we can hold the temple and make the reliquary safe, I believe some of the people will make their way there."

"And just how will they know to do that?" She asked sarcastically. The assassin wasn't sure why she felt quarrelsome with the priest. Perhaps it was the fact that she'd just seen him do something she'd seen a thousand charlatans fake, something she'd never thought was real. Now, seeing a priest use healing magic by his faith made her irksome, perhaps because it was a commentary on how far humanity had turned from the deities that they had once worshipped. Whisper was an unbeliever and proud of that fact.

Seeing him heal Bandur had shaken her more than she liked to admit.

Cenric wasn't biting. If he was aware of her feelings, he did not show it. "In the same way that the Pallid have no doubt sensed the power of the reliquary, the people of Wend will be able to sense it as well." He shrugged. "At least I hope that they will.

With an arched brow, the assassin said acidly, "I sense no such feeling, priest."

Turning away from her, he intoned. "There are those who won't sense it."

"Such as?" Whisper said, pressing the issue. She had a feeling of what he was going to say but wanted to make him say it aloud.

The priest's voice was neutral when he answered. "Such as those whose souls are, unreceptive, to its power."

"Like an assassin whose hands are stained with the blood of innocents?" She said in mocking tones. "If it's not able to save the lost, then is it really an artifact of the gods?"

Despite his calm, she was getting to the priest, who turned and bit back. "I did not say that it couldn't save you." Modulating his tone, he added, "I simply said that perhaps you couldn't sense it."

Perhaps their argument over the implications of such a divine object upon those whose souls were night dark would have continued. However, at that moment, Venaro appeared at the gates. His face was drawn and he looked sad. "I am ready." The merchant said simply.

Turning her ire to Venaro, Whisper said rather too sweetly, "Did you say goodbye to dear Delia?"

"Yes." He replied simply, obviously not wanting to talk about it further.

Cenric began walking down the cobbled street. "We must go." He said. Without another word, the melancholy merchant trailed after him and after a moment, the caravan guard followed as well. This left the vexed Whisper fuming for a time in front of the gates, half wishing the guards would come out and challenge her so she could take out her frustration. When they didn't oblige, she stalked away, murmuring beneath her breath.

All along the north wall of Wend, chaos had broken out. In most places, the Dregs had completely overrun the walls and poured over, heading out into the street. The resistance the guards had mounted had held them briefly but in the end, it had just been a matter of time.

'Perhaps if we'd known they were only hitting the north wall.' Hedolf thought to himself. *'We could have pulled men from the south and east gates. Maybe it would have been enough...'* The guard's thoughts trailed off and he knew he was lying to himself. They'd held here along this stretch of wall but it had been a close thing. The dead and dying lay all around them, the bodies of brave guardsmen strewn amidst the monsters they'd fought. Looking around for a moment, he thought he might be the only living thing left here. Most of the Dregs were now past the walls, into the town. He stood alone with sword and torch in hand and marveled that he still lived somehow.

Hedolf thought then of Oled, his wife of almost twenty years. *'I've done my duty here.'* He thought then. *'We've failed but maybe I can save my wife.'* They'd never had children and she was all he had in the world. Sometimes, Oled would laugh and say that he was all the child she needed but sometimes he would catch her crying and he knew the truth. He loved her with all his heart and he was getting her out of this doomed town. It wasn't that the guardsman was a coward or had no sense of honor but it was clear to him now that this was the price a town paid when those in charge were greedy and corrupt.

Heading down the wall toward the stairs, he saw something stir and cautiously slowed his pace. A half burned Dreg was trying to crawl free of a pile of bodies. There was little left of the monster and it was so badly burned that it was hard to tell what it had been. It had one arm left that it was using to pull itself forward. Sheathing his sword, Hedolf plucked up a spear from the ground and pinned the monster through its back. Then he kicked the remnants of a bucket of oil over onto the thing and thrust his torch forward. The thing went up anew but this time was charred so badly that it finally, mercifully stopped moving.

"Anyone else down there still alive?" A gruff voice asked, causing Hedolf to look up. He saw a figure that he thought he recognized.

"Oso?" Hedolf asked and despite the carnage all around him, he smiled when the other guard nodded. Then, his smile slipped as he looked around helplessly and shook his head. "All dead." He said simply and started heading toward the other man.

A foot long shard of sharp bone burst through Hedolf's chest tearing through his vital organs. As he was lifted off his feet, he heard the strangest sound. The dying guard tried to focus on it but he was fading. He tried to speak but blood poured from his mouth and a gurgling sound was all that came forth. 'Oled...' He thought and then his head slumped forward.

Seeing Hedolf die, Oso gritted his teeth. "You filthy bastard!" He growled, stalking forward. The guard had a long handled cavalry axe that he'd grabbed from the armory. He'd discovered that it was a wonderful thing to hack apart these monsters.

Seeing a living target, the hulking Dreg dropped the dead guardsman. It was a massive creature with the body of a blacksmith. Its body was almost all of a piece save for the thing's right arm, which had most of the meat stripped back from the forearm. There, several bones, including a femur had been fused together and where the hand would have been, the arm came to a needle sharp point. The most horrifying thing was that where the head of a man should have rested atop that heavily muscled neck, the thin, sallow face of a sickly young boy rode instead. Reflexively, the thing kept coughing, the sound of a perpetually sick child. This was the sound, Hedolf couldn't figure out as he was dying.

As Oso stepped forward to face the creature in the fitful light of the torches along the top of the wall, he heard a voice behind him. "Another one?" He didn't have to turn to recognize Umfrey's voice. They had fought together along that nightmare wall against the tide of monsters.

The coughing Dreg moaned like a sick child, the sound sending shudders up both men's spines. It took a step forward, extending the bloody shard of bone along with its other hand like a boy who expects his mother to hold him.

Now Oso did turn, although he kept one eye on the approaching monster. "Go on, lad. Get out of here."

Umfrey couldn't take his eyes off the oncoming horror. "We'll fight it together."

"No!" Oso barked. "You go, I'll deal with this thing." He gestured down to a wound on his leg where one of the horrors had bitten him with incisors like that of a bear. "I can't run so I'll just stay for a bit." He said with false bravado that sounded hollow to his own ears.

"I'm not going to leave you!" The young guardsman swore, now looking at his friend. He seemed a very different person from the complaining boy that had stood the gate watch with the veteran.

Smiling through his pain and grief, Oso clapped the lad on the shoulder. "You fought bravely, lad." Then he shoved him back. "I'll be damned it I let you die up here. Go!"

"Oso…" Young Umfrey began.

The Dreg was close now, within a few steps. The monster's arms were still outstretched and it was coughing sporadically, sounding for all the world like nothing more than a boy who was very ill and needed his mother.

"*GO!*" The veteran ordered and Umfrey fell back with tears in his eyes. He was a brave lad but he was in a state of shock after the horrors of that night. Oso could hear the youth make it to the stairs and his footsteps as he went down. He hoped the lad would fare better in the town below, though part of him doubted it. Right now, though, he had to stop this coughing thing that had killed old

Hedolf. He had to stop it because he knew he couldn't outrun it and he didn't want to die with that hideous shard of bone in his back like his old friend. He had to stop it because he couldn't take the sounds coming from it any longer, the sounds of a lost, sick boy.

"Come on then." Oso said, his voice surprisingly gentle as he stepped toward the huge monster.

The Dreg spread its arms wide as if about to receive a hug from its mother and the drooling smile on the thin face of a boy was madness inducing. The two rushed toward each other amongst the twitching parts of dead monsters and the still forms of dead men.

Oso swung the long handled axe low, aiming for the Dreg's left leg. He'd meant to hit the thing at the kneecap but was himself hampered by his leg wound and his aim was off. The axe bit into the monster's lower leg but had the effect he'd hoped for as it toppled forward. The veteran tried to leap back then but his weak leg gave and he fell backward himself with a groan.

Still coughing sporadically, the horror reached out with its massive, gnarled hand and grabbed Oso by the foot. The guardsman struggled up to a sitting position and brought the axe down, seeking to split the thing's skull. Again, he was off the mark and chopped into the thing's shoulder instead.

Incapable of feeling pain, the Dreg held him there with its hand while it brought its other arm forward. The onrushing shard of bone slammed into Oso's stomach with such force it parted the chainmail links of his armor as though it were made of paper. Gritting bloodstained teeth, the guardsman tried to lift his axe again but found that he lacked the strength. He watched numbly as the monster with the face of a child drew back the awful bone spear of an arm again.

There was no one to hear the crunch of the sharp bone hammering into the guardsman's forehead. Mercifully, there was no one to hear the sounds the Dreg made as it began to feed on the fallen warrior. Sounds that were horrifyingly similar to a delighted child who has been given sweets.

Rushing down the street, the barbarian recalled the innkeeper's directions. Soon he found himself standing before a house with wooden shingles and a porch painted blue. It had been chaos all along the street and Tanoc had been forced to fight his way past several Dregs already. He hadn't tried to destroy them but had focused on getting past the creatures. Now, he stood before Lilli's home and hesitated as he saw the front door was broken in. There was light from within and shadows danced there. Something was moving within. Dreading what he'd find, the Northman trudged forward, his axe and shield in hand.

Within, the house was a shambles. An oil lantern gave dim illumination to the interior not far from the front door. The entryway led into a front room with a small fireplace and several chairs. There were several doors that led off of this main room and a narrow staircase on the far wall. It was a simple place, quite small really but these details were lost on Tanoc.

The barbarian's attention was riveted on the scene in the center of the room. Several Dregs were busily feasting on the corpses of an old woman, a boy and a young woman that he instantly recognized. So intent on their feeding were the monsters that they hadn't even noticed his entry. For a long moment, the Northman was frozen, as he looked at the girl's face. It was pristine and untouched, save for a fleck of blood on one cheek. Her body moved with a gently rocking motion as the vile creature fed and he remembered the last time he had seen her face, the smile she wore for him.

With a savage cry, the barbarian fell upon the Dregs. As the gore streaked head of the creature that had been feasting on Lilli came up, he severed it with a single stroke. The thing's head flew into a corner, snapping still. As the other Dregs rose, the powerful Northman laid about him with his axe, hacking through limbs and torsos in a frenzy of rage and grief. His strength and speed were such that it was over in seconds and the remnants of the creatures were strewn about the room that had become a slaughterhouse. The body parts still twitched and thrashed but so thorough had Tanoc been in his work that there was nothing that could do more than spasm.

Looking down at Lilli's cold face, the Northman might have been carved of stone. He shed no tears, though his face was lined with grief. His muscles were ridged as he gripped his axe and shield tightly and bunched his jaw. He was unsure how long he stood there before he saw a twitching hand clenching and unclenching near his foot. Tanoc strode to the oil lantern and without looking at the girl's face again, shattered it on the floor near the mess. As the flames took hold and began to burn, he turned and headed for the door.

By the time the barbarian reached the street, the house was beginning to catch fire in earnest. Perhaps the thought flitted across his mind that the flames might spread to other houses but if it did it was only the briefest of thoughts. His face bore a terrible mien as he stalked down the street. Lilli was gone and nothing would bring her back. Woe to any creature that crossed his path as he made his way toward the temple!

Past the north gate, near the barracks, Fina stood amid the carnage, a flawless vision of dark beauty. A frown stained her beauteous features as she looked to the south. It was still there, that steady thrum of something that was inimical to her and her kind. She'd never felt its' like but the Pallid had heard of such things.

Kast found her there, her lips pursed and her petite brow furrowed in thought. "The Dregs are getting out of hand." He noted, absently shaking a spatter of blood and gore from his blade.

"Their lust for flesh and blood will be sated soon enough." Fina noted distractedly. "Then it will be time for harvesting and adding to their ranks." She still looked toward the south part of the town pensively.

Gazing that direction, Kast spoke. "I sense it too." His voice had a curious edge to it. "Though I cannot tell what it is."

"It is a relic." Fina said bluntly then. "A remnant from an age long gone. It cannot stop us."

His doubt radiating from him, Kast looked over at her. "Should we ignore it then?"

"No." She replied firmly. "You will deal with it. I must keep the Dregs in line lest they leave nothing to be gathered."

Kast was surprised now. "What shall I do?" He asked simply but allowed his query to radiate from him. He didn't even know what was there to the south or what caused the sensation he was feeling. "You say it is a relic?"

Her expression still troubled, she was silent for a moment as the pondered. "I believe it is an artifact of the feeble beings that men call gods." Her face twisted. "They are dying or dead and have little power to affect this world."

"Yet, apparently, they still have some strength." Kast replied wryly.

Fina's voice was sharp. "*Very little!*" Her very being radiated loathing when she thought of the deities that men paid homage to. "Their presence is all but gone and such artifacts are little more than memories of their past glories."

Kast's tone and manner turned curious. "Yet how did we not sense it until now?" He too found his attention pulled south. The sense of that power was of something that would destroy him if he ventured close. "Vok never spoke of it when he visited this place and met with Malken on his way north." Looking around, as he thought of the Pallid who had been Malken, he then asked, "Where is Null?"

The two of them looked around but there was no sign of the fledgling Pallid. Fina snorted. "It matters not." Kast nodded in agreement. They'd both known that he would go off on his own. "I haven't seen him for some time." She stared at Kast then, letting her sense of urgency envelop him. "We've no time for that. Dawn is not far off."

The other Pallid grimaced. "The guards put up a stiffer defense than I would have expected." Kast admitted. "There were some brave warriors in their midst. In the end, it didn't matter."

"Yet they slowed our advance." Fina sniffed. "We've the reaping to tend to and we cannot afford to fight any who rally in the light of the sun." They both knew it was true. Dregs were slow and sluggish in the daylight compared to their prowess at night. "We are here to add to the multitude not return with fewer than we started with."

Sensing that she had made a decision, Kast quirked an eyebrow. "Well then?" He intoned sardonically.

"Out there somewhere is someone who knew not only how to find the relic of the fading gods but also knew how to trigger it. They must have only recently discovered it and activated its power." Fina let Kast think on her statement for a moment. "Such men and women of true faith are rare these days." She tapped a long fingernail on the pommel of her slender sword. "Whoever this is will seek to rally the people to the relic. It will draw them even as it repels our kind."

"I see." Kast murmured then. It made sense to him as he could feel the warning of that not too distant hum telling him to keep away. It would be like a lodestone drawing the mortals to its perceived safety. "If I kill the one who has called out to the old gods?"

"Precisely." Fina replied, smiling. "With them gone, the relic will become an inert item again. It is faith that channels such things."

Kast nodded and then asked, "What if they are hiding?"

"They won't be." The other Pallid assured him. "They know that the artifact is vulnerable, being only a focus of their faith. They will have to protect and defend it." Fina's will washed over Kast as she commanded him. "Take what Dregs you can bring to heel and go. Slay all who defend this relic and destroy it."

Though he nodded, Kast asked, "Will the Dregs approach

such a thing?" It was a valid question as they both could feel the artifacts forbidding power from here. Left to their own devices none of the creatures would willingly go near it. It was doubtful that many of them could be forced to approach it and it would be an act of sheer will to force them.

"That is up to you." Fina said dolefully. "If your will is equal to the task, you should be able to leash enough to your will to complete your task."

The insult was clearly implied and Kast's eyes narrowed. Fina knew how difficult it would be to bind many of the Dregs to his will enough to approach the power that had bloomed to the south. "And what shall you be doing, my lady?" He asked mockingly.

Imperiously, Fina answered. "I shall marshal the Dregs and begin the harvest as planned." Without sparing him another glance, she added, "I shall leave this town before dawn."

"Very well." Kast replied in clipped tones.

No more words were spoken between the two as Kast left Fina amid the butchery at the north gate. He could feel her will rising as she began to call to the Dregs and knew it would take her some time to bring them to heel. He thought no more of her then. He had work to do.

CHAPTER TWENTY-FIVE

The stout door of the Crooked King was made of solid oak, banded with iron. Its windows were narrow and now were boarded up. Jorun and his employees, along with a few patrons who had holed up there. They were all armed with an assortment of weapons that the old innkeeper had stashed long ago and now made ready to defend themselves.

Outside, they could hear the sounds of screams and cries of agony punctuated by terrible, inhuman noises of the creatures that were attacking the townsfolk. Those near the windows had looked through the cracks to get confused glimpses of scenes from out in the streets. What they reported was terrifying. Now, they waited.

As it turned out, they didn't have long to wait. The front door shuddered as something large hit it. Nearby, one of the boarded up windows thumped as hands and other appendages beat against it. One of the toughs that worked for Jorun as a bouncer jumped back, startled as discolored fingers wedged themselves through the cracks between the boards.

"Easy, lad." Old Jorun said with a calm that he did not feel.

The brawny young man stared back at the innkeeper in disbelief. "Easy? There's nothin' easy about it!" He held a short sword in one trembling hand while he pointed at the scrabbling fingers at the window. "We're trapped in here while those…*things*…are killing everyone out there!"

Jorun, who held a solid woodsman's axe was still behind the bar. Before him were more weapons, though most were now clutched in the hands of those within the taproom of the 'king'. "We don't know what's goin' on out there." The old man said firmly. "There are probably a lot of folks doin' exactly what we are." He looked at the others. "The priest told me we got to hold 'til dawn and that's what we'll do."

The others nodded doubtfully. They'd closed and locked all the inner doors, as well as the door that led to the upper floor. Jorun had pointed out that they didn't have the numbers to defend the whole inn. Their best chance was to block off the main barroom and hold it.

There was a crash from somewhere toward the back and one of the barmaids screamed. "They're going to get in here!" Her voice was panicked. "They'll kill us all!" The girl was barely into her twenties and terrified.

"No, they won't." Jorun soothed. "Remember, we got the inner doors locked and barricaded." He reminded her, gesturing to the inner doors that were nailed shut with boards from the inside and furthermore had stacks of heavy furniture piled against them.

Then, one of the boards over a nearby window cracked. "They're coming through!" Another of the bouncers shouted and stabbed with a boar spear through the opening. "I got him!" He said triumphantly but then his voice became tinged with dread. "I stabbed that big bastard right in the head and he's still coming…"

"Remember what the priest told us!" Jorun shouted at them all. "We have to hack them apart and burn them!" He eyed them all then. "But we have to make sure we don't burn the 'king' down in the meantime!"

Then, more of the boarded up windows began to be broken open and the inhabitants of the Crooked King rushed to hold the terrors in the night at bay. They did remember the words of the priest but words seemed a feeble defense against the horrific things they saw reaching in toward them from the night.

"Hold them back!" Jorun yelled, hacking off a hand that reached through. Kicking it away, the old man saw the arm withdraw. Meanwhile, he didn't see the hand, still moving as it flipped itself over and started crawling toward him like some kind of insect. Then a knife drove through the hand, pinning it to the floor. The old innkeeper turned to see the barmaid step back, leaving her dagger in the still writhing hand. "Thanks Moll." He said to the girl.

There was no time to deal with the hand as more of the monsters threw themselves against the building, sensing the humans inside. The door thudded continually beneath the assault there and the sounds of splintering wood could be heard amid the yells and cries.

The mayor gave a start again as he looked toward the door to his office. He'd heard something out there again, he was sure of it. He'd come there after being awoken earlier. He sat at his desk with a bottle of strong wine and a loaded crossbow. The shutters to his fine glass windows were closed and locked. He did not want to see what was happening to his town. Edber had given his guards strict orders to guard his home and keep anyone from disturbing him. Then he had withdrawn to his sanctuary.

As the noise from outside had grown, he had steadily drank more and more. The mayor couldn't help but think of the tall stranger who had met with him that evening back in the dead of winter. He remembered the man's interest in Wend and how he'd claimed to be a wealthy merchant. Malken had assured him that Vok was part of a trading consortium from the west who were trying to gain a foothold in the trading in the area. Both he and the shabby, little man had been paid handsomely for information that had at first seemed innocuous and innocent enough. He remembered only too well that meeting. How many people lived in Wend? How many guards did the town boast? What kind of weaponry did they have?

What machines of war, if any could Wend bring to bear?

Thinking back, he clearly recalled wondering at the questions but the man called Vok had assured him that he was trying to protect his interests. After all, if he were to bring business and trade to the region, he would need to know how well guarded the town was. The towering man had also asked about the other settlements of the region. Edber remembered how the man had made him ill at ease but also how the gold he'd given him had made that unease fade so quickly.

Now, as he sat getting drunk as a lord, he asked himself the questions that he'd forced himself not to ask. Why had he never seen Vok again or any other member of his consortium? What happened to the merchants who were supposed to have shown up in Wend to represent their interests? Why had the towns and villages to the north begun to go silent? Then there was the real question that currently plagued him; could this attack have something to do with the dark stranger who had paid him a visit that wintry night?

It all began with Malken. The mayor knew it and wished again that he'd never made the acquaintance of the vile man. He'd never been liked in the town from what Edber had heard of him but when he'd come to the mayor, claiming to be old friends with Vok, the latter's gold made him ignore his misgivings about both of them.

"Malken." He growled half to himself. Setting down his fine cup, he placed a hand on the crossbow as he thought he heard a faint noise again and something that sounded like a thump. He hadn't fired the crossbow in some time but he was taking no chances. Another soft thump sounded almost too quiet to be heard by his straining ears but he was sure of it this time; he'd heard something beyond his door. The mayor knew that he should have heard his men if they'd been attacked but he'd heard nothing. Struggling to focus through the haze of alcohol, Edber realized that it was deathly silent. He had heard nothing for several minutes, not the strange thumps or rustles or the low voices of his men...nothing.

Standing to his feet a bit unsteadily, the elected official of Wend lifted the loaded crossbow. "Erd? Tarin?" He queried, calling his guards names. "Belun? Dolm?" In reply, the door handle began to turn. It only went so far, as the door was locked. "Who's there?!" The mayor half shrieked, startled by the unsteady sound of his voice. Incredibly, the handle continued to turn slowly and then, with a shriek of tearing metal, was no longer there!

The door opened slowly and a figure stood there shrouded in the darkness. There had been a lantern in the hall but it was no longer there.

"Who are you?!" Edber demanded. "I've a loaded crossbow here! Show yourself!" As the mayor barked this command, his voice steadied a bit, pleasing him to no end. If this was a looter, they would rue the day they came to his home!

"You don't recognize me?" A familiar voice asked slyly then.

"I don't..." The mayor began but then trailed off as it dawned on him that he did know the owner of the voice. "Malken?"

Walking forward, the shape resolved into the very man the mayor had named. He looked different somehow, though. Malken stood taller, no longer hunched and his face was relaxed and did not have the greedy pinched look that Edber had come to associate with the man.

"That isn't my name anymore, mister mayor." The shabby man replied.

"What are you talking about?!" Mayor Edber snapped, detecting the snide tone in the other man's voice. "Where have you been, Malken?" He demanded then. "Do you know what is going on out there?"

"I told you, that is not my name." The little man hadn't stopped walking and was getting alarmingly close. Then, the mayor saw the blood on his hands and pointed the crossbow at him.

"Stop right there!" Edber commanded. "I'll shoot you, Malken! I swear by Tilva I will!"

"I told you..." The other man growled then. "That's not my name!" He came on toward the mayor with astonishing speed and

Edber pulled the trigger. The mayor's look of astonishment as the little man dodged the projectile turned to one of fear. The shabby man grabbed the crossbow and twisted his hand. The solid wood front piece of the weapon snapped like a dry chicken bone.

Falling back behind his desk, the mayor held up his hands. "Please, Mal...please sir!" He begged, amending the name he'd been about to use.

"Sir..." The shabby little man savored the word. "I like that, Mayor Edber." A twisted smile crawled across his face. "You calling me sir." He stepped around the desk and though the fat mayor was much taller than him, the man seemed to wilt. "My name is Null."

Edber stepped back until he bumped into his chair and half fell into it. "P...please...sir...Null..." He said stuttering with a fear he couldn't comprehend. He didn't understand how the shabby little weakling could twist off his door handle, dodge a crossbow bolt and then snap the weapon like a dead stick.

"Please, what?" Null asked sarcastically, mimicking the trembling man before him. "Please don't belittle you?" Then, he slapped the pudgy man in the chair so hard, the mayor's head turned and it left a handprint. He went on in a caustic voice, punctuating each question with a harder slap. The force of the blows was incredible and the big man rocked in the chair. "Don't mock you? Don't look down my nose at you? Don't threaten you? Don't intimidate you?"

Null slapped the man in the chair back and forth now, his victim's head whipping back and forth. When the mayor tried to throw up his hands, they were batted aside as easily as if he were a babe in arms. Null stopped for a moment and looked with disgust at the quivering wretch before him. The mayor's nose was broken and bent to the side. Blood and snot flowed freely from it as tears too flowed freely from the sobbing man's eyes. His mouth was a mashed and bloody thing now and as he mumbled something, teeth fell from it.

"What's that, mayor?" Null asked in a hard voice. "I can't

understand you."

Looking up through swollen eyes, the mayor looked to have been worked over by a gang of toughs using their fists. "P...pleath...do...don' hurk me."

"Don't..." Null began and then realized what the pathetic thing before him was asking of him. "Don't hurt you?" Seeing the once proud mayor's head nod pitifully brought him a savage joy but not as much as he'd thought it would. "You used to stand so tall." He said, leaning down to look closer at the weeping man. "Now, you can't even defend yourself from someone you once called a conniving little rat. Do you remember saying that to your guards?" When the mayor shook his head in denial, the Pallid laughed. "Oh, I think you do, sir! I think you remember all too well!" He laid a hand on the mayor's shoulder then and the man flinched. "Don't hurt you?" He said, mouthing the words again. "Mayor, I've just begun to hurt you!"

The screams the mayor gave as Null began soon turned to whimpers and moans and then gave way to gurgles and pained murmurs. The mayor begged for death before the end but it was a long time coming.

Out beyond the doorway, his dead guard's eyes saw nothing and their dead ears heard nothing. There were no witnesses to tell of the horrible end the corrupt mayor of Wend met as he died along with his town that night.

So great was the brutal joy the Pallid took in his vengeance that Fina felt it streets away as she worked among the Dregs. She smiled briefly but it was soon gone as she exerted her will on the massed creatures as a rancher will round up his herds with dogs and rope.

The milling mass around her was growing slowly, as those who had feasted deeply on the inhabitants of the doomed town were more easily controlled. The others were hearing her mental summons and would answer in due time. Once she had enough, the Pallid would begin to use the Dregs to capture and not kill.

The harvest was at hand.

Dulwen didn't think he'd ever run so hard in all his life. The pudgy guardsman had fled the wall without a backward glance. He knew what the others would think of him but he also knew they were fools who wouldn't survive what he'd seen coming over the wall. Knowing better than to go near the barracks, Dulwen had run back to his rented room where he lived above a butcher's shop. As he passed by the people on the street, he never thought to warn them or even speak as he ran by. A few of them asked him what was happening on the wall or why the warning horns were sounding but he ignored them.

As he arrived at butcher's shop, Dulwen rushed around to the back. Normally, he liked to linger at the shop when he had the time. He'd often get free food from the owner and flirt with his daughter but now he had no time. Wheezing with the effort, he trudged up the back stairs that led to his apartment. Fumbling with his key, he opened the door and entered. He leaned there with his back to the door for several moments, just breathing, fighting to calm himself. The fat guard couldn't get the image of those nightmare creatures out of his head. The vision of those horrid, deformed things clambering up the walls was seared into his mind.

"Have to get out of here!" Dulwen wheezed to himself, though there was no one to hear him. The guardsman tore off his guardsman's tunic, thinking that he'd wouldn't be stopped by the townsfolk with it off. More importantly, he'd be less likely to be recognized and brought to task for desertion. He grabbed a bag and began stuffing clothes and valuables in it. Then he went for his cache of hidden coins. It was a fair sum that he'd built up over years of bullying and extortion on the side. Dulwen never felt an ounce of guilt for his actions. After all town guards didn't make much coin and besides, everyone did it. Of course, Dulwen knew in his heart that there were men like Hedolf that refused but such men were, in his professional opinion, fools. What man in his right mind wouldn't try to get some extra coin on the side?

It was Dulwen's greed that was ultimately his undoing. He struggled with leaving his ill-gotten gains behind and quite a lot of it wasn't in the form of coins. An antique candelabra chased with real silver, a set of fine platters, a painting that he'd looted when a local merchant went missing. It all made for a cumbersome load and he couldn't figure out how to take it all in one trip.

The butcher's shop, for all that Dulwen had nearly expired running there, was only a few streets from the north wall. It didn't take the Dreg's long to get out into the streets after sweeping aside the guards defending the wall. Had Dulwen simply fled, he might have made it to the east gate and made his escape, though he also might have fallen over dead from a heart attack. Neither of these things happened, however, as he was still looking over his treasure as he heard a crash from below followed by screams. By the time, he realized he'd taken too long and ran toward his door, the monsters were already coming up the back stair. Again, he could have, perhaps, barricaded himself in and kept quiet but quick thinking was no more a trait of his than moving quickly. The Dregs caught him halfway down the stairs.

The man thought of as Dullard by a certain priest met his end in a most gruesome manner. He was alive when they began to devour him.

Cenric and the others reached the temple and saw that there were lights there already. They drew up short for a moment, staring down the street. The buildings around the place seemed empty but the crumbling church did not seem so.

"I thought you said this place was deserted." Bandur growled, his hand straying to his sword hilt.

"Easy…" The priest said thoughtfully. "Neither the Pallid nor their servant creatures need lights to see."

Venaro asked, "What then?"

"There is movement." Whisper stated, pointing toward the temple. Her eyes were sharper than the others, who hadn't seen what she had. "It looks like there are people there in the church."

Cenric smiled broadly and then explained to the others. "It is as I told you. Some can sense the emanations of the reliquary." He gestured toward the lights. "It has begun already."

"Won't they be in danger when the Dreg's come?" Bandur asked bluntly.

The cleric's face was sad. "Yes. Though they feel drawn here and safe, they'll be in danger while we battle the Pallid and their minions." He started walking toward the temple. "We must warn them."

The other three followed Cenric and they soon were standing on the grounds of the building. Here and there amid the ancient graves and monuments were people. They were clumped together in small groups mostly just talking quietly, huddled around torches and lanterns. The people looked like a sample of everyone within the town. There were young and old, rich and poor, men and women. They noted this new group with nods and little more. It was clear that they were all afraid but that for a reason they could not comprehend, they felt better here.

The priest led them inside the church, past the shattered doors, though 'inside' was perhaps a stretch. They saw, as Cenric had earlier, the caved in roof, broken and rotting remnants of furnishings and the general vandalism. Within, they saw more lights and more people, still congregating in groups. These too, noticed them as they entered but one of them recognized the cleric.

"Father Cenric!" A familiar voice called out causing him to turn. He smiled then to see the skinny form of a young man that he recognized.

"I told you, Juriel," the priest said with a smile, "My order doesn't use such terms." There was genuine warmth in his voice as he introduced the youth to the others. He only gave the names of the other three to the lad.

Smiling at the gently rebuke, the lad replied, "I'm sorry err, sir…"

"Just call me Cenric." The priest said gently."

"Right." Juriel said, nodding, "Sorry Cenric. I'm glad to see you here, though!" His eyes were troubled. "No one knows what's happening but people are saying monsters have attacked the town! I ran when I saw some of them down my street and made my way here." His words were a torrent tumbling from him.

All around them, the other groups were falling silent as they recognized Cenric as a priest. Here and there, they whispered amongst themselves but it was clear they wanted to hear what was being said to the young man. Most edged closer and all listened intently.

Venaro asked him then, "What made you come here?"

"I don't know, sir." Juriel replied with a shrug. "I just felt like I should…it felt…safe…" He trailed off and then, after a moment, looked at the priest. "I don't know why but a lot of us felt it…felt like we'd be safe here."

"Well, you're not safe!" Bandur grated, causing the lad to give a start.

Glaring at the warrior, Cenric put a hand on the Juriel's shoulder. "Much as I hate to admit it, Bandur is right." He gazed steadily upon the youth. "You and these others need to get out of the temple. You aren't safe."

"But…" Juriel began, a confused look in his eyes.

Cenric gently interrupted him. "I know it feels safe but the same thing drawing you all here will surely draw the creatures here as well." He looked around at the others and raised his voice. "Do you hear me?" His voice was rich and full of power and authority. "It isn't safe here, at least not within the temple proper."

"What are we to do?" A woman asked, clutching at her two small children.

A man in a tradesman's coat stepped forward. "There's no place safe in Wend! I saw them come over the walls with my own eyes!"

"At least here, we can feel something…" An older man began, his voice confused as he grappled with what he wanted to say but growing stronger as he went along. "…Something of the old gods and their ways. They can protect us!"

"*Listen to me!*" Cenric said, not quite shouting to be heard above them all. "The very thing that makes you feel so safe will draw these creatures here!" His gaze swept over them all and his eyes flashed. "They will come here to make it stop!"

Amid cries of "What can we do?" and "Where can we go" along with "We're all doomed, were mixed weeping and hoarse sobs. The priest felt his heart lurch. These people had come here seeking hope and safety and were now terrified.

"You should all go to the grounds behind the temple!" Cenric shouted then, noticing that now some of those from outside were coming in to hear him speak. He realized it had been some time since he'd given a sermon and while this was a very different circumstance, he felt more fervent that he ever had behind a lectern. "These monsters will come within the temple, seeking what you also feel. They will come to stop it and we will face them." He gestured to his companions as he said it.

"How can you stop so many?" A stocky young man asked. "There are only four of you."

"Five." A deep voice answered from the doorway. Tanoc stood there, head and shoulders above even the tallest of the inhabitants of Wend, looming in the doorway like a herald of doom. He walked toward the others and they could see the blood and gore on him. The townsfolk shrank back from this towering apparition.

Venaro grinned wryly, gladder to see the Northman than he'd ever thought possible. "It took you long enough." Then he saw Tanoc's face. "The girl?"

Ignoring the question, the barbarian grimly pointed with his blood smeared axe back the way he'd come. "They are coming." It was all the answer he would give.

Looking the direction that he'd pointed, the inhabitants of Wend saw twisted, shambling things heading down the street from out of the darkness. Screams and cries sounded within the church and the priest turned to them once more.

"GO!" He commanded. "Stay on the church grounds but keep your distance from this place!"

As the others left Juriel paused. "Cenric, sir. I have something I have to ask you."

"Now?" The priest asked. Bandur, Tanoc and Whisper were readying their weaponry and looking about for the best place to make their stand but Venaro hadn't moved yet and stood near the priest. When Juriel nodded, Cenric gave his assent. "Out with it then."

"Remember the house that you and I and Dulwen went to?" Juriel asked, the question surprising the priest, who nodded thoughtfully. "Well afterward, I kept looking around and I found out that every one of the houses with a mark like that one all had the same thing in common."

Cenric nodded absently. "Yes, someone who lived there was very sick or had some other health problem." He was gazing out toward the oncoming forms of the Dregs, trying to ascertain how many there were. It was difficult to pierce the gloom. "Just as you found that crutch in the upstairs room that day."

Venaro looked mystified and intrigued all at the same time but Juriel was impatient. "Yes sir but there's more." He lowered his voice a little to make sure no one else heard him but then realized the townsfolk were fleeing out the sides of the church, through the broken doors and rents in the wall. "Almost all the families in those houses with the strange marks were gone! Most of them were empty and the few folks who hadn't left were awful tight lipped. One sick, old man told me he'd been visited by a tall stranger in black and someone from the town, I think his name was Malken."

The priest looked at him then. "You want to know what it means, don't you?" When Juriel gulped and nodded, Cenric spoke. "I must be brief but I'll explain what I know. The marks are put there by one from within the town who works for these creatures or rather their masters. These masters, known as the Pallid, will have these people who do their bidding find any who are desperate enough to try anything."

The young man gave a start as Cenric spoke of the mythical Pallid. Venaro nodded as he began to understand more.

Cenric turned and set his pack on the ground then. He continued as though lecturing to acolytes. "These wretches, who serve the Pallid out of greed will later lead one of their masters to visit the homes of the desperate and dying. Later, those who believe the lies of the Pallid will follow them out into the wild where the undying masters wait for them."

"What..."Juriel began in a whisper, "What happens to them?"

In answer, Cenric pointed at the oncoming Dregs. "It is time for you to go now."

Juriel shook his head. "I'll stay and fight with you!" He was deathly afraid and pale as snow but his voice was firm and his jaw set.

"No, Juriel." Cenric said calmly. "This is no place for you." The boy might have said more but Bandur walked up and shoved him then, the big ex-soldier not giving him a chance. The boy left with a wounded look in his eyes but as he glanced at the oncoming monstrosities, he was glad to go, though he hated to admit it. "GO!" Cenric shouted at him then.

The priest pulled his warhammer and went to stand with the others. Venaro finally drew his sabre as well. "Remember." Cenric said calmly then. "They will seek the reliquary."

"Where is it?" Bandur asked, glancing around the interior of the temple.

Cenric smiled grimly and glanced back toward the doorway on the back wall of the sanctuary. "There is a hidden stair back in the chambers beyond that door."

"Shouldn't we go there now?" Venaro asked quickly.

"No." The priest answered. "Not yet."

At the merchant's somewhat confused stare, Bandur interjected.

"He's right sir." He gave the cleric an approving look. "We should face them here first and not fall back until we have to. We have space to move and take cover here." His voice was bleak. "We might not have that below."

"We will not." Cenric confirmed with a nod.

"Here they come." Whisper announced and just like that, the time for talking was over.

CHAPTER TWENTY-SIX

Facing the oncoming Dregs, each of the reluctant heroes, though they would have laughed to hear themselves called such, made ready. They might not have thought of themselves as heroic but to those citizens of Wend who were huddled behind the temple, hiding amidst the fallen stones and monuments that was exactly what they were. They formed a ragged line ten paces or so back from the entryway of the temple.

On the far right stood the priest, Cenric. He held his heavy warhammer in one hand and with the other hand made movements with other. The priest spoke strange archaic passages in a language that none of the others understood. When the cleric finished his preparations, he noted, "The sign of the Hammer protects us and the favor of the gods is upon us." It was a cryptic statement and his comrades didn't comment.

Next to the cleric and a couple of steps forward was the mighty barbarian. Facing the oncoming horrors, he stood with axe and shield in hand. Tanoc said not a word, his teeth bared like a hungry wolf's. His earlier dread of the creatures seemed to have vanished and now he seemed ready, his muscled frame taught as a drawn bowstring. As the Dreg's got closer, Tanoc clashed the head of his axe against the face of his shield rhythmically.

In the middle of the group stood Venaro roughly even in line with the priest. The merchant slowly drew his sabre and looked around him at the others. The normally verbose trader struggled for something to say, though he felt pride to stand with such valiant souls. Finally, he glanced over at the Northman and quipped, "At least you had time to repair your shield while we were here." Tanoc said nothing but continued to slam his axe into his shield. "Looks like they did good work too." Venaro mumbled and then stopped talking and brought his sabre into a guard position.

At the merchant's left side and slightly in front of him stood faithful Bandur. The former soldier bore his sword and shield at the ready and was still marveling at his newly healed wrist. He occasionally swiped the blade at the air in front of him as if he thought the pain would return but it did not. Though Bandur's smile faded as the monstrosities drew nigh, he stood firm, all doubt gone.

The far left was taken by Whisper, who stood slightly farther away from the others. Whether this was by design or an unconscious will to fight alone no one could be sure, including the assassin. While the others had talked to Juriel and readied themselves, she had gone through a complex set of stretches and now bounced on the balls of her feet like a dancer. The assassin had drawn her short sword and from somewhere had found a hatchet. She left her rapier and daggers sheathed as she'd paid close attention to the instructions on how to kill the monsters.

None of them bore bows or other ranged weapons. They knew the monsters facing them were all but immune to such attacks. This would be settled up close and no other way.

Cenric spoke, as the Dregs reached the door. "Remember, they must be incapacitated and then burned." He glanced around at the many torches and lanterns that the townsfolk of Wend had left behind when they fled. "I was going to light the few torches that I had but that won't be necessary."

"Shouldn't we all have torches at the ready now?" Venaro asked, his calm voice almost but not completely masking his fear.

"Keep your hands free for combat." Whisper hissed then.

The priest nodded. "Time enough to burn them after."

As the tide of Dregs reached the door, Bandur murmured, "There has to be close to twenty of them."

The monsters had seen their prey and swept in past the entryway and Tanoc leapt to meet them, his axe hewing left and right amongst the Dregs. Thick, clotted blood spattered all about him as he wrought red ruin amongst the creatures.

Bandur came on more cautiously, his shield up. Seeing several rush past the raging barbarian, He blocked a swipe from a clawed hand and chopped through the leg of the monster. When it fell, the caravan guard then hacked through the Dreg's outstretched arm. Another of the monsters caromed off his shield and knocked him back a step.

Whisper was there then, lunging in with incredible speed and half-severed the other arm with a vicious slash of her sword. Her blade was made for stabbing and didn't cleanly cut through but the arm now flopped uselessly about. Spinning around the creature's useless appendage, the assassin swung the axe in her left hand down to chop into the back of the monster's knee. When it stumbled, she took full advantage and her hands became a blur as she began carving the Dreg apart.

As the assassin and guard fought with the two opponents in front of them, Venaro rushed past to meet the third head on. "Remember!" He shouted, wondering at how steady his voice sounded "Go for their limbs and heads!" The Dreg facing him was a vile thing with no arms but a long, sharp bone grafted onto the head of a once beautiful woman. The creature let out a shriek as it rushed toward him, lowering its head like a lance. Venaro side-stepped at the last instant and brought down his sabre in a two handed stroke that severed the head from its shoulders. The merchant kicked the flailing body over.

Meanwhile, Cenric had run forward to aid the barbarian. He dare not get to close to the whirling engine of fury that was Tanoc but began to deal with any of the Dreg's that got around him. The others might have wondered what good his warhammer would do when they needed to incapacitate the monsters, but they soon saw that the cleric knew his business. The first of the creatures that met the priest was hit by the head of the hammer square on the top of the head. The force of the blow, wielded by the squat, powerful man practically exploded the Dreg's head like a ripe melon and drove it to its knees. Without hesitating, Cenric stepped back slightly and swung his hammer sideways, crushing the thing in the chest and knocking it backward. As the twitching thing struggled to rise, the priest brought the hammer down on first its right leg and then its left. So great was the ruination wrought by the cruel weapon that the legs were so badly damaged it could not rise. The hammer's head was not flat but had a point in the middle and then was concaved out to its sharp edges. It was designed to tear and crush and in the hands of the skilled warrior priest, it did its job well.

Three Dregs were down quickly before the berserk Northman's charge. Now, as more and more pressed him, he threw down his shield and wielded his axe with both hands. Powered by the incredible strength of the barbarian, each blow struck was devastating as a limb or head was severed. Then, spinning, Tanoc lodged the weapon in the collarbone of an oncoming Dreg. As the thing fell, the axe went with it, stuck in the tough bone. Without, hesitation, the reaver released his hold on the weapon and fell back, drawing his sword. Laying about him with the broadsword, the warrior's circle of carnage widened.

The heroes did not have it all their own way, however. In the press, they sustained injuries as well. Bandur was bitten on the leg by a Dreg with fangs from some wild beast. The needle sharp teeth were so long, the creature's jaw was distended and it constantly thrashed forward like a shark. The caravan guard went down to one knee as the teeth clamped onto his lower leg but hacked the head and neck of the Dreg apart in recompense.

Venaro too was wounded but his injury was less severe. The merchant's shoulder was clawed into by a nasty looking Dreg whose hands and arms were almost skeletal. The finger bones had been bonded together and the monster swung them like hooks. He fell back before the creature, parrying further attacks until Bandur hacked through its legs.

The barbarian was bleeding from a dozen small cuts and nicks but his speed and armor had served him well and none were serious. Neither Cenric nor Whisper had sustained injury.

As quick as it had begun, the fight was over. More than twenty Dregs lay strewn about the temple floor, their severed limbs and torsos still convulsing and writhing. Cenric was quick to pour oil from a nearby lantern about and then smash it on the pile. Tanoc quickly bent to retrieve his axe and shield from the flagstone floor. Then, as the assassin and barbarian went about, kicking stray parts into the burning pile, the priest went to check on the injured. Venaro waved him off, motioning toward Bandur.

"This looks bad." The priest said gravely as he examined the caravan guard's leg. The bite had gone in deeply on both sides and the warrior could not stand.

"Do...tell..." Bandur rasped painfully.

Cenric laid his hands upon the wound and spoke in that strangely divine tongue again. As the whitish light bloomed, the warrior gasped as the pain eased. However, the injury did not fully heal and the priest stepped back, his face drawn.

Holding his injured shoulder, Venaro stepped close to help Bandur rise to his feet. The warrior could do so but he favored the leg.

"It is all I can do." As he saw their questioning glances. "It is taxing to use healing magic and I must hold something in reserve for more...serious wounds."

Knowing little about such things and grateful that he was able to stand at all, Bandur smiled and nodded.

"More coming." Whisper murmured as she looked beyond the stinking blaze of burning Dregs.

"Good!" Tanoc said and started walking toward the door. He

was stopped by the compelling voice of the priest, who had stooped to retrieve his pack.

Cenric's voice was reasonable yet insistent. "Now is the time to fall back." He pointed toward the door at the back of the main sanctuary. "We'll funnel them to us."

Bandur and Whisper nodded in approval as Venaro wore a doubtful expression. "Is there a way out back there?" The merchant asked, trying and failing to mask his dread.

"There are a couple of doors that I didn't try." The priest answered. The answer mollified the merchant, who went to help Bandur who was already heading that direction, albeit painfully. "Tanoc." The cleric said then. "We need to get back."

The barbarian hesitated a moment longer, straining as he gazed out into the night. "There are more of them this time." He said, finally turning to join the others heading toward the rear door. Tanoc's countenance was grim. "And there's something else with them."

It had been difficult to tear the Dreg's away from their feed. Like beasts, most of them would gorge until they could barely move and this could not be allowed. Kast fought to tether as many as he could to his purpose. He could likewise feel the implacable resolve of Fina as she corralled more of them. It perturbed him that her ability was so much greater than his but he didn't worry about it for long. She had been a Pallid for longer than he and he had other things than pride to think about.

The Pallid had welded together a large group of almost two dozen Dregs together as he swept down the streets of the doomed town. He left those too rooted in their feast and instead pulled on those who were hunting or had already devoured much. Their movements were more torpid once they'd gorged and their will more easily controlled. Using his resolve like a whip, Kast drove that group toward the emanations that they had felt earlier. Striking at the mindless Dregs with piercing mental commands, he fixed his goal in their minds and turned them loose. As they barged away like a pack of unruly hounds, he had next turned to collecting the next group.

It had taken Kast a bit longer to seize control over the next pack of Dregs as it was a large one. Once he'd accomplished his goal, he added to the herd as he stalked ever closer to his destination. He could feel the forbidding power not far away now and he knew that the Dregs would never have willingly come this way on their own. Those he had sent ahead had dawdled along the way so much that as wasn't far behind them at all. As he entered the street with the ruined temple at its end, he saw and felt the last of them fall to those defending the church. He didn't quickly move but observed them from a distance, reaching out his senses to taste…defiance!

Angrily, the Pallid chivvied the throng of Dregs forward. Nearly fifty of the creatures moved along with Kast and he had no doubt that he would easily deal with these fools who thought they could stand before the might of the Pallid!

With hoots, grunts and moans, the horde descended on the temple.

Wend was now truly a dying town. Though most of its buildings were intact, few still had doors that had not been smashed open as the Dregs broke through to feast upon their occupants. Here and there, fires raged in the town as those who fought the Dregs sought to use fire against them and lost control of it. There were still distant screams and yells but it was much quieter now.

Fina glided down the street with an ever widening circle of her minions about her. There were less of them now but the losses seemed to be about what Vok had estimated. Within the sphere of Dregs was a growing group of townsfolk. It had been difficult at the beginning to muzzle the appetites of the Dregs but as they had satiated themselves on the flesh of the townsfolk, it became increasingly easier for the Pallid. In the beginning, the survivors who'd found themselves in this inner circle would try to run back out or attack the darkly clad woman they found at the center of the maelstrom of twisted flesh. Fina allowed her servants to tear those who fled apart while she dealt with the few foolish townsfolk who attacked her. A few broken necks and snapped spines and one graphic disemboweling cowed the rest of the people and they had fearfully followed her then.

It was a marvel to Fina how easily the humans fell in line. As her will washed over them as well as the Dregs, she fought not to bathe in the sensation of their horror and despair. The Pallid was disciplined, however and continued in the reaping. Soon, she had most of the Dregs around her, hundreds of them, more than two thirds of what they'd attacked the town with. Fina also had well over two hundred townsfolk with her as well and that pleased her to no end. She conjectured that by the time she was finished with her slow, revolving sweep through the town, she would have close to four hundred or more.

The bleak smile that writhed across her lovely features was ghastly enough to cause those humans nearest her to stumble back away from Fina. She was pleased, though the problem of that distant pulse still gave her pause. The Pallid could sense Kast and his Dregs moving closer to it as well as the insolent defiance of those who stood against him. She was certain that he could deal with it and gave it no further thought. Dawn was not far off and the stars had begun to disappear from the sky, the moon hiding her face.

It was time to leave. Fina and her massive circle of minions and prisoners slowly moved back to the north of the town.

Delia jumped as she heard a hoarse scream and knew that another of her guards had been wounded. She lay there in the bed fretting and fuming, feeling more helpless than she ever had in her life. She'd ordered one of the guards to fetch her a sword and he'd obliged but she felt no better as she'd never been much good at fighting. With her injury, she knew beyond the shadow of a doubt that she would be less that useless in a fight. The merchant thought of Venaro but then forced the man from her mind. He had chosen to leave her, she reminded herself.

Amice had come to the room where she lay and told her that there were guards outside her door as well as those defending the manor. Delia saw that the old woman bore a sword as well, though she too seemed uncomfortable with it.

"How do they fare at the gates?" Delia asked.

The governess turned horror filled eyes on her employer. "The…they're gone mistress."

"What do you mean they're gone?!" The merchant snapped

"The gates…" Amice said numbly. "They're overrun…the guards there…they were all killed."

Delia's voice was an incredulous hiss then. "Those creatures are on the grounds?"

"Everyone outside the manor house itself has been slain, mistress." Amice said bluntly then, shaking her head. "The guards are fighting to keep those…those creatures out of the house."

"Can they keep them out?" Delia all but whispered the question. In the distance, shattering glass was her only answer.

Cenric led the way through the door beyond the main temple. The others followed him, knowing that not far behind were more of the monstrosities. As they neared the side cloister, the priest paused and after a moment, opened the trap door. The priest had retrieved a torch as they'd made their way back and thrust it toward the darkened stair.

"At the bottom is a passage that leads to a large chamber." The priest said as he fought to catch his breath. "There are two passages that lead out of that chamber and the room with the reliquary is to the left." Schooling his breathing, he added, "The doors are long since rotted away so they will offer no barrier.

"Of course." Whisper said derisively.

Wincing as he leaned against a wall, Bandur asked, "Why are you telling us this?"

"We must seek to hold the Dregs here." Cenric replied. "I believe there is a Pallid with them. If we are unable to hold them, we have to get down into the funerary chambers and stop them there."

None of them liked the sound of that. "Funerary chambers?" Venaro said.

"Yes." The priest answered. "We must be ready to quickly go down the stairs if it seems that we will be overwhelmed. We must keep them from the reliquary chamber at all costs." His gaze was steady. "The creatures will be loath to touch it but they will try to knock it from its pedestal and profane the chamber with their presence. This must not happen for it is all that keeps the majority of unfettered Dregs at bay."

"Make ready." The barbarian intoned as the shadows of misshapen things could be seen heading closer. The slobbering grunts and howls of the Dregs echoed from the stone around them.

"Remember." Cenric reminded them. "We must hold until dawn."

As the Kast and his Dregs entered the temple, several of the creatures shied back at the presence they felt within. The Pallid knew full well now that something, some remnant of the ancient divines that once held such sway was active here. He drove his minions forward ruthlessly through the still burning flesh of their fallen. As he looked past the flickering and dying flames, he saw figures move through a doorway at the back of the temple and a grin lit his face. Like scurrying beetles they fled from before him but they would not escape. Feeding his Dregs the taste of his wrath, Kast whipped them into a frenzy as they rushed toward their quarry.

The Pallid vowed to leave none alive.

Tanoc met the first of the Dregs as they came through the entry to the cloister. The chamber was long and narrow and the trapdoor was toward the back. The barbarian hacked and slashed two handed with his axe, having slung his shield on his back. The others could not get close enough to aid him as there wasn't the space and watched, appalled and admiring at the same time, the butchery he wrought.

As the mangled, twisted and broken bodies of the Dregs began to pile up at the entry, they began leaping over their fallen to get at the barbarian. They could only come in one or two at a time and this had allowed the ferocious Northman to reap a bloody harvest. Even now, as they came over the growing mound of writhing body parts, he hacked limbs, clove skulls and rent torsos like a man possessed.

Yet, the barbarian was only flesh and blood and he was beginning to tire. Through the red haze, he saw a dark figure driving the monsters on and his concentration slipped.

A large, Dreg with heads attached to its wrists where fists should have been leapt over the rampart of twitching flesh, colliding with the weary barbarian. The heads were screaming as they came in to bludgeon Tanoc. With superb reflexes even in his exhausted state, the northern reaver hacked through one oncoming arm but the other smashed into the side of his head.

Pitching backward to land near his companions, Tanoc shook his head as Bandur and Whisper leapt forward to attack. Venaro said something but he couldn't make out the words through the ringing in his head. The merchant removed his helm and the held it out before the dazed barbarian. One of the horns was broken off and the side was crumpled in.

"You're lucky you've got such a hard head!" The merchant said with black humor.

Tanoc tried to nod but the motion made the whole room seem to swim. Growling, the warrior fought to clamber to his feet and it was a demonstration to his iron physique that he was able to stand there, though he swayed as he did.

Whisper leapt past Bandur who had blocked the screaming 'fist' of the Dreg as more of its kind crowded in behind it. As the head slammed against his shield, the warrior could see the features bloodying and breaking against the hard steel as teeth flew. Hardened warrior though he was, his stomach turned at the sight. Suddenly, the head was gone from the arm, severed by the axe in the assassin's hand.

As the two fought to stem the tide, Cenric roared, "Down the stairs!" As he did so, he took the stumbling barbarian by the arm.

"My axe!" Tanoc yelled in confusion, casting his gaze back to where he'd dropped the weapon.

Pushing the injured barbarian down the stairs after the priest, Venaro shouted, "Leave it!" In his addled state, the Northman allowed himself to be bulled along by the merchant and the cleric.

Falling back, Whisper lopped the arm off of a reaching terror and sought to decapitate it but instead wedged her axe into its shoulder. Bandur shoved her back behind him and the weapon was wrenched from her grasp.

"Get down there!" The ex-soldier bellowed like a bull as he slashed the hand from a reaching Dreg. "I'm right behind you!" The assassin nodded and turned to leap down the stairs, following the light from Cenric's torch. She had the presence of mind to grab a lantern that she'd brought from the main temple and dashed down the darkened stairway.

Bandur backed slowly toward the stairs himself, blocking several attacks from the wild Dregs. Then one of them slashed at his injured leg with claw-like fingers. The former soldier brought the rim of his shield down hard on the monster's arm and heard something snap but it had left him exposed.

Bounding over the carpet of fallen Dregs a long limbed monstrosity with the torso of a bull orc slammed into Bandur, bearing him backward off his feet. The canny warrior had managed to get his shield up and between them but knew that within seconds more of the creatures would be on him. Frantically, he slashed and cut at the thing as it grappled him, finally shearing through the clutching hands that held him.

Regaining his feet, Bandur saw that more of the monsters were already boiling down the stairwell like angry ants. He realized that he was cut off from his comrades. Then he heard dry, raspy chuckle that froze his blood as a black clad apparition stood before him.

"Not bad." Kast said to the human warrior that stood unsteadily before him. As several Dregs lurched forward, he glanced at them and they backed away. His gaze swept over the stairs and they moved to crowd behind the others at the trap door.

Realizing that he was in the corner of the room several strides from the opening, Bandur looked that way as well. "I'll kill you demon!" He growled at the Pallid who blocked his way and slashed at him.

Kast's arm was a blur as he drew his blade and blocked the human's blow in one smooth motion. His riposte was breathtakingly fast as he drove the point toward Bandur's shoulder but the man managed to throw his shield up to block. The warrior brought his own sword around but the Pallid easily blocked it. Then, the movement so quick that his opponent couldn't follow it, Kast stepped in and stabbed forward. The strange green blade bit into the man's arm below the bicep.

With a hoarse cry of pain, Bandur dropped his blade but tried to shield-bash his foe. However, the Pallid was far too quick and stepping under the clumsy attack, plunged his blade into the man's stomach! So hard did the dark warrior strike that the links of chainmail snapped easily and the wicked Pallid slowly drove the sword forward to the hilt.

Bandur weakly tried to grab at his enemy but the Pallid laughingly slapped his hand away. "I could have slain you when I was still living." The creature said in disappointment. "Perhaps your companions will provide better sport." Stepping away, he ripped the sword from the dying man's torso. As he did so, he slewed the blade from side to side, casually disemboweling him. Bandur screamed as he fell forward amidst his entrails.

Stepping away from the dead man, Kast saw the last of the Dregs pushing toward the stairs. Some were milling about and he noted how slowly they'd begun to move while he'd killed the man. Like a whip, he cracked his will against them to get them moving more quickly.

Below, Whisper backed away from the slowly moving Dregs on the stairs. She waited until they were packed into the passage leading to the large circular chamber and then threw the lantern full of oil into their packed midst. They burned and knocked each other and a few were trampled down beneath the others.

Beyond the chamber, she saw light down another passage and quickly made her way there. The Dregs seemed slow to follow and for that Whisper was glad. A tortured scream from above made her hasten down the hall and she found the others within the reliquary chamber. In the center, she caught a flash of silver and her mouth quirked into a smile in spite of everything.

"A pitcher?" The assassin asked drily. "It couldn't have been a magic sword or something?"

Cenric ignored her as he knelt and laid his hands on the barbarian, calling out to his gods in that strange ancient language. The blood from Tanoc's split scalp ceased to flow and his eyes lost that hazy look. Looking around wildly, the Northman stood to his feet.

Venaro looked back at the passage. "Bandur?" He asked, glancing at Whisper. When she shook her head in negation, a sad look came over his face. "Are you sure?" He pressed, even though they'd all heard the scream.

"The Dregs are still coming and that Pallid is with them." The assassin said in answer. "How do we kill that thing?" She demanded of the priest, her eyes flashing. She hadn't known Bandur long but he'd been a brave man.

Cenric was still kneeling, going through his pack. "Much the same as the Dregs." He said as he drew several torches forth. Lighting them with the torch he'd carried down, he set them in sconces about the chamber. "They must be cut apart and burned to slow them."

"That only slows them?" Venaro's voice was shocked.

Whisper demanded caustically. "How do we destroy them permanently?"

Returning to them, the priest answered. "Silver injures their kind greatly and if they are cut open with silver and burned they'll begin to die." They could hear the sounds of approaching Dregs now. "If they're brought into the sunlight in such a state, they can be completely destroyed."

"Oh." The merchant practically whispered. "Is that all?"

Cenric held his hammer forth. "My warhammer is chased with silver and can bring him down." He looked at the others. "The rest of you must help me slow him enough so that I can strike."

Whisper grinned wickedly and drew her rapier, its silver scrollwork flashing in the torchlight. "I plan to do more than slow him, priest."

CHAPTER TWENTY-SEVEN

Reaching the ruined north gate, Fina paused to look at the wholesale slaughter there. Bodies were strewn about, most half eaten and blood was spattered everywhere as though an insane painter with an obsession with red had been set loose. Darkness was quickly retreating as the sky began to gray presaging the coming dawn.

Fina mused as she thought of how the Pallid had always been cautious to take smaller settlements, leaving little sign of what had transpired. The fall of Wend had been nothing like those and there was plenty to show that the town had been attacked. Yet the Pallid master had explained to her that the quiet taking of small towns and villages was a thing of the past. They were conquerors now.

As the first of the Dregs and their prisoners passed through the destroyed gates, a presence caused Fina to look up. There, atop the gore streaked wall sat Null, swinging his legs absently back and forth.

"So you took your vengeance?" Fina asked.

Null smiled at her. "Enough to satisfy me." He spoke absently and she knew that he'd realized the hollowness of such petty things. "We're leaving?" He asked her then.

"We must be away east." The Pallid answered. "Vok awaits."

Watching the stream passing beneath the gate, Null stood. "I suppose he does." The fledgling Pallid jumped from the high wall easily and landed like a cat. Walking toward Fina, he could sense her disapproval. "I am sorry I left."

"No." She refuted. "You aren't."

Hurtling through the archway, the monstrous Dregs came on like a herd of cattle. They were driven by the implacable will of Kast and so great was their dread of the force within that chamber, they had no semblance of defense but rushed to attack. The four heroes met them before the reliquary and stopped their charge, their weapons taking a horrible toll on the remaining creatures.

In a storm of carnage, the terrible creatures were torn apart, though they took a recompense of blood. By the time the last Dreg fell, Venaro's arm was torn open, though he thanked the gods it was not his sword arm. Meanwhile, Tanoc who had once again strode to the forefront of the battle, bore wounds on his arms and shoulders, though none were serious. Cenric too had been wounded when one of the final surviving monsters drove a spear-like shard of bone into his thigh. Such was her amazing agility that Whisper remained unwounded. She went to bandage Venaro's wounded arm while the priest did the same with his leg. Meanwhile, Tanoc ignored his injuries and stood with sword and shield at the ready.

A slow clap sounded from down the passageway, somehow seeming ironic. It continued as it got closer and Tanoc tensed to leap forward.

"Wait!" Cenric barked. "We must face him together if we're to prevail!" The barbarian hesitated and then nodded grimly. Whisper finished tying the scrap of cloth around the merchant's arm and drew her rapier and short sword while Venaro once again pulled his sabre from its sheath. The cleric limped forward, leaning heavily on his warhammer.

"I must say…" A sardonic voice said as a shadow filled the entry. "Well done!" The scarred Pallid that stood before them was of middling height and build but he exuded menace and power. His face might have been accounted handsome but for the cruel mocking expression it wore. The Pallid ceased clapping and drew forth a strange sword of greenish metal in his hand and it was bloodstained. Holding it up before him so they could see the red ichor, he smiled. "Your friend is dead."

"You will pay for his death!" Venaro said, feeling foolish and more than a little afraid as the Pallid's cold regard turned toward him.

"Will I?" The Pallid warrior mocked. "My name is Kast, by the way. I thought that you should know before I kill you all."

With a roar like a lion, Tanoc charged, slashing down with his broadsword. With a look of surprise at the speed of the attack, Kast leapt lightly to one side, dodging the blow.

"You're fast for such a big man." The Pallid noted. "Made it all the way from across the sea did you?" He said cruelly then, "It didn't go well in your homeland did it? You must have run like a dog to make it this far!"

Whisper came in, leading with her left hand, the short sword seeking the Pallid's side. Kast blocked the attack, though his voice held admiration. "I see this town saved the best for last." As he beheld her. "You certainly are a lovely thing." Venaro and Cenric moved in more carefully due to their wounds.

Laughing maniacally, the Pallid sprang forward between the barbarian and assassin and his blade took the merchant in the chest. Venaro sank to his knees, clutching at the wound as Cenric swung his hammer in a deadly arc. Kast blocked the blow, though he felt its strength. "Of course there would be a priest of the dying gods here!" He regarded the cleric. "You were the one who activated that relic, weren't you?" He said then, glancing toward the silver pitcher. "Dreadful thing is made of silver isn't it?"

Whisper had gritted her teeth as Venaro fell and with blinding speed was upon the Pallid. Three times they crossed blades, their swords forming blurring arcs. Cenric took the opportunity to attack again and when the Pallid moved to block him, Whisper's rapier plunged into his shoulder.

As the Pallid fell back, hissing in pain, the assassin grinned.

"That's not all that's made of silver!"

The priest and the assassin tried to press the attack but the infuriated Pallid wove a skein of glittering green that blocked every attack. He caught Whisper a backhand glancing blow that slashed open her left arm, causing her to drop her short blade. "You could have survived the remaking, my dear." Kast said then as he sidestepped another swipe of Cenric's hammer and casually chopped down into the priest's right shoulder. As Cenric bellowed with pain, the Pallid stalked forward. "But you're going to die screaming!" Kast had forgotten Tanoc though.

The barbarian had waited, not wanting to hit his allies as they circled the impossibly fast Pallid. Now, he rushed past the retreating assassin and rammed into Kast full force with his shield. For all his speed and grace, the dark warrior couldn't move aside in time and was knocked backward to land a full ten feet away.

Stunned, Kast sat up, his mad eyes wide. It had been a long time since anything or anyone had hurt him much less knocked him down. However, Tanoc wasn't done and bulled forward, chopping down with his broadsword into the fallen Pallid's leg. Though not made of silver, the force with which the powerful barbarian struck with was enough to chop deep into the bone of Kast's lower leg.

Screaming in with rage and hate, the Pallid lunged up inhumanly fast and drove his blade deep into Tanoc's side. Dropping his shield, the barbarian grabbed Kast's hand and held it there so that it couldn't go in further. Astonishment bloomed on the Pallid's face. No human could be so strong! To add to his amazement, the wounded Northman actually began to pull his hand away.

Whisper had wasted no time and had dashed to the side and her rapier came it quick as the strike of a viper. Kast threw his arm up and the silver blade pierced his forearm. Cenric shuffled forward moving slowly but before he could get there, Kast released his hold on his sword, twisted like a serpent and pulled away from them, Whisper's sword still piercing his arm!

The indomitable Pallid grasped the weapon and pulled it free, hissing in pain as it came out. As soon as he had it out, he cast it behind him, the silver burning him. Then, he flinched as several daggers flew at him. He was able to dodge the first two but a third pinned his chest.

Roaring like a devil, Kast rushed forward at Whisper, his hands outstretched like claws. She writhed and tried to dodge aside but he was too quick and swept her arms up in a bone-crushing embrace. The assassin felt her spine creaking and knew that the fiend was going to break her back.

As suddenly as he'd grabbed the assassin, the Pallid released her as the priest's warhammer slammed into his back. It lacked the force it would have had as the wounded Cenric could only swing it one handed but the burly cleric was strong and the hammer crunched into Kast's lower back. The dark warrior shuddered at the force of the blow that drove the hated silver into his flesh and he made to turn.

Now, though, the mighty barbarian had regained his feet and swung Kast's own sword in a mighty arc that sheared through his already wounded arm! "I like your sword!" The Northman said savagely through gritted teeth.

Still not done, Kast struck the barbarian in the face with his palm and the mighty Tanoc flew backward to land on his back. He sat up slowly and shook his head, stunned at the strength of the Pallid.

"You think you can destroy me!" Kast hissed then, "I am immortal! I will..." His words were cut off as clear water splashed into his face. Cenric had snatched up the silver reliquary from its pedestal and thrown water from the blessed vessel into the fiend's face.

Kast fell to the side, writhing and screaming as smoke roiled from his features. The blessed water ate through him like acid and he crawled like a worm to escape it.

"*Now!*" Cenric bellowed and Whisper, who had retrieved her rapier and Tanoc rushed forward. The priest joined them and as the whack and thud of silver hammer and rapier joined with that of Kast's own sword, the Pallid's screams died as they hacked him apart. Finally, the three stood back, weary and wounded to regard their handiwork. The ruined form of Kast was no longer recognizable as having been even vaguely manlike. Cenric then doused the remains with water from the reliquary.

A weak voice spoke then. "If you…don't…mind…" They all turned to see Venaro lying on the ground still clutching his chest. "I'd…rather…not die…here."

As they passed through the broken gates, Fina and Null paused. They had both sensed it and the fledgling Pallid looked at her.

"Is he destroyed?" Null asked, his incredulity coming off in waves.

Fina's look was neither sad nor happy. "Yes." She said simply and turned away. As Null followed her out of the town, she sensed his troubled emotions. "Kast wasn't strong enough to defeat those who defended the relic, though he accomplished his purpose."

There was fear in his voice and it troubled Null that he could still feel such a thing. "I didn't think there were any left who could destroy one of our kind."

"It is surprising." The older Pallid admitted. "It is of no import." She said then. The sheer worry and amazement from the fledgling made her pause. "Kast did as he was bid and so must we all. We serve a greater power and we will prevail in the end." With a contemptuous glance back at the fallen town, she added, "The greed of men will see to that."

"What if they come after us?" Null asked, loathing the sound of his voice and unable to mask his fear.

"They will not come after us." Fina said patiently. "They think they've won a great victory here even though they do not yet realize what we have taken." She let her certainty wash over him.

"You have much to learn."

The newly created Pallid turned to look at the remnants of the place he'd once called home. He felt nothing as he gazed upon that ruined place. Not anger or joy…nothing. "I want to learn." Null murmured.

"Then…" Fina's voice replied, "Follow me."

As the dawn broke over the shattered town of Wend, four people walked from the ancient temple. A crowd had gathered around the place as it had been silent for some time. The first to exit was the priest, who helped a wounded merchant along. They were followed by the bloody form of the huge Northman who carried a bundle wrapped in his cloak at arms-length. Last to leave was a woman in dark garb who no longer moved with quite the same grace as she had.

"I'm glad you saved some of that faith for me." Venaro said, wincing as he spoke.

The priest, who was as much leaning on the merchant as the other man leaned on him couldn't even laugh. "I told you it was taxing." His teeth were gritted in pain as they walked along. "You're lucky I didn't pass out before I could get to you."

Tanoc strode past them into the sunlight and unceremoniously shook out his cloak onto the cobblestones. The remains of the Pallid fell with a wet thud and began to burn and smoke in the sunlight.

The people around them watched the remnants of the evil thing burn for a while as the heroes sat and saw to each other's wounds. None were overly serious, save for the merchants and the priests healing ability had kept him from dying. More people began to gather near the temple. Young Juriel and those who had hidden behind the temple came forth and brought bandages and water. Jorun and the survivors from the Crooked King showed up, including most of the merchant's drovers and guards. Old Jorun was wounded from a gash on one arm but alive and in good spirits. A few of Delia's guards even made an appearance, telling Venaro that their mistress still lived, much to the disgust of Whisper.

A short time later, when the bones of the Pallid had liquefied and were nothing more than a dark stain on the cobble, Venaro looked back toward the church. "It's a shame about Bandur." They'd passed his eviscerated corpse on the way out but none of them had had the strength to carry him. The merchant had covered his remains with his blue cloak and wept.

"He was a brave man." Tanoc said then and the merchant looked over in surprise. He knew there was no love lost between the two but the barbarian nodded. "His valor will not be forgotten."

"I'm sorry about the girl, Lilli was her name wasn't it?" Venaro said softly then. Tanoc nodded slowly and it was quiet for a time. "I'm going to bury him right here, on the grounds of this temple." The merchant said and the others murmured in agreement. Then, Venaro looked at them. "What now?" He asked the others.

Cenric spoke firmly. "I'm going to stay and see what I can do to help the survivors." He had noticed the crowd gathering around them, though they kept a respectful distance. Lowering his voice, he added, "I must contact my order so a decision about the reliquary can be made."

The merchant looked at the barbarian, who grimaced. "I'm getting the hell out of this cursed place!' He growled and cared not a whit for the shock written on those nearby.

Venaro couldn't quite suppress a smile. "What will you do?"

Tanoc thought about it for a few moments before answering. "I'm going south." He said then.

"Do you think you can go south far enough?" Venaro asked quietly, glancing at the sword of green metal that rode at the barbarian's belt.

They were both thinking of the Pallid and Tanoc growled, "I'll go as far as I can." He glanced at the assassin and then to Venaro. "What of you, merchant?"

"I have business to the east I must see to." Venaro answered neutrally.

Whisper started a little. "East?"

"Yes." The merchant replied simply. "That is where we must go, my dear." Venaro didn't bother explaining the statement to the priest or the barbarian and they didn't ask.

For her part, Whisper fixed him with a challenging stare. "East then."

Bandur was buried near the old temple and most of what remained of the shattered town turned out. Cenric said the last rites and commended his body to the earth and his soul to the gods. Venaro was surprised when Tanoc showed up, though the barbarian looked ready to travel. Whisper didn't come, saying that she loathed funerals and waited for him with the remainder of his men back at the Crooked King. Apparently there were very few of the town guard left and the mayor had been found dead, torn apart as though by a rabid bear.

"Take care of yourself, Tanoc." The merchant said after the funeral. When the barbarian extended his arm, Venaro clasped it in a warriors' handshake.

Smiling, his gray eyes calm, Tanoc replied, "Farewell...Venaro."

The merchant laughed out loud when he heard the towering warrior say his name. They said no more and the Northman turned to go. Cenric walked up then and waved as the barbarian walked to his horse and swung into the saddle. Miraculously, most of their horses had survived the attack, the monstrous Dregs seeming to prefer the abundance of human flesh.

Tanoc waved and rode away and the merchant and the priest stood together for a moment on the cobbled street. Looking back at the temple, Venaro found it surreal that he was still alive, though his still painful wounds proved he was.

"Did we win here?" Venaro asked the priest softly. He was troubled as they'd discovered how many had died. The merchant had been very sorrowful when he'd heard how many had been taken by the Dregs and their masters.

The priest sighed and didn't answer for a time. When he finally did, there was sorrow in his voice but hope as well. "Yes..." He said hesitating and when Venaro looked at him. "...and no." He finished. Cenric shrugged, the movement paining his injured shoulder. "We did not completely stop the Pallid and they did get what they came for, I suppose."

"It sounds like we lost." The merchant said, raising an eyebrow.

Cenric nodded. "Yet, we slew one of them, which has not been done for an age." His voice was strong as he considered the implications of what had transpired in the town. "We know that the Pallid are behind the disappearances and that here in Wend, they have declared war."

Venaro's voice was doubtful. "The realms of men are so shattered and divided." He felt helpless as he thought of the wars men had prosecuted on one another. "Is there anyone left to fight such a threat?"

"We were ready to stand against them, my friend." Cenric said warmly. "Others will take up arms against this darkness and Wend will be avenged, I assure you. My order will not let this stand."

Venaro smiled then, though there was a wry twist to it and a dryness in his voice. "I'm glad that 'others' will take up the fight." He said and turned to go. "Because I'm done."

Cenric laughed and the two men said their farewells. He hoped in his heart that Venaro would find peace but he doubted it. For danger was all around them and the Pallid were just beginning to arise. The priest walked back toward the temple enjoying the warm spring breeze that contained just a hint of summer.

ABOUT THE AUTHOR

Brad Farley lives in Michigan with his lovely wife and children, accompanied by a menagerie of pets. His favorite thing to do is spend time with his children and grandchildren. He has many hobbies which include avid reading, playing guitar, and song writing and composing.

Brad Farley originally contracted with Dream Big Publishing to unleash The Iron Kingdom Saga upon readers everywhere. On March 13, 2015, *Iron and Blood*, the first of the six epic novels arrived as e-books and paperbacks. The second in the saga, *Iron and Stone*, emerged on September 4, 2015, and the third, *Iron and Fire*, is in the works.   Brad's contract with Dream Big ended on September 3, 2016, and he is excited to see what new opportunities arise.

Both books are available on CreateSpace and Amazon in paperback, and are available in Kindle format.

In addition to The Iron Kingdom Saga, Brad has been working on a set of stand-alone novels set in the imaginary world of the Sundered Realms. The first of these, *A Pallid Moon* is what you have just read, with more stories to come!

For more information about Brad and his current and upcoming library, please visit http://www.realmsofiron.com.

Happy Reading!